MASTERMIND

A
Robert Ricks
Novel

 BLACK PEARL BOOKS PUBLISHING
www.BlackPearlBooks.com

This book is a work of fiction. Names, characters, places and incidents are products of the author's imagination or are used fictitiously. Any resemblance to actual events or locales or persons living or dead, is entirely coincidental.

MASTERMIND

A Robert Ricks Novel

Published By:

BLACK PEARL BOOKS INC.
3653-F FLAKES MILL ROAD – PMB 306
ATLANTA, GA 30034
404-735-3553

Copyright 2005 © Robert Ricks

All Black Pearl Books titles, imprints and distributed lines are available at special quantity discounts for bulk purchases for sales promotion, premiums, fund raising, educational or institutional use.

Special book excerpts or customized printings can also be created to fit specific needs. For details, write to Black Pearl Books: Attention Senior Publisher, 3653-F Flakes Mill Road, PMB-306, Atlanta, Georgia 30034 or visit website: www. BlackPearlBooks. com

FOR DISTRIBUTOR INFO & BULK ORDERING

Contact: **Black Pearl Books, Inc.**
                  3653-F Flakes Mill Road
                  PMB 306
                  Atlanta, Georgia 30034
                  404-735-3553

Discount Book-Club Orders via website:
         www. BlackPearlBooks. com

ISBN: 0-9773438-0-4   LCCN: 2005936492

Publication Date: December, 2005

ACKNOWLEDGEMENTS

First and foremost I would like to thank God for denying me death on my own terms, and for placing me in jails and institutions to keep me safe, and restoring me to sanity. I would like to thank the late great Mary Alice Ricks, my mother, who bought me a second- hand word processor and a desk and called me her author. Who died some years later of a broken heart because she poured all she had into three no-good-ass kids.

I would like to thank Brenda Costanza and Angela Green, the mothers of Jarred Robert Ricks and Kumani Rayona Ricks, two of my children; two women who always had my back. Who said write that damn book boy, we got these kids. A special thanks to my oldest son Robert, who is not only my child but my friend, and his mother Mary Brooks, my first love. Both of them bare the scars of my distorted perception of love.

I would like to thank my sister, Humdia Williams, who always said how much does it cost and what do you need, disregarding the fact that she was a single mother raising three kids and working two jobs. My niece Nijimah Williams, who came out in a snowstorm to pick up fifty pages of the book and unceasingly told me how good it was.

I would like to thank Amy D'Amico for her unwavering faith and excellent editing ability, and her husband Gordy Quackenbush for his marvelous insight and for keeping the baby quiet for four days while we did a read-through at their house.

I would like to thank Tani for doing everything that the above people did with the exception of having my child. We went blow for blow night after night and day after day, some time fighting over one word one period or one coma. You put in work girl and for that I am eternally grateful and forever in your debt.

I would like to thank Tim Wright for his editing skills and for his patience with my ignorance.

Wendy Low, who believed in me when I didn't believe in myself, who gave me opportunities to practice my craft and hone my skills even before I knew I had skills. My arts mother.

I would like to thank my sister Cynthia Green, who strokes my ego and keeps me grounded at the same time, and my niece Mary Ann, who constantly reminds me in words and deeds how important family is and what love looks like before you cut it and water it down.

I would like to thank all the youth who have worked with me over the years, I can say without reservation you have helped me far more than I have helped you, and thank you Susan for just being Susan.

Last but definitely not least I would like to thank Joe Bivins, Larry Clayton, and James Perkins. Together these men showed me what it meant to be a man, a black man. A special thanks to Mr. Perkins from all the children that he went, and continues to go, above and beyond for, even the ones who are now adults.

MASTERMIND

A
Robert Ricks
Novel

 BLACK PEARL BOOKS PUBLISHING
www.BlackPearlBooks.com

CHAPTER 1

The Promise

AKA

Mr. Kittles pulled into the freshly paved parking lot of the Saints and Sinners Baptist Church, turned off the air, rolled down the windows, and sat for a moment, savoring the smell of the new black top. He loved the strong pungent aroma and how it glistened when the sun hit it. Sort of like him, he thought as he grabbed the briefcase from the back seat and pulled his 5'11 frame from the red Lexus.

His new black Timbs made a crackling sound as he trudged his way to the church door and punched in the last four digits of his social. He took the stairs two at a time until he reached the third floor, then punched 1987 into the second pad.

That was a date that not even old timers disease would allow him to forget.

By the time the green light flashed, the lock clicked, and he entered, the transformation was complete. He was no longer Mr. Kittles, nor little Clarence Kittles, A+ student. He was no longer a barber, a boyfriend, nor a brother, but the equivalent of all the above marinated in pain: He was Clear.

He walked through the door and made his way around the oblong redwood table, greeting his captains one by one. He sat, opened his briefcase, pulled out four manila envelopes and passed them to his right.

The soft white light illuminated his Tootsie Roll colored skin, as he scanned faces looking for signs of confusion. Although he knew nothing about stocks, bonds and Dow Jones reports, what he did know was that nine ounces of cocaine, thirty thousand dollars in cash, and twelve years had made him very wealthy. Oh, he thought, let's not forget about the well-educated white broad and the street-wise fat kid. Clear followed the Henry Ford philosophy. He didn't need to know everything he just needed to surround himself with people who did.

Black, South-Side captain, pushed the papers forward a bit, and sunk into his chair.

Marwon, East-Side captain, stuck up a finger indicating he needed another minute and continued reading.

Daemon, West-Side captain, looked at Clear, smiled and said comically, "We some rich motherfuckers. We white folks rich."

Big Mack, the fat kid, North-Side captain, second in command, sat expressionless, saying nothing... Doing nothing.

"Any questions?," Clear asked. Silence confirmed comprehension.

"Okay, gentlemen, if you would pass all that incriminating shit forward, I'll retain a copy which you are free to examine at any time." Then with a slight smirk, he asked, "What in the hell is white folks rich, Daemon?"

Daemon looked up from the paper and smiled, which made him look much younger than his twenty-six years. He was the newest member of the organization, but he had served faithfully for nearly eight years. He was only eighteen when Clear and Mr. Roebuck magically turned manslaughter into self-defense, and twenty-five to life into five years probation.

"Well let me tell you," Daemon responded. "See, 'cause I'm an authority on white folks. I study their greedy asses. I believe they wipe their butts from side to side to preserve toilet paper, but that's an ongoing study. Now there's three kinds a rich; white folks rich, black folks rich, and nigga rich: white folks rich is when you got so much damn money you got to build little tax shelters to hide the shit. Black folks rich is when you got a house next to the white folks with the money. And nigga rich is when the bill collectors ain't on your ass, you got a stash under your mattress, two blunts on the dresser, and a half a bag of party wings deep frying in Crisco."

"Nigga, you crazy," Black said between chuckles.

"Excuse me? I'm eccentric. Poor folks go crazy," Daemon elaborated.

As the balance of the envelopes came forward, Clear sat staring at his Rolex, waiting for the second hand to make its way around for the second time. Calming himself as he looked across the table at Mack, he attempted to crawl into his head, looking for the screw that was loose or the bulb that was blown, because Mack was his man, and he would rather repair him than junk him.

"What's up wit' you, Mack?", he asked, trying to establish boundaries where once no boundaries existed.

"What you mean, what's up with me?", Mack responded.

"You okay?"

"Yeah. I'm straight", Mack said, tilting his head a little and adjusting his fitted baseball cap.

"Then why are you selling dope out of the hotel, man?"

Mack looked around the room and exhaled loudly as if the question aggravated him.

"Because I'm their man. Thousands float in and out of that hotel, and I decided it looked better in our pockets."

"You decided! You fucking decided…"

Clear paused, leaned back, once again composing himself, and nodded his head.

"So you doing your own thang now. Kinda liberating yourself from the mundane activities of this organization," he said.

Duplicating Clear's actions, Mack leaned his chair back.

"Naw, it ain't like that. I figure I can make some decisions to keep shit moving, too."

"But you can't," Clear said, leaning forward, throwing diplomacy to the wind.

"Why fuckin' can't I?"

Clear stood up, placed his hands on the table and pressed forward. "This organization didn't change when you went to the penitentiary for that bullshit, Mack. We're like the Borg and once you're assimilated, the collective needs to know everything you think! In fact, everything you think you thought. Therefore, from this point forward, you can disregard any thoughts you might have concerning day-to-day operations. I disseminate information around this bitch. I am the collective."

The heat from Clear's words obviously burned Mack's ego. Clear could see the fire in his eyes as nouns, verbs, and adverbs danced in his head, authorizing a response that could possibly get him killed.

This nigga didn't know nothing about hustling. He was one of them burger flippin', French fry shakin' motherfuckers. I should have just jacked his ass way back then. That's what Mack probably thought. And he was probably on the verge of giving voice to his thoughts when Clear noticed Marwon's and Daemon's hands simultaneously sliding underneath the table. Mack had obviously noticed too.

"You. . .you right, man," Mack said. "I...I just feel a little pressured Clear, feeling like I'm not holding my weight. I been home damn near six months man and every time I look up, y'all lacin' my pockets and shit."

Clear sat back down, licking his lips to conceal the smile forming on his face. He knew Mack well, thirteen years well, and he was fully aware that he was being served some heart warming, melodramatic, bullshit. So he called him to the carpet.

"Don't give me that shit, Mack. You doing exactly what you wanna' do. The same shit you were doing before you went to jail, parlaying and chasing ass. But you're fucking with the illusion, and when the illusion is gone, we're nothing but common street thugs throwing bricks at the penitentiary."

Mack bobbed his head up and down, as if he was in perfect agreement with what Clear was saying. Clear glanced over at Marwon, Daemon, and Black, whose eyes were veering neither left nor right, and defying the principles of blinking.

Clear got up, walked around the table and placed his hands on Daemon and Marwon's' shoulders.

"I'm not about to do a day in jail behind your bullshit, Mack. And if you never sell another bag of dope, or make another financial contribution, your presence will always be felt in this organization. But remember… this shit is until death do us part… and please don't make me do us part."

Clear proceeded around the table, collected the envelopes, and embraced his Captains once more. But the warmth that once confirmed him and Mack's camaraderie was now gone. And in that instant, Clear knew, and he walked out attempting to embrace the inevitable.

He didn't stop to talk to Pastor Williams, he walked straight out of the church, hopped in his car, got on the expressway and headed for the highway.

The windows went up, the air came on and the seats in the 1998 Lexus coupe went back. Pac blasted through the Boeing speakers, cruise control initiated and the speedometer read minus 120 miles per hour, the odometer was going backwards. Backwards into endless streams of yesterdays, back to a time where memories were buried deep inside of harsh realities that weren't really real.

The night he crawled into the dumpster behind McDonalds looking for food to feed his little brother and sister wasn't real.

The standing in the lines at the Open Door Mission, silently praying that they didn't run out of stale bread and almost spoiled hot dogs wasn't real.

The garbage bag of day old donuts resting against the wall at the House of Mercy wasn't real. And the sparkle that appeared in Dayja's eyes when the kind lady gave her two donuts just for being four and a half, wasn't real.

The diaper rash that was still discernable even after Dayja entered Miss Nash's first grade class wasn't real.

The head lice and ringworm that left bald spots in Brandon's head weren't real.

The degenerates and derelicts and prostitutes who were way past their prime weren't real, they only appeared real when they burrowed themselves in the living room. Smoking, drinking, and geekin' as if their house was a clubhouse for society's rejects.

His little brother's blood splattered all over the family-size boxes of Tylenol and Advil wasn't real. But... it all seemed real then.

The only thing that was real was The Promise. . . Oh, and of course, the psychological disfiguration that comes from living a nightmare.

CHAPTER 2

A Clear Sunday

"You here because your Mama on welfare and you can't afford a hair cut?". Toby said to Wakim.

"I can afford to kick your ass. The only reason you talking smack is because I'm in this chair," Wakim responded.

Clear shouted from the back room. "Wakim! What I told you about cursin' in my shop?"

"I'm sorry, Mr. Clear, but Toby said I was on welfare."

Clear walked out from the back and onto the barber floor.

"Why you here, Toby?", he asked walking over to his station to retrieve his car keys from the drawer.

Toby cocked his head to the side and announced without any apprehension, "Because my Mama said if you crazy enough to cut hair for free then she smart enough to send me down here."

"Is that so?", Clear said.

Black laughed as he continued to cut Wakim's head.

Clear dropped the keys back into the drawer then turned and patted his chair. "C'mon, Toby," he said.

"You not my barber, Black my barber."

"I'm gonna be your barber today," Clear responded.

Toby got up and climbed into his chair. Clear took the edgers, shaved one side of Toby's Afro off then handed him the mirror.

"You like that?", Clear asked. " I call it the crazy man cut." He tried hard not to laugh.

"Mr. Clear, you not gon' leave my hair like this, are you? My Mama gonna spaz-out on you."

"Tell your Mama the crazy man did it, and if she got eight dollars, he smart enough to fix it."

"Come on, Mr. Clear, it's Sunday. I'm gonna have to go to school like this tomorrow."

Clear handed him one of the many baseball caps that hung on the coat rack in the corner. Toby looked up at him, climbed out the chair, walked to the door then shouted "Fuck you," and ran out.

Clear and Black laughed but Wakim wasn't amused at all.

He turned to Clear and said, "I'll catch him and beat his ass if you want me to, Mr. Clear."

"That's okay, Wakim. Life is gonna beat his ass."

He hung his barber jacket on the coat rack, retrieved his keys, shaped up Wakim and headed home.

Clear hated cutting hair on Sundays. The getting up and getting there was one of the problems. But once he was there and all the little boys said, "Good morning Mr. Clear," and all of their tired, over-taxed Mamas looked at him as if he were the best thing since peanut butter and reduced daycare, that made the mornings worthwhile. Sure some of their parents had the eight dollars to pay for their kids' haircuts, but most of them didn't. And for Clear those were the ones that really mattered.

Clear pulled into the driveway, turned off the car and sat for moment. He moved his head from side to side trying to work out the kinks in his neck as he turned to retrieve the flowers from the back seat. He often bought Porsha flowers, just as a small token of his appreciation. She cooked, cleaned, washed, smiled, laughed, scratched his head, massaged his shoulders, and spent his money. Ain't no cheat in a fair trade, he thought, smiling as he stuck the key in the door.

"Hey, Boo," Porsha said while she ran down the stairs.

"Hey, Baby," Clear responded.

"Are those for me?." she asked.

"Oh, shit," Clear responded and stuck the flowers behind his back. "Naw, they for our new neighbor, a housewarming gift."

"Oh," Porsha said cheerfully. She walked up to him with her lips puckered and arms extended. She pressed her lips to his and put her arm around his waist. Then she snatched the flowers from behind his back.

"Bitch won't get these, you're not tracking hair on her carpet," she said, and turned and went in search of a vase.

"What's for dinner?", Clear asked, following her into the kitchen.

"I don't know, go and ask the bleached blonde next door."

"You know her number?", he asked, teasing.

"Keep it up, Clear, and you'll be wearing these flowers and this vase."

Clear laughed and put his arms around her waist as she leaned over the sink to fill the vase.

"How was your day, baby?", he asked as he pulled her to him and kissed the nape of her neck.

"It was good, until the cable went off and I was stuck with four channels. Football, football, golf, and an infomercial about zits or wrinkles, some kind of face stuff."

"Did you call the cable people?", Clear asked as he walked over to the stove and lifted the top on the stewed pork chops.

"Time Warner's people don't work on Sundays. Nobody works on Sundays except you, and all the little Clear wannabes at the barbershop", Porsha smiled, then took Clear's hand and led him into the dining room.

"Why you dissin' my boys, Porsha?", Clear asked, pulling out a chair from the table.

"I'm not dissin' em," she said with a smirk. "If I was a man I would follow your crooked ass too."

Porsha went into the kitchen and pulled two plates from the cabinet. She piled the mushroom and onion gravy on top of the Uncle Ben's rice, and laid two stewed pork chops neatly beside the diced green beans that she had seasoned with beef bouillon, just the way her man liked them. She placed two medium sized slices of Jiffy corn bread in a saucer, because Clear didn't like his corn bread soggy. One small scoop of rice, one pork chop and a thin slice of corn bread was all she had, because her figure was bangin' and she intended to keep it that way.

Porsha stood at the refrigerator all of two minutes, tortured by the choice between pink lemonade and diet Pepsi. Pink lemonade won and she retrieved another glass from the cabinet and filled it with her weakness.

She sat across the table from Clear, silently praying over their food.

Clear didn't start eating until she was finished, but he didn't indulge in the prayer ritual.

"Some lady called. I wrote her name on the pad by the phone. She said she turned in the plane ticket and was taking the bus, and she told me to tell you that if God intended for her to fly, he would've made her an angel."

"If God intended for her to travel he would have gave her some damn money," Clear responded.

"Some things are more important than money, Clear," Porsha said, setting him up.

"Like what, Porsha?"

"Love, family, eternal life."

Clear looked at her and shook his head. "You definitely need to get out more. Love is a feeling. You can't eat it, sleep in it, nor drive it. And if I'm broke, show me you love me by giving me some money. And eternal life? The jury's still out on that shit. If I'm gonna pay ten percent of my gross earnings for my whole life to secure a place when I'm dead, I need to see that shit in writing."

"It is in writing, read your Bible," Porsha responded.

"Which Bible? From which religion, or which translation from which religion?", Clear asked, sounding a bit more abrasive than he probably had intended.

"We're awful hostile today," Porsha responded.

"I'm not hostile, Porsha, I'm real. Religion in the black community has become an excuse to sit around and wait for something to happen. Instead of getting off your ass and making something happen. You ride through the ghetto and the only thing you see black-owned is the Churches. Not the houses we live in, the businesses we slave at, not even the cars we drive. You would think, that if we can take ten percent of our salary and invest it in the hereafter, that we probably could take another ten percent and invest it in the right fucking now."

"I'm not even going there with you, Clear," Porsha said as she got up and walked into the kitchen to get the hot sauce.

"I would suggest that you didn't, because you would lose."

Porsha knew exactly where Clear stood in reference to the black church, the black community, the black non-profit organizations, and so forth and so on. They had had that discussion many times before. She couldn't say she felt any differently, but tonight, she had bigger fish to fry.

"You need something?", she shouted from the kitchen.

"No I'm fine, baby."

Porsha strolled back into the dining room and picked up the conversation. "It's not that I would lose, I'm just not in the business of contemplating how I'm gonna save the world. I've decided I'm gonna take care of you, and you take care of the world. Comprende'?"

"Comprende'," Clear responded with a smile.

Porsha sat picking at her food as she pondered different approaches to the subject. Then finally she decided--subtle and indirect.

"What about family?", she asked.

"What about family?, he responded.

Porsha looked down into her food. "I spoke to Dayja today."

"Come on, Porsha," Clear said almost pleadingly. "Didn't we just make a deal? I take care of the world, you take care of me."

"Since when did Dayja become not a part of you, Clear?"

"The day she decided she could do whatever she wanted."

"She was fourteen, Clear, that's what fourteen-year-olds do."

"No, that's what assholes do."

"Dayja's the victim, Clear, just like the rest of these bad ass kids you bend over backwards for."

"How is she a victim, Porsha? I gave her everything a fourteen-year-old could want."

"Did you give her mother back, her brother back, her daddy back?"

"Hell, no… I gave her Fendi, Gucci, Phat Farm, private school, dance lessons, etiquette classes and anything else she thought she wanted."

"Those things don't mean nothing after the price tag is ripped off. Dayja needs you."

"What Dayja needs is her ass whipped," Clear responded.

"Well bring her home and give her an ass whipping. Don't quarantine her off from the only two people that love her."

Clear picked up his knife and fork and proceeded to cut his pork chop. Porsha raised her voice and continued in spite of knowing she was over-stepping boundaries.

"You know you got some double standard shit going Clear. You embrace every bad ass, nappy head, snotty nose kid in this community, but when it comes to Dayja, you just cut her off. Do you not realize the girl's been in foster care for a year?"

"And she'll probably be there another year. Before I allow what happened to Brandon to happen to her, I'll chain her to the wall in the fucking basement. If that doesn't work, I'll put a bullet in her head my goddamn self!"

Clear slammed his fork on the table, got up and walked out the door.

Porsha sat watching the clock and dicing grains of rice with her fork. After a moment she got up from the table, picked up the plates and walked into the kitchen.

The garbage disposal will eat good tonight, she thought as she raked Clear's barely touched plate in the sink. Then she slowly sauntered out of the kitchen, through the dining room, living room, and up the stairs. She kneeled on the side of her bed in a prayer position, as memories added depth and weight to her present discomfort.

You're a selfish, self-centered little bitch. Nothing matters but what Porsha wants. If you stop fanning your fat ass around in here like that, he won't be looking at you, if he was.

It had been years since she'd spoken to her Mom, but the cruel things she used to say were permanently etched in her head. And anytime the wheels of misfortune turned, her mother's unoriginal quotes were randomly selected and played.

"But I am being selfish," Porsha said as she fluffed her pillows--noticing the diamonds that adorned her fingers, the bedroom she designed, and the furniture she selected.

Porsha crawled into bed, closed her eyes and thought of Clear. She thought of all the things that Clear had done for her. How she never really wanted or needed anything. She thought of all the little luxuries that were now necessities, the clothes, the shoes, the jewelry, and the trips. How he would lift her chin and say, "Keep your head up," when she was having a bad day. How with just a mere mention to him, all her problems mysteriously disappeared. How today she felt safe and secure and knew she was loved. How he made her feel like a woman.

"Get a grip, girl," Porsha said to herself, and shook her head slightly as if to rearrange her thoughts.

Leaving Dayja in foster care had to be one of the hardest decisions Clear ever had to make, and he's probably feeling like shit now. She looked at the phone, then looked away, then looked at the phone, then looked away. "Why do I always have to be the one that says I'm sorry?", she said as she picked up the receiver and dialed.

"Hello."

"I'm so sorry, baby. I just love Dayja so much. I feel like she's my child, and every time I speak to her it hurts, and I just want her to come home."

"Yeah, I know," Clear said.

Obviously, he wanted her to understand what he was trying to do. He had spoiled the shit out of Dayja and consequently she had turned into a little bitch. She reminded him of her daddy, and though he would never admit it, sometimes he wished he had left her in foster care when his mother died.

A somber silence loitered on the corner of Nextel and AT&T Drive as Porsha held the phone and quietly pondered their conflicting views, in search of a resolution.

The bedroom door opened and Clear walked in. Porsha looked up at him and hit the end call button on the cordless phone then laid it down beside her. Clear closed the flap on his Nextel and sat down on the bed facing the mirror, with his back to Porsha. She moved closer and put her arms around him.

Only she could see the invisible tears rolling down his face, despite the stoic expression reflected in the mirror.

"Winners do what they have to do, losers do what they wanna do, and my baby sister will not lose, she might hate me before I'm done, but she will not lose," Clear said.

Porsha got up and walked around the bed. "You hungry, baby?", she said.

"No, I'm fine."

Porsha pulled his shirt over his head, folded it neatly, and laid it on the corner of the dresser. Then she kneeled, untied and took off his boots, scooped his legs and guided them to the bed. He turned over as she straddled him and started kissing his neck and massaging his shoulders.

"I have a visit with Dayja on Wednesday, will you come with me?", she said.

Clear laughed. "Do you ever give up?", he asked.

"Nope, if I gave up you would probably still be with that pale ass white girl."

"Now you know she ain't pale, why you hatin', Porsha?"

"Because I can."

CHAPTER 3

The Brown Family

The mortar and cinderblock foundation was off just a little bit, so the shack rocks just a little bit. And every time it went up and came down the tin roof made a thunderous sound, but no one seemed to mind at Aunt Maulee's and Uncle Benny's Juke Joint. The jukebox was jimmied and for fifty cents you could dance all night, and dance they did.

All the Brown family needed was a couple jugs of moonshine, some Remy and some Heinekens, and before you knew it, stilettos and Stacy Adam's were strewn in the corner, and bare feet were burning holes in the linoleum floor.

The man right there doing the Crazy Rooster or the Funky Chicken, that's Benny, but everybody calls him Uncle

Benny. And the lady over there pulling the plug on the jukebox, that's everybody's Aunt Brenda Gail. She says Uncle Benny embarrasses her when he gets that fire water in him.

Uncle Benny and Aunt Brenda Gail are like the president and the first lady in this family, but this is a dictatorship not a democracy. There's no voting, no discussion, no deliberation. They rule, from Opelika to Montgomery. The only decision that takes precedence over theirs is God's and he needed to show up to deliver the message in person. But that ain't the case when it comes to Uncle Benny or Aunt Brenda Gail. When someone says, "Uncle B, or Aunt B" the whole Brown family stops breathing to make sure they get the message fully and clearly. That's not because they're mean people. In fact, they're two of the finest people the south ever produced they just mean what they say.

Uncle Benny will give you the shirt off his back, and so will Aunt Brenda Gail. Even though they believed that a man should never ask another man for nothing but directions to a job.

Uncle Benny got shot in the head in the war, so everybody says he's crazy, but they know he's not. Even when he tells the story about the angel who resuscitated him, he's given the benefit of a whole lotta doubt.

He says, "One of dem goddam Koreans caught me snoozin' and put a bullet straight through my thinker. And a Angel named Presumptuous resus-ti-tated me." He says she told him to come home and raise some men. He came home from the war, married Brenda Gail, and put his foot on the neck of every male child her and her four sisters pushed out. As a result, Bud, Homer, Willie-Lewis, Jimmy Dickey, Magic and little Benny Jr. are some of the most respected young men in Alabama.

Uncle Benny is a dinosaur, the last of a dead breed. He was raised during a time when morals, values, and ethics were as

MASTERMIND

plentiful as the dropped consonants and the omitted vowels in the southern dialect. A time when men and women had positions and neither was any more important than the other. A time when black folks knew that they were all they had.

Aunt Brenda-Gail is a dinosauress. She says, "Don't be sittin' around me like you ain't got nothin' to do. Go home and mop dem filthy flo's. Do some laundry. Wash dem dirty draws. Y'all just nasty, nasty, and don't no man want no filthy woman."

But no matter what they say, any day of the week you can go to her and Uncle Benny's house and get a hot plate of food, and help with whatever problem you may have. It's like that at all the sisters' houses.

Unfortunately, Aunt Brenda Gail's sister Peggy isn't here. She's dead. They say she was found up in Rochester NY. in an abandoned building. Say she had a big smile on her face and a syringe in both arms.

Peggy was the oldest of the four girls, and she had a lazy streak that ran through her like a second spine. Her mom used to tell her she was going to hell for being so slothful. "Hell couldn't be too much worse than this," she would mumble under her breath. She was also the prettiest, even when she was little. She had long sandy black hair that waved up and shined like a full moon when she put a little Blue Magic on it. She had dimples deep enough to hide something in, and her legs were long and lean like the stalks of corn planted in the fields across from their house in them days. She sort of glowed, like their daddy's shoe's when he spit-shined them for church on Sunday morning, but she lost her glow when her parents died.

Their Mama and Daddy went over to Montgomery one Friday to attend a freedom march. That next Monday a man came to their house and said they got beat to death and her and Brenda Gail had to go identify the bodies. After that neither her nor Brenda Gail was the same. Brenda Gail became the mother, even though Peggy was the oldest.

Brenda Gail made sure her sisters were at church every Sunday morning. It didn't matter that the church was a little over a mile and a half away from their house. They would start out before the sun peeked over the trees and generally get there before the pastor. After service was over, a couple of the members with cars would drop them off at home. But on this particular Sunday, in spite of the fact that they knew Katy and Maulee would be whining and complaining before they got a third of the way back home, they decided to walk.

The mile and a half walk was divided by oak trees, pine trees and farm land, and once you came around the bend the tall pine trees turned into corn fields almost magically.

The Alabama sun seemed to sit a little lower than usual on this Sunday. So they concluded that it had baked Peggy's brain when she stopped in the middle of the road and said, "I ain't eatin' no mo' goddam fatback and fried bread." Then without an explanation she turned and headed back toward the church.

About two hours later the pastor dropped her off. She looked a bit disheveled and a little happier than usual when she walked into the house and pulled a brown paper bag out of her panties. She emptied the bag on the kitchen table and called Katy in from outside. Katy was the best reader out of all the four girls. Her and Maulee took turns going to school while their sisters worked in the fields, sometimes from sun up to sun down.

Katy was obviously surprised to see all the little envelopes lying on the table. The same envelopes her mother and father used to drop in the basket as they marched around the church while the choir sang. The same basket that her parents insisted she put her penny candy money in.

Katy read all the names on the envelopes while Peggy tore them open and made neat stacks of nickels, dimes, quarters and paper money. She let Katy and Maulee split all the pennies, and gave half the paper money to Brenda Gail. That day Peggy decided it was much easier to spread her legs across the pew and let the pastor have his way with her, than it was to work in them fields.

Eventually, all the men started calling her Sugar Mama, and all the women called her a hoe. She stopped going to church and Brenda Gail stopped taking her money. She said it was as filthy as the things she did for it.

When Uncle Benny and Aunt Brenda Gail got married, they did all that they could to help Peggy change. Every Sunday Aunt Brenda-Gail would ask the church to say a special prayer for her sister. Most of the women would toot up their nose and not join the prayer circle, but Brenda Gail didn't care as long as they didn't say anything to her or none of her sisters.

Uncle Benny, Aunt Brenda Gail, and half of Opelika had one known enemy, a slick talking northern boy name Big Percy. Uncle Benny blamed every bad thing that happened to him on Big Percy. He said Big Percy won the deed to their land from his drunken father in a card game. He said Big Percy slithered into town through the sewer with two baboons he called prostitutes, and to add insult to injury Peggy hooked up with him. By the time Uncle Benny and Aunt Brenda Gail found out, she had a kid and was well on her way to living miserably ever after.

Uncle Benny and his best friend, Double Barrel, went to see Big Percy. Aunt Brenda Gail, Aunt Claude May and Aunt Katy went to see their sister. Uncle Benny told Big Percy he would blow his head off and bury him in the woods. Aunt Brenda Gail and her three sisters took Peggy and her daughter to the Greyhound bus station, and put her on a bus with two black eyes.

If you look straight ahead, see the man slumped over the bar. That's Maulee's son Jimmy Dickey, and this is his birthday party. But If you look to the right of him, right there stuck between the jukebox and the bar. You see the lady sitting there adorned in the beautiful summer dress with the cold, wintry eyes? That's Peggy and Big Percy's daughter. Her name's Peggy, too, and like her Mama, her picker is broke when it comes down to picking men.

CHAPTER 4

She Got It From Her Mama

Peggy sat thinking, and sipping on her third cup of Remy, wondering if Uncle Benny's portrait of her father was accurate. She often found herself trying to balance what her Uncle Benny said with what her mother had told her. But her mother was a liar; God bless the dead. And her Uncle Benny was an 'Embellisher'. He told the truth but added a lot of his own stuff.

Peggy noticed the semi-stranger staring at her from the other end of the bar. It was one of them Duke boys. She could tell because of his big watermelon head. All the Dukes had watermelon heads, even the girls. Big heads and big feet.

She picked up her cup and placed it to her lips. Realizing that the semi-stranger looked better and better every time she lowered the cup and glanced in his direction. He even seemed to have grown into his watermelon head.

She turned and flirted a little bit, batting her eyes and smiling. Then panicked, as he wasted no time making his way around the bar and pulling up beside her.

"Hey, beautiful," he said.

She looked into his hazel brown eye's thinking, This country ass nigga is wearing contacts, but it had been a long time since someone referred to her as beautiful, so it wouldn't have mattered if he strolled over with a seeing eye dog.

"Hi," she said nonchalantly.

"And what's your name?", he asked.

Peggy took a mint from one of the mismatched bowls on the bar, opened her mouth and stuck her tongue out just enough to place the mint. "Miserable," she said as sensuously as miserable could be said.

His lips cracked into a small smile. "Miserable," he repeated, apparently giving himself a chance to formulate a response and weigh what she said against how she said it.

Peggy popped another mint in her mouth and it almost lodged in her throat. She raised her hand to her mouth and coughed prissily.

"You okay?", the stranger asked, and she nodded clearing her throat. "Can I get you a drink?"

"No thank you. I think I've had enough," she said, clearing her throat once again. She picked up a napkin off the bar and dabbed her eyes, trying not to smear her make-up.

"And what's your name?", she asked.

"Happy. Genuinely Happy."

She looked away, over to her uncles, aunts, and cousins. They also seemed genuinely happy, or genuinely drunk.

Peggy watched in silence as everyone finished eating. The old folks were preparing to go home because the jukebox had worked its way through the sixties, seventies and the eighties. Now Tupac, Biggie and Nas were spitting venom through the speakers and upsetting their spirits.

She stood up and brushed some of the wrinkles out of her dress.

"Do you dance, Mr. Happy?", she asked, sashaying out to the dance floor, certain that he would follow, and he did.

They danced and danced all the way back through the seventies and the eighties.

Peggy remembered all the dances she'd learned in Fat Pam's basement. She remembered the running-man, the cabbage-patch, the butterfly, and the bump. She also remembered the flashing-lights, the Malt Duck, and as soon as Phillip Bailey hit the high note, she remembered Magic Sr.

Her cousin Homer knew that Earth Wind and Fire was her favorite band and Reason was her favorite song. He played it just for her, she thought as she closed her eyes, firmly caressed the back of the stranger, laid her head on his chest and thought about Magic Sr.

She didn't hear the door open, nor did she see the stream of moonlight that illuminated the back of her dress. But she felt his stark stare cutting the heads off the high notes as they rang through the woofers and tweeters. She eased her head up from the stranger's chest and tried to put some space between them.

"Let's go," Bear said.

Peggy backed away and Bear brushed the stranger's arm as he pushed past them and walked out the Juke Joint.

Twelve o'clock had come and gone. Cousin Jimmy-Dickey was slumped over the bar with his face buried in a bowl of breath mints. The elders had gone home and were probably fast asleep. Dreaming of Sunday morning service at the Saints and Sinners Baptist Church. Peggy walked around acknowledging everyone that was sober enough to say goodbye to, and consciously avoiding the stranger's watchful eyes.

She hurriedly walked out of Aunt Maulee's and Uncle Benny's Juke Joint, got in the truck and silently began praying to the alcohol God. She asked him to stop her stomach from churning and her head from spinning.

"You just oughta hadda pulled your draws down and fucked him right there in the middle of the dance floor," Bear said. "This ain't the goddamn Bronx, Peggy, and in Alabama decent womans don't do dat."

His thick country accent and terrible grammar made her more nauseous, and the anger in his tone let her know that not even the Gods could help her tonight.

"You just a hoe. A New York hoe. And you know what we do to hoes in Alabama, Peggy? You know what we do?" He turned and spat in her face.

She didn't flinch, didn't move, she just sat there staring straight ahead as the slime rolled down her cheek, bracing herself. She knew that him spitting in her face was not in lieu of, but would be chaperoned by, 'The Ass Whippin'.

He reached for her as she grasped the door handle and grabbed the collar of her dress, ripping it from her body as she leaped from the car, landing in thick brush. She crawled down into a ditch and laid there silent and still, blanketed by the dark Alabama night.

She heard the tires dig into the gravel as the old Ford pickup came to a halt. She heard the door slam, and the sound of him raking through the brush. She lay there listening as the Monsta drew closer. Then, prompted by the stench of his Old Spice cologne, she sprang to her feet, grabbed a patch of weeds and attempted to pull herself out of the shallow ditch.

He jumped in, grabbed her by the hair and yanked her to the ground. Then he started slapping her. He slapped her until her cheeks were numb and her head flip-flopped from side to side. He stomped her and buried her face in the muddy marsh. Then he yanked her head from beneath the water and plunged it back in again. Peggy heard the knife opening, he snatched her head back and stood straddling her like the king of everything. He pressed the razor sharp knife to her neck and announced with true conviction, "Bitch, I'll kill you, cut your ass up and use you for fish bait." He released her head and her limp naked body lay in the mud, defenseless. She was almost too tired to breathe.

He grabbed her by her legs and dragged her to the truck. She gasped as the gravel penetrated her panties and peeled her skin. Not bothering to lower the hatch, he threw her in the back like a bundle of shingles, got in and pulled off.

The cool night air played like a symphony. It was supported by all the sounds of the creepy-crawly night things. She gently touched the throbbing gash on the side of her head. She felt the blood trickling down her face, mingling with her tears. She cried and cried and cried, then rested her head on an old bag of concrete until her sadness found refuge in sleep.

The snoring bounced around the living room then proceeded down the hall where Little Cory sat in the middle of his bed, staring into the darkness, eyes big as cupcakes.

His little feet hit the floor, One... two... three... jump. Now he was safe, safely in bed with his big brother who would protect him from the Monsta. The Monsta who had found its way into their house and was now in their living room, growling.

"Cory, get your butt out my bed!" Magic yelled.

"It's da monsta! It's da monsta!", Cory cried as he buried his face in Magic's chest, holding him with all the strength he could muster.

"That's your daddy in the living room snoring, boy. Let my neck go!", Magic yelled.

"Uh, uh, dat da monsta, dat da monsta."

Magic pried the covers from between him and his little brother, tucked him in his arms, and headed down the hall to the living room.

"Now you see?"

"Dat my daddy, dat my daddy, Magic," Cory responded.

Magic carried him back to their room and laid him in his bed.

"Cory sleep with Magic?", Cory asked.

"No. Now go to sleep."

"Where Magic goin'?"

"Um, going to the bathroom."

"Cory gotta pee."

"You ain't gotta pee, boy, go to sleep," Magic said just below a yell.

"Cory do gotta pee," Cory responded, covering his head with his blanket.

Magic slipped into his pants and headed back down the hall. He looked in his mother's room--she wasn't there. She probably exhausted herself and fell asleep on the way home, he thought. He slipped on a pair of old boots and headed down the driveway.

The brisk night air caught him off guard. "I should have put on a shirt," he said, rubbing his arms as the goose bumps popped up. Just as he went to open the truck door, he heard soft breathing coming from behind the cab. He turned quickly to find his mother lying motionless in the back of the truck.

"Mama, Mama," he said softly and gently touched her shoulder. She sat up slowly. She had bruises on her face.

"I think you should come in, it's almost morning," he said as he lowered the hatch while avoiding her eyes. Because all the frightful details of the evening would be catalogued in her eyes.

He placed his arm around her shoulder and they walked toward the house, acting as if it was perfectly normal that she was arrayed in only a bra and panties, and her beautiful sandy-red hair, that she had teased and combed and teased and combed was now plastered to the side of her head by coagulated blood.

Not a word passed between them. He dropped her off right beyond the threshold and gave her a hug and a kiss, as if it were prom-night. Then he walked back to his room, crawled into bed with his little brother and held him close like a favorite pillow, thinking, I'm telling Uncle Benny, as he drifted off to sleep.

CHAPTER 5

A Magic Sunday

On most Sundays, Magic thought, life would be traipsing up and down the halls of this house. The smell of freshly brewed coffee, bacon and eggs would be settling into the upholstery and flowing out of the window. Cory, Magic, and Peggy would be listening for their ride to church and the Monsta, Cory's dad, would probably be stalking some helpless animal in the woods over by Black Creek. But this morning would be different. Magic slid his arm from underneath his little brother and sat up in bed.

He slipped on some pants, walked quietly down the hall to his mother's room and pushed the door open just enough to peek in and make sure she was alone. Then he crept into the dimly lit room, closed the door behind him and leaned on the dresser in silent observation.

The bloody towels from last night were neatly folded and laid on the floor beside the bed. Rouge, lipstick, and tons of other beautifying stuff sat on the dresser, rarely used by the woman that just didn't feel beautiful any longer.

Bears' closet was sickening to him, everything matched, stacked, and laid out in numerical, alphabetical order; black shirts, blue shirts, white shirts; blue jeans, dress pants, khakis neatly pressed and separated by race, creed, and color.

Their room was like a mortuary. Impenetrable. Dark blue carpet and dark blue walls, black curtains concealing black blinds that attempted to suppress the bright sun. But on this day, neither Magic nor the sun complied. A single stream of light illuminated the welts on the face of the woman that just didn't feel beautiful any longer. And in spite of being told since the age of five, 'What goes on in this house stays in this house,' he was gonna tell his Uncle Benny. Because he had also been told and constantly reminded, 'If Uncle Benny says jump, you don't ask how high, just start jumping high as you can.' And his Uncle Benny had made it perfectly clear that day after the church picnic, when his mother wore sunglasses long after the sun went down. And the black and blue marks were too many to hide.

He'd put his arm around Magic's shoulder and walked him to the back of the church. He looked Magic squarely in the eyes, and expressed to him in no uncertain terms, "If dat man lay a hand on yo Mama again, and the sun sets and you haven't killed him, or I ain't on my way to kill him, I will beat you like you ain't my family." Then he turned and walked back around to the front of the church and over to the truck where Bear and his mother sat waiting. He opened the door to the truck on the side where Bear sat, "Real men don't hit woman," he said, then turned and walked away.

Magic picked up the telephone from his mother's dresser, walked out of the room and dialed.

"Hello," his Aunt Brenda-Gail answered.

"Hi, Auntie."

"Hi, Magic."

"Can I speak to Uncle Benny, please?"

"Yeah, just a minute. You ready fo' church, boy?"

"No, ma'am, not yet."

"Well you need da git a movin', Benny," she shouted, "Peggy's boy want you."

Magic slid down the wall outside his mother's room and sat on the floor, strongly considering hanging up.

"Hey, boy," Uncle Benny said cheerfully.

"Hi, Uncle Benny," Magic responded. "I just called to let you know that we won't be at church today."

"Why... Is everythang alright?"

"No," Magic replied, hoping that was all he had to say.

"Where your mama?"

"She layin' here."

"And Cory?"

"Sleepin'."

"Where his daddy?"

"Hunting, I think."

"You think... look in the gun cabinet and see is any guns missing, boy."

Magic got up and walked to the living room.

"Yes sir, two shotguns and a pistol."

"Did dat man put his hands on your Mama again?"

Magic hesitated, then, "Yes, sir."

"Put your Mama on the phone."

Magic walked back into the bedroom and tapped his mother gently on the shoulder. She rolled over and Magic laid the telephone beside her and left the room.

Peggy picked up the phone; she could hear Uncle Benny talking to her Aunt Brenda-Gail.

"Brenda-Gail, talk to this fool child, and tell her… I will kill dat man dead today, or she can leave Alabama. And when you get off the phone, call all your sisters and tell dey son's I said meet me at Black Creek… And bring dey guns."

"Hello, Peggy," Brenda Gail said.

"Hi, Aunt Brenda Gail."

"You okay, baby?"

"I'm fine, and how are you?", Peggy said, resigned with what was to come.

"You lying, Peggy."

"I'm fine, Aunt Brenda Gail."

"Peggy, you ain't fooling no damn body."

"I'm fine, Aunt Brenda Gail."

"Don't fix your mouth to lie to me, girl."

Peggy sat up. She gasped as a sharp pain shot across her lower back and down her leg.

"Peggy! You alright, baby?", Brenda-Gail asked.

With childlike simplicity and words that were barely discernable, Peggy cried out, "I didn't do nothing! I didn't do nothing, Auntie Brenda Gail. I didn't go nowhere, I didn't even come visit yall. I didn't talk back, I didn't fight, I didn't cheat, I didn't do nothin…"

"Peggy, dat don't matter!", Brenda-Gail interrupted. "Dat don't matter, baby, dat man crazy. His daddy was crazy, and his mama was crazy fo' just stayin' dare, and lettin' dat man take her to a early grave. And you know ya Uncle Benny will kill dat man.

"Aunt Brenda-Gail, that's Cory's daddy!"

"I wouldn't give a damn if he was the Pope. Your Uncle Benny will kill dat man, bury him in the woods, and be at church by eleven o'clock, and you know it."

"Auntie, that's my baby's father, please don't let Uncle Benny kill him," Peggy pleaded.

"Peggy, once a man start puttin' his hands on you, he don't wake up one day and just stop."

"Aunt Brenda-Gail, I'll stop him, please!"

"If you coulda stopped him you'd a done did it. So you can kiss his ass goodbye, or you can leave Alabama. Those your choices."

"That's not a choice, Aunt Brenda-Gail."

"Peggy, you heard what I said, and I ain't about ta sit here and listen to your back talk. You can either pack or I'll have Benny mark his grave for you and Cory. "

"I'll leave," Peggy said.

"Well git-da-packin', and I'll call all your kinfolks and tell 'em to meet me at cho' house so we can all see you off. I'll fry you some chicken and make you a cake fo' ya trip."

The telephone went silent. Peggy held it to her ear until the dial tone returned, which solidified the fact that there was nothing else to be said. She got up and walked into the living room, where Magic sat watching the firewood smolder in the fireplace.

"We got to move. I guess you satisfied," Peggy said.

Magic continued to stare into the fireplace.

"You always got your nose stuck in other people's shit. I told you about running your damn mouth," Peggy shouted as she paced across the living-room floor.

"All I did..." Magic said, and Peggy interrupted.

"All you did was make me have to uproot from my damn home."

"This ain't no home, Mama. Ain't no love around here. That man got us trained like one of his huntin' dogs. He drop somethin', we fetch it. He holler, we run in the corner and tuck our tails!"

"Bear been good to us, Magic."

"What's good, Mama? What's good?", Magic responded, scowling. "When he kicks your ass every other week, or when he's calling you every name in the book? No, I guess good is when he comes home and changes his clothes and leaves without even a how was school, dog, or how was your day, cat!"

"No, good is putting a roof over your head, food in your mouth, and clothes on your back!", Peggy shouted.

"Damn, Mama, are you losing your mind? This is Uncle Benny's house, and everything me and Cory gets comes from Uncle Benny and Aunt Brenda-Gail. I ain't stupid, and though you acting like it, you ain't neither!"

Magic got up from the couch, stalked out the door, jumped over the banister and headed down the driveway.

"Magic, get your ass back here... I said, get your ass back here and pack your clothes, boy."

"Leave 'em for the good man your imagination done created," Magic responded, and continued across the road and into the woods.

Peggy turned and walked back into the house.

Cory stood in the doorway rubbing his eyes.

"Magic said a bad word, Mommy."

"Never mind Magic, baby, he a little upset."

"Cory a little upset, too."

"What's wrong with Mama's baby?"

"Magic peed in Mamma's baby's bed, see," Cory said, turning around.

The dark yellow stain ran all the way up the backside of Cory's oversized T-shirt, and Peggy couldn't help but laugh. She picked him up, pressed him solidly against her and kissed his cheek. Just like she used to do to Magic a long time ago, when she needed to feel loved after a long night of demanding sexcapades. As she held Cory close, Magic's words played in her head. 'This ain't no home, Mama, ain't no love going on around here.'

She had known that for a long time, but at some point, it stopped mattering. She had a house on two acres of land, plenty of food to eat and two healthy boys that she didn't have to sell her ass to take care of. Which was more than she thought she deserved.

"Did Daddy hit chu right dare?", Cory asked, pointing to the welt on her face.

"No baby, Mommy ran into the screen door," Peggy lied. Then asked, "You wanna take a bath?"

"No," Cory said.

"So what you gonna do, walk around smelling like pee all day."

"Yep," Cory said, then lifted up his shirt and smelled it. "I don't stank."

"Yes you do," Peggy said, smiling.

"No I don't," Cory said, lifting his shirt and sticking it in his mother's face. "Smell."

"Peeeeee U," Peggy responded and carried him into the bathroom.

"Mommy, I want lots a bubbles. I want dem all da way up dare," Cory said, pointing to the ceiling.

Peggy smiled and headed to the kitchen to get the dish washing liquid, which worked fine as bubble bath.

She returned to the bathroom, undressed Cory, placed him in the tub and gave him a rubber Mickey Mouse, a Trans-former Autobot, and a few other toys to keep him occupied while she packed.

Peggy took her toothbrush from the cup on the sink and opened the medicine cabinet to get the toothpaste. Catching a glimpse of her reflection in the mirror, she started rubbing the bags underneath her eyes. She moved in a little closer and touched the scar just above her right eyebrow-- her one-year anniversary present from Bear. She gave him gold cuff links and a double-breasted suit.

She continued down to her neck and touched the claw marks that countless tubes of cocoa butter hadn't removed, remnants of when he choked her unconscious then panicked and poured a can of Budweiser in her face. It was as if she had never seen these scars before. On the verge of tears, she turned away from the mirror and away from Cory.

"Mommy's going to make some phone calls. When you want to get out, just call me."

"Okay, Mommy," Cory said, fervently trying to stuff Mickey Mouse into a big gulp cup from Piggly Wiggly's.

Peggy walked out of the bathroom, pulled her suitcases down from the closet, and frantically began emptying her drawers.

The woods were the only place Magic felt safe to think, because sometimes thoughts generated strong emotions that he couldn't control. And Uncle Benny said real men's tears flowed backwards, silent and invisible.

He used to come out here with his twelve-gauge shotgun and just shoot stuff until he felt better, but Cory's father put a lock on the gun cabinet. Now he came and watched the wild blueberries grow fat, bending their branches and kissing the ground. He watched birds soar from weeping willows, to oaks, to pines. He watched wild squirrels as they played charades before scurrying up the Pecan trees.

Magic walked and walked and walked until sweat poured off him like a melting ice cube. Then he sat underneath the biggest tree he could find. A cool breeze danced around his neck almost apologetically because the late morning sun had marched in, showing no mercy.

It was so peaceful here, and he knew that at some point the little committee in his head would quiet down. Then clear thoughts would flow. When they finally did, he dusted off his pants and headed home.

CHAPTER 6

Bear

It wasn't the sex. It was the surge of power or the temporary abatement he felt from the moment her blond hair flipped into his face and slowly flowed down his body. Her soft pink lips followed, alternating from right nipple to left nipple in soft circular motions. Her blue eyes looked up periodically, saying, moan, damn it, moan.

Down, down in a zigzag motion, gentle bites meant to arouse as soft, skilled hands and prissy pink florescent nails stroked, stroked and stroked... Lips, tongue and cheeks moving in unified motion, faster and faster and faster.

"No, no, no!", the Monsta said as he sat up and grabbed her head.

"What's wrong, baby?", she asked, looking more aggravated than concerned.

"Nothing," he replied. "Just start over."

"Start over? That's another fifty dollars."

Bear woke from his ecstasy-induced daze. "Bitch, I ain't ask you how much it cost. Don't I always take care of you?"

"Yeah, Daddy," she responded seductively. She started sucking on his earlobes and worked her way back down.

Carla had serviced men for years; she knew every lewd and lascivious act ever performed, whether it was written down or passed down. She knew it, had practiced and perfected it.

"Close your eyes, babe," Carla said, "and loosen those butt cheeks. I ain't gonna hurt you."

Bear smiled, complied, and soon arrived at that place. That place where yesterdays and tomorrows don't matter-- where problems, worries, fears, and doubts send letters or postcards, but never do they visit.

She moaned, he moaned, she groaned, he groaned.

"Now," she said, then shrank the circle about two centimeters; the adjustable circle that fit perfectly around cucumbers, carrots, hotdogs and slim neck coke bottles. She stopped swallowing and allowed her saliva to flow freely.

Her pale complexion blended perfectly with the white sheets and her head moved so rapidly up and down, up and down that it became merely a blur. His thigh muscles tensed as his toes curled and his body shivered. She geared down from five...to four...to three...to two then skipped one, went to neutral and backed out from between his legs. She rolled over, took a couple of deep breaths while gently rubbing his legs. Then she got up, and left the room.

Bear laid there feeling like he had taken a big bite of happy and wishing he had brought another fifty dollars.

Carla returned shortly and handed him a damp rag and a shot of gin.

"Thank you, baby," he said.

"My pleasure," she responded, smiled and strolled off to the bathroom again.

Bear wiped himself, folded the face rag and laid it on the dresser. Then he went in to his wallet and placed the five twenty dollar bills beside it. He turned up the shot glass and got dressed.

Bear could hear the running water and the buzzing sound of the electric toothbrush up until he reached the front porch. He smiled and hopped into the old Ford and put the pedal to the floor. The back tires started to spin, kicking up dust and gravel as the truck hurtled forward.

Peggy heard the gravel crackle from the weight of the old Ford Pickup. She rushed to the window, although there was no need. The sound of that truck pulling into the driveway was very familiar to her. As was the dreary feeling that seemed to engorge the whole house as soon as the left turn signal was engaged. Her first thought was to hide. To run to her room and crawl under the bed or in the back of the closet with the mice. But she stood there paralyzed.

His footsteps played in stereo. And with each approaching step her body weakened and her eyes darted from the door to the suitcases lined up against the wall like exhibits A. B. and C.

The screen door opened and the Monsta's eyes went straight to the suitcases.

"Bitch, where you think you goin'?" he shouted. A disconcerted stare was her only response.

"Goddammit, Peggy, I'm talkin' to you," he said, kicking the Donna Karan suitcase into the TV.

The gin bottle and ammo box hit the ground.

The coffee table took flight and shattered the glass in the china cabinet.

Peggy started to run toward the kitchen when his steel-toed boot caught her in the stomach and her hundred and thirty pound frame buckled as she gasped for air.

"Gitcha motherfuckin' ass up and put dees clothes back where dey belong," he shouted.

Then with, "No more!" ringing from her lips and years of pent-up anger controlling her actions, she jumped in his chest and dug her nails in his face.

"Bitch, I'm gonna kill you," he shouted, slamming and then straddling her.

Peggy fought back with kicks, scratches and screams, until all her will to fight was erased. He slapped her, choked her, and spat in her face until she begged and pleaded and begged and pleaded some more.

The screen door slammed… the glass from the gun cabinet shattered…and the cocking of the shotgun echoed through the house.

"Get the fuck off my mother!" Magic shouted, pushing the twelve-gauge into Bear's jaw.

"Git that goddamn gun out my face, boy," Bear shouted and then repeated, "I said, git that goddamn gun out my face, boy." He turned and his lips grazed the barrel of the gun.

"I said, get the fuck off my mother."

"Magic… Magic," Peggy whispered as he stood there with the shotgun pressed firmly against his shoulder; just like his Uncle Benny had taught him.

There was no evidence of fear, no sweat formed on his brow. He was calm, prepared.

"Magic... put the gun down, baby," Peggy pleaded. Her words didn't register.

"Get the fuck off my Mama," he repeated.

Bear reached for the gun and Magic pulled the trigger.

The force sent the Monsta's half-headless body flying across the living room. It hit the ground and jerked and jerked and jerked, then stopped. The blood oozed from the Monsta's head onto the hardwood floor, getting bigger, and bigger, and bigger. Panic replaced anger and minutes replaced moments as they stood there in shock until the pitter-patter of little feet running down the hall seemed louder than the ringing in Peggy's ears.

With a mud pie in one hand and a stick in the other, Cory leaned over his father's dead body and with tears in his eyes, summed the morning. "Magic, you kill my daddy. You kill my daddy!"

Magic dropped the shotgun and walked out onto the front porch. Peggy sat on the floor next to the body, her back resting against the couch and Cory tucked in her arms. His tears soaked the front of her shirt and his.

Magic watched as the brigade of shiny trucks pulled into the drive way. Benny Jr. and Cousin Willie-Lewis took the body and buried it in the woods. Cousin Jimmy-Dickey and Cousin Homer burned down the house. Aunt Brenda-Gail and Aunt Maulee took Peggy and Magic to the bus station. Uncle Benny took Cory, kicking and screaming.

CHAPTER 7

In Search Of....

A foul mouth lady and her four bad kids occupied the first three seats on the bus, one of them tried to bathe a stuffed animal in the toilet. This caused the toilet to overflow, and little shit balls rolled up and down the bus for at least the first eight hundred miles. The bus driver— was very apologetic as he walked through spraying Glade potpourri fragrance all over everybody—He stopped to let the bus air out. This caused them to miss their connecting bus and they had to sit three and half-hours waiting for the next one.

They boarded the second bus about three o'clock in the morning and sat in front of some newlyweds who spent most of the night arguing. Their conversation ended when he said to her, "Your father needs to be in an old folk's home and not rolling around in a damn wheelchair insulting people." She cried, he cursed and Magic drifted off to sleep.

He was awakened by a woman sitting in front of his mother holding a conversation with a person that wasn't there. She sounded like the woman at his Uncle Benny's church, who stood up every Sunday morning and uttered some gibberish that they called speaking in tongues.

Magic closed his eyes and laid his head on his mother's shoulder. He managed to amass about four hours of sleep before his mother awakened him with a kiss on his forehead.

"Good morning, Magic," she said with a smile, a new smile that almost looked genuine.

"Good morning, Mama," Magic responded, matching her smile for smile.

"How'd you sleep?", she asked.

"Good, but my butt hurts," Magic said.

She chuckled.

"I'm going to that restaurant," she said, pointing out the window at a little Mom and Pop place across the street. "I need a cup of coffee. You want something?"

"Yes ma'am. I'm about tired of chicken and pound cake."

She kissed him on the forehead again then slowly walked toward the front of the bus. Magic turned to the window and watched her as she waited for a break in traffic, thinking that he couldn't remember the last time his mother had kissed him or even rubbed his head like she'd done half the night.

He could tell she was tired: she had dark circles and a reddish tint to her eyes. He wondered if it was from crying or lack of sleep. She'd had a real problem leaving Cory, but Aunt Brenda-Gail said she needed to 'git settled' before she dragged that child down the road.

50

Uncle Benny and Aunt Brenda-Gail tried to get his mother to stay, Uncle Benny told her he would build her a brand new house, a better house. She called him a dictator and said she didn't want nothing else to do with Opelika. But that didn't stop her from taking the money Aunt Brenda-Gail pretended to slip her when they boarded the bus. As if Uncle Benny didn't know.

Aunt Brenda-Gail didn't do anything without Uncle Benny's approval. Her sisters often mocked her; they would say, "If I want a damn glass of water out yo' house, you got to ask your husband." And she would respond, "Git one, a real one, and you wouldn't piss out the water I give ya without his permission." Which was a joke, because they always asked for Uncle Benny's advice, and they turned their sons over to him as soon as they were old enough to speak.

Magic's Uncle Benny say 'everybody disrespectful up north', he say he 'wouldn't live there if you paid him'. Magic's mother said they lived in Rochester, N.Y. up until he was five. Him, her, and his dad, but he didn't remember. She says, 'that's why I don't talk country.'

According to their bus tickets, they would get to Rochester Wednesday morning about eleven or twelve. Probably have hemorrhoids by the time we get there, Magic thought.

He laid his head up against the window, placed his feet in his mother's chair, and closed his eyes. Then he heard someone say, "Young man... Young man..." He wasn't sure, but it sounded like the crazy lady from last night, so he acted as though he hadn't heard her. But she raised her volume and called again, "Young man."

"Yes ma'am," Magic responded quickly, feeling as though he had done something wrong.

"Would you please join me?" she asked.

Magic got out of his seat and stood in the aisle next to her. "Please sit," she said.

Magic sat down hesitantly, one foot in the walkway and the other one pointed in that direction, turbo jets on and ready.

She sat with her eyes closed and her hands together in her lap. She was probably in her early sixties and her face looked as if it had lost most of its elasticity. But she was very well dressed and smelled pretty good for a crazy lady.

Quietly, she said, "You slept with me last night," then paused.

Now that's just nasty, Magic thought as curiosity replaced his fear. She sat perfectly still, eyes closed. Nothing moved but her lips as she continued. "Evil hovers over you like a dark cloud, and the demons that are in front of you are far worse than the ones you left behind. Don't be afraid of your dark side."

The loose skin under her neck jiggled a bit as she continued, "Your path was chosen prior to Saul's, and dark angels rest on your shoulders. The pillars will rot, the foundation will weaken, and the house will fall on you. You are the rightful heir."

She filled her lungs, held it for a moment, then exhaled slowly as if she were cleansing her body of a toxic chemical. Magic sat there for a minute, then made his escape. He walked hurriedly off the bus and looking neither left nor right, bolted out into traffic.

"Boy, you look like you saw a ghost," his mother said.

"Mama, who is Saul?" Magic blurted.

"Saul from the Bible?"

"I guess."

"He was a persecutor of Christians, until God spoke to him one day. Why you ask?"

"Just asked," Magic responded.

CHAPTER 8

Home Sweet Home

They pulled into the Greyhound bus station in Rochester, New York, about two o'clock in the afternoon.

"We're home," Magic's mother said. She looked over at him and in her eye's he saw what appeared to be hope at half-mast.

The crazy lady got up and looked over at Magic as she gathered her stuff from the seat next to her. "Nice to have met you, Magic Junior," she said.

"Nice to have met you, ma'am," Magic responded as she walked past.

"Do you know her?" Magic asked his mother.

"No," she said as she pulled their suitcases from the overhead compartment.

"Well, how she know my name Magic Junior?"

"Don't play with me, boy," his mother responded. Then she turned and walked off the bus.

The bus station was cheerless, illuminated only by dirty white walls that cried out for a fresh coat of paint. It sat in what appeared to be an alley adjacent to a monstrous building and was about as big as a nice size living room. Fourteen dingy chairs were bolted to the ground with small TV's protruding from the front, and for fifty cents you could watch twenty minutes of television. But the people there were much more entertaining.

A woman stood at the counter cursing out the ticket lady because she wouldn't give her a refund on a ticket that was clearly marked non-refundable. But she didn't have anything on the guy with a wine bottle in each of his back pockets, and a sign hanging from his neck saying, 'will work for food.'

After about fifteen minutes, a taxi pulled up and Magic and his mother loaded all of their stuff in the trunk and hopped in.

"Where to?" asked the driver.

"The Department of Social Services," his mother responded, then asked. "Is it still on Westfall Road?"

"Yes, but there's a new one on St. Paul," he answered, his accent so thick his words barely resembled English. He was Jamaican or West Indian--some kinda different breed of black.

All the houses were so close together that privacy obviously wasn't a big thing here, and stoplights seemed to impede every effort made to get anywhere. Stop signs lurked around every corner.

"No, keep straight," Magic's mother shouted to the cab driver through the thick glass window that separated the driver in the front from the passenger in the back; which made no sense to Magic.

"You no drive, I drive," he responded.

Magic's mother sat up in the seat, pressed her lips against what appeared to be air holes, and said, "I no fucking pay, you pay!"

The speedometer went from thirty-five to fifty-five. Apparently, there were no more stop signs or stoplights.

Magic and his mother got out of the taxi and retrieved their four suitcases and the Tupperware bowl of stale chicken. His mother handed the driver a twenty-dollar bill and said, "Keep the change."

He smiled and nodded graciously. "Tank you, mon," he said in good tip language.

Before they could pick up their bags, a dirty-looking man with a cigarette stuck between his lips walked up.

"Can I help you with those, gorgeous?" he asked.

Magic thought he had seen his mother's entire range of facial expressions, but he had never seen this one. She looked at this man as if he was cow dung, and said, "You at the welfare. Obviously, you're having a problem helping yourself." She stuck the Tupperware bowl under her arm, picked up her two suitcases and proceeded into the building.

All eyes were on them before they could get through the second set of doors. Magic looked at his mother. She was dressed in a pair of straight leg blue jeans that fit her perfectly, a powder blue sweater, blue suede pumps, and a matching purse. Magic had always been the best-dressed boy in his ninth grade class. And he had made high honor roll every year since seventh grade. So, the appropriateness of his attire could not have been in question. So what were they looking at? he wondered.

Magic studied the room and realized that they were the only people there with suitcases. He wanted to ask his mother where they were, but decided against it. People were packed in this building like they were giving away money. Drinking soda, reading the paper, picking their noses, chit-chatting and socializing while babies ran around like they didn't belong to anybody. Others sat watching the color TV that was chained and mounted in a steel box on the far wall.

They got in the line that said, 'Drop off, Pick Ups, and New Applicants,' right behind Miss Congeniality. "Hi," she said, and stepped forward a bit trying to give Magic and his mother a little space.

"Hi," his mother responded.

"Girl, I picked the wrong day to come here. I just need to drop off some check stubs and I been in this line for damn near an hour."

Magic's mom and her struck up a conversation about hairdressers, nail shops and nightclubs.

The long line went rather quickly in spite of the teeth sucking and the fuck you's, and the fuck thats, and the fuck its, that seemed to end every other conversation carried on through the thick glass with air holes that separated them. It was very apparent that the middle-aged gay looking man who stood well protected behind the glass window, didn't like his job.

Wearing a fake smile, Magic's mother stepped to the window and spoke into the air holes.

"Hi, my name is Peggy."

"Hi. I'm late for break, can I help you?"

His mother paused for a moment, licked her lips then continued. "My son and I just returned here from the south and we don't have any place to stay. I would like to apply for emergency housing."

The man stepped back, put his hand on his hip and did a little gay thing with his face. "Okay, honey, let me make sure I'm hearing you correctly. You came here from another state, knowing that you didn't have no place to stay?"

"Yes, that's what I said."

"Well, Miss Peggy, we only do emergency housing if there's a fire or an eviction. Sorry, but we don't do accommodation for out of town guests. Is there anything else I can do for you?"

That's when his mother lost it.

"No, you can't do shit for me! I need to speak to your supervisor."

"My supervisor is on break, where I should be."

"Well, I need to speak to your supervisor's supervisor before I come through that little-bitty hole and kick your ass."

All of a sudden a security guard about 6'2" looking all of 300 pounds came running from the back with a little Spanish woman who was about half his size trailing. Magic's mother was escorted to the back by the little Spanish lady, and the security guard just stood there looking like a black Barney.

Magic looked around the room, trying to find a spot big enough to accommodate the luggage and him.

'Kenya Graves, window three,' came bellowing out of the static filled intercom, and a black lady who appeared to be about twenty-six, got up with her two small children. This cleared a spot for Magic right on the end. He watched everyone who came out the back hall.

About twenty minutes later the guy from the window came prancing out with a cigarette in one hand and a can of soda in the other. He walked out of the building, Magic right on his heels. Magic walked up behind him and tapped him on the shoulder. He turned around with the unlit cigarette stuck in his mouth and Magic tried to take his head off. He hit the ground and wobbled, trying to get up. Magic stood over him and talked like his Uncle Benny used to talk to him when the long walk in the woods didn't work.

"Don't disrespect my Mama," he said. "I don't disrespect yours."

The next thing Magic knew he was dangling in the air, barely breathing. On the verge of losing consciousness, he heard someone say, "Let him go, let him go."

The big security guard dropped him hard and he lay there trying to catch his breath.

"You okay, Peace?", some man said, standing over him.

"Yes I'm fine, sir," Magic responded, struggling to push whole words through his windpipe.

The stranger turned, walked over to the security guard, said something then went back into the building. The security guard shuffled over to Magic and said, "Listen, little nigga, you should be in handcuffs on your way to jail. So take your ass back in there, sit down and don't move, you understand me, boy?"

"Yes, sir," Magic responded.

When Magic walked back in the building some people started to clap and the man who had asked if he was alright turned and looked at him.

His stomach was sitting below empty; he hadn't eaten for way too long, but the last thing he wanted was more chicken, and he was afraid to move. The man who asked was he all right, was sitting in front of him watching The Rosie O'Donnell Show. Out of desperation, Magic leaned forward. "Excuse me, sir, you know where I could get something to eat?"

"It's a Mickey D's up the street," he responded.

The volume on the television went up and everybody started singing along with Usher. Even the little kids were sliding across the floor singing and dancing to the beat. A couple of minutes later, Rosie walked out on stage, asked Usher about his new album, made a fool of herself trying to do a dance move, and said her farewells. Then the guy in front of Magic turned and said, "Yo, Peace. I'm, Clear. What's your name?"

"Magic," he said, slightly delayed and off balance.

"Magic, Magic," he said with a bit of question in his voice and a little chuckle.

"Check this out, Magic. I'm a little hungry myself, so I'm gonna run up here to Mickey D's. My peoples should be ready to pull up out of here in about twenty minutes. If I'm not back, tell her to chill."

Clear stood up and headed for the door.

"What she look like?" Magic asked.

"You'll know her," he responded.

Magic nodded as he turned to walk out, escorted by the eyes of every black, white, and Hispanic female in the building.

He returned about fifteen minutes later with two super-sized double-cheeseburger value meals.

"How much was it, sir?" Magic asked.

"Small thang, Peace, don't sweat it," he said, and Magic wondered if he thought his name was Peace instead of Magic.

Clear looked to be about 30 years old, and he got a real kick out of Magic calling him sir. Magic sat there and told him his story. And with the patience of a priest appointed to a confession booth, Clear listened. Magic talked so much he all but forgot about how hungry he was.

Clear told Magic where he shopped, and how to get dreads. And that he drove a Lexus Coupe; Candy Apple Red, with butter soft leather seats that vibrated and heated up with the push of a button. He told him his mother died when he was twenty-one and he didn't know who his father was. He asked Magic about his grades in school, what he wanted to be, what he liked to do, if he went to church, and if he believed in God. Magic guessed he answered all the questions correctly because the last thing Clear said was, "I like you, Magic, you a good kid. We need to hang out sometime."

They sat there talking for about ten minutes more before Clear's girlfriend walked out from the back. He was right, she looked like his girl. She was about 5'3" waxed and buffed. She shined like a picture in a magazine, and her oversized butt accentuated her Roca Wear sweat pants.

She walked over, stood behind them, placed her hands on Clear's shoulders then leaned forward and kissed him on the cheek.

"Hey, baby, what's up?"

"You," Clear responded as he pulled the straw from his mouth. "You straight?" he asked.

"Yeah, I'm straight," she replied with a touch of uncertainty in her voice.

"How's Dayja?" Clear asked.

"Not good."

Clear seemed to ignore her response and continued. "Porsha, this is Magic, Big Magic from the south," he said teasingly. "Magic, Porsha."

Magic stood up to shake her hand and his orange soda and French fries hit the ground. He stood there with his double cheeseburger in his hand, stuck between dumb and dumber.

Magic started to kneel to pick up his trash, but Clear grabbed his arm and said to Porsha, "Get that for me, baby."

She walked around the chairs to where Magic stood and began picking up the soggy French fries. She then walked over to the desk where the security guard had posted himself and asked him for a mop.

Magic stood there thinking that that was something his Aunt Brenda-Gail would do. But his Uncle Benny wouldn't have had to ask her. Moments later a brother who looked to be in his mid–forties, wearing a faded blue uniform, came walking out with a mop and a bucket.

Porsha met him as he turned the corner and insisted that he give her the mop. After several, 'I'll do its, the maintenance man surrendered and handed it to her. She cleaned the floor and returned the mop and bucket to the custodian.

"Thank you," Porsha said with a smile.

"Thanks, baby," Clear said.

"Thank you, ma'am," Magic added.

"Ma'am!" Porsha responded, laughing. "How old are you, Magic?"

"Fourteen."

"Fourteen? Damn! They grow 'em big down there," she said. "Just call me Porsha."

"Yes, ma'am, I mean, I mean Porsha."

They laughed a small but genuine laugh. Like Mama and Magic use to when Cory did silly baby stuff.

Clear threw his arm around Magic's shoulder and said, "Come on, Peace, take a walk with me."

"What about my stuff?" Magic asked.

"Yo, Rock," Clear yelled. And the big security guard's head snapped up from the book he was reading. Clear pointed to Magic's things.

"Got you," the security guard responded.

"You ready, baby?" Clear asked, as they turned to leave. Porsha didn't say anything, nor did she move. Clear turned to face her.

"Dayja made me promise we would stay until she came out," Porsha said.

"You playin' me Porsha?" he said. His face hardened as he stared into Porsha's eyes, visibly upset. She looked away, then established herself in the nearest chair and assumed a humble but steadfast position. Clear walked over, stood behind the chair and put his lips to her ear.

"I ain't got time for you or Dayja's bullshit. Call me when you ready to leave," he said, and turned, and walked out of the building.

Magic walked beside him, Porsha was about five paces behind.

They were standing in the parking lot across the street when Porsha decided to plead Dayja's case.

"So, what are we gonna do, Clear, just let her rot in foster care?"

Clear turned abruptly, but Porsha didn't flinch.

"I know plenty people that's been in fuckin' foster homes and it ain't kill' em."

"Dayja's a girl, Clear."

"She ain't no girl, she's a bad ass! I spent four years trying to make her into a girl. For what, for what Porsha? So she could skip school and suck those little bum-ass niggas' dicks on the corner. Far as I'm concerned she can do what she want a do as long as she ain't slobbin' on my pillowcases."

"All she wanna do is see you, Clear," Porsha said, tears rolling down her face as she turned and walked back toward the building. When she got to the middle of the street, she turned back around and headed back. She stopped about four feet from Clear, put her hand on her hip, and said, "Did you ever wonder where she learned to suck a dick, Clear? My step-daddy taught me. In my room. In my house. Right under my mother's nose, and I'm damn good at it, ain't I?" She turned to walk away and the way she swung her hips wasn't nuttin' nice.

Clear grimaced, smiled, and shook his head as he hopped up on the trunk of an Intrepid that was parked next to his red Lexus.

He looked Magic up and down, as if he was sizing him up for a suit.

"You know I like you, Peace, and that's big shit, because I don't like teenagers. I got a sister and I can't stand her ass. But you," he said softening his voice, "you got that lost boy look in your eyes, just like my brother Brandon had." Clear hopped off the Intrepid, reached into his shirt pocket and handed Magic a card which read, *Precision Cuts*, then continued, "Welcome to the Rock, Big Magic. A concrete jungle financed by the villains and maintained by the suckers they refer to as employees. Come see me when you settle in." He smiled and said once more, "I like you kid."

As the candy apple red Lexus pulled off, Magic began replaying everything he had said over and over and over in his head. He even found himself practicing his gestures in the mirror when he went to the bathroom. He was bedazzled by his walk, his words, his over-sized shirt, sagging pants, and Timberland boots. At that moment, he knew exactly what his future entailed. He was going to be a barber and marry a woman with a big butt and an attitude.

When he went back into the Department of Social Services, Porsha was standing talking to Rock, the Security Guard. Magic took his seat next to their luggage, kind of watched TV, and kind of watched them. About twenty minutes went by and a middle-aged lady walked in and over to Porsha. Her and Porsha talked for a minute then they walked toward the back, in the direction his mother had gone. Five minutes later they walked back out with the prettiest girl Magic had ever seen. She had bone-straight hair that caressed the back of her neck and her complexion was the same as the pecans he stole from Mrs. Molly's tree. She had big, pretty, oval-shaped eyes and beautiful lips--the only thing missing was a smile. So hurriedly, Magic rambled through all his smiles. His smiley smile, his thank you smile, his I'm smiling just to be polite smile. He tossed them all to the side. And there it was, in the back, in the corner, in the dark. It had never been used before. His 'I love you' smile. His 'I will fade your clouds and brighten your days' smile. He put it on hoping he would be given the opportunity to give it to her.

Porsha had her arm around Dayja's shoulder, Dayja's head was lying on Porsha's chest, and she walked right by him, never even glancing in his direction. From behind they looked to be about the same size, her butt wasn't quite as big. But it was big enough, and it would grow.

CHAPTER 9

Heart Break Hotel

The big sign in front read Clemar's Hotel, Your comfort is our only concern.

They stepped out of the taxi and apparently into an elderly man's dining room. He sat on the sidewalk with his back resting against the hotel, sopping the juices from a can of cat food with what appeared to be a honey bun. Magic's staring obviously offended him.

"What you looking at? What you looking at? You want to buy me something to eat?" he said.

Magic's mother grabbed his arm and directed his attention to the suitcases sitting on the ground beside the taxi.

"Nine Lives--that's the good stuff," his mother interjected."

He smiled and showed about twelve very stained teeth.

The cat-food man hopped up and wiped his dirty hands on his dirty pants as they started into the hotel.

"Can I help you with that, ma'am?" he asked.

"Sure," Magic's mother said, and handed him the two suitcases.

Just as they entered the foyer, a beautiful white lady in her early thirties with long purple fingernails stood up and shouted, "Po' boy, get your stinking ass outta here!"

The cat-food man dropped the suitcases and ran out of the hotel while Magic and his mother stood there, startled.

Magic couldn't help but think that this hotel, the bus station, and the welfare building were related. You could almost hear the mildew growing underneath the filthy gray carpet. The squeaky ceiling fan seemed to play mortuary music as it limped in a circular motion, carrying cobwebs of extinct spiders and years of dust piled up and running over the side.

This place is nasty, the people are nasty, and I don't want to stay here, Magic thought as his mother stepped up to the counter in her normal fashion.

"Hi, ma'am, my name is Peggy, and I was sent here by the Department of Social Services."

The pretty lady behind the desk extended her purple fingernails to Magic's mother.

"I'm Marge," she said, smiled and looked over at Magic. "And how are you, young man?"

Magic wanted to say, 'I'm nervous, and I don't want to be here'. Then a vision of Clear popped into his head, so he stuck out his chest and put a little bass in his voice.

"Fine, thanks, and you?"

"What a polite young man," she said as she ruffled through some papers. "That's hard to find in this city. And what's your name?" she asked.

"His name is Magic," Magic's mother answered.

"And how old are you, Magic?"

Magic looked at his mother and his mother looked at him. Marge turned and took some papers from the fax machine. Her butt stretched the seams of the purple pants she wore.

"Seventeen," Magic said. His mother almost choked.

"Are you okay?" Marge asked.

Clearing her throat, Magic's mother responded, "I'm fine," looked at Magic and smiled.

"Okay, ma'am, if you could just sign here."

She handed Magic's mother a piece of paper and a pen, and handed Magic a key.

"This is the best room in the hotel," she said. "When I work late and don't want to go home, I sleep in this room."

"Thank you," Magic said as they turned and walked toward the elevator. Magic looked back, not really knowing why, but she smiled and winked. Magic felt himself blush. He stumbled and his body seemed to overheat. He went to sleep that night counting purple sheep. He danced on purple clouds and found a pot of gold under a purple rainbow.

They stayed at Clemar's Hotel for three months. In those three months, Magic learned more about life and people than he had in fourteen years. The first two weeks his mother and him hung out a lot. They went to the mall, to the movies, and out to eat. Then she hooked up with one of her old friends name Candy, a cousin, his mother said, but she didn't resemble anybody he knew in their family.

Candy would come to the hotel smelling like she had bathed in perfume and wearing just enough clothes to keep from being arrested. The Dentyne Ice did nothing for the searing smell of alcohol that slapped him in the face when she repeatedly told him how fine he was. And how she had robbed a few cradles in her day.

Magic and his mother went to her house a couple of times, once for a party. It was a beautiful house with a pool in the backyard and statues of oversized frogs and pink flamingos in the front like the rich white people's yards in Alabama. It was clean, like his Aunt Brenda-Gail's house. The basement was like another apartment. It had a kitchen, a bathroom, a big TV, furniture, and a pool table. His mother made him stay down there almost the whole party. It was a pool party with women running around in bikinis while fat old men drooled.

Monday through Saturday Candy and his mother went out, so for the most part Magic was on his own. He cruised the halls getting familiar with his surroundings. If you entered the hotel from the back, the stairs that led to the lobby were on your right. On your left was a big steel door with four dead-bolt locks. One afternoon he saw some guy installing a security camera aimed directly at the door that led to the basement. It was the only place he installed a security camera and the monitor sat in Marge's office. He told Magic his name was Blast. Magic said, "Blast what?" He said "Blast Blast." This made Magic curious, so he watched the activities in the basement closely. Every two weeks two couples would come to the hotel and go in the basement and stay from Monday to late Wednesday. The only way Magic knew they were there was because Marge would unlock the door and let them in and Magic was normally at the front desk. The only other time he saw someone in the basement was when two church vans came and dropped off some big boxes. Magic asked Marge what was in them and she told him to mind his own business.

Marge would go in the basement three or four times a week and bring up boxes that were much smaller than the ones the church vans dropped off. A big truck with UPS on the side would pick them up.

The second floor was the prostitute and crackhead floor. The crackheads, prostitutes, and their petrified dates entered from the back and took the stairs. The normal people entered from the front and took the elevator. Most of the crackheads were there for emergency housing, which was set up by the Department of Social Services.

Marge and Magic hit it off from day one. And once she realized that his mother was out half the night and slept half the day, she really tried to keep Magic busy. When he wasn't sweeping the halls or cleaning the vacant rooms, he was in her office playing rummy or go fish. It sometimes took them hours to finish one game because she was always on the phone talking about money, stocks and bonds, buying and selling. She sounded like a stockbroker or Mrs. Greenspan. Magic had hoped that one day she would call him into her office and gently guide him into manhood, but it never happened.

The maintenance and upkeep was the same throughout the building--very little. But more attention was given to the second floor because crackheads 'lived like animals', Marge would say, which was the truth.

One evening Marge called up to Magic's room and asked if he wanted to make fifty dollars.

"Sure," he said.

Magic's mother was out looking for an apartment and he had fallen in love with this little funny looking kid named Bart Simpson. Magic turned off the television and took the elevator to the first floor.

Diana, who managed the front desk, was standing there doing what she did, which was nothing most of the time.

Magic asked her where was Marge, and she pointed to her office.

When Magic entered the office, Marge was on the telephone telling 'the story' to one of her friends. She gestured for Magic to have a seat.

"Girl, we didn't see that man for twelve days and at about two in the morning on the twelfth day, the same girl who came in with him crept off the elevator butt ass naked. She had most of her clothes in her hand and her eyes were racing around the room like something was going to emerge from the woodwork. All she said was, 'that motherfucker crazy! That motherfucker crazy!' She stood in the middle of the lobby putting on her panties and skirt, then she crept out the front door with her shirt barely over her head.

"When day broke, Diana and I went up to check on him. Girl, I could smell the cocaine seeping out through the cracks between the doorframe." Marge stopped for a moment, shook her head and then continued to tell the story as Magic sat there totally caught up. "I knocked on the door and said who I was, but I ain't get no answer. I tried the passkey, but the door was jammed so Diana and I went back downstairs and called Big Mack. He had to come down and kick the damn door in.

"Girl, this man was standing in the corner on his tiptoes with no clothes on, a stem in one hand and a lighter in the other, dried shit running down his legs. Chil', he had to be at least twenty pounds lighter than when he came in." She laughed. "The room smelled like straight up shit, and it was covered with crack vials and empty bags. There were maggots crawling around the toilet, and used condoms beside the bed. Spoiled food all over the place, it was awful. Made me sick to my stomach. I couldn't even go in there, and Diana made me pay her triple time just to get the man dressed."

Magic imagined the person on the other end of the phone must saying, 'Why didn't you call the police?' because Marge said, "Call the police and tell them what? That I let a man stay in my hotel and smoke crack until he was damn near dead? I don't think so. Anyway, my little boyfriend's in the office, and he's gonna go and clean the room for me. I'll talk to you later. Bye, girl."

Marge didn't exaggerate at all, how anyone could stay in that room was beyond Magic's comprehension. He soon realized that this was a different world and many things would be beyond his comprehension. He cleaned the room, got his fifty dollars, and swore never to say yes to anything in the blind again.

A few days later one of the ladies on Social Service didn't show up for her work assignment and the welfare wasn't going to pay for her to be at the hotel any longer. When Marge came in that afternoon, she called up to the ladies room to tell her, and when she got her on the phone, the lady went off. She called Marge all kinda white bitches, and the last thing she said was, "Bitch, try and put me out!" Marge just slammed the phone down.

Diana was about 5'10" and weighed about 170 pounds. Her butt covered the whole screen of the nineteen-inch TV that sat in the lobby. She was Spanish with an Italian temper, and when Marge put down the phone, Diana said, "I know dat bitch didn't just say put her out."

Marge turned to her, and in her best sassy sister persona said, "Oh yes she did."

Magic was sitting at the computer behind the front desk typing a letter to Magic's Uncle Benny and Aunt Brenda-Gail when Marge turned to him and said, "Watch the desk." Then they took the elevator to the second floor.

About twenty-minute's later the elevator door opened, and Marge walked out with a weave ponytail in one hand and a bag of clothes in the other, followed closely by Diana who was dragging the unconscious lady by her feet. They dragged her out of the building, propped her up on the side and marched back in.

The third floor was reserved for Big Mack, one night stands and overnight group parties. Mostly the younger patrons were given those rooms on Friday and Saturday nights. The hallway always smelled like marijuana, and you could hear the headboards banging against the walls all night long. If it got too noisy or too rowdy, Marge called Big Mack. She never called the police.

Magic met Big Mack one day while sweeping out the elevator. He had it on emergency stop. Big Mack tarried into the lobby looking like a well-dressed gorilla, a six pack of Molson Ice in one hand and a bag from McDonalds in the other. He was immaculately dressed, with cream and brown reptiles on his feet and a chocolate-colored velour sweat suit. Head bald and shining, like the diamonds on his pinkies.

He stopped abruptly midway between the counter and the elevator and turned to Diana, who was standing behind the counter doing what she did.

"What's up, you Puerto Rican princess?" he said.

"Hi, Mack," Diana responded nonchalantly.

"When you gonna come up to a player's pad and play?"

"I ain't seen no players around here. But if you talking about you," she said, putting her finger on her chin and rolling her eyes upward. "Uhmm... never."

"Oh, that's cold. That's cold," he responded, sort of walking and sort of sliding onto the elevator. Magic reached to disengage the emergency stop button and said, "Do ya job, Peace. I'm just gonna stand here and stare at that stuck-up little bitch right there."

"This is one bitch you'll never get your fat ass on top of," Diana replied.

"You know what, fo' real fo' real, I don't even want you. I want yo' Mama," he said.

Diana's eyes went to confused. Magic really expected her to say something, or throw something, but she didn't. She picked up the newspaper from the counter and pretended to read.

Big Mack laughed a real insulting laugh, then he sat the Molson Ice on the floor, went into the McDonalds bag, pulled out a Big Mac, and took a gaping bite out of it. He leaned against the elevator wall, smiling, taunting Diana.

The only person Magic had heard refer to anyone as Peace was Clear, and his mother always told him that association brought about assimilation. So, feebly, without turning around, he asked, "You know a dude name Clear?"   The smacking stopped, and something was visible in his voice, though Magic couldn't detect what it was.

"Why, he been here?" he asked, his voice muffled by the processed meat.

Suddenly Magic's voice took on a more serious tone. "No, I just asked," he said.

"We don't ask questions just to ask."

Detecting some menace in his voice, Magic gripped the handle on the steel dustpan. If Big Mack made a wrong move, he was going to try to push it straight through his big ass.

Magic had heard lots of stories about Big Mack on the third floor and none were nice.

"I met him at the Department of Social Services," Magic said, and Mack laughed.

"Clear? At the welfare? You got jokes, little nigga," he grumbled, the other half of the sandwich stuck in his mouth.

Magic walked off and hit the third floor button on the elevator panel. He just stood there connecting the dots as the numbers lit up and the elevator ascended.

The cat-food man and Magic ate ham and cheese subs from the deli next door almost everyday. His real name was Michael Breedlove and he was a veteran.

"I was in the Army, World-War II, an infantry man, toe-to-toe, face-to-face," he would say, as he brought up his fists and moved them in a circular motion preparing for combat. "I was in the crazy house, too. They fucked me up, They fucked me up, Magic."

Almost every time they talked, he would cry. He said he had three grown kids that lived somewhere, but he didn't know where.

"But I live under the Clarissa Street Bridge, they just finished fixing it and it's beautiful. Sometimes I spend the night in the dumpster behind the hotel. But not on Wednesday because they dump the dumpster on Thursday at eight o'clock, and I might oversleep like my friend did one time, and he almost got dumped in the garbage truck. The suit people give me money early in the morning, mostly pennies, nickels and dimes and sometimes they give me dollars."

Then without fail, he would say, "I was in the Army, World-War II, an infantry man, toe-to-toe, face-to-face. They fucked me up, Magic, they fucked me up."

CHAPTER 10

No Place Like Home

Magic boarded the elevator feeling very ambivalent, weighed down by two suitcases and a heavy heart. Though the people he met here were cloaked with mystery and some walked the fine line between crazy and crazy, most of their hearts were full of love and compassion.

When the crackheads experienced moments of clarity they would take baths, change clothes and take their kids down the street to Manhattan Square Park. Or they would just sit in the lobby and watch TV as their kids played with their happy-meal toys or the old box of toys that sat in the corner. Sometimes Big Mack would come through and buy enough pizza and wings to feed the whole hotel. And the cat-food man was always inviting people to dine with him. Magic thought they dreamed dreams of fathers that stayed, of happily ever after and houses on hills with white picket fences. Nevertheless, life continued. And the reality of the hard times and bad times of yesterday would seep in and they'd return to the discomfort which had become comfortable.

Magic also learned about another type of people. The people who were poised for success, like Marge's son, little Brandon. He was eleven and went to private school. Took piano lessons from a private instructor and tennis lessons three times a week. His father was a surgeon, and his grandfather on his father's side was a surgeon. And Brandon said he was gonna be a doctor.

Marge said that Brandon's father divorced her because she was a nigger lover and that she acted like one sometimes.

"That's the way he was raised," she said. "But I'll beat Brandon black if I ever hear a prejudice statement come out of his mouth."

Magic was surprised when she told him he was prejudice because they would laugh and talk when he came to the hotel to pick up Brandon. He was the kind of person that his Uncle Benny couldn't stand. Uncle Benny would say, 'You just can't trust 'em, dey smile in your face all day while you doin' da' mule work, and dey talk about you like a dog at their dinner table.'

Magic was relieved when he stepped out the elevator and saw that Marge wasn't at the desk. He really didn't want to say goodbye. He walked to the counter, his suitcases in his hand and Diana came around and gave him a big hug and a kiss. She handed him a card and insisted that he read it and when he opened it, a hundred-dollar bill fell out. The card had a little kid on the front standing on top of a mountain with climbing gear on. On the inside, it said, 'The Sky's The Limit,' and underneath Marge wrote.

Dear Magic

Thank you for all the help you gave us here at the hotel.

You are such a bright young man with wisdom that far exceeds your years.

Your mother told me your fifteenth birthday is in a couple of months. Please buy yourself something on me. If there is ever anything I can do for you feel free to call or come by.

P.S. We have a mutual friend so I'm sure our paths will cross.

Love, Marge

The cat-food man was coming up the street with his cart half full of bottles and cans as they walked out of the building. Magic stopped and waited as his mother beckoned him from the passenger side of a white Expedition driven by her 'new friend', as she called him. The cat- food man walked up to Magic, embellished in the posture of powerlessness. He looked thoroughly beaten by the hot summer sun and Magic went into his pocket, pulled out a twenty-dollar bill, and handed it to him.

"Magic's my friend," he said.

"Yes, Magic's your friend."

He looked into Magic's eyes. Magic smiled, he smiled, and a single tear rolled down his worn face and disappeared into the mostly gray mustache. He pulled out a soiled handkerchief, wiped his mustache and blew his nose while simultaneously going into a little grocery bag that hung from his cart. He took out his dog tags from the Army and held them up by the rusty chain.

"These good luck, Magic," he said, attempting to qualify the gift and his act of kindness. Then he came closer and put them around Magic's neck.

"Thank you," Magic said.

He turned, walked back to the front of his cart and resumed his life.

Magic got into the back seat feeling as if he were abandoning his friends.

"You and Marge got pretty close," his mother said.

He could see the contemptuous look on her face through the rearview mirror.

"Yeah, she was a really nice lady."

"A hundred dollar bill tells me how nice she was, now how nice were you?"

Magic was thrown off by that question so he didn't respond.

"That's all right, I don't think I want to know. This is my friend Bruce, Magic," she said. Magic could see her smiling from the rearview mirror.

"How you doing, Mr. Bruce?"

"Fine, young fellow, how you?"

"Fine, thank you," Magic said. His mother rang back in with a smirk on her face.

"You know, Magic, Bruce is a really nice man too, but he ain't never gave me a hundred dollars."

Magic felt like that was meant for Bruce, but he was thoroughly aggravated at this point so he decided to test his boundaries.

"Mama, I worked for that money. I cleaned filthy rooms, vacuumed the halls on all three floors, swept the elevator, signed people in, and answered the phones. Do you do all those things for Bruce?"

"Hell no," Bruce responded.

His mother looked up and adjusted the rearview mirror so that she could see Magic, and said, "No, I do other things for Bruce, but that ain't none of your business."

Magic wanted to stop right there because he was soliciting information that he really didn't want. But the test wasn't complete.

"You would have known how much I did at the hotel if you hadn't been out doing other things for Bruce."

"Next time I'll get your ass a babysitter, okay stank a boo boo?" she said.

At that moment Magic realized that he really didn't know this New York Mama with her pager, cell phone, and her new friends and he questioned whether he liked her or not.

They pulled into an old raggedy house on some street, it was a dingy gray with dark blue trim. Magic's mother got out and Magic got out behind her and started to get the luggage out of the back.

"Leave the luggage," she said and stuck her head into the truck to talk to Bruce. Magic felt totally lost at that point so he sat down on the front steps and watched a group of boys standing on the corner and periodically running up to cars.

"See you later, Magic," Bruce said.

Magic threw up his hands as his mother reached across him and ripped a for rent sign from the overworked screen, held shut by a man's blue dress tie that matched the house perfectly.

His mother sat down beside him and put his hand in hers. And suddenly he was four years old again and the center of her universe and they were holding hands while skipping down the street on a bright sunny day. He talked to her and she talked to him and they laughed and frolicked until his nightlight played Twinkle, Twinkle Little Star and morning found her beautiful face looking blissfully into his.

"Magic, I love you," she said. "More than I love me and I'm gonna take care of you. Please don't question that. I need to know that you believe I can do this. There's a big difference between Opelika and Rochester and there's no Uncle Benny or Aunt Brenda-Gail to protect us. It's just me and you, baby. We all we got." She turned to Magic, pulled his head to her chest and kissed his forehead. He felt the sincerity as they got up and went inside.

The inside of the house looked a little better than the outside but none of the furniture matched. Some rooms had curtains, others didn't, and as Magic went to turn on the TV, his mother told him there was no electricity. Before he could muster up the guts to ask her what was going on, there was knock at the door. She rushed to answer it.

"Miss Graham?" asked the clean cut white boy with the buzz cut, dress shirt, penny loafers, acid washed blue jeans and crooked tie.

"That would be me," Magic's mother responded.

"We're from Rent-A-Center and we have your furniture."

"Oh, good."

"We just need you to sign right here," he said, handing her a clipboard with several pieces of paper on it. "Would you like for us to set it up for you?"

"No, that won't be necessary. I'm not quite sure where I want it to go and I believe we might have to take the box-spring through the bedroom window upstairs."

"Okay, that's fine, ma'am. Where would you like for us to put it?"

"Just put it all in these two rooms." She pointed to the living room and dining room off the kitchen.

They piled it all in the two rooms. Magic helped with one of the mattresses and brought in a few pillows.

"Now we just need the first week's deposit," the stocky little blond-haired white boy said.

"That's thirty dollars a week for each set, am I correct?"

"That's correct, ma'am."

Magic's mother walked over to the counter, got her purse, pulled out a wad of cash, counted off a hundred and twenty dollars then handed it to him.

After they left, Magic and his mother walked down the street. She slowed to use her cell phone and Magic went in the store and got a honey bun and a Nutty Buddy. He smiled as he walked past the cat food and up to the counter.

As they walked around the block, she showed him a boarded-up house where one of her good friends lived when they were younger. Magic dreaded the thought of living in this neighborhood. It was scary. There were boarded up houses everywhere and most of the ones that weren't boarded up looked like they should be. There were very few trees and hardly any grass. Beer bottles, potato chip bags, Little Debbie treats and bubble gum wrappers were the only things that stimulated a pleasing thought.

"This used to be a much nicer neighborhood," his mother said as they turned the corner on Bay and Seventh Street. "But just like all inner city neighborhoods, the white folks move out and take the weekly street sweeper with them. The city crews that used to come out and mow the lawns of the vacant lots stopped coming. The landlords don't care because they don't live in the city. Poor blacks move in and they don't know they have rights as renters. They're just happy to find a place that they can afford after Uncle Sam, Rochester Gas and Electric, Rochester Tel. and Wally's World split their sad forty-hour paychecks. Their parents lived like this and their parent's parents lived this way. So, what makes them think they should live any better? It's just a vicious cycle, Magic."

Magic could feel the sadness in her voice.

By the time they made it back to the house, Bruce was in the driveway. He was sitting in a U-Haul with two men that looked like he'd scraped them off the sidewalk and all of their new furniture was on the truck. They moved into the Canterbury Apartment building on Lake Ave. and Clay, in a building with grass and trees in the front yard. The walls were freshly painted and there was brand new carpet on the floor.

CHAPTER 11

Magic Sr.

He'd served under General Cocaine and Major Heroin and they had marched his ass in and out of every crack den and shooting gallery in Rochester. After spending his teens in juvenile jail and all his twenties in rehabs, mental institutions, and state prisons, he decided not to reenlist. He accentuated his life experiences with some text book dribble and at forty-one graduated from the University of Rochester with a Masters in Social Work. He was voted most likely to take no shit. For fifteen years, Mr. Ashby had been a drug and alcohol counselor. But in his fifty-six years he had never seen the likes of Magic Sr.

Magic Sr. sat in the Hot Seat, directly across from Mr. Ashby. Stephanie, Donna, and Larry sat to his right, and Karen, Robert and Benny to his left. The room was unusually quiet, no one had expected Magic Sr. to make it past the first week. So, everyone was shocked that he was still there after twenty-nine days and would be graduating from the program in less that twenty-four hours.

Magic Sr. smiled as he looked across the room at Stephanie. He had manufactured a dream and she had bought it. I'll have her ass jumping through hoops in no time flat, he thought. Maybe I'll take her with me tomorrow when I leave, a good looking bitch is like a stacked deck. He winked and she blushed, which confirmed that his incantation was still in effect.

"So how you feel, Magic?" Mr. Ashby asked.

"I'm cool," Magic responded.

"Cool isn't a feeling, it's generally used when making reference to the weather. Example; It was a cool fall day. So, how do you feel, Magic?"

"I'm cool, like a cool fall day," Magic responded.

"Bullshit accepted. Let's move forward," said Mr. Ashby. "Now everyone knows how this works. Mr. Magic, your peers will express to you their concerns regarding your ability to stay clean outside of this controlled environment. After each individual expresses their concerns, you will be given the opportunity to embrace or rebut their assessments. We'll start with you, Stephanie."

Stephanie looked up at Mr. Ashby, then over at Magic. "I really don't have nothing to say. I've only been here a little over a week and I really don't know him."

Mr. Ashby looked up from the clipboard, scanned the room and stopped when his eyes met Karen's.

"Karen, bring Stephanie up to speed," he said.

Karen looked straight at Stephanie, uncrossed her legs, and leaned forward.

"Listen, Stephanie, the hot seat is about saving asses not saving faces. Now having said that, I believe you know Magic better than I do, and him and I came in on the same day. Y'all been grinnin' in each others face since the first day you got here. He's your spade partner, Y'all eat breakfast, lunch and dinner together every day. In fact, you jacked his dick last night during the movie."

"You a lyin' bitch," Stephanie responded.

Karen smiled, sat back in her chair, and crossed her legs. Mr. Ashby looked at Magic, but directed his words to Stephanie.

"She ain't lying. That was the first thing I heard when I came in this morning." Then he turned and looked at Stephanie. "The only reason you still here is because my responsibility is to teach you how not to use dope. And hopefully when the fog clears, you'll learn how not to be a hoe on your own. But I'll come back to you." Mr. Ashby scanned the room again. "Robert, what about you?"

"Yeah, I got a couple of concerns, but not about him getting high. I really don't think that he's gonna get high, and if he does, I don't think he's gonna smoke crack. My concern is his attitude. He got this I don't give a fuck attitude and that shit will get you dead far quicker than crack. It was a lotta days up in here I wanted to do you, and I'm not a violent person. That's all I got."

"Would you like to respond, Magic?" Mr. Ashby asked.

"Naw, I'm straight."

"Can I go next?", Donna asked anxiously.

Mr. Ashby nodded and Donna got up and walked over to Magic. She stood about four feet in front of him and crouched down until their eyes were level. She spoke slowly and meticulously.

"I love you, my brother, you're an African King, but you are one of the most charming, grimy motherfuckers I have ever met. And it's a good thing I didn't feed into all that bull you was serving me when I came up in here. Because if I did, I would be trying to figure out how to get some undetectable poison in your system and this building wouldn't be big enough for Stephanie and me. For your sake, it's a good thing I ain't dumb." She looked over at Stephanie. "I might be a crackhead, but I ain't dumb."

Donna stood up and walked back to her seat. Magic Sr. sat there appearing impenetrable, with hard face intact as the character assassination continued.

Mr. Ashby allowed silence to give birth to the perfect moment. He glanced up at the clock on the wall directly across from him, then looked intently into Magic's eyes. Don't look for no remorse or dismay here, Magic Sr. thought. Ain't gonna find it here. So, the verdict was in.

"How you feel, Magic?" Mr. Ashby asked calmly.

"I'm straight," Magic said, sounding as brazen as ever.

"No you're not. In fact, you're even more fucked up than you were when you walked up in here twenty-nine days ago. Because now, there's one more person whose life you've effected with your bullshit. You probably haven't effected Stephanie as severely as you've effected little Magic Jr. and his mother, whom you haven't seen in about eight years. Or your dead Mom, who you manipulated until the day she died. Or your Dad, who won't even accept your phone calls. Oh! I neglected to tell you that I called him and tried to set up a conjoint between the three of us. He said, and I quote, 'I ain't got no son,' and hung up."

Mr. Ashby studied Magic's face, which had become harder and colder. Magic sat like a ticking time bomb, you could almost see the steam rising from his head as Mr. Ashby advanced forward with flames spewing from his tongue.

"You know, I considered giving you a thirty day extension," he continued, his words soaked in sarcasm.

"You know I can do that, considering you were mandated here by drug court, but I'm gonna do you a favor." He got up and walked around the inside of the circle as if considering the severity of his favor. "I'm gonna let you go a day early," he said. "In the hope that you will return the day before your good looks and charming personality takes your ass out. See, because you think you got another winning move. Maybe some old fake left and roll right shit, but at any rate, I refuse to deny you your pain another second. Go pack your shit, you outta here."

CHAPTER 12

Reconciliation

Peggy snapped the straps of her G-string, making sure every dollar was present and accounted for. Then she laid down on the leather couch that was nice and cool thanks to the newly installed air conditioner. The ceiling fan was just decoration, as were the mirrors that lined the walls in a checkerboard design. She looked up at her reflection and smiled. The mirrors told her that she didn't look a day over twenty-five.

Sometimes they lie, she thought. She remembered going to the house of mirrors as a little girl. Some made her look short and fat and others made her look tall and skinny.

"But I always looked good," she said to herself.

A bitch look better flat on her back, butt ass naked, wit' a bank role, than serving time on an assembly line, barely payin' the rent. This was one of her mother's fundamental principles. Not quite her own, but who knows, she thought, as she seductively walked over to the table and quickly drank two of thirteen glasses of Hennessy sent to her by different men, all vainly hoping to put whip-cream on top of Miss Hot Chocolate.

She smiled as she pictured thirteen men spraying whip-cream all over her body while she laid there naked, tied and gagged. Then they'd empty their cans and begin licking it off. She started feeling flush so she got up, put her money in the safe, and started to change into her Miss Hot Chocolate costume.

Peggy placed the James Cagny broke down brim on her head and started to lace her brown stiletto boots. The door flew open and Candy walked in.

"Bitch, you got thirty seconds to get your ass on the runway or your show will start without you."

"This we know is a lie," Peggy said, slowing almost to a halt. "Good as them drunks out there chanting, Hot Chocolate, Hot Chocolate, Hot Chocolate."

"That sounds pretty cocky coming from the woman that ran off the stage crying like a baby her first night out."

"Oh, bitch, don't hate," Peggy responded.

"You ain't got to worry about me hatin' until they stop chanting Candy, Candy, Candy."

"I know that's right," Peggy said. They laughed, slapped each other up and Candy turned to walk out.

"Oh, there's a fine ass brother out there. He told Red, who told me to tell you that if you give him a chance he would give you the world." Peggy laughed.

"Yeah, that's what they all say, until you super size the value meal one time too many."

"Good one," Candy responded and continued out the door.

Miss Hot Chocolate hit the runway in a full body suit that zipped off in halves and matched her complexion perfectly. Too damn tight would be a modest assessment of how it fit. If anybody had another dollar, she wanted him or her to know she wanted it.

She licked the pole, split the pole, went up the pole right side up, and came down the pole upside down. She placed her hands on the stage, braced her back against the pole and spread her legs for the extra point. The song was saying 'lick it, lick it good, lick it real good,' and the men started to go crazy. Even Red (the cute little bisexual barmaid) threw a five-dollar bill on the dance floor.

The first thing she saw was the hundred-dollar bill, but she knew that hand. The long, lean fingers and freshly manicured nails. The even, cream-colored tone that perfectly matched her son's. Those hands guided her from adolescence to womanhood. They had rubbed her young shoulders and stroked her young vagina, penetrating periodically as she moaned climatically. His tongue had made small circular motions around her fully erect young nipples. She knew the love line was short and the lifeline was long.

Her movements were off, nothing like she had rehearsed them. She had practiced this dance, to this song, excessively over the last two weeks. Now she was upside down, leaning against a pole, legs wide open, totally lost.

She ended the dance before the song was over, scooped up her money and ran off stage.

"Damn," she said, grabbing Candy by the arm, and dragging her into the dressing room.

"What's wrong?" Candy asked.

"Girl, that's my baby daddy," she responded, sounding and looking shocked.

"And," Candy said in her 'who gives a fuck' tone.

"I haven't seen that nigga in over eight years."

"That was even more of a reason for you to shake your ass. You just fucked up a perfectly good dance routine."

"Girl, you don't understand, the last time I seen him he was cracked out, weighing a buck forty. Now he look good as a bitch."

"So take off that hot chocolate shit and go get your man. Because I was checking his ass out when he walked in, and I'll damn sure take him."

"I'm sure you will, skank."

"Mrs. Skank to you," Candy responded, as she tossed her weave back and headed toward the bar.

Peggy threw on her white sandals and the off-white form fitting summer dress that she'd worn to work that day. Did a couple of turns in the full body mirror, and thought, Damn, I look good, trying to boost her confidence. She walked over to the table, picked up one of the shots of Hennessy, placed it on her bottom lip, tilted her head back, and headed for the door.

Just as she reached for the knob, she turned, went back to the table, picked up glass nine and did a toast with her reflection. "Here's to me," she said.

The club always looked different when you were dressed as a civilian and you were walking parallel with the patrons and co-workers licking a pole you just finished spreading your legs up and down. It seems somewhat nasty, Peg thought as she slowly walked over to the fifth table in the second row, twelve steps from the pool table and sixteen from the bar.

"Hi, Magic."

"Hi, Peggy," Magic Sr. responded.

"Would you like a drink?", Peggy asked.

"No, thank you, I'm allergic to alcohol. Every time I drink I break out drunk."

Peggy laughed, thinking he still had his sense of humor.

"Do you mind if I have one?", she asked.

"Of course not. Can I get it for you?"

"No thank you. Around here we let everybody do their job."

Peggy turned to summon a waitress. The bar had thinned out, and all remaining eyes were on her.

"That big mouth ass, Candy," she said aloud.

"Excuse me," Magic said, looking a bit confused.

"Nothing. Are you driving?"

"No, but we can catch a taxi," Magic Sr. said as he reached for the cell phone dangling from his hip.

"That's okay, it's a nice night, we can walk. I'll be right back."

She left the table and headed back to the dressing room.

Candy walked up to the table where Magic sat and stuck out her hand. "Hi, I'm Candy."

"I'm Magic," he said, extending his hand.

"I know. Can I get you a drink?"

"No, thank you."

Candy turned and yelled to the bartender, "Yo, Red, get this brother a cute seven-up. I don't like to drink alone." She pulled the chair out and sat down.

"Please join me," Magic said sarcastically.

"Don't mind if I do," Candy said, fighting the urge to stick her tongue down his throat and write her home number on his tonsils. Damn this nigga fine, she thought. Let me qualify and set up some boundaries before the hoe in me takes over.

"That's a hell of a boy you and Peggy got," she said.

Magic nodded in agreement as Candy continued.

"He's a straight A student, but you wouldn't know that. And his Mama's a real stand up woman, which you possibly would know. Now as for me, Peggy calls me sis, and your son calls me Auntie Candy. I'm the type of person that if I can't help a situation, I damn sure ain't gonna stick around and hinder it. Now what about you?"

Magic sat back, rocking on the hind legs of his chair. Contemplating whether he should dice her ass up into little pieces, or take a more subtle approach. He knew that if he didn't handle this situation properly, it would come back to bite him on the ass.

"Actually, I'm not accustomed to a woman questioning my character. Where I'm from, the only time you find a woman in a man's face is when she's ready to turn her life and her money over to his care. So if you ain't ready to drop those kibbles and bits you made sliding your ass up and down that pole, I would suggest you get the fuck out my face."

She smiled, obviously to let him know that he wasn't dealing with a bitch crafted from paper maché and that Kool-Aid wasn't the substance that pumped through her veins.

"Nigga, you've read too many Donald Goines novels. This is the twenty-first century, Pussy, crack, and credit rules this motherfucker, and this pussy will get your globe cracked. Think it's a game?" She pushed the table just inches away from Magic's chest, spun out of the chair and headed toward the bar.

She was just in time to catch Red as she made her way over to the table with the seven-up. She snatched it off the serving tray.

"Don't give that nigga shit," she said. She walked behind the bar and poured it in the sink. Damn I like that nigga, she thought. I wish I had met him before I went into retirement. He could have gotten all my hoe money.

Candy was a third generation hoe. Her mama was a hoe, and her grandma, half-senile and confined to a wheel chair, still caught a date every now and then at the North Side Old Folks Home.

She was the oldest of fourteen kids, a trick baby. And she was promised to a pimp named Main Street at age seven. Main Street fed her and clothed her until she was twelve, and at twelve she was put in the back of a rust-colored Cadillac and taken to Binghamton N.Y., where she went through Basic Hoe Training. She had a soft round ass and firm perky tits by the age of ten, and by the age of twelve, she was fully developed.

Tricky Tracy was top hoe in Main Street's stable, and she took Candy under her wing from the first day they met. That night they went to a club where pimps and hustlers were radiant and confidence oozed from their pores like perspiration. They passed straws in neatly folded hundred dollar bills packed with white powder, and everybody sniffed and sniffed and sniffed and told stories of hoe's and dates, and dollars and cents. After two double shots of Hennessy and two greedy scoops and sniffs, heaven seemed to open her pearly gates. Candy went straight to the tree of life and bit the apple.

That night, her, Main Street, and Tracy made love over and over and over. And between licks, sips and sniffs, they talked about dreams that would never come true, and a future that would be so bright, if they pursued it with the desperation of dying men.

She learned to walk like a hoe, talk like a hoe, dress like a hoe, and most importantly, think like a hoe. For almost six years things went as well as could be expected. Then Tracy started getting thin and sickly looking. She died of AIDS, Candy knew now. But at that time, nobody knew what that shit was. Main Street never recovered from her death. He searched for comfort in a heroin-filled syringe. Last she heard he was a lifer in the methadone maintenance program. Candy graduated from marketing and promoting her body, to the marketing and promoting of bodies of the young, old, housewives, or hoes at the Peek-a-Boo Club.

"Call me in the morning, you know we have a nail appointment," Candy said to Peggy, as her and Magic walked toward the door.

"Since when?", Peggy asked.

Candy sucked her teeth and responded, "Since I'm gonna call in the morning and make it."

"Oh, it's one of those appointments," Peggy said as her and Magic stepped out the door and into the dismal reality of those who work the night shift.

The neighborhood's bottle and can man couldn't figure out whether to push, pull, or slide his latest invention. 'The Cycle-Crate-Cart-Mobile,' fully equipped with a spray bottle, and coffee mug holder. Maximum capacity one hundred and fifty aluminum cans.

"Hi, Hot Chocolate," Carla, the happy crackhead shouted as she walked down Lyell Ave. like a fashion model, heel toe, heel toe. She was going to be a figure skater in the Olympics. At least that's what it said in the yearbook she carried around from time to time, showing people how beautiful she once was, and would one day be again.

Mr. Executive Director of some department at ABC or CBS or M&T cruised by and slowed down. Eyes zooming in, and zooming out, looking for Miss C.E.O of S.T.D.'s.

"So how you been, Miss Hot Chocolate?" Magic asked teasingly.

"Fine. And you, Mr. Dope Fiend?"

"I guess I had that one coming."

"Naw, you don't want what you have coming," Peggy replied.

"What the fuck I got coming, Peggy? I just spent the last two months kissing my father's ass, trying to get back in his good graces, twenty-nine days in a rehab, and seven years in hell. So whatever else I have coming, bring it on."

"I just spent the last seven years getting my ass kicked by a goddamn hillbilly, because you choose dope over me and your son."

Magic looked away.

"Why?", Peggy asked.

"I don't know," he responded, and they turned the corner heading into the alley.

"Yall straight? I got that heat," announced a too-big pair of jeans, and a too-big Phat Farm shirt, wearing a precarious juvenile delinquent. Neither Peggy nor Magic responded.

"Well fuck yall then," he retorted. Magic stopped, turned, pulled the nine from underneath his shirt, took three giant steps and was in the little boy's face with the pistol pressed against his forehead. That little boy embodied every drug dealer that had ever called him a fiend, that had ever shot his dope on the ground, and said, fetch it, fiend.

"Fuck who, little piece of shit? Fuck who?" Magic said, smacking him with the pistol so hard his head hit the wall and his body followed.

"Please, Mister! Please! Don't kill me! I'm sorry, I'm sorry! Please, Mister," the little boy cried. He lay on the ground covering his face and pissing his pants.

"Don't shoot him, Magic!" she whimpered, but her eyes glowed.

Magic stepped back and watched the urine roll down the stoop, then carefully placed the pistol back in his pants. He turned to look into his son's mother's eyes as the too, too big pants and shirt rose from the stoop and darted out the alley.

Peggy's eyes said all is forgiven, and Magic walked over and placed his arm around her waist. She laid her head on his chest and they stood there in the street on the corner, holding each other as if nothing or no one occupied this space in time. Tears started to flow down her face, and she said, "Please don't hurt me, I can't take it."

He gently kissed her tears and uttered, "I love you, Miss Hot Chocolate."

CHAPTER 13

Are?

The Sunday morning sun never seemed as bright as Saturday mornings. The birds that chirped in the Sunday morning choir always seemed to be missing a soprano or two. 'Maybe they were tired, as I was,' Magic thought. Maybe their mothers woke them up at four in the morning tweeting frantically, chirping erotically, and chattering the name of some well-endowed Blue Jay.

It wasn't the first time he had heard his mother having sex. But it was the first time she sounded as if she was really, really enjoying it. And the smell of bacon pounding on his door at 9:15 told him that she had.

The last thing he expected to see was a man sitting at the kitchen table with his mother. But they didn't say anything, so he didn't say anything back. He just stood there in a wife beater and boxers for what seemed like forever. He looked at his mother, then him, and they just returned his stare as if waiting for him.

He'd never witnessed another man being in this house since they'd moved here, but for some reason, this man seemed oddly familiar. He had thick, dark, high-arched eyebrows that looked like his. And the way his lips were perfectly aligned with the cleft in his chin, was what separated his lips from all the boys in his class. At least that's what the girls told him.

He looked at his mother and she looked away, then he looked back at him as he picked up the napkin and wiped the bacon grease from his lips.

"Hi, Magic," he said in a tone that inferred they had met before.

"Hi," Magic responded. He looked at his mother again expecting her to do something. She got up, slid past him, and went to her room.

He looked over at Magic and said very nonchalantly, "Have a seat."

Magic looked at him thinking, who are you to offer me a seat in my own damn house?

"My name's Magic. Magic Senior," he said.

Right then any and everything Magic thought concerning feelings was up for re-evaluation, but what he felt, he stuffed. He pushed it down so hard he felt his big toes swell. He wanted to say something like--Where you been? What happened, and why are you here now?--But he didn't, he said, "Pleased to meet you," turned, walked over to the stove, picked up the plate of bacon, and went back to his room.

CHAPTER 14

Auntie Abigail

The Canterbury Apartments sat on the corner of Lake Avenue and Clay Street. A big oak tree that provided plenty of shade sat in the front yard. The hedges went all the way around the building. It had a driveway, a medium-size backyard and a deck. But the most distinguishing characteristic about it were the people who lived there.

Fat Shirley was the building bully. Her apartment was full of bikes, scooters, shovels, toys, boots, and sneakers. Anything that was left in the hall she confiscated. There was a sign taped to the entrance door that said 'Anything left in this hall belongs to Shirley, and if you don't like it, see me in apt. 4A.' A lot of people went in to try and retrieve their stuff, but no one ever came out with anything.

Then there was Mr. and Miss It, in apartment B6, who were actually the same person. On Friday and Saturday Mr. It became Miss It. He would put on his high heels, short skirts, blond or black wig and come and sit on the front stoop like it was perfectly normal that he was wearing women's clothing and there wasn't enough foundation in the USA to hide the razor stubble.

Miss Pitney--aka--Miss Cravats, was about sixty and she sometimes came downstairs and sat on the front stoop with her panties on over her polyester pants. The landlord said that as long as she had sense enough to pay her rent he didn't care. She was also nosier than Mrs. Cravats on 'Bewitched.' No one came in or out of the Canterbury apartment building without her knowing. She could tell you the height, weight and shoe size of everyone that came in or went out of the building. Mama said every building needs a Miss Cravats.

There were also some normal people living in the building, like Magic's Aunt Abigail. Aunt Abigail moved in about four months after Magic and his mother did. She pulled up in a 22" U Haul truck, threw it in reverse, and ran over all the garbage cans in the front yard. Then she hopped out the truck in a pair of blue jeans short shorts that fit like gristle on a chicken bone.

She had a little too much cleavage and butt showing for most of the women who lived in the Canterbury Apartments, but just enough for the men and boys. So her popularity was split from the very start.

"Hi," she said. "I'm Abigail, Abigail Pride. Could I possibly get any of you gentlemen to give me a hand moving my stuff? I don't have a lot of money, but I can buy pizza and soda or maybe beer."

Magic and the others lined up at the truck.

Aunt Abigail was classically beautiful. She wore no make-up, no weave, no false eyelashes or false fingernails. She had shoulder length charcoal black hair and a sedating smile, with milky white teeth. When she walked, her tits bounced, and her hips swayed in perfect harmony.

Aunt Abigail and Magic connected from day one. Magic just liked her. Maybe it was a little lust initially, but that soon gave way to admiration and respect. She gave him his first lesson on how to use a condom.

One day she called him into her apartment. "Sit down, Magic," she said.

Magic sat in the chair by the door, pretending not to notice the condom and a cucumber sitting on the coffee table.

"You know how to use those?" she asked.

"Use what?" Magic responded. She pointed to the table.

"Sure, Mama puts hers in salad, but I like mine with salt and pepper," Magic said, trying not to laugh. "And a little vinegar."

"Good answer, Magic," she said. "Have you noticed how these old bags be looking at you like the fresh batch of crab legs at the Chinese Buffet?"

Magic smiled, trying not to appear cocky, and she tore open the condom, placed the vegetable between her knees, sat the condom on top and rolled it down the cucumber.

"You need to leave a little space at the top to catch your...your."

"Semen," Magic said.

"Yeah, your semen," she said, and smiled.

Magic thought she was coming on to him, so he didn't want to appear totally oblivious, but she cleared all that up when she held up the cucumber, and said, "A man got to be packing like this to satisfy a woman like me."

Magic knew right then that he didn't fit the bill.

Aunt Abigail was real about everything. She reminded him of his Aunt Brenda-Gail and she insisted that he call her Auntie. She said Mrs. Abigail was too formal for her.

From the first day she came over and Cory was home she treated him like he was her son. She took him everywhere and was always buying him stuff. At first Magic was jealous, but between his mother, his father and his friend Clear, he didn't want for anything.

Auntie Abigail couldn't stand his father, she called him Frostbite. Said he was as cold as the winters in Rochester. But after spending a winter here, cold became a new creature for Magic. One that his father couldn't touch.

They had winters in Alabama; sweater, jacket winters. Thirty, forty degrees was cold, and a few snowflakes was exciting. Below zero, wind chill factor and lake effect snow were new concepts; concepts Magic could have lived without. It was so cold in this city during the months of November, December and January, he determined hibernation must have originated here.

During the winter Magic's Aunt Abigail put a treadmill and a Bowflex in her living room and very rarely came out for air. She said she didn't do anything in the winter but workout and wait for summer. She was strong, bench presses, leg lifts strong, and her biceps were bigger than his. Cory treated the Bowflex and the treadmill like toys, Magic treated them as if they weren't there.

One day Magic asked her why she worked out so much. He expected some vain answer, but she looked at him like he had ripped a bandage off her forehead.

"I'm a victim the first time, but the second time I'm a volunteer," she said, as she traipsed up the stairs in her black spandex and black sports bra.

She was also a proficient, tenacious type strong. She was an, I'm able to handle any shit that comes down the feeding tube of life, type strong. About six months after she moved in, the women of Canterbury Apartments made her prove it.

It was a Sunday, women's day on the front stoop. All the females would gather in front of the building and gossip. Any woman that wasn't present and accounted for was fair game. They talked about her, her kids, her mom, her dad, and her man if she had one. It didn't matter, all you had to do was not show up for this Sunday ritual and your ass was getting talked about.

This was a well-known fact throughout the apartment building, so normally what was said there was taken with a grain of salt. Magic's mother and Auntie Abigail never partook in this communion. His mother generally slept until two or three in the afternoon on Sunday, and his Auntie Abigail said she had better shit to do with her time.

On this particular Sunday, Magic was sweeping down the stairs. The landlord paid him five dollars a week to keep the hallway clean, and Auntie Abigail was coming down to take out her garbage. Garbage pickup day was Monday.

As Magic approached the first floor landing, he heard Miss Banks speaking.

"That Abigail needs to change her name to Jezebel, and yall better watch yall men. She just oughta come outside butt ass naked like Miss Pitney, that little skimpy shit she be havin' on. And yall know don't nothing keep a woman's teeth that white but cum."

Magic's Aunt Abigail didn't wait around to hear anymore. She propped her garbage against the wall, went in her pocket, and stuck a fifty-dollar bill in his hand.

"Gather all of the kids playing outside and take them to the McDonalds down the street. Not the corner store, Magic," she emphasized. "I want them to stay there and eat."

Aunt Abigail turned and headed up the stairs. Miss Banks was about to get her butt kicked, and Magic wasn't about to miss it. Therefore, he delegated the trip to McDonalds to one of his protégés, Little Calvin, who lived three doors down. Magic helped him gather the kids and claimed he was paying for their lunch.

Aunt Abigail went to her apartment and put on a pair of baggy blue jeans, an oversized shirt, and a pair of tennis shoes. She put her hair in a ponytail, slapped some Vaseline on her face, walked straight down the front stairs, out the front door, turned to Miss Banks, and said. "Bitch, I hope you can fight," then punched her in the mouth. Miss Banks hit the wall and came off swinging wildly. Aunt Abigail stepped back, turned, walked off the porch and gestured for Miss Banks to come on down. Miss Banks came off the porch with her arms going around and around like a windmill. Aunt Abigail came straight through the center with a jab to her nose. When Miss Banks grabbed her face, Aunt Abigail scooped her up, body-slammed her, and the fight was over. Miss Banks' 160-pound frame hit the ground and became one with the concrete. Then to add insult to injury, Aunt Abigail placed her foot right on Miss Banks' neck.

Everyone seemed to be in a state of shock. Cars pulled over, a small crowd had gathered, and Aunt Abigail wasn't even breathing hard when she started.

"First thing I want you bitches to know is that I don't play the dozens. You bitches been cup a sugar-in-me, cup a flour-in-me, couple a dollar-in-me everyday since I moved into this

108

goddamn building. Now you out here smearing my name like dog shit. For the record, your poor ass, beer guzzling, pot smoking, minimum wage job working ass boyfriends can't afford me. I'm an aristocratic bitch, a steak tar tare bitch."

This must have struck a nerve with Fat Shirley, who was always in Miss Banks' AMEN corner. She headed down the stairs coming for Aunt Abigail, who reached under her T-shirt and pulled out a pearl-handled 25 automatic.

"Bitch, if you breathe hard in my direction I will air your fat ass out."

Fat Shirley, looking like a stuffed grizzly bear, came to a screeching halt and stood perfectly still.

"I hate nigger women. You bitches should be going to parenting classes or seminars on how to get a fucking life instead of standing around polluting each other's mind with all this negative bullshit on a Sunday afternoon."

Aunt Abigail paused for a moment and looked deeply into the eyes of every woman in the crowd.

"And we wonder why our kids so fucked up. Apples don't fall far from the tree," she said, lowering her arm slowly, but never taking her finger off the trigger. She raised her foot from Miss Bank's neck, turned, and walked back into the building.

Less than a month later Miss Banks moved out. And Fat Shirley and Aunt Abigail became something resembling friends.

CHAPTER 14

Who's Who and What's What

The year was eventful, and it flew by. Magic's mother and father took good care of him. They argued a lot but never anything physical. Most of the time his father wasn't even home, especially after he got the white Bonneville. They rode together a couple of times, but anytime they were alone, there was an uncomfortable silence. So consequently, there was an unspoken agreement to avoid each other. Magic was fifteen and near grown now so the best his father could do was 'try and be his friend', so he said during one of their rare father-son talks.

Most of Magic's days were spent at the barbershop with Clear, Marwon, Black, and Daemon. He learned a lot about music, clothes, and talking shit. He also learned how to cut hair, but no one believed him so he never got the opportunity to practice. Clear and Magic would ride and talk for hours sometimes, mostly about life, money, and school. Magic never really had a philosophy on life, or the black plight, he just never thought about stuff like that. But Clear did all the time.

Sometimes their conversation would get intense; or rather Clear's conversations, because most of the time Magic would just listen. The things Clear had to say were much more interesting than anything Magic learned in school.

Clear had a favorite restaurant called 'Grandma's Kitchen. The food there was so good that Magic convinced his mother, his father and his Aunt Abigail to go there. Then they started eating there all the time. Clear said one day he was going to franchise it like the Country Buffet. He was always talking about buying this and buying that and building this and building that. He said that black people were the world's greatest consumers. He said 'white people take our shit and sell it back to us.'

When Clear and Magic first started hanging out, he called Magic Brandon a lot, so frequently that Magic started answering to it. First he was Peace, then he was Brandon, and eventually he became Magic.

About five months after the move into the Canterbury Apartments, the family took a trip down South to pick up Magic's little brother. Magic didn't realize how much he missed him until he ran and jumped in his arms, totally ignoring their mother. She was visibly hurt by that, but Magic was the closest thing to normal in the household.

Cory, Magic thought, must have been instructed not to talk about what happened, because after Magic picked him up and told him that he missed him, he put his arms around Magic's neck, got as close as he could possibly get to his ear, and whispered, " You killed my daddy." Magic handed him to his mother as the gray matter started to replay all the events of that morning.

They stayed for three days. Magic's aunts, uncles, and cousins treated them like royalty. Magic and his Uncle Benny took a walk in the woods on their last day there. He told Magic he didn't like his father, said his father didn't respect his mother.

"You watch him, Magic," he said, "and I'll come up there if I have to."

He asked Magic to tell him about the north and they reminisced about all the things Magic did when he was little. They laughed about how afraid Magic was of guns when he first started teaching him to shoot. And how he would make Little Benny beat Magic up until he started to fight back. "Take care of your Mama, boy," he said and they walked back to the house.

CHAPTER 15

School

School, Magic decided, was a joke. Teachers were afraid of students, and police paraded up and down the halls brandishing guns and metal detectors. It was like daycare for juvenile delinquents, a very aggravating situation. He had a college level vocabulary, and if you could pronounce a word correctly, he could spell it correctly. He was the spelling bee champion in Alabama.

As far back as he could remember, he wanted to know everything there was to know about everything. So he read voraciously and listened intently and for fifteen he was pretty damn smart. This wasn't a problem as long as he sat in the back of the class and acted as dumb as his peers. But as soon as he started raising his hand and answering questions, he became very unpopular with the cool dumb boys, but the cool dumb girls admired him from afar.

Miraculously, he got dumb and started raising his hand a lot less after his run in with, 'The Knockouts.' Whom he referred to as 'The Soon To Be Dropouts.'

He left lunch early that day, whatever he had eaten that night was dying to come out. His stomach had been bubbling and gurgling all morning. He was standing in front of his locker looking for something to read while he sat on the toilet.

"What's up, cutie?" she said.

"Hey," Magic responded.

Her name was Jackie. She was one of the popular girls from his math class, where she slept, talked, or admired the new design on her fingernails.

"So what you up to?" she asked.

"I'm about to go and take a shit," Magic said. She sucked her teeth. Magic laughed and proceeded to the bathroom.

Magic lined the seat with toilet paper, pulled his pants down and was getting ready to sit when she came busting into the stall with this big smile on her face like she had hit the lottery or something.

Magic stood up, mushed her in the face, closed the door and didn't think anything of it.

An hour or so later, while Magic was leaving his fourth period class, a kid just walked up and sucker punched him. Magic came off the locker and commenced to beating his ass, then about six other boys jumped in and just started kicking and punching him.

Magic folded up in the corner against a locker, and took their best for the next five minutes. Then he heard Jackie yelling, "Disrespect me, motherfucker, disrespect me."

Moments later someone yelled, "Five O! Five O!" Magic opened his eyes and all he saw was the bottom of Timberland boots and little Nike signs in flight.

Then Flash, a Puerto-Rican sentry who was cool with all the students but not much liked by faculty, came running down the hall. "You all right?" he asked as he tried to help Magic up.

"I'm straight," Magic said, jerking away as the kid escorted him to the office.

Magic tried to explain to the vice-principal what had happened, and why it had happened, but he said he didn't care.

"Fights are more common than A's in this school, and it's always the other person's fault," he said. "And you're going to be suspended for at least five days no matter whose fault it is. Now what's your home phone number?"

"For what?" Magic asked.

"I need to let someone know you're coming home."

"It's in my records, look it up," Magic responded angrily and walked out the office.

The vice-principal walked out behind him and asked one of the receptionists for his file. She gave it to him and he went back to his office, about five minutes later he came out and told Magic his mother was picking him up.

Magic sat there for about fifteen minutes, then he walked down the hall to the payphone and called the barbershop.

"Precision Cuts."

"Hey, Black, is Clear there?"

"Yeah, hold on a minute man... You okay?"

"Naw. Can I speak to Clear, please?"

The telephone went silent as if someone had placed their hand over the mouthpiece.

"Magic?"

"Yeah."

"What's wrong?"

"I got jumped, man," Magic said and he burst out laughing.

"Welcome to the Roc, baby," Clear responded.

Magic slammed down the phone, even more pissed off. He walked across the hall to the boy's bathroom to assess the damage. His lip was swollen, and he had a couple scratches and a small cut over his right eye, nothing major.

When he came back to the office, his mother was sitting on the bench. Probably wanted to see the supervisor's supervisor, Magic thought, because they were ushered into the head principal's office.

He sat behind his big mahogany desk with plaques hanging over his head like halo's, implying that he was qualified to do this job, which Magic questioned everyday he walked into this mad house.

"Pleased to meet you, Miss Brown," he said. He stood up to shake Magic's mother's hand.

"Please to meet you," his mother replied.

"Have a seat," he said. "And how are you, Magic?"

Magic didn't respond to the dumb question. He just took his seat on the witness stand.

"I'm very sorry about what happened to your son, Miss Brown. I'm even sorrier that we're going to have to suspend him." He paused, looked down at the folder in front of him, then continued. "My preference would be that you take him with you now for safety reasons. Unfortunately, the young men he had a confrontation with are members of a little gang."

Magic's mother looked at him and shook her head. Then she looked at Magic and asked, "Magic, are you okay?"

"Yes ma'am."

"Would you like for me to take you home?"

Magic sat there for a minute with the words, 'hell yeah' dangling from his lips, but all of a sudden, he could hear Clear's voice. "Never surrender your turf, Magic. If you ain't willing to fight for it, then you don't deserve it." And this was his turf. His school.

"No," Magic said, but with a 'hell, no' look on his face. His mother turned to Principal Morgany and spoke slowly, as if she were talking to a retard.

"Now what you're telling me is that because my son was jumped by four known gang members, he's going to be kicked out of school."

"That's policy, ma'am," the principal responded. "You fight, you get kicked out of school."

"If that's policy then the policy's crazy! You're telling me that my son, straight A student, four point 0, GPA has to go to school with gang members. And when gangs do what gangs do, you're gonna kick him out of school?"

"All kids are entitled to an education, ma'am," he said as if his responses were scripted.

"You're right. But I'm gonna take it one step further, my son has the right to an uninterrupted education, unless he's the one causing problems. At that point, you're free to suspend him forever. In fact, you wouldn't have to, I would keep his ass home if he didn't come here to learn."

"But, but," Mr. Morgany stuttered.

"No buts, Mr...." She leaned over to read the nameplate on his desk. "Mr. Morgany, I don't believe in policy. I believe in right and wrong. And if you feel it's right for you to kick my son out of school because he got jumped, then I believe it's right for me to take your ass to court, win, lose, or draw. Obviously, you can't protect him, and he's not allowed to protect himself. So what should he do?" She stood there staring at Mr. Morgany, waiting for his answer, but none was forthcoming. "That's what I thought," she said, "Are you sure you're okay, Magic?"

"I'm fine, Mom."

She got up and walked out the door without another word.

Mr. Morgany sat there chastened, studying Magic's file that sat on the desk in front of him.

"You're a good kid, Magic," he said after a few moments. "But if something happens to you on school grounds after that confrontation, I could lose my job. But your mother's right. I want you to stay in the office until your next period class and give me a chance to round up all these little knuckleheads."

"Thank you, sir."

Magic hadn't made any real friends so he was quite surprised when a kid walked up to him after his sixth period class.

"Your name Magic?" he asked, sounding like a COPS commercial.

"Yeah," Magic responded with his hard face on.

"You know a dude name Clear?"

"Yeah."

"He told me to watch your back. My name Muscle," he said, going into his pocket. He pulled out a knife that was about six inches long, handed it to Magic then turned and walked away.

When Magic came out of his last period class, Muscle was right outside the door leaning against the wall.

"You ready to do this?" he asked.

"Do what?"

"I heard them niggas gonna be waiting for you after school, but if you represent properly today you won't have to worry about this shit no more this year."

"Let's do it," Magic said.

"You got that thang I gave you?"

"Yeah." Magic stuck his hand in his pocket to make sure.

Muscle turned and gestured for him to follow, and they pushed their way through the crowd and ducked into the first floor bathroom.

"Take it out and open it," Muscle said.

Magic slowly took the knife out of his pocket and pulled the blade out manually. He grinned and stuck out his hand. He laid it in his palm. He closed it, and then it snapped open. He closed it again and it snapped open.

Magic looked at the knife thinking, 'do that shit again, I'll get it next time.'

Muscle looked at Magic and asked, "You never seen a switch blade before?"

"A what?"

"A what-fucking-planet you from?" He opened his palm, showed Magic the button on the side of the knife and handed it back. Magic hit the button, and it popped open like, well, Magic. Magic smiled and Muscle smiled with him, or at him, one of the two.

"You right handed or left handed?" Muscle asked.

"Right."

"Leave the knife open, and put it in your right hand pocket, tighten your belt so your pants won't be falling down, and less roll."

As they approached the double doors, all Magic could hear was the track coach saying, "Keep your head down and your legs moving." Magic's specialty was the hundred-yard dash and if all else failed, running was always an option.

Muscle stopped abruptly, as if he'd seen a ghost. "Yo, that's Clear."

Magic looked out and over all the heads gathered in front of the school. Parked right in front of the building was Clear's candy apple red Lexus and behind him were three black Acura Legends with tinted windows, twenty-inch rims, and spoilers. Looking fierce, like they could fly and shit.

Muscle looked at Magic and said, "He came up to the school for you. Who the fuck are you?"

Clear stood outside his car talking to one of the officers that worked at the school. He directed the conversation as soon as they were within hearing range.

"What's up Bro, hey Nephew," Clear said, then pulled both boys to him and put his arm around their shoulders. "Officer Fontane, this is my little brother, and my nephew."

"Hi, Officer Fontane," Muscle said and reached to shake the officer's hand.

"Hi, Muscle," he said. "And you must be Magic."

"How you doing, sir," Magic said, looking around as everybody stood and watched like star-struck fans.

"I'm good, and you?"

"I'm good too," Magic responded.

"Let's keep it that way," he said and moved in a little closer. "If one of these motherfuckers look at you hard, you let me know, alright."

Magic nodded, then Fontane walked over to Clear and extended his hand. "Have a good day, Mr. Kittles."

"You do likewise, Mr. Fontane," Clear said and ushered the boys into the car.

They pulled out of the circle and made a right onto the street. Clear picked up his cell phone and said peace, and the three Hondas behind them turned off at the next side street.

"Why you hang up on me like a little bitch, Magic?" Clear asked.

"Because you made me mad."

"Every time someone makes you mad you act like a little bitch?" Clear said. Muscle snickered. "Why you back there snickering like a little bitch, Muscle? That's why them niggas up in that school think they can handle yall, because yall be acting like bitches."

Muscle didn't say a word, Magic didn't say a word, and Magic was sure that both of them were hoping that Clear was finished.

"How's your aunt, Muscle?" Clear asked.

"She's good."

"And your cousins Rachel and... Rocky, they must be about eight or nine now."

"Rocky's ten, and Rachel's eight," Muscle responded, sliding over to the center and sticking his head between the seats as Clear continued. "I was at the hospital when Rocky was born, did you know that?"

"No, but Auntie got a couple pictures of you holding him when he was real little. She say them was the good old days."

"They all good if you sucking air," Clear said as he sped through the yellow light.

"You two know each other?" he asked.

"Not really," Muscle responded.

"Well get to know each other," Clear said as he pulled over in front of the store down the street from Magic's house. He pressed a button on the steering wheel. After the glove compartment popped open, he leaned over and pulled out a stack of bills, the bank seal still attached. Then he slid two crisp hundred dollar bills from the stack and handed one to Magic and one to Muscle.

Magic sat there for a moment thinking he had made a mistake. Muscle stuck the money in his pocket and started out the car.

"Thank you, Uncle Clear," he said.

"Tell your aunt to call me if she needs me."

"I will," Muscle said as he got out of the car.

"Thanks," Magic said, holding the money in front of Magic, making sure he saw that it was a hundred.

"Not a biggie', Magic," he said, and Magic hopped out.

Magic went in the store and got a Mr. Goodbar and two bags of potato chips. Muscle stayed outside and waited for him. When Magic went to stick the change in his pocket, he felt the knife. He pulled it out and handed it to Muscle.

"You can have it, I got about five," Muscle said.

"Why so many?"

"I don't know, some I bought, some I found," Muscle responded, hunching his shoulders.

Magic stuck the knife back in his pocket and joined Muscle on the wall.

"I got a nine too," he said. "My Uncle Mack gave it to me."

"Your Uncle Mack?"

"Yeah, my Uncle Mack."

"Do he live in the hotel downtown?"

"Yeah, but he own the house we live in, too."

"You live in?"

"Yeah, I live with my aunt. Well she's not really my aunt, she's my Uncle Mack's baby's Mama. They own that hotel, too."

"Your aunt and uncle own a hotel?" Magic asked.

"No, the Black Mob owns the hotel."

"What's a Black Mob?"

Muscle ignored the question and came with one of his own.

"How you know Clear?"

"I met him at the welfare when me and my mom first moved here from down south."

"And the welfare sent you to the hotel?"

"Yeah."

"It's fucked up down there, right?" he said, but Magic didn't respond.

His question sent Magic back to the hotel and he started thinking about Marge, Diana and the Cat-Food Man.

"That's how you met my Uncle Mack?" Muscle asked.

"Yeah."

"He just got out of jail; he did three years for shooting some kid in his hands."

"For what?" Magic asked, trying to conceal his shock.

"For touchin' my aunt on the ass."

"He shot somebody in the hand for touching his wife's ass?"

"Both hands, my Uncle Mack crazy," Muscle said with a hint of pride in his voice. "They not married, they ain't even together no more. She say he crazy, too."

Muscle smiled and shook his head slightly as if crazy was the place to be. "When I turn eighteen… my Uncle Mack gonna make me his second lieutenant. Maybe Clear'll make you a lieutenant," he said.

Magic stood there feeling real uninformed as the local boys started to circle and give them dirty looks. They entered and exited the store with their bottles of liquid courage wrapped tight in brown paper bags. No hellos. No what's ups. Just dirty looks.

"Um, 'bout to bounce, man, see you tomorrow in school," Muscle said and turned to slap Magic up. "You got first or second lunch?"

"First."

"Look for me, alright?"

"Alright," Magic said and headed up the hill toward home feeling like someone had picked him up and dropped him off in a foreign country without a map.

CHAPTER 16

Muscle

Muscle and Magic became really good friends. He coached Magic through his first year cool, and they created another tier on the high school food chain. The Smart Cool Boy's Tier. But the picture he painted of Clear and the person that Magic had come to love and respect were two different people. To Magic, Clear was a hard working entrepreneur with dreams of one day becoming rich and powerful. The person that Muscle described was a hardworking Kingpin, who was already rich and powerful.

Magic had known Clear a little over a year, and there was nothing about him that said drug dealer. Drug dealers didn't cut little kids hair all day Sunday free of charge and spend time hangin' out with boys like him. Yeah, Magic decided, he got a nice car, a nice house and a fine girlfriend, but he ain't flashy, and everybody likes him, even cops.

He often asked himself why would Muscle lie to him about something so crucial? And he never came up with a reason that made sense. At first he thought Muscle was a little off or maybe addicted to fantasy, but Muscle was smart as hell in two languages, actually three. English, Thug and French. He learned French at a private school that his Uncle Mack sent him to, but he got kicked out in the seventh grade because some kid called him a nigger and taped a noose to his gym locker. He said he beat the kid up and tried to strangle him with his own rope. He learned Thug living in the hood, watching BET, MTV and his Uncle Mack.

After a little while Magic realized that Muscle was just angry. Angry at his mother, who he referred to as the bitch that traded him in for a crack pipe. Angry at his father, who he didn't even know.

One day they were walking down Main Street on their way to Footlocker to get the new orange and white Uptowns. Muscle just stopped as a guy walked by with a big Rottweiler. He looked at that dog as if he was trying to send him some kind of telepathic message or something. Then he looked at Magic with a straight face and said, "That's my motherfuckin' daddy." Then he growled and showed his teeth, and they burst out laughing.

CHAPTER 17

Princess Dayja's Home Visit

Magic shuffled through the bootleg CD's, found the best of JadaKiss, slid it into the CD player and sat back as the Lexus Coupe glided through the raggedy city street like a magic carpet. He watched heads doing double takes and females squinting, trying to see who was flossin' inside. Magic loved this car. It had a five-deck CD player, DVD player; two TVs on the headrests and one that slithered down from the roof between the passenger and driver seat. It had a sunroof, climate control, and a mini-bar in the back.

"Why you got all these bootleg CD's?" Magic asked.

"Fuck them niggas, they don't know what to do with their royalty checks anyway. Niggas starving in the ghetto and they running around buying platinum chains and million dollar automobiles."

Magic laughed and looked over at Clear. "The more I hang around you the less I understand you, man," he said.

"You only sixteen, it's a whole lot of shit you don't understand. That's why I like you, lil' nigga, because you smart enough to know you don't know."

"O...K...," Magic said stretching out the O and the K as he reconfigured Clear's words and translated them into a language that he could understand. "So what's on the agenda?" he asked.

"I thought we would go down to the zoo and look for some ostrich eggs and sniff some elephant farts," said Clear.

"Man, drop me off at the basketball court, you trippin'," Magic said.

Clear laughed and adjusted his sideview mirror. "Just sit back and enjoy the ride, it ain't every day you get to cruise in a chromed-out Lexus Coupe."

"True, true," Magic responded, leaned back, closed his eyes, took a deep breath and blurted out, "What's The Black Mob?"

Clear laughed but Magic was still sitting there with his eyes closed trying to hide the nervousness he felt from his stomach up.

"It's an equal opportunity employer," Clear responded, then he hit the volume button on the steering wheel, and started bopping his head to Jada Kiss.

The cell phone was barely audible over the crisp lyrics pumping through the powerful woofers. Clear brought the music down, picked up the phone, looked at the number and then handed it to Magic.

"Who is this?" Magic asked.

"Just answer the phone."

"Hello?" Magic said.

"Hello?"

"Hello?"

"Who is this?" "Who is this! And can I speak to my brother!"

Magic offered Clear the phone. His heart started to race as he realized that that was the girl from the welfare office.

"Talk," Clear said, not even looking in Magic's direction.

"Here, man," Magic said, and Clear just continued to drive. Magic changed hands, wiped the sweat from his palm, pressed the recline button and pulled smooth out of his top hat.

"Hey, Dayja," he said soft and airy with a touch of bass.

"Who is this?" she asked.

"My name's Magic, I'm a friend of your brother."

"Oh, I know you, you're that fine square boy Porsha told me about."

"You got something against fine square boys?"

"No, I don't have nothing against nothing."

"That's a good fundamental principle," Magic responded. He looked over at Clear who was wearing a smile.

"Why you use all those big words, you trying to perpetrate a smart person?" Dayja asked.

"I am smart," Magic responded, "and I attribute my extensive vocabulary to the fact that I'm an incessant reader."

Magic knew girls liked smart boys with a twist of thug, because they got the best of both worlds, at least that's what Muscle said.

"I don't read books, I read people," Dayja said.

"Oh, you're a psychic."

"No, I didn't say I was a psychic, I said I read people. There's a difference."

"Okay... Can you read me?"

Dayja giggled like a little girl.

"Sure," she responded. "Put the phone up to your chest."

"Hell, no. You trippin," Magic said.

"No for real, everything real comes from the heart. Game like you kickin' comes from the head."

"You playin' right?" Magic asked.

"No, I'm serious, put the phone to your chest," Dayja insisted.

Magic pressed the phone to his chest and looked over at Clear again. Clear looked back, smiled and shook his head as he pulled over.

Magic raised the phone and put it back to his ear. "What did my heart tell you?" he asked.

"It told me I got your ass shook, because the pulsation far exceeds normal rapidity. Tell my brother I see his car, and I'll be out in a second." She hung up.

The phone went dead, and Magic proceeded to stare out of the right passenger side window.

Moments later Clear tapped him on the shoulder and pointed to Dayja who was coming from the other side of the street. Magic licked his lips and took a quick glance at himself in the rearview mirror as Clear got out the car. Dayja walked into her brother's arms and they embraced.

"I'm sorry, Bro," she said.

"You should be," he said.

They leaned against the car and Dayja's arm stayed around her brother's waist, then she grabbed his arm and placed it over her shoulder. She moved in so close that she could probably hear his heart beat, and his words vibrate in his chest. She obviously missed her brother so much that it hurt inside.

"Listen, baby girl," he said while gently rubbing her shoulder. "I've been the best big brother I can be, and for a long time you were the soul motivating factor in my life. Until I realized we didn't hold the patent on pain. There are children growing up under worse circumstances than we did. I can't change the world, but I can change some lives. I got a plan, baby, and anyone that stands in the way of that plan I will erase, including you. But as long as you are doing what you know to be right, in here," he said pointing to her heart, "I will die, kick down the gates of hell and poke the devil in the ass with a hot ice pick for you."

Dayja stood there smiling as warm salty tears mixed with black mascara, raced down her high cheekbones. They dipped into her inherited dimples, collided to caress her strong feminine chin, then splashed like black raindrops onto her superwoman shirt. She wiped the tears from her face and said, "I understand."

"I need to change my shirt," Dayja said, then turned and walked back across the street, into the house and up the stairs to her room. But the tears wouldn't stop, because the memories wouldn't stop. She remembered him and Porsha sprinkling gold glitter from the front door, through the living room, up to her bedroom, and telling her it was fairy dust. They did this every time she lost a tooth…

She remembered when she was nine and her brother played hopscotch with her because all the other little girls in the neighborhood said she thought she was all that.

"You are all that," he said. "Get the chalk. I'll play with you."

She remembered the night she told her brother that he couldn't tell her what to do and he wasn't her motherfucking father. She remembered him telling her, "If you walk out that door, don't come back."

She remembered a couple months later the cops breaking up the fight between her and the girl with the second worst reputation in the neighborhood. Second worse because by that time she had the first.

She remembered that she was no longer fourteen and sexually frustrated and her name wasn't Princess Dayja any longer. It was Dayja, tramp, slut, hoe.

She remembered when the police brought her to her brother's door and he wouldn't even let her in the house.

She remembered him looking her in the face and saying 'I ain't your motherfucking daddy,'and slamming the door.

She remembered calling from the children's shelter and him not accepting any of her phone calls or responding to any of her letters.

She remembered telling everybody, "Fuck him, I ain't got no brother." And she remembered her counselor saying, "Listen, you spoiled little bitch: for your information, your brother is paying me a hundred and fifty dollars an hour to de-program your spoiled ass! He pays all your medical bills, purchases all those Applejacks and Fruit Loops that your ass seem to be addicted to. He has sent you more goddamn clothes than I have in my closet and I have a six-figure income, so you need to recognize, straighten up and get the fuck out of here!"

She remembered Miss Kay, her foster mother saying, "If it wasn't for your brother your little spoiled ass wouldn't be here."

She remembered Porsha saying, "If me and your brother didn't love your spoiled ass, do you think I would be sitting in the welfare on such a nice day?"

Dayja put on her pink Capri's and her pink shirt, and white sandals. She accentuated her outfit with her white shades, gold bangles, gold hoops and gold necklace. She went downstairs and gave her foster mother Miss Kay a big kiss, then walked out of the door like the princess she was.

As she approached the car, a slight shimmer from the gold medallions that hung from her brother's neck caught her eye. Then the memories that resided in the murky cesspool pushed forward, and tried to pollute the moment. Quickly, she put on her tough skin and deceptive smile and proceeded to stop traffic.

Magic turned to get out the car so Dayja could sit in front with her brother. Clear grabbed his arm. "Play your position. First class niggas don't ride coach," he said.

Dayja got in, leaned forward, kissed her brother on the cheek, and extended her hand.

"Hi, Magic, I'm Dayja," she said.

"Pleased to meet you, Dayja," Magic responded and caressed her hand gently.

"Okay, where we going? To the mall?" she asked.

"Girl, you ain't got enough clothes?" Clear responded.

"Yeah, but did you ever think that I might need some shoes, some socks, some underwear, some belts, some bras, some tuck combs."

"Okay, okay, okay. I get the picture," Clear said as he backed into a driveway and shot out into traffic.

"Dayja, call Porsha, tell her we're on our way. Tell her we're going to the mall and bring her own damn money."

Dayja leaned forward to retrieve the phone from the cup holder and Magic said, "You smell nice."

Dayja laid the phone down on the back seat, went into her purse, pulled out the bottle of lotion, and handed it to Magic.

"Peaches and Cream, Frederick's of Hollywood, Market Place Mall. Ten seventy-one with tax, and thank you," she said, then picked up the phone and began dialing.

"Hello?"

"Hello, Porsha."

"Dayja!" Porsha said excitedly

"Princess Dayja to you."

"Princess, my butt. Where you at?"

"Whipping in the red Lex, girl."

"So he did come and get you. I thought I was going to have to jump on your brother about you today."

"No, he straight."

"Is Magic with yall?"

"Yep."

"Ain't he fine."

"Yep."

"You like him, don't you."

"Yep."

"Girl, you bad," Porsha said.

"Yep," Dayja responded and they laughed.

"When yall coming to get me?" Porsha asked.

"We on our way now, and my brother said bring your own loot because all of his is reserved for me."

"That's cool, ask him is it right, left, right or left, right, left."

"Bro--Porsha said is it right, left, right or left, right, left something like that."

"You tell Porsha if she touch my safe I'll kick her ass."

"You heard that, didn't you, girl?"

"Your brother ain't gonna swat a fly, so you know he ain't about to be messing with me."

"Bro, Porsha said..."

"Oooh, Oooh, Dayja don't tell him that."

"Yeah, that's what I thought."

"You little traitor."

"I'm down with the money."

"Okay," Porsha said.

"Love you."

"Love you too, Dayja, see you in a minute."

They went to Darien Lake, shared a hot dog and a snow cone, and held hands on the Ferris wheel. She screamed Magic's name on the Superman Ride of Steel, closed her eyes, and pressed her soft sweet smelling body against his. They both had Lobster Cantonese at China Gate, and maple walnut ice cream at Carvels. The night resembled a storybook, Dayja thought as he walked her up the driveway to the door.

They stood there well hidden, blanketed by night and the manicured hedges, totally consumed by puppy love. Magic moved in, arms extended and lips puckered, ready to solidify the relationship. As he advanced, her heart said yes, yes, yes. But her head said no, no, no. Miss Kay always said, "They'll never buy the cow if they can get the milk for free." Dayja stepped back, almost pushing the flowerpot off the stoop.

"I had a wonderful time, get my number from Porsha and call me," she said. Then she leaned forward and kissed him on the cheek, turned and went in the house.

CHAPTER 18

Deja vu

Magic levitated up the stairs and could barely find the keyhole in the dimly lit hall. Peaches and cream had him drunk. He pushed the door open quietly and malicious assertions circled the house, shot through the hollow halls and slapped him square in the face.

"Well, why the fuck you here?" he heard his mother say.

"Peggy, you ain't about to hold me hostage in this damn house. If you want someone to wine you and dine you twenty-four-seven, you better try dial a date," his father said.

"Fuck you, Magic!"

"Fuck you!"

"You can kiss my black ass!" his Mama said. And that was it.

The fake wooden door slammed shut, shaking the pictures of Martin, Malcolm, and Marcus almost off the wall.

"Listen, Peggy, you got one more time to invite me to your ass!" his father said, and before Magic's petition could reach the pearly gates, she said it again, but this time with a twist.

"Kiss my hot chocolate ass, Magic," and they collided like bloodthirsty gladiators.

Magic rushed to the bedroom door as the words exploded in his ears. "Bitch, hoe, stankin' bitch," he yelled. Magic's pounding heart protested as his trembling hand reached for the doorknob. But fear swallowed him whole, and carried him back out the door and down the stairs, to the front stoop where the intrusive sounds of the city streets confirmed his cowardice.

The front door flew open and his father blew past him without looking in his direction. The white Bonneville roared, the tires screeched and kicked up dirt.

Magic turned and slowly walked up the stairs and into the house. Cory stood at the door with his little fists balled up, pounding and pounding on their bedroom door crying, "Mama, Mama."

Magic walked slowly down the hall then reached to pick him up. The pain in his face was indescribable.

"Your daddy beat up my mama," he cried, "and I'm gonna kill him just like you killed my daddy."

Then he turned and walked into his bedroom. Deep down inside rage had found a home and nestled itself on the crux of Magic's heart, tuned itself to the pulsation of his vascular organ and waited, and waited, and waited.

CHAPTER 19

Old News

Big Baby sat on his mother's porch and popped the top on the last can of Old English. He patted his pocket to make sure that the six hundred and ninety dollars was still in place. He raised his foot up off the stairs to check for scuffs, and to give his new Jordan's the once over. He laughed, exposing the gaps where teeth use to be.

Big Baby had always been fat, black and the brunt of someone's jokes. His fighting career started in pre-school and he lost his first tooth in kindergarten. I knocked the hinges off that motherfucker, he thought as he closed his eyes and turned up the can of Old English, determined to consume every drop.

The first slug from the automatic weapon pierced the bottom of the can and white foam shot out, reaching far beyond the second square of the concrete walkway and into his mother's tulips. His body hit with a loud thump and warm blood poured from his head and onto his mother's freshly swept and mopped porch.

Little Big Baby, who was only five, had just turned away from the window. He was going to tell his grandma that his daddy was drinking beer on her porch. His little body stiffened when the piece of steel ripped into his little back, ruptured his spleen and lodged itself in his heart.

Now Grandma's hope for the future rocked in her arms, and lay dead on her porch. Blood stained the white apron and smoke from burnt chicken wings filled the room. It was chicken wings Tuesday. Little Big Baby and Big Baby loved chicken wings.

Sirens filled the air. Sorrow filled her heart and white men in blue suits filled her house and emptied her days.

CHAPTER 20

That Black Mob Shit

After Dayja's first home visit, she started coming home once a week, then twice a week on Wednesdays and Saturdays. Saturdays, Magic and Dayja would spend most of the day together at the mall or at the movies. It didn't matter, whatever she wanted to do or wherever she wanted to go was fine with him. She was the first thing he thought about in the morning and the last thing at night. Thoughts of her invaded his day and he'd drift into la la land. On Wednesdays, the four of them would go out to eat, play pool or rent a movie.

On this Wednesday, they decided to go and see the 9:00 P.M. showing of Love and Basketball. Clear and Porsha were discussing how the movie ended as they walked to the car.

Dayja and Magic were masterminding a plot to get her curfew extended. She had to be back at her foster parent's house by twelve. They knew that Clear had implemented the curfew and could be abated only by him.

They got into the car and just as Dayja sat up and stuck her head between the seat, the phone erupted. Clear picked it up and looked at the caller ID.

"Officer Campbell. How are you, my dear fellow?"

"I just rolled up in here and I need to make my rounds, but your boy Mack's name is poppin' like Orville Redenbacher around this motherfucker. I don't know how he's connected, but it has something to do with that double homicide yesterday over on Ravine. Um-out, but holler back."

Clear hung-up and sat for a moment. No one said a word until he pulled off.

"You okay, baby?" Porsha asked, but Clear didn't respond. He hit memory on the cell phone, scrolled down until he came to Black's number, then hit dial.

"Hey, Clear," Black answered, sounding half-asleep.

"We need an assembly and a Tuesday's paper, breach of protocol, East Side, dogma, midnight. Breach of protocol, East Side, dogma, midnight," he repeated.

Clear hung up, turned around in the next driveway and headed back toward the city. He pulled in front of his house and Porsha and Dayja got out of the car without question or hesitation.

"Git Dayja home, Porsha. I'll drop Magic off," Clear said and pulled off heading for the expressway.

Magic sat in the passenger seat with curiosity churning in his stomach to the point of discomfort. This is that black mob shit, he thought, as he sat and watched Clear go through a gamut of different emotions. As Clear made the sharp turn onto the expressway, Magic, unable to restrain himself, asked, "What is the Black Mob, man?"

Clear glanced at the Movada on his wrist then he looked at Magic and his face softened.

"Magic, you're asking for information that could possibly get you killed," Clear said. "Now I can give you a bunch of surface shit, but that wouldn't satisfy your curiosity, eventually you would begin to theorize and speculate. So tell me what you want to know."

"I wanna know everything you know," Magic responded.

Making up his mind, Clear exited the expressway and pulled into a dimly lit parking lot, hit redial on his cell phone and told Black he'd be there at 12:30. Then he reached under his front seat and pulled out a Mack 10. He hit the button on his dash and the glove compartment popped open.

Magic flinched as Clear reached across him and pulled out two stacks of hundred dollar bills then laid the pistol and the hundred dollar bills neatly on the armrest.

"This is the Black Mob. So, once again I'm gonna ask you, what do you want to know? Because there's an invisible line, Magic, and once you cross that line, death is the only way out."

Magic could feel the adrenaline flooding his system. Clear's words and persona were like a slow dripping IV jammed into his main vein. Pumping in courage, style, finesse and knowledge. He didn't know this Clear, but he knew that this man would never let anybody put their hands on his mother. Clear placed the pistol back under the seat, picked up the hundred dollar bills and shoved them back in the glove compartment.

"You going home?" he asked.

And once again Magic said, "I want to know everything you know."

"Say no more."

Clear put the car in reverse, turned around and started out of the parking lot. Magic sat there for a moment juxtaposing this short, short story. Filling in the blanks and holes with bits and pieces of information he had stored from the first day he set foot in Rochester. Starting with his conversation with Clear in the parking lot at the welfare. The conversations he'd had with Muscle. The hundred dollar bills in the glove compartment, and the black Acura Legends at his school, all of which simply confirmed what Muscle had told him. Clear was no one to fuck with. So that meant the Black Mob was nothing to fuck with. And as a member, he would be nothing to fuck with.

CHAPTER 21

The Sacrifice

Clear pressed the buzzer at the Saint and Sinner Baptist Church then turned to scan the parking lot making sure everyone was present and accounted for. Magic scanned also noticing that the same trucks that were at the barber shop was now at the church. Pastor Williams approached the door wearing the same smile he had worn for the last twenty years, and the same suit.

"Saint Clear, how are you my friend?" Pastor Williams asked as he came to the door.

"I'm doing well, Pastor. And yourself?"

"Couldn't be better," the pastor responded, looking agile but aged.

"Pastor, this is a friend of mine, his name is Magic."

"How are you, young man?"

"Good, thank you," Magic said.

"Polite young man, must be from out of town."

Clear and Magic smiled.

"So, Pastor, how is the flock?" Clear said.

"Good, very good. We've finally finished remodeling the basement, and we started opening up in the evening for recreation about three months ago. Our adult population had increased by twenty percent."

"Yeah, and the monthly generated revenue has increased by almost thirty percent," Clear said.

"I don't know what happened, Clear, but once we started the teen-program and started giving dances on Saturday night, people started paying tithes. Shock the shit out of me. God knows I can't stand that music, but if they're here on Saturday night, it's highly likely they'll be living Sunday morning."

"You're doing a great job, Pastor."

"Thank you, Clear, and so are you."

The pastor turned and walked down the stairs as Clear and Magic walked up past the sanctuary and into the specially constructed, sound-proof room. Clear punched in the code and entered, hard face intact. He walked around the table slowly and embraced his Captains while Magic stood by the door. Clear sat down in the chair at the head of the table directly across from Mack, who was reclining in his chair, his hands locked across his belly and his face shielded by the beak of his baseball cap.

"Gentlemen... Magic," Clear said, and waved his hand as if Magic was behind curtain number two. Daemon moved down, then gestured for Magic to take his seat. Magic approached the table feeling very apprehensive.

"Hey, Magic."

"What's up, Black...Daemon, Marwon, Mack," Magic responded with a slight nod.

Magic and Marwon generally greeted each other by pounding on their chest two times, which meant much love in ghetto jargon, but not tonight. This room was occupied by the same jolly fellows that cut hair and talked shit from eight to eight at 'Precision Cut.' But the atmosphere was very different, so much so that it made Magic nervous.

"What's up, little Nigga?" said Mack, never raising his head nor showing his eyes.

"Chillin," Magic said, using one of his newly acquired phrases.

He had only seen Mack about four or five times since he had come to Rochester. Twice when he came to the barber shop to talk to Black, once at Muscle's house, and at the hotel.

Clear leaned back in his chair, stretched his arms over his head and yawned loudly. He spoke before his yawn was complete. "We all know Magic, and have discussed him on several occasions. He has decided to join us much sooner than we expected, but you know my motto. I would like to snatch'em straight outta the pussy if possible." Black smirked, Marwon smiled, Daemon laughed, and Mack lifted his head slightly. "Any objections?" Clear asked, and all heads moved from side to side.

"Okay, now let's get to the business at hand." Clear gestured to Black and he pushed the copy of Tuesday's paper across the table. Clear opened the paper to the local section. The picture of the grandmother, her 26-year-old son and her five-year-old grandson had made the front page.

Clear sat and slowly read to himself. When he neared the end he started to read aloud. "It was probably drug related. The grandson had served two jail terms and had a record that began when he was twelve. He was currently facing a seven-year sentence for a charge of possession with the intent to sell.

"Thanks to a neighbor sitting on her porch doing a crossword puzzle who wrote down the license plate number, the shooter was apprehended a short time later. The grandmother is presently in the hospital suffering from shock, but is expected to make a full recovery."

Clear laid the newspaper on the table in front of him and searched the faces on the front page.

"What happened, Mack?" Clear asked.

Mack cleared his throat. "Well, this is the way it came to me."

"Are you telling me that you really don't know what happened?"

"Yeah, I know what happened, man," Mack responded with aggravation in his voice.

"My boys CJ and Smooth was at the spot over on Alexander and somehow the dude in the picture got in the back hallway. His partner came to the side door where they were serving the product and was beefin', saying that the bag was too small or it wasn't good or somethin'. Then the kid in the picture burst through the back door and got the drop on CJ.

"Smooth said the kid in the picture was acting crazy as a bitch. Said he stuck a pistol in CJ's mouth and told him to suck it like he was sucking a dick, while he went through his pockets. They told Smooth to call his mother and tell her to start making funeral arrangements, and when Smooth refused, he bust him in the head with the pistol and knocked him out."

Mack blew hard, slid down in his chair, adjusted his baseball cap and continued. "Smooth said when he woke up CJ was driving him to the hospital, and after he got stitched up, CJ was nowhere to be found. He said he tried to call him, but got no answer so he caught a taxi home. Then about four in the morning CJ called him and said he was in jail."

Clear fingered the gold medallion around his neck, eyes searing, attempting to bring all of this into focus.

"How much money and product did we lose, Mack?" Clear asked.

"About sixteen hundred in cash and about four in product," Mack said.

"So, two people were murdered for two grand. A thousand dollars a head. What kinda shit is that, Mack?" Clear said, releasing the medallion as he leaned forward. "First of all, second-lieutenants don't sell dope, they pick up and deliver. Lieutenants and second-lieutenants are on call twenty-four hours a day. Have you ever called me and didn't get an answer?" Clear snatched his cell phone off and slammed it on the table. "That's what this motherfucker is for, we established these rules."

"Clear, you act like I pulled the trigger, man."

Clear pounded his fist down on the newspaper. "Do you think this woman gives a fuck who pulled the trigger?"

"Man, it wasn't my fault. I can't be every fuckin' where," Mack said.

Clear got up, walked around the table and placed his hands on the back of Marwon's chair.

"Marwon, if your spot gets robbed, your lieutenant gets knocked the fuck out, you got a demented second-lieutenant with a bruised ego running around shootin' at a motherfucker that ain't worth their weight in peanuts dead or alive, and a four-year-old baby gets caught in the crossfire, your second-lieutenant is locked the fuck up and singing louder than Brittany Spears. Who's fault is it, Marwon?"

"It's mine."

"Why is it yours, Marwon?"

"Because it was my responsibility to make sure that the apartment was secure before I allowed any business to be conducted there. My first lieutenant is my responsibility, and I don't know about anybody else but my second-lieutenant knows we don't have shootouts in the streets, we have cops and paid killers who do dat."

"Whose fuckin fault is it, Mack?"

"It's mine. But..."

"But my ass! Whose fault is it, Mack?"

"It's mine, man," Mack said just above a whisper.

"You breached protocol, Mack."

Mack stood and simultaneously Black, Marwon and Daemon stood with pistols drawn. "Section seven: damage control, page nine of the Black Mob Bible reads: Kids don't die, neither directly nor indirectly, precipitated by any action we performed or fail to perform. That's your fucking rule Mack, that's what separates us from them. Damage fucking control!"

"What's going on, Clear?"

"You know what's going on, Mack. There are rules and regulations. Procedures, protocol, gangster etiquette, motherfucker, that's what you call it."

Clear rubbed his head with one hand and gripped the medallion with the other. He looked up into Mack's eyes for the last time and nodded slightly. There was no hesitation, no gap between the nod and the command.

Mack stood there resolved and mute, gripping the edge of the redwood table as pieces of steel riddled and decimated his massive frame. Severing the bond that was permeated approximately a decade ago, when him and Clear clicked together the barrels of their brand new nines and swore to kill any motherfucker that stood between them and the legacy... Even if that meant one another.

Black, Marwon and Daemon set their guns on the table, allowing them to cool as Clear sat, trapped in his own mind, attempting to quiet his conscience. And there was a moment of silence, a quiet moment. Not a customary moment of prayer and reflection, a shit-fuck-damn moment of silence. A stop...and begin again moment.

In the midst of that moment, Magic opened his eye's, and saw the automatic weapons lying on the table, smoking like old men pipes, and filling the room with barely breathable air. He looked at Mack's dead body slumped over in the chair, and for the first time he saw the resemblance between him and Muscle. And all his mind would allow him to think was damn, damn, damn.

Clear sat, fucked up. Teeth clenched and eyes closed. This wasn't the first time he had to order the assassination of one of their own, but Mack was a pillar, a cornerstone, a founding father. No one could know and truly be impassioned for what Clear was feeling. Him and Mack's friendship had eroded over the years, but when they reminisced, they told stories of swashbuckling ghetto adventures, The Crack Crusaders fighting poverty in the hood. But at some point, Mack defocused and his vision became obscured. He wanted a reputation, but the plan was for a legacy.

"You okay, Magic?" Clear asked.

Magic moved his head up and down and up and down until he found the lie. "Yeah, I'm straight man," he said, trying to sound like a big boy.

"Magic, Daemon," Clear said as if he were introducing them for the first time. "East Side Captain. Seven Gates, fourteen foot soldiers, one second-lieutenant, seven corporate connections. Annually generated revenue five point five million. Magic, Black, multi-county marketing, twenty gates, four per county, two second lieutenants. Annually generated revenue eight point two million. North Side Captain. Magic, Marwon, multi-narcotic distributor, twelve gates, two female Captains annually generated revenue six point four million."

Clear stood up and walked over to the chair that contained Mack's body. He picked up Mack's baseball cap and placed it on the table then posted himself at the back of the Mack's chair. He spoke slowly, making sure every syllable was annunciated.

"Magic, my friend, meet Big Mack, my friend, South Side Captain. You've just stepped over that invisible line. Welcome."

Clear walked back around the table and as he passed, he scooped Black's 45 automatic to take its temperature.

"A new piece?" he asked.

"Naw," Black responded.

Clear popped out the clip and just as he had suspected, not a single round had been fired. He popped the clip back in and pushed the pistol back across the table and sat down.

"Any new business?" Clear asked.

"I got something, but I need to pull it together before I bring it to you," Daemon responded.

"You do dat," Clear said as he looked around the room, assessing faces. "Black--put an APB out on that kid, Smooth. Marwon and Daemon, call down to the crematorium and see when we can get this body properly disposed of. Daemon, since you're the better driver, put the body in your trunk until my man can get us in down there. I'll take care of this room and that snitchin' motherfucker in the county. Our meeting will be at Black's spot next week. Black, you got the south side until further notice. If there's nothing else, I'm out."

Clear stood up, walked around the room and embraced all his captains. And even when tempers flared and dead bodies were sprawled over the furniture like throw pillows, the embraces were long and warm. Marwon, Daemon, and Black embraced Magic, which eased some of the discomfort that bounced around in the pit of his stomach. Clear walked down the stairs, unlocked the door to the church and proceeded to the car. Magic followed. He looked over the hood and into Magic's eyes, which were full of questions. And though it was faint, he saw a semblance of pain. Not the pain derived from death, but the pain derived from life.

The ride home just wasn't as comfortable, Magic thought. The red Lexus seemed like a coffin with an Italian leather interior. As Clear turned the music down, Magic cracked the window. Morbid feelings hung in the air while soft music rapped itself around the bellowing sounds of the city streets. Thoughts stimulated feelings, feelings stimulated feelings and gut-wrenching emotions grasped for words that weren't in the English language.

"I'm not ready for this, Clear," Magic said as Clear pulled in front of the Canterbury apartments.

"You're right, Magic, you're not," Clear said.

"So why you let me get involved in this shit?"

"Because it's not about you, Magic."

"Well what the fuck is it about, Clear?" Magic asked just below a shout.

"Even if I told you what it was about you couldn't see it, because your life experiences have blurred your vision."

"Well fuckin' try me," Magic said with tears welling up in his eyes.

Clear was obviously shaken by Magic's tone. He closed his eyes for a moment, then, "Magic... I come from a place that's dark and scary. A fucking cesspool full of one-ways, dead-ends, and do not enters. Half the niggas I grew up with are either dead or in jail. And I look around, and shit just gets bleaker, and bleaker, and bleaker. And everybody running around with their thumbs stuck up their ass as if they don't know what the problem is."

"So what's the problem, Clear, since you got all the damn answers?"

"I'm the fuckin' problem. I'm the by-product of that dark, dark place where nobody wants to live, where nobody wants their children to live. Whole fucking countries have gone to war to keep from living in that place."

"What fuckin place?"

"The place where there's never enough of nothing. And want and need to carry pistols and pull triggers. A place where your environment forces you to make decisions when you're too young to make good decisions. A place where hunger pains are louder than the squeaking mattress where your Mama is fucking just to get one more bag. And you don't know whether it's gonna be a bag of groceries or a bag of dope. But you never lived in that place, Magic, and you will never live in that place."

"What fucking place, Clear? and don't talk to me in metaphors and shit."

Clear dug his fingers into the armrest, clenched his teeth, took a deep breath, and began again.

"Magic, open up your country-ass eyes and see what you're looking at. Read the paper, watch the news, and listen to the rhetoric of the politicians. Listen to what your Mama ain't saying. Don't nobody give a damn about us, Magic, and as a result, we don't give a damn about each other. A motherfucker will kill you for that Averix jacket and them Timberland boots, and it shouldn't be like that."

"So what does all of that have to do with me?"

"It has nothing to do with you, but everything to do with your uncanny ability to know what X plus Y minus D to the third power means. And if you have your way, you'll get your little degrees, and your corporate executive job, and move out to the 'burbs and lobby for more prison and welfare reform and against affirmative action."

"So the answer is to sell dope and murder your friends?" Magic said and Clear lost it. He sat up in his seat and tossed diplomacy to the wind.

"I sell dope because it was the first and most lucrative trade I learned, besides flipping hamburgers for five fifteen an hour. My brother and sister came out my mother's crackhead-ass needing shit. I needed meat, potatoes and rent money, not fucking college credits. My little brother lost his life trying to get sneaker money. And I swore my little sister would never want for shit again in her life. As for Mack, I murdered that fat bastard because he forgot, he fucking forgot. He didn't even want to give his wife and kids money when he went to prison. I sent her money every week out of my pocket. When he came home he didn't even go and see his kids, he moved into the fucking hotel. Why, because he wanted to be a big-balla and fuck every car-hopping rim-chasing hoe that would open her legs. He became the man we swore we would never be and he got careless, and he got dead. Any more questions, little nigga?"

"Yeah, what the fuck does this have to do with me?"

Clear shook his head and then hit a button on his steering wheel. The dash popped open and he reached across Magic, pulled out the stacks of hundred dollar bills, and dropped them in Magic's lap.

"Obviously, you're too pain-ridden to hear what I'm saying, but the bottom line is this, Magic. I'm building a legacy, and I'm taking you with me whether you like it or not. And the only thing you need to remember is this: I'm a fucking kamikaze nigga. I don't give a damn about dying or killing. I will kill you, your Mama, and your little brother. Then I'll take a busload of niggas just like me down to Opelika, Alabama and annihilate everybody down there with similar DNA to yours. Now get the fuck out my car."

Magic hopped out and slammed the door. Stuffing the two stacks of bills in his pocket, he turned to watch the red Lexus fade into a haze of distant cars, headlights, and street lamps. Dazed, he staggered onto the stoop and glanced at his watch as he reached to open the door. He walked up the stairs, unlocked the lock and headed down the hall to his room.

"Morning comes early," his mother said.

Startled by the sound of the voice in the darkness, he jumped. "I…I know, Ma, I'll get up."

"I know you will, and bring your ass back here," she said turning on the lamp light by her chair.

Magic was halfway down the hall when the light came on. He turned and pulled down his shirt, making sure his bulging pockets were covered.

"Do you know what time it is?" she asked.

Magic looked over at the fake antique grandfather clock.

"Two-forty," he said.

"Don't you ever come walking up in my house at this time of morning no more. You ain't got no damn job."

"Yes, ma'am," Magic said and turned to walk away.

"Wait a minute, I ain't say you could go no where."

"Come on, Mama, I'm tired."

"You should have thought about that three hours ago, and why your eyes so red? Come here, Magic."

"Come on, Mama."

"I said come here, Magic," she repeated.

Magic reluctantly walked over to where his mother was sitting.

"Why are your eyes so red, and what is that?" She stood up, licked the tip of her thumb, wiped it across his cheek and then turned to examine it in the light. "This is blood, Magic."

"Where?" he asked, leaning over into the light to examine her fingertip.

"Where'd it come from, Magic? And don't lie to me, boy."

Magic stood there as all the events of the day ran through his head at an accelerated pace. He wanted to tell her. He wanted to crawl onto her lap, lay his head on her shoulder and tell her everything. He would start with the trip to the movies, the phone call, the dead body and end with the two stacks of bills in his pocket.

"I'm tired, Mama. I went to the movies and fell asleep, now I'm going to bed, if that's alright with you."

"You went to see a movie that had real blood popping out of the screen. Magic don't make me call your Uncle Benny."

"Call him, Mama, and don't forget to tell him I got straight A's on my report card, and that nine times out of ten I'm home before ten o'clock and I watch my little brother when you're at work most of the time. Yeah, call him, Mama, but make sure you tell him everything," Magic said and headed down the hall.

"You just make sure you have your midnight movie-going ass up at seven o'clock in the morning," Peggy shouted down the hall.

"I will," Magic responded as he turned on the light in his room. "Where's Cory?" he asked.

"He's at Abigail's. I thought you were coming home at a decent hour and I told her to bring him to you when you got here."

"I'm sorry, Mama, you want me to go get him?"

"At three in the morning, Magic, you can get him right before you leave for school."

"Okay, love you."

"Love you, too."

"Good night."

"Good night."

CHAPTER 22

No Better Killer Than A Cop

Clear pulled into his driveway, pulled out his Nextel, scrolled down, and hit dial.

"Hello."

"What's up, Officer Campbell?"

"I don't know, you tell me. But give me a minute, man, I got this rookie looking in my mouth like he a throat specialist or some shit! Yo, partner, Officer Campbell said turning to the rookie. "Why don't you go and get us a cup of coffee, two sugars two creams for me." A pause, then, "Okay, what's up, boss man?"

"I hear there's a fifteen thousand dollar price tag on that kid's head who murdered that little boy over on Ravine, and twenty if the story makes the morning news."

"Oh, yeah," Officer Campbell responded.

"Yeah."

"Tell Porsha I like cheese with my grits, over-medium eggs and I prefer sausage to bacon. And I don't take checks. Peace."

"Peace."

CHAPTER 23

Money, Money, Money, Money

Morning did come early, and six snoozes weren't enough. Peggy burst through the door and snatched the covers off Magic's bed.

"Get you're black ass up, Magic, and turn off that alarm!"

"Okay, Mama, gimme my covers."

"I ain't giving you shit. Get up right now," she shouted.

After his mother left, Magic sat up in the bed, stretched and yawned. He dragged himself out of bed and over to his closet to decide what he would throw on because time was working against him. The cream-colored khakis lay across the old la-z-boy recliner in the corner. He walked over and pulled the two stacks of bills from the pocket.

"Damn!" he said as he counted the three zero's behind the five on both stacks of bills. All of a sudden, he was wide-awake. He took a quick shower, got dressed, and went to get Cory from Aunt Abigail's.

Abigail embraced the bite of the steaming hot water beating down on her celestial brown skin. Sometimes she took three or four baths a day, and still didn't feel clean. She closed her eyes and tried unsuccessfully to stop thinking. She placed her hands firmly against her ears in an effort to stop the sounds that echoed in her head, even though the nightmare was over. But a recurring nightmare was a small price to pay for such a lavish lifestyle. They robbed me of all desire to ever allow another man to touch me, she thought. They wanted pussy, and to retain their reputation. I wanted stocks and bonds. Ain't no cheat in a fair trade.

She stepped out of the shower, dried off, and sprayed herself down with body sprays. "This that good shit, not that Kmart, Wal-Mart cheap shit," she said.

A soft knock at the door temporarily emancipated her from the omnipresence of gloom and doom that were always there. Pointing their accusing fingers, calling into account all of her iniquities and all of her transgressions, damning her to that fire and brimstone hell. The hell created by this loving and caring God, the same God that allowed her to be raped, and raped, and raped by a bunch of little dick white boys.

She tied her housecoat and walked to the door.

"Who is it?" she asked.

"It's Magic, Auntie Abigail, I came to get Cory."

"Magic who?"

"Come on, Auntie, you gonna make me late for school," Magic said and she opened the door.

"I ain't got no nephews that stay out all times of the morning."

"How you know?" Magic asked as he walked into the apartment.

"Your little brother walked half the night. Every time he heard a noise in the hall he ran to the door until he tired himself out."

"I'm sorry, Auntie."

"I'm sorry my ass, Magic, don't start doing shit and not considering other people," she said and walked away, appearing totally disgusted. "He's in my bed and his clothes are folded up in the chair."

Magic went to her room, scooped Cory up and rushed back to their apartment, deciding not to say anything to Aunt Abigail until she cooled off. He laid Cory down gently and kissed him on the forehead. When he did, his little brother's eyes opened.

"Hey, little bro."

"Where you was at?" Cory asked.

"Just out with some friends."

"I thought somebody had kill'ded you," he said, and Magic smiled reassuringly.

"Ain't nobody gonna kill'ded me. But I got to go to school and you got to get up in a little while. But when you get off your bus this afternoon, I'll be the first person you see, okay?"

"Okay," Cory said.

Magic grabbed his book bag and headed for the door. Just as he reached for the knob, he thought about last night. He went back and knocked on his mother's door.

"Stop knocking on my damn door and go to school."

"Is my dad in there?"

"No, and if you miss that bus, Magic, I'm gonna kick your ass."

Magic opened the door just enough to stick his head in.

"Tell him I said pick me up from school."

"Boy, if you don't get out of my house I know something."

CHAPTER 24

Freestyle

Magic hadn't had any major problems since Clear had come to the school. Most of the cool kids from last year were in jail, or had dropped out. New cool kids had come and taken the old cool kids' place and were busy making sentries and teachers earn their babysitting checks.

Muscle and Magic were in the eleventh grade. They had two years of seniority and pretty much kept to themselves, so their problems weren't physical confrontations, they were academic blockades. All you needed was one or two knuckleheads in a class, and they would bring the learning process to a grinding halt on any given day.

Magic walked into homeroom, dropped his book bag on the floor, flopped down in the chair, laid his head on the desk and fell asleep.

"Magic, Magic."

"Five minutes, Mama, just five minutes."

"If I was ya mama you wouldn't be sleeping in my class."

Magic raised his head and yawned in his homeroom teacher's face.

"This ain't class, this is homeroom, that's what we supposed to do here," he said, trying to sound sharp and alert.

"Whatever, Magic," Miss Hutchins said and turned to the new kid standing beside her. "This is Bryant, Bryant Sapp. He just moved here from Compton and both of you have the same schedule. He's all yours for the day. And you just slept through the bell, so get moving before you're late for your first period class."

Magic looked up at the clock and sprang to his feet as he extended his hand to Bryant. "What's up man?" he said.

"What's up, Magic," Bryant responded. "They call me Freestyle, but you can call me Free."

"You rap?" Magic asked.

"The best that ever did it, but I'm also nice with these," he said holding up his fists.

Another knucklehead, Magic thought as he raced through the hall trying to get to first period before the second bell rang.

First period was English, Mr. Foster's class. If you didn't come to his class to learn, then you skipped. There were kids that Magic had seen the first couple days of class that left and never came back. He didn't take any shit. If you didn't do your homework, he put you out with a dittoed copy of your next day's reading and homework assignments. You didn't come to his class late, you didn't talk when he talked, girls sat on one side, and boys on the other.

To Magic's surprise, Freestyle was smart and focused. He listened, finished his class work and started on his homework. Magic finished his class work and homework. Second period was Social Studies, Mr. Barone's class. This was Mr. Barone's second year teaching high school, and his first in the inner city. The first semester there was a blazing fire in his eyes. He was so zealous about teaching that it was funny. You could tell that he was a good teacher, but his enthusiasm was short lived. After being threatened, slapped, cursed out, having his car keyed and tires slashed, the blazing fire was now just a flickering flame focused on a paycheck and the last day of school. All classwork, homework and reading assignments went on the board. If you didn't say anything to him, he didn't say anything to you.

It was totally chaotic when Freestyle and Magic walked into class. They went to the back of the room and Magic pulled out his social studies book and started to read what was written on the board.

"This shit is crazy, man. Is it always like this?" Free asked.

"Every day," Magic said.

"How do you learn anything?"

"Most of us don't, but most of us don't want to. They come to school to socialize and get phone numbers."

"And the teacher just sits there and watches?" Free asked.

"All your work is on the board and if you have any questions just go ask," Magic said.

Freestyle got up and started walking toward the teacher's desk.

Malcolm, who was at least six feet and weighed about 210 pounds, stood in the walkway with his foot on Carla's chair.

He was blinding her with his gold fronts and attempting to talk her out of her panties.

Freestyle stood there blocked in for about fifteen seconds. "Excuse me," he said.

Malcolm looked over at him then went back to talking to Carla. Freestyle stood there for about five more seconds.

"Excuse me," he said again.

Malcolm turned and said, "Go the fuck around, nigga."

Free looked at Magic, who just shrugged. Free wasn't sure if Magic was looking or not, but Magic knew he didn't even see him swing. He heard a crack and he saw Malcolm crumble in Carla's lap with drool and blood coming out his mouth while Freestyle tarried up to the front of the room.

"Hi, Mr. Barone. My name's Freestyle," he said and stuck out his hand.

Mr. Barone's hand trembled as he reached for Free's, and very politely Free said, "I came to school to learn, and if you're my teacher then you need to teach me."

Then he turned and walked back to his seat. Mr. Barone got up and walked over to the phone on the wall by the door.

"Hello, this is Mr. Barone, the Social Studies teacher in room 245. There's a young man lying in the middle of my floor. Actually he's not even one of my students, so if you could send someone up to escort him out, I would greatly appreciate it."

Then Mr. Barone picked up his ruler and started explaining what was on the board. This was the first time in a very long time that it really felt like school, Magic thought. Especially in this class. The funny thing was, most of the kids seemed to enjoy it.

After about five minutes, Malcolm got up and staggered out of the room, mumbling something barely intelligible. When the sentries came about fifteen minutes later, Mr. Barone simply said that the student had got up and walked out.

It was like a different school that day, the teachers didn't know how to act, especially Mrs. Smith, their third period Global Studies teacher. She was running around the class answering questions and patting students on the back for figuring out shit they should have already known. Several times she had to consult her teacher's textbook, probably because she hadn't actually taught anything in so long she had forgot how to do it herself.

Fourth period was study hall and Free and Magic ran into Muscle. He was on his way to Global Studies, which of course he skipped after running into Magic and Free. During the course of the day, Magic thought a lot about the night before. He thought about Mack and the things that Clear had said. He thought about the way he treated Diana at the hotel that day and what Muscle had told him about Clear. He concluded that he really wasn't a nice person. He was the kind of person that his Uncle Benny would kill and bury in the woods. But even with all that in mind, Magic was still pissed off at Clear. He felt tricked, manipulated, betrayed. And although he knew all of that was bullshit, he was still pissed off. He thought it was the Muscle connection and the abrupt slaying of his illusions.

Magic introduced Muscle to Freestyle. At first he was a little standoffish, but after a while he warmed up. Magic learned that Free was the last of his mother's three sons. His two brothers were killed, one right in front of their house. The other one was shot in the head at a stop light in L.A.

He said his mother and him left the funeral home and got straight on a plane. He said his brothers had paid for him to go to private school because they wanted him to be somebody and that's why he wasn't going to let nothing or nobody stand in the way of his education.

"My mother wouldn't take a dime from them, she said it was dirty money. The first year I went to private school they would pick me up at the bus stop in the morning and drop me off at LA Catholic Charity School. My mother thought I was going to Fredrick Douglas Middle School, but after a while she knew, she just didn't say anything. My grades were so good after the first year she just went along. She wouldn't take any money, but she sure cashed in them insurance policies," he said.

By lunch, Free's name was ringing throughout the school, which was most apparent when him, Muscle, and Magic walked into the cafeteria. All eyes were on them and a hushed fanfare occupied the otherwise noisy lunchroom. The girls did everything but open their legs, lay on the table and say take me. The boys were clearly disinclined because Malcolm had quite a reputation. He wasn't top notch but he played the second rung real close.

Magic chose pizza and two ice cream sandwiches, Muscle the same, and Free decided on an Italian sausage, a bag of chips, and two chocolate milks. As they left the lunch line, Freestyle noticed Malcolm standing against the wall on the other side of the room, watching his every move. He nudged Magic and motioned in Malcolm's direction.

"That's where him and his crew always stand," Magic said.

"They don't always stand there watching me," Free responded. He set his tray down and headed towards Malcolm.

Magic's mind started telling him stuff like, It isn't your fight. He ain't your friend. But he was fighting for what Magic believed and never had the courage to stand up for. Then Clear's elevated assertions started to reverberate in Magic's ears louder than the ringing bells that now signaled the end of another lunch period.

'We don't stand for shit, Magic, we just go with the flow like fucking tumbleweeds. If it ain't worth fighting for it ain't worth having.'

"Damn," Magic said aloud, and took off behind Freestyle with Muscle on his heels.

Magic saw the knife go up and come down in one smooth motion. Freestyle's arm went up in front of his face and the knife plunged into his side. He did some old karate shit and Malcolm's arm snapped like a dry twig. Muscle, Free and Magic were standing back to back, ready to take on anyone who stepped forward. Then someone yelled, "The Jakes, The Jakes," and everybody took off running accept Freestyle. He collapsed and when Magic looked back, his white Nikes were red. Muscle tried to go back, but Magic grabbed him by the arm and damn near had to drag him out of the cafeteria.

Muscle met Magic as he walked out of his last period class.

"They took Free over to Strong," he said. "If we can get his last name, we can go see him."

"I know his last name, but I'm not sure I want to go and see him. Suppose he dead or some shit."

Just as the words left his mouth, Magic saw Mack's body slumped over in the chair. He looked over at Muscle wondering if he should tell him.

"Why you looking at me like that?" he asked.

"Just thinking about Freestyle," Magic said.

Magic's father had given his mother his old Bonneville and bought himself a Black Cadillac that talked to you and shit. It was really nice, Magic thought, and he'd only had it a couple of weeks, so when he pulled up beside them it took Magic a minute to realize who he was.

"Hey, Dad," Magic said.

"Your mother said you wanted me to pick you up."

"Yeah I did, can you give us a ride to the hospital?"

"For what?" he asked.

"One of our friends had an accident and we want to go see him."

"Is that why you wanted me to pick you up?"

"No, this just happened today," Magic said.

"Come on, get in."

Muscle hopped in the back while Magic walked around to the passenger side.

"How you doing, Mr. Brown?" Muscle said.

"How you doing, young man?" Magic's father responded.

"You seen my uncle today?" Muscle asked.

Magic's father adjusted his rearview mirror so that he could see who was talking to him.

"Who's your uncle?"

"Mack," Muscle said. "He introduced us one day when yall was riding together. Yall picked me up down on Jefferson and dropped me off at my aunt's house."

"Okay... Muscle, right?"

"Yeah," Muscle responded and smiled.

"No, I haven't seen him today, but we suppose to get together later on this week."

Magic adjusted his seat as his brain started dropping flags and pointing out penalties. Something was wrong here. He had no idea what it was, but something was wrong.

"Thanks, Dad," he said as they pulled in front of the hospital. Magic turned to get out of the car.

"I thought you wanted to talk to me," his father said. Magic grabbed hold to the first lie he could find and went with it.

"I just wanted to see you, maybe take a ride in your new ride," he said.

His father was an asshole. He acted as if he was afraid of his own son, not physically afraid but afraid to get too close. They never did anything or went anywhere together, but Magic had no desire to see him dead, and that kamikaze shit sounded believable.

"Okay," he responded, poking out his lips and nodding. Then he went into his pocket and tried to give Magic some money. Money was his answer, he always tried to give Magic money, guilt money, 'I'm sorry I'm an asshole' money.

"I'm straight," Magic said, got out the car, and closed the door.

They had to lie to the receptionist and the security guard to see Freestyle. Magic was his brother and Muscle was his first cousin. He was still in one of the emergency cubicles when they got there. The curtains were drawn when they came to the partitioned section. They stopped when they heard voices.

"Little boy, I have a son your age."

"And I have a mother your age, so we have something in common."

"Would you roll up your sleeve so I can check your blood pressure?"

"I got some mighty pythons up under here so you better be careful," Free said.

"I'll take my chances," the nurse responded as they walked into the room.

"Hey, fellows, nice of you to come and see your old dad. Nurse Patty, these are my sons, Magic and Muscle," Free said with a straight face.

Everyone burst out laughing. His laughter ended with him holding his side saying, "Ow, Ow, Ow."

"That's what you get, you little Casanova," the nurse said. "Now you need to behave before that wound starts to bleed again." She finished his vitals and left the room.

Muscle and Magic walked to the foot of his bed and just stood there. Magic wondered if he should have brought him a card or something.

"You niggas looking like I'm about to die or some shit. Snap out of it," Free said, snapping his fingers.

"You alright, man?" Magic asked.

"I'm good, man, nothing but a flesh wound."

"Flesh wound my ass, nigga, you was bleeding like a stuck pig," Muscle said as he sat down in the big gray chair in the corner. "And we bitched up. That nigga had already stabbed you by the time we got on the scene."

Free looked at Muscle, a smirk on his face. "And my brothers said you New York niggas were soft. I didn't expected yall to roll wit' me. You cats don't even know me."

"So what you sayin', you wouldn't have rolled with us?" Magic asked as he sat on the arm of the chair.

"That depends, you can be my best friend, and if you wrong I'll watch you get your ass kicked, but if you right, I'm down."

"So was you right? Magic asked.

"Don't be silly. I'm always right," Free said, and everyone laughed.

They sat talking about how the day unfolded, and between the I should haves, the I could haves, the what ifs, and if onlys, a bond was forged. No vows were given, no blood was mixed, and nothing was said or signed. It just was.

The nurse gave Free pain medicine just before his mother arrived. He drifted in and out while she sat on the edge of his bed rocking, crying and holding his hand. Muscle and Magic introduced themselves and she apologized for her tears.

"This is my last son, and I'm so afraid of losing him to these damn streets," she said. "I thought it would be better here, but it's not better. The ghetto's the same all around the world and it just keeps getting worse, and worse and worse. Yall just gotta stop. You gotta stop. Just stop," she said as she got up and walked out of the room.

Magic looked at Muscle, his eyes mirrored his feelings. He wanted to leave so bad, but for some reason he just sat there wondering if worse and worse and worse, was the same as bleaker and bleaker and bleaker. She returned with a wad of toilet paper, blew her nose, wiped her eyes, and resumed her position--crying and holding her remaining son's hand.

Magic left the hospital sadder than he could ever remember being. On any given day that could be his mother, and he could be the one laying there with a hole in his side. He thought about Malcolm and wondered if anyone had ever told him what 'excuse me' meant.

His Uncle Benny and Aunt Brenda Gail were sticklers for stuff like that. If you came to their house and didn't speak, they put you out. If you didn't say pass me, please, you didn't get none. If you didn't say thank you, whatever they gave you, they took it back. The funny thing was, most of the adults in this city didn't have good manners and his Uncle Benny always said, "You can't give what you don't have."

Muscle and Magic stood at the bus stop. Muscle seemed to be off in la la land, as was Magic, but then Magic thought about Cory.

"Shit," he said.

"What's wrong?" Muscle asked.

"I told Cory that I would be the first face he saw when he got off the bus."

Magic looked at his watch--he was an hour late. He could get there in time enough to play a few video games with him, or maybe walk down to the basketball court before dark if they caught a cab.

"Let's catch a taxi," Magic said, and headed back toward the door where the valet stood.

"I ain't got no money, man," Muscle said. "That's why I'm looking for my Uncle Mack."

"Your Uncle Mack?" Magic repeated then paused. "Your Aunt don't give you money?"

"She do, but she broke too."

Magic stuck his hand in his pocket to give Muscle some money, and thought about the knife he had given him almost two years ago. He visualized it sitting in his top dresser drawer and made a mental note to himself: 'put knife in pocket.'

Magic had concluded that if someone's mother was going to be sitting in the hospital rocking and crying, he would prefer it not to be his.

Magic handed Muscle four of the five hundred he had.

"Damn, where you get all this money from?" he asked, examining the hundred dollar bills.

"You don't want it?"

"Yeah, I want it, but I want to know where you got it from."

His Uncle Benny had told him friends don't lie to friends. If you can't tell 'em the truth, then don't tell 'em nothing. And just as Magic was about to tell Muscle nothing, a taxi pulled up.

"I'm gonna get this one and you get the next one," Magic said and hopped in the cab.

CHAPTER 25

Black's Spot

Black incorporated the bald head after viewing his first episode of 'Spencer for Hire'. He fell in love with the chilling, no-nonsense character Hawk, and shaved his head, grew a goatee, and brought his voice down from a baritone to a bass. Black was forty-four years old, but could easily pass for thirty-five. Grecian Formula kept his goatee shiny, black, and gray free, and the low maintenance bald head fit perfectly atop his six-foot frame. Black was blue-black, good looking, rich and resentful. A lethal combination.

He had come into the organization on the ground level, when Clear was green and didn't know Peruvian flake from fish scale or rock from re-rock, the motherfucker had never even seen a triple-beam scale. Never cut, cooked or bagged shit but a Happy Meal, Black thought, as he closed the folder containing the financial report.

"Any questions?" Clear asked.

Black felt Clear's eyes, but he refused to look up.

"Okay, yall know the drill," Clear continued, "pass all that shit forward." Clear waited until all the folders were stacked in front of him before he continued. "Any new business?"

"Yeah, I got something," Daemon said. He looked over at Clear and waited to be prompted.

"Go ahead, man," Clear said.

"It's this new dude makin' moves around my way. He got spots on damn near every street I got a spot on. Which wouldn't be so bad, but he got some banging ass product. In the last couple of months I've lost damn near a third of my customers."

"What do you mean, he got a spot on damn near every street you on? That implies it's the same person."

"It is."

"Who the fuck is it?" Clear asked. Daemon hesitated.

"Magic's father," Daemon said. "That's what I needed to find out before I brought it to you, and I didn't want to put it out there while Magic was here, anyway."

Clear had never been introduced to Magic Sr., but everyone knew him by reputation. He'd supplied Mack before he fell off.

Clear could hear the frustration in Daemon's voice, so he needed to be perfectly clear about what he wanted done. Because at this time, doing anything to Magic's father wasn't even an option. But something about this just didn't sound right. There were always new hopefuls on the horizon, popping up here and there, but this sounded like some inside trading shit. Which meant somebody was selling stock, so Clear decided to go fishing.

"Anything else?" he asked as he panned the table to choose a victim. "What about you Marwon, what's going on on your side?"

"Nothin', I'm straight," Marwon responded, shaking his head.

"What's up with you, Black?"

"Um, all good, just missing my man a little bit," Black said. And for the first time he met Clear's eyes. And he was obviously trying hard to hide what he was feeling.

Mack was Black's man, his methodologist. Mack had put him down as soon as he hit the streets after doing seven years in Attica. He gave him a half-ounce, a piece, a car and didn't ask for nothing in return. But Black only tolerated Clear. And recently, neither him nor Mack was able to do even that.

Clear studied Black for a moment before he made his incision and began surgery.

"Okay…you all good... Missing Mack… I miss him too, and I'm ready to join him. What about you?" Clear could see the contempt in Blacks eyes, but he'd always seen contempt in his eyes. Black was quiet and most of the time had a calculating look on his face, which made it real hard to trust him, but he was a go-getter, which made it real hard not to respect him. Or at least, tolerate him.

"Is a man ever really ready to die?" Black queried.

"I stay ready... and willing," Clear said turning to Daemon. "Find out what he's selling, where it's from, and who supplies it. Get that information to me and I'll take it from there. But until then, let him eat."

CHAPTER 26

Training Day 1

Malcolm never came back to school, at least not back to East High. Free's mother had to go down to the Board of Education and act up in order to get Free back in. He'd told them that he didn't know who stabbed him, or why they stabbed him. Finally, they said he could come back to school when the doctor released him from his care. It would be about a month if Free took it easy, his mother said, and they agreed to give him a tutor while he was out.

Free's mother wouldn't let him do anything or go anywhere the first two weeks, so Muscle and Magic would stop by every day after school and sit with him. After that she told him no sports and be home when his tutor came.

Free's mother was fifty-seven, and looked every day of it. She worked two jobs. One as a cashier at a grocery store called Al's on Reynolds and Bronson Ave. and at an industrial cleaners, where they cleaned uniforms and big floor mats. They had to go there one time when Free locked his keys in the house. She also cooked every day, accept Saturday and Monday when she went straight from one job to the other. She wouldn't let Free get a job. She said he needed to focus on school so that he could get a good job on the plantation.

Muscle's aunt was nice too, Magic thought, but she was modernized. She wasn't into the cooking and cleaning, that 'domestic shit' she called it. She was from the happy meal, straighten up the house while smoking a blunt, generation. But she worked everyday and took good care of her kids and Muscle too.

In the three weeks that Free had been out of school, him, Muscle and Magic had gotten really close, but Magic thought he subconsciously started to gravitate toward Free. All Muscle wanted to talk about was the Black Mob and his Uncle Mack. Sometimes Magic just wanted to say shut the fuck up. He would relinquish parental rights of his first born child to be a part of the Black Mob. Magic thought it was about feeling like he belonged somewhere. Even though Muscle had his own room, his own key, and his own stuff, he didn't feel like a part of the family, especially since his Uncle Mack wasn't there.

Magic hadn't seen Clear for almost three weeks, and he missed him. So when Magic walked out of school and saw him sitting on the back of his car, he was happy and nervous all at the same time. Comparing him to his Uncle Benny had sort of cleaned him up in Magic's eyes, and in a lot of ways he was just like his Uncle Benny. He was kind, generous and would kill your ass, and that was Uncle Benny in a nutshell.

The only time Magic had a problem was when he saw Muscle. Just like the only time Magic had a problem with him killing Cory's father was when he saw Cory. Which was all the time, but Magic had learned to deal with it, and he would learn to deal with seeing Muscle, who stuck to Magic like glue.

Magic stood there for a minute and watched Clear watch him. Then he waved his hand and Magic walked over.

"What's up, Peace?" he said, extending his hand.

"What's up, Clear," Magic said with a faint smile and a touch of enthusiasm in his voice.

"What cha' doing?"

"Waiting for Muscle."

"You niggas like Siamese twins these days."

"Yeah, we pretty close," Magic responded as Clear hopped off the car.

"Come ride with me," he said.

"What about Muscle?"

"Muscle was finding his way home from school long before you met him," he said and got in the car.

Clear took Main Street down to Jefferson, made a left and pulled over. He turned off the car, adjusted his seat to a reclining position, turned on some old Tupac, leaned back and stared silently at a dilapidated building. He hadn't said a word since they got in the car, but true to form he appeared certain about where he was going, how to get there, and what to do when he arrived. Which today meant sitting and listening to music, Magic assumed.

After about the fourth song on the Best of Tupac CD Magic started getting anxious and agitated, so he reached to turn off the music.

"Wait, wait, listen," Clear said and started singing along with the music and moving his head to the beat. "Here's homage to my sisters on welfare. Clear cares, if don't nobody else care," he sang. Then he turned the music off, sat back and closed his eyes.

Magic didn't know what the motivating factor behind him bringing him here was, but it must have provoked some old deja vu shit because he started spoon feeding Magic excerpts from his life. And the stuff he said turned Magic's stomach. He told him he picked roach eggs out of boxes of cereal and wiped mice terds off the countertops before Brandon and Dayja would get up in the morning. He told him about weeks with no diapers for Dayja, no wet wipes or wash rags. That they slept on a pissy mattresses with no sheets.

He went back almost twenty years, back before Dayja was born, and the memories seemed crisp in his head as if it was yesterday. The shit scared Magic. Not because he felt threatened or because he screamed or shouted, or cried out, but because what he saw was right now pain, not pain from past experiences. What was even scarier was that there was no visible expiration date.

"What happened to Brandon?" Magic asked.

Clear didn't answer, he just looked at Magic, apparently searching for the fast forward button. Because when he picked up the story he was in a completely different place and the pain seemed to subside as he brought Magic current.

"I soon learned, Magic, that the person who sold the best dope and had the most courage controlled the streets and crack was like pussy, it sold itself. Mack was fearless, born that way, but I was driven by a hundred different forms of fear and countless demons. Number one being poverty. So my primary purpose was to stack dead presidents and dead niggas just didn't matter.

I was nineteen years old and had a reputation that said I was nothing to fuck with. I had three bodies and a hundred dollar two week notice that I gave to every nigga that worked for me. If you owed me a hundred dollars and didn't pay within two weeks, you might as well invest it in your arsenal because you were gonna need it. The only thing I cared about was my money, and my little sister, who was still in foster care. But her foster parent would let her come and spend the night with Porsha and I.

"One Saturday I was coming down Jefferson Avenue dirty as hell. I had just finished making drops on Sawyer and Barton Street. I had product under the seat for the gates on Columbia and Troup St. When I turned off Plymouth Ave. onto Jefferson, cops were everywhere. All the side streets were blocked and a crowd of people was standing in front of the store on the corner of Magnolia and Jefferson. I turned into the liquor store parking lot and got out the car.

"I walked down the street to where the crowd had formed and pushed my way up to the front, and there laid Dayja. She was covered in blood with a cherry flavored blow pop in her mouth, ponytails, white barrettes, and a cream-colored short sleeve shirt. I saw Dayja exactly how she looked earlier that day. I had gone by her foster parents' house to give her some clothes I had bought from some boosters not even two hours prior. I gave her foster parents two hundred dollars because they were going somewhere. I saw Dayja, and nobody could tell me I didn't.

"A cop stopped me when I tried to go under the yellow tape. That's my sister, that's my sister!" I yelled. 'You can't cross this line,' he said with his hand in my chest.

"Then I looked again, and it wasn't Dayja. I wiped the tears from my eyes and looked again. It wasn't Dayja and that freaked me the fuck out. I backed away thinking I was losing my mind.

An old lady was standing just outside of the crowd, and she called me by my name and extended her hand. I figured she was one of my mother's old friends or one of the ladies from the missions I use to go to or somethin', so I reached to shake her hand. And Magic, it was as if someone said, 'We now conclude broadcasting on this station.' I went blank for a minute, and when my head cleared and my eyes could focus, something had changed.

"Up until that day my conscience and me had an understanding. It didn't fuck with me and I didn't fuck with it. When I came out of that daze, it didn't matter that the little girl laying there wasn't Dayja. She was every little girl and every little boy that had to endure the shit that my brother and sister had to endure growing up. And I cried and I cried and I cried for hours. It was that day Magic that I realized I didn't hold the patent on pain. After days of seriously considering joining the church and becoming a priest, I thought about the fact that there were more churches than liquor stores in the neighborhood when I was growing up. And more churchgoers than drug addicts. But the liquor stores and drug addicts made more of an impact on the neighborhood than the churches and the churchgoers. It was sad, but it was true, and I was determined to make an impact.

"By this time money wasn't an issue. It was coming faster than I could count it, but envy, jealousy, and careless recruitment produced unjustified homicides. Dissention and the lack of unity equaled snitches, which sometimes meant long prison sentences, confiscated product and down time. So, from these realities, the Black Mob was created.

"One first lieutenant, one-second lieutenant, one captain for each side of town, and constant recruitment of frontline soldiers. Captains were responsible for first lieutenants, first lieutenants were responsible for second lieutenants, second lieutenants were responsible for foot soldiers, and there was not a gun fired, nor a punch thrown without my authorization.

"Creed of conduct, by laws, rules and regulations were implemented. If you breached protocol, there was no verbal or written warning; you were murdered. Reward systems were set up and ten percent of all profits came to me. Ten percent was funneled back into the community through our religious affiliations. Forty percent is compensation for services rendered. Services rendered by police, politicians, judges, and lawyers. Some push pencils, others push dope, but all are necessary. The other fifty percent is invested.

"I stopped trying to build a reputation and began laying the foundation for an empire. And in spite of everything that you've seen, that's the Black Mob."

CHAPTER 27

Dayja's Homecoming

"Did I tell you I love you?" Dayja said to Porsha as Porsha handed her one of the credit cards from her wallet.

"If I had your platinum plus card in my hand I would love you too," Porsha said teasingly.

"No, for real Porsha, this don't mean nothing," Dayja said holding up the credit card. "I've always had things, my brother made sure I had lots a things."

Porsha had spoiled the moment, so Dayja stood there quiet, trying to recapture the courage to say what she needed to say to this woman. This woman who wasn't her mother, her sister, or officially her aunt. But she had been there for her, even when she didn't know she was there.

Over the last two years, Porsha called her at least three times a week. Sometimes just to say that she loved her. Even in the beginning when Dayja wouldn't accept her phone calls, she would still call and leave messages.

"Will that be cash or charge, dear?" said the Kaufmanns cashier disturbing Dayja's reminiscent moment.

"Charge, please," Dayja said, handing the cashier the Visa Card.

"Are you Porsha Hines?" the cashier asked

"No, that's my mother," Dayja responded, smiling.

"I'm sorry, dear, but your mother must be present when you are using her card."

Dayja turned to Porsha and said, "Mom, the cashier said you must be present when I'm using your card."

Porsha stood there looking through her purse for her wallet, obviously very amused by this exchange. She handed the cashier her ID.

"This is your mother?" the cashier asked stupidly.

"Yeah, she started doing it early. She was hot in the butt," Dayja said, trying not to laugh.

With a 'that was too much information' look on her face, the cashier took the ID from Porsha's hand and examined it. She smiled politely, swiped the card and started to hand it back, but Porsha took it instead.

"You good, but you ain't that good," Porsha said.

The three of them laughed as the register started spitting out the receipt. Porsha signed it and they headed out of the mall.

Dayja seems different, Porsha thought. She wasn't that same little brat that was cursing her brother out from the police car. She was more like the little, little girl that would run down the hall, jump in her arms and almost knock her over if her book bag was full of books that day. The little girl that would knock at every door in the apartment building and say, "You got some candy?" like trick-a-treat was whatever day she wanted it to be.

As they approached the doors, a neatly dressed, well-groomed, medium complexioned boy, flavored with a twist of thug, almost tripped staring at them. His demeanor stimulated thoughts of Magic who she hadn't seen in over two weeks. She had hoped that their relationship wouldn't be effected by his relationship with her brother, but she knew that was too much to ask. Her brother controlled everything around him, except the weather. She had talked to Magic last night, and he had said that he would make himself available. "Don't do me no favors," she responded and hung up.

Though she wouldn't admit it to a living soul, sometimes she would sit by the phone in her room writing him love letters while anticipating his calls that came everyday about four thirty, and every night about nine. She masked her excitement, and never mailed the letters. She sealed them in an envelope, and put her lip prints where the stamp would be. Sprayed them with body spray and dropped them in her hope box, with all of the other skyscraping aspirations and re-awakened dreams.

Dayja gazed out of the window feeling warm inside as she passed familiar scenery. No longer was she a ward of the state and never again would she be. Princess Dayja will be my title and I will carry myself as such.

A canary yellow Range Rover pulled into the driveway. A banner taped to the garage door read, 'Welcome Home

Princess'. Tears started to well up in her eyes and she covered her face. Porsha put the truck in reverse, pulled out of the driveway and parked a couple of blocks down the street. She leaned over and pulled Dayja into her arms.

"It's okay, baby, it's okay," Porsha said. Dayja closed her eyes and held on tight. Hoping that the honey that pumped through Porsha's veins would ooze through Porsha's pores and contaminate her.

"I just want to be a good girl, Porsha, and make you and my brother proud," she said.

"Dayja, you are a good girl."

"No I'm not, I'm a little bitch."

"Dayja, that little attitude you got. At its best it's, it's simply bullshit repellent. Its function is to keep people from getting close enough to hurt you, but it doesn't work, because we get hurt anyway. Such is life."

Dayja sighed and sat back. Porsha turned, placed her hand on Dayja's chin, turned her face and wiped the tears from her eyes.

"Dayja, your brother and I just want you to be the best you're capable of being, and I'll teach you everything I know about being a strong black woman. All that I don't know, we will learn together, okay?" Porsha said.

Dayja didn't respond.

"Okay?" Porsha repeated a little more sternly.

"Okay," Dayja said between sniffles. They sat there for a moment as Dayja composed herself.

As they pulled back into the driveway, Dayja saw Magic standing on the porch. She hopped out the truck, walked up to him and put her arms around his waist.

Obediently, he put his arms around her neck. "Hi," he said.

She pressed her lips to his, plunged her tongue down his throat and lost herself in his arms just as she'd said she would do in the letter she wrote the night before.

"Wow!" Magic said.

Clear stood in the doorway, leaning against the frame as Porsha got out of the truck with a bag and a suitcase. Porsha walked up to Dayja and said teasingly, "You need help. Good girls don't do that."

"I beg to differ," Clear responded, pushing open the screen door. He ran toward Porsha as she backed up.

"Don't play, Clear," she said backing into the truck.

He grabbed her, threw one arm around her waist and the other around her neck. Then he placed his lips to hers and lowered her like in a movie. Porsha dropped the suitcase and assumed her position in the synchronized lip dance, as Dayja and Magic watched, smiling.

"Porsha, you are so fired. How you gonna mentor me?" Dayja said.

"Do as I say, not as I do," Porsha responded, and they laughed.

Dayja walked over, wedged herself between them and put her arms around both of their waists. "My luggage, please," she said to Magic and they walked around him and into the house.

The dining room was decorated with balloons; a small cake sat on the table with pink frosting and a picture of Jada Kiss painted on top. Kelly, Dayja's best friend sat in the living room playing. DJ and Muscle sat beside her giving her his best, which didn't seem to be good enough.

Dayja walked in and lost it, and Kelly crushed three CD jackets trying to get to her. They screamed, hugged, jumped up and down then screamed, hugged, and jumped up and down again.

"Girl, you gonna git it, why you haven't called me, Dayja?"

Dayja shook her head and said, "I don't know."

"That ain't no answer, why you didn't call me, Dayja?"

"I don't know, Kelly, I didn't call nobody."

"I'm not nobody, Dayja, I'm your girl."

Kelly turned to Porsha as she walked into the dining room from the kitchen. "And your aunt and your brother was no help," she said.

"That's not true, Kelly, we told you she was out of town and would be home soon."

"Soon is two weeks, a month at best, not almost two years."

"Well we're sorry, Kelly, the next time we want to send her somewhere, we'll have our people contact your people. Just to make sure it's okay."

"You do that," Kelly responded.

"Come on, girl, let's take a walk so I can catch you up on the what's what," Kelly said as she grabbed Dayja's arm and pulled her toward the door.

"Wait a minute, Kelly, I just got home, and who is that in my living room?" Dayja asked, when she saw Muscle sitting on the couch.

"Oh that's Muscle. He can come, and where's that Magic boy, he can come too," Kelly said as Magic came waddling into the living room with two suitcases and a plastic bag.

"Can a brother get a hand?" Magic asked, and simultaneously everybody started to clap and Muscle hopped up to greet Dayja.

"Welcome home, Dayja."

"Thank you," she said and looked at him strangely, "You're Uncle Mack's son, right?"

"I'm Uncle Mack's nephew."

"I remember you from when you were a little boy."

"Ya'll the same age, Dayja," Clear said.

"Yeah, maybe physically," Dayja responded.

After Muscle helped Magic with the rest of Dayja's stuff, they decided to walk down to the store.

The tank tops were inappropriately measured with reference to the flesh that bulged from the top, and the short shorts confirmed that summer had muscled in on spring. It was a perfect eighty-one degree day and Magic and Muscle played the back as the four of them walked to the store.

"Girl," Kelly said, "those private school bitches are so shady. They got you in Alaska selling your ass to Eskimos, pregnant and about to have not one but two snorkel-wearing Eskimo babies. I got my ass kicked two times trying to defend your honor."

"Girl, you know you ain't no fighter," Dayja responded as she looked back to make sure that Magic was still in tow.

"I thought I wasn't, but I know it now," Kelly said. They laughed as they basked in the comforts of their old relationship.

"So what's up with that Magic kid? He look good."

"I don't know. My brother introduced us, but I'm feelin' him. In fact, I'm feelin' him a lot, but I don't know. I think all men got brain damage, especially my brother."

"He seems alright," Kelly responded. "And so does his buddy, Muscle. His rap is kind of weak, he's kind of short, but he cute."

"Yeah, cute," Dayja replied, thinking about a time when cute, gear, and a car was all that mattered.

"You coming back to school this year?" Kelly asked.

"Hell, yeah! I just left the mall, I'm gonna hurt 'em when I walk up in there next week."

"I know that's right, girl," Kelly said as she stuck out her hand, beckoning for a high five.

"What you wearing?" Kelly asked.

"I'll show you when we get back to the house," Dayja said.

"I'll have my mother drop me off at your house and we can catch the bus together."

"My brother's probably gonna drop me off. I'm sure he has a few trust issues."

About a half a block away from the store, Dayja noticed that the corner was packed. She slowed down, because even from that distance she could tell that some of them were dark spots from the past.

She looked back and noticed that Magic and Muscle had fallen way behind. Good, she thought, because if anything was said, she didn't want Magic to be privy to the conversation. She picked up her pace.

"Slow down, girl, they ain't gonna run out of fucking Snickers," Kelly said.

"Just come on, Kelly."

"What's wrong, Dayja?"

"I'll tell you later, just come on."

MASTERMIND

Just as Dayja feared, Misery was posted up on the corner. He sat on top of a newspaper dispenser with a forty-ounce bottle between his legs and his flunkey Rod glued to his side.

This was the last person in the world Dayja wanted to see. He was a factor in her walking out of her brother's house that night. He had pumped her head with all kind of garbage, and made her all kinds of promises, none of which he followed through on. But in spite of all that, she called him every night after she got out of juvenile jail and went to the foster home. He never returned any of her calls.

She could hear whispering and snickering as she approached the store, but it was too late to turn around.

"Losers," she said softly. Then she held her head up, stuck her butt out and walked into the crowd.

"What's up, Dayja?" Misery said as he took the forty-ounce of Schlitz bull from his lips.

Dayja didn't respond. She continued into the store, grabbed some stuff, and headed to the register.

Magic obviously wasn't very familiar with this crew. He simply said, "What's up?" and walked into the store.

Muscle, Dayja knew, used to live in this neighborhood. He went to elementary school with Misery, Rod, K.K, and Lawrence, so he stayed outside and got reacquainted.

Magic, Dayja and Kelly walked out of the store together and continued just past the crowd, then stopped to wait for Muscle. Misery turned up the forty-ounce. and finished it off.

"Dayja?" he shouted. She watched, as he held the bottle just above his mouth and let the foam ran down onto his chin. He grabbed his throat as if he were choking and, mimicking her, said, "You're choking me, you're choking me."

Laughter resonated like thunder in Dayja's head and she headed toward Misery. K.K. stepped into Dayja, ramming her

Pepsi bottle into the side of her head. She grabbed her face, staggered back and hit the ground. Without breaking stride, Dayja lunged forward. But before she could do anything, Magic had snatched her off her feet. He handed her off to Muscle, who handed her off to Kelly, but Kelly couldn't hold her, so Magic took her back.

"Stay the fuck outta this, Dayja," Magic said. He pushed her back toward Kelly and walked up to Misery.

"What's up with that, nigga?" he said.

Misery jumped off the newspaper dispenser, backed up into the street and broke the forty-ounce bottle.

Magic went into his pocket, pulled out his switchblade, and snapped it open. Then he moved forward, eyes locked on his target. Rod rushed in from the side, but Muscle rushed in from the back and stuck the nine in his face.

"This is gonna be a fair one," Muscle said. "I know how you motherfuckers roll!"

Rod started to back away, but Muscle grabbed his shirt as he turned to run. He threw his arm around Rod's neck, and stuck the barrel of the pistol in his ear.

Misery charged, but Magic sidestepped him and scuffed his baby blue Timbs trying to cave in his chest. Misery turned, holding his chest with one hand and the broken bottle with the other, and they went round and round in circles like championship wrestlers. Magic swung the knife and just missed Misery's face, and in that off balance moment, Misery plunged the sharp jagged edge of the forty-ounce bottle into Magic's leg, dropping him to a knee. Dayja rushed in from behind and pushed Misery forward, right on top of Magic.

Sirens blanketed the streets like a thick winter quilt. Blood ran down Magic's arm, warm, thick, and slimy.

CHAPTER 28

The Moment She Feared

Candy had taken the night off. The white girl Eve had moved to paradise with a rich computer guy from out of town, and the Peek-A-Boo club was jumpin'. Any time there was a businessmen's convention in town, everybody got paid; strippers, hoes, transvestites, and all in between. Even the girls with no T and very little A had full G-strings.

Miss Hot Chocolate had long become the drink of choice at the Peek-A-Boo club. "You 'jitter bitches ain't got nothing on me," she'd say when they tallied their earnings and paid the house. It was only 11:00 and she'd made a week's wages and the rest of the night looked so bright she decided to put on her

Raybans. She strutted around the pool table in her lime green bodysuit and matching pumps as if she owned the spot.

"Eight ball corner pocket," she said, winking at old man Bubba. "The only reason yall keep lettin' me win is so you can see my ass tooted up in the air," she said as she chalked her stick.

"Actually, I'm a titty man myself," Bubba said from across the table, obviously waiting for her to bend over.

Hot Chocolate pulled the neck of her bodysuit down a little and leaned over as she aligned the cue ball with the eight ball.

"Is that enough cleavage for you?" she asked.

"Not quite," Bubba responded.

"Well that's all you gonna get for fifty cents," she said as the eight ball slowly rolled into the corner pocket. "Bag him up and get him outta here."

Tammy, Red's newest girl toy, walked up and tapped Peggy on the shoulder, then pointed towards the bar where Red stood waving the phone. Peggy handed the cute dyke the pool stick and walked over to the bar. Red leaned and spoke into her ear.

"I just accepted a phone call from the county jail. It's your son."

"Don't play with me, Red," Peggy said.

"Do you see me laughing?" she said and grabbed for the phone.

"Pick it up in the back, it's too noisy in here."

Peggy turned and started pushing her way through the crowd. When she got to the dressing room, she snatched the phone off the receiver.

"Hello!"

"Hi, Ma."

"Magic, what in the hell's going on?"

"Nothing, Mama. I'm alright."

"Where are you, Magic?"

"I'm downtown."

"Where downtown?"

"In jail, Mama."

"For what, Magic?"

"They say attempted murder."

"What! Attempted murder!" Peggy yanked the phone from her ear and pressed it into the couch cushion. Compose yourself, she thought. Just get a grip, Peggy.

"What happened, Magic?" she asked calmly.

"I don't know, Mama, I got into a fight."

"With who?"

"Some kid name Misery."

"About what, Magic?"

"I don't know, Mama, some dumb stuff."

"You almost killed somebody over some dumb stuff?"

"It happened so fast. I had a knife, he had a broken bottle, the next thing I knew I was in handcuffs and he was in the ambulance.

"Mama I got to hang up, but it's all on the answering machine. I just didn't want you to get home and bug out after listening to it. I'll be in court on Monday."

"Do you have a bail, Magic?"

"No I can't get a bail until I see the judge, and don't worry about that, Clear said he'll take care of the bail and the attorney."

"And what the fuck does Clear have to do with this?"

"Come on, Mama, it's not Clear's fault, but I gotta hang up. I'll call you tomorrow if I get a chance."

"You straight, Magic?" Officer Campbell asked.

"Yeah, I'm straight, just tired and kind of hungry."

Magic rubbed his eyes and walked over to the chair next to the fingerprinting equipment. Officer Campbell took the phone from his hand and made a call.

Magic listened in, but he couldn't hear the other guy.

"If I was a woman and had a last name like Cox," Campbell said, "I would be placing want-ads, looking for a husband."

A pause, then, "You can stop being so damn mean and give a brother a play."

Another pause then Officer Campbell laughed, and started over.

"How are you tonight, Sargent Cox?"

Campbell smiled, then, "You got any extra rookies over there?"

He looked at Magic while the other guy spoke, then said, "I need one of them to run out and grab something to eat. Hold on a minute." He took the phone away from his mouth. "You smoke, Magic?"

"No, Sir."

"What you want to drink?"

"It don't matter," Magic said as he shook his head and cursed himself out. Stupid motherfucker, stupid motherfucker, you don't even know what you were fighting for.

To his right he saw some kid standing, gripping the bars, staring into the bright lights that lined the ceiling. Knuckles bruised, lip swollen, shirt torn, grass stained pants sagging, revealing the almost white boxers.

To his immediate left was some black kid. He'd stand up then he'd sit down, his hands in his pockets the whole time.

Mr. Drunk and Disorderly sat on the potty to his far right, going through toilet paper like crazy.

"That damn Hormel Beef Stew," he said. "Can't eat that shit straight out the can." He wobbled and wobbled but didn't fall down.

Officer Campbell came from behind the desk and the Spanish kid cried out, "Officer Campbell, can I make a phone call? I'm trying to get bailed out."

"Sit cha ass down, Pedro. You don't know nobody with no fucking money."

"You let that kid use the phone about three times, that's fuckin' discrimination," Pedro shouted.

"He's a visitor, you live here. And If you call my name again, I'm gonna wipe that old man's ass with your face," Officer Campbell said as he gestured for Magic to follow him.

They walked down the hall and made a quick right into a well-kept TV room.

"This is the trustee's lounge, you can sleep in here tonight. Officer Cox is bringing you over some food and a mattress. You can turn on the TV, but keep it low." That said, Officer Campbell was gone.

The steel door slammed and made a clamoring noise that said beyond a shadow of doubt, I'm locked. Magic turned on the TV and sat down in one of the ugly orange chairs. All the special treatment made him feel uncomfortable, although he knew it was designed to do the opposite. He felt uneasy, but he knew that everything would work out as long as Clear was at the helm. He laid his head on the big orange arm of the big orange chair, and fell asleep.

"Magic," a soft malleable voice whispered, and Magic opened his eyes.

"Hi, I'm Officer Cox."

"Please to meet you, ma'am." Magic quickly sat up in the chair and wiped his face, making sure there was no dribble running down his cheek.

"Here's your food. I would say enjoy, but it's a garbage plate."

Magic smiled as politely as possible, considering he could barely keep his eyes open.

"There's your mattress," she said, pointing to the floor. "You have two pillows, a sheet, wash rag and a towel."

"Thank you."

Sargent Cox went into her pocket and handed Magic her cell phone. She stood there in her tight blue uniform, thick like a sister. But her hair and complexion said that there was some commingling of the races going on during her conception, or just before.

"Clear wants you to call him," she said. "When you're done, just tap on the window. I'll be right there in that office."

She looked at Magic as he took the cell phone from her. "You'll be okay," she said confidently, which in a small way made him feel better. He opened the flap on the Nextel and called Clear's house.

"Hello."

"Hi, Porsha."

"Magic!" Porsha responded. The heartiness in her voice made him feel even better. "You okay, baby?"

"Yeah I'm chillin," Magic said.

"You chillin ha'?"

"Yeah, I'm chillin."

"You've come a long way boy. Here's Clear. Keep your head up kid."

"I will."

"What's up, man?" Clear said. "How they treating you?"

"I got a garbage plate and I'm watching David Letterman. I guess that's good as it gets."

"They ain't got cable?" Clear asked.

"If they do, not in this room."

"Some time tomorrow my attorney, Mr. Roebuck will be in to see you. After you talk to him, call me and let me know what you think."

"I trust you man, if you say he's a good attorney, then he's a good attorney."

"Okay, but if you have any problems hit me on my cell, alright?"

"Alright man, let me speak to Dayja."

"She asleep," Clear replied harshly. He paused, then, "I don't know whether she asleep or not, Magic, but I need some time to consider your relationship with her."

"What you mean, man?"

"What I mean is I got plans and I don't know if those plans include you and Dayja being an item."

"So you decide who me and Dayja see?"

"No, I decide who the fuck you see."

"You sound like you mad or something."

"Naw… Just disappointed,"

"You disappointed because I took up for your sister."

"No, I'm disappointed because you didn't think."

"I did think, and my thoughts were I wasn't going to let nobody disrespect my man's sister."

"Who in the fuck is Dayja, is her picture on the back of some foreign currency or is she some new cuisine? Because if you can't spend it, chew it, digest it, and shit it out, I don't want to hear nothing about it because it ain't gonna pay your attorney fees or your bail."

"So what was I suppose to do, Clear?"

"You should have let her get slapped on her ass, then picked her up and brought her home. Those were consequences of her own fucking decisions."

"That's your sister," Magic retorted angrily.

"You damn right, and I know her, just like I know you, and presently she's worthless to me, and association brings about assimilation."

"You don't fuckin' know me, man."

"Magic, I know more about you and yours than you know. I know the nurse's name that treated you when you were five and almost died from eating rat pellets. I know the name of the man that mysteriously disappeared when you and your Mom took the Greyhound bus up here. I know your Mama got a bank account at Chase Manhattan and it's a hundred and twelve dollars and forty-six cents overdrawn, and Mrs. Dayja didn't get me that information. Mr. Benjamin did. I'll talk to you tomorrow," Clear said and hung up the phone.

Magic hit the end call button and immediately dialed his mom's cell phone.

CHAPTER 29

Unfaithful - Anything He Can Do I Can Do Better

Peggy sat at the bar with a glass of Hennessy and a tear chaser, staring beyond the flashing Budweiser sign in the window. So, consumed with guilt, she didn't even see the taxi pull up, but somehow the horn penetrated the fog in her head and got her attention. She stood up to leave and Red walked from behind the bar to give her a hug.

"If you need me, call," she said.

"I will." Peggy looked at her watch--12:15 A.M.. For a moment she thought about all the money she was going to miss.

"Where to, ma'am?" the cabby asked.

"Lake Ave. Canterbury Apartments."

Peggy's cell phone went off. She tore through her purse to find it before her voice mail picked up.

"Hello?"

"Hi, Ma."

"You okay, baby?" Peggy asked.

"I'm fine, Ma. I just need to ask you something."

"What is it, Magic?"

"Was I in the hospital when I was five for eating rat pellets?"

"Why, Magic? Who said you were?"

"Please, Mama, just answer my question."

"Yes, but it wasn't my fault."

"I'm not looking for fault, Mama, I'm looking for some answers. Do you have a bank account at Chase Bank?"

"Why, Magic?"

"Please, Mama, just answer my question."

"Yes, Magic. But why?"

"Is it overdrawn?"

"Yes."

"Okay, I'll talk to you tomorrow," Magic said and hung up the phone.

"Magic, Magic," Peggy shouted, as the cab driver glanced at her through the rearview mirror. She glanced back, and closed the flap on her cell.

It was late arriving, but she'd seen it coming. It was often referred to as 'getting to big for you britches or smelling your

214

own musk.' A subtle defiance that had many causes, but the only cure was age. She stuck the cell phone back in her purse and turned to look out of the window as she ran comparisons between herself and Magic when she was his age. She concluded that her little boy wasn't a little boy any longer. The city streets had begun the process of transforming him, and what he became would be accredited to the company he kept. Miss Harper, her seventh grade social studies teacher, always told her, "A hard head makes a soft ass." She would stop Peggy and her girlfriends in the hall, fold her arms, smile, and say to them, "You girls are metamorphosing into nothing right before my eyes."

I wish I had listened, Peggy thought as the taxi pulled in front of the Canterbury apartments.

She handed the driver thirteen dollars and got out. On her way up in the elevator, she decided to go in the house, put on her nightclothes and relax for a moment before she picked up Cory from Abigail's. She walked into her house and immediately knew something wasn't right. The strong smell of perfume and the two wineglasses on the coffee table confirmed it. She stood there still and quiet, listening to the soft moans, and squeaking bed frame. Her heartbeat accelerated and caught in a whirlwind of adrenaline. She flew down the hall and burst through the bedroom door.

Peggy grabbed a handful of Candy's blond weave, then dragged her off Magic and onto the floor. Screaming, Candy escaped underneath the bed. At the same time, Peggy ran out of the room and headed for the kitchen. She could hear Magic Senior heading down the hall. As he turned the corner, she sliced his arm with a butcher's knife, then instantly backed away, trembling.

"Come on, motherfucker," he said, "I told you not to hurt me. I'm gonna kill you and that back stabbin' bitch."

Magic's hand was pressed against his arm; blood gushed from between his fingers.

"Gimme the knife, Peggy."

"I'm gonna give it to you, motherfucker."

"Gimme the knife, Peggy," he repeated.

The knife went up, but Magic Sr. stepped to the side and threw a hard right that caught Peggy between the temple and left eye. Her head hit the wall and over Magic's shoulder, she saw Candy's terrified face. She lunged forward, again swinging the knife wildly. Magic Sr. seized her arm in an upward position and floored her with an overhand right.

The apartment door flew open and as it did, Candy turned to get away and ran straight into Abigail and her pearl handled twenty-two. She stood there motionless like a nude figurine and instinctively Abigail knew what was going on. The barrel of the pearl handled twenty-two caught Candy square in the mouth, broke a tooth and propelled her backwards over the couch.

Abigail hit the light switch to the left of the door, igniting the dimly lit room and pointed the gun at Magic Sr.

"Git the fuck outta here, you trifling motherfucker," she said.

Magic started backing up, his hands partially extended in the air.

"I got to git my shit," he said.

"You gets nothing but a bullet in your ass if you don't get up outta here."

Candy crawled out the door and into the hallway that was now filled with nosy neighbors. Magic Sr. sauntered behind her looking bruised but not beaten, and Abigail escorted them down the first flight of stairs.

"Did anyone call the police?" Abigail asked as she made her way back into the apartment.

"Hell, yeah," Old Miss Pitney announced. "I told her to come down and see me. I could have told her, yeah, I could a told her dat ain't the first time that hussy been in her bed," she said.

Long standing neighbors walked into Peggy's apartment, lingered for a moment offering words of comfort, planting seeds of revenge, then left. Abigail closed the door and walked over to the couch where Peggy lay. Her eye had begun to swell and her lip was busted and swollen. Tears saturated the soft cream throw pillow that she held tightly pressed against her chest.

"I'm going to go and get Cory, unless you want me to keep him," Abigail said.

"Bring him home," Peggy uttered.

A short time later, Abigail walked back into the living room.

The tears had stopped and Peggy lay there in a fetal position with her eyes closed. Abigail opened the door.

"Where you going?" Peggy asked.

"Home," Abigail replied. "Where should I be going?"

"Don't leave," Peggy said.

Abigail closed the door, walked over and sat on the edge of the couch. Peggy laid her head in Abigail's lap. The light in the corner made her tears glisten as they began to roll down her face and melt into Abigail's silk pastel nightgown. The Liz Claiborne perfume complimented the cherry red Victoria Secret body spray. Abigail gently placed her hand underneath Peggy's head and the other one across her shoulder to the center of her back. Tenderly, she pulled Peggy's soft bruised face into her firm spherical breast and rocked her affectionately, just as she liked to be rocked when her heart was bruised. She kissed her gently on the forehead, but the tears continued to flow. Peggy looked up as Abigail looked down and their eyes told a similar story. A story of a lifetime of lies and half-truths and loveless relationships and relationships that they refused to dispose of long after the expiration date.

Peggy had been curious ever since the night she sat at a table counting her money after the bar closed and Red walked up and gently massaged her neck and shoulders. Then Red leaned over and began suckling on her neck with perfectly gauged suction until her insides screamed and she pulled away.

"I'm strictly dickly," she said to Red that night but tonight she wasn't sure.

She pressed her lips to Abigail's and Abigail pressed back and Peggy though of the many nights Abigail had romanced her soul, caressed her thickness, and laid with her naked on sandy beaches in her dreams. Abigail shifted from underneath her, kneeled beside the sofa, and slowly began to unbutton Peggy's blouse. Then hard, authoritative knocks extinguished the moment.

Peggy sat up and began buttoning her blouse. Abigail stood and stepped away from the couch, their eye's converged in the dimly lit room and mutually agreed that it would happen soon.

"Who is it?" Peggy asked.

"Police."

Peggy got up, cracked the door, and peeked out. As the police entered, Abigail left.

"Call me when they leave," she said.

CHAPTER 30

Flex

The purple blouse and purple Levi's and purple scrunchies Dayja wore made Clear smile, and sift a fond memory of a person, from a place and a time when everything seemed bleak and grim. Dayja stood in the living room staring out the window.

"You look nice Dayja," Clear said.

"Thanks, just something I threw on."

He walked over and gently tugged her ponytail.

"What you looking for, baby girl?" he asked as he pulled the curtain back just enough to see what she saw.

"Baby girl looking for Baby girl," she responded.

"I think I see her over there hiding behind that tree."

"Naw, she not over there, but eventually I'll find her," Dayja responded.

Clear left the living room and went into the kitchen.

"What time does your bus come, Dayja?" he asked.

"My bus came over an hour ago. I'm going to court with you."

"No you're not," Clear responded, and before he could turn around with the carton of orange juice, Dayja had made her way into the kitchen.

"Why, Clear? And please don't give me that because I said so shit."

"Because I said so is more explanation than I owe you."

Clear walked toward her, set the orange juice on the table, and got up in her face. "The last thing I need this morning is your bullshit. Have Porsha drop your smart ass off at school," he said, and like a gush of wind, he blew past her, fighting the urge. Clear passed Porsha as she was coming down the stairs and headed out the door.

"Clear, Clear," she said. "Clear," she repeated as she stood on the stoop in her housecoat.

"What is it, Porsha?" he said.

"What's wrong, baby?" Porsha asked as she walked up and grabbed his hand.

"You need to talk to your daughter before I beat her ass," he said as they walked toward the car.

"Baby, you got too much going on to let Dayja distract you. You take care of the world, I got Dayja," she said then stopped and caressed his face with both hands, kissed his lips and went back into the house.

"Dayja!" Porsha shouted.

"I'm changing. I'll be down in a minute."

"Get your ass down here now!" Porsha said. She stood at the bottom of the stairs with one hand on her hip, tapping her foot. "Dayja!" she repeated.

"Just a minute!"

Porsha took the stairs two at a time and stormed into Dayja's room. Dayja reached down to pick up her book bag. "I told you I was coming," she said.

"Sit down, Dayja!" Porsha roared.

Dayja dropped her book bag and plopped down on the bed.

"First of all, I know that's your brother, but that's my man, and when you've gone on to the next episode of how to fuck up Dayja's life, he will still be, My Man. Now listen to me very closely because this is the hook, the shit that needs to play in your head repeatedly like the verse of your favorite song. The next time you disrespect him in this house, I will kick your ass. I will not put you out. I will simply kick your ass."

Dayja tried to stand up but Porsha pushed her back on the bed.

"Don't put your hands on me Porsha," Dayja said.

"I didn't. I put my hands on that thirty two dollar blouse I just bought."

"You want it?" Dayja responded.

"Hell no I don't want it, I got six or seven of them in the closet with the price tags still on. What I want is for you not to make me whip your young ass up in here."

"Porsha, you ain't gonna do nothing to me."

"Rise up off that bed again and I'll show you."

Porsha stood there poised to give Dayja the ass whipping she felt she should have gotten a long time ago. Dayja sat with her head down and her elbows resting on her knees.

"I just wanted to go see Magic," she said.

"Do you realize, Dayja, that if it hadn't been for you, Magic wouldn't be in jail?"

"I didn't tell him to fight that boy."

"So what was he suppose to do, just stand there and let you get your ass whipped."

"No, but…"

"But my ass, Dayja, your brother ain't never had to defend my honor, because I don't do dishonorable shit. I'm a lady, and I act like a lady at all times."

"Porsha, you don't understand."

"What don't I understand, Dayja? Tell me what I don't understand."

"It's different now."

"It ain't different, Dayja. The same knucklehead kids that you deal with had knuckle head parents that I dealt with, and most of them are dead, in jail, or cracked out. The same place your ass gonna be if you don't slow down."

"You slow down around here and you get ran over."

"Not if you on the right track. You're sixteen; get on the sixteen-year-old tracks. Your brother risked his life and his freedom to make sure you straight."

"My brother's an undercover drug dealer, he ain't no better than the rest of these niggas around here."

"Your brother's a man that grew up with a crackhead Mama, an absent father, and two kids he had to take care of.

And regardless of how he did it, he did it. Do your research, Dayja, before you start labeling people. Your brother pumps more money back into this neighborhood than United Way. He's a damn good man and a damn good big brother, and if you don't like the way he gets his money, stop fucking spending it."

Porsha turned, walked out, and slammed the door. She walked into her and Clear's room and slammed that door too. She stood in front of the mirror hoping that silence and solitude would smother the fuse protruding from her head. She stood there and watched her nose swell and her temples bulge as thoughts of putting her foot knee deep in Dayja's ass overloaded her head. She opened a drawer and pulled out a white blouse. Slammed it closed and opened another drawer and pulled out a pair of pink sweatpants. She opened another drawer and pulled out a pair of white socks then went to her scrunchies holder and grabbed a pink scrunchie. She gathered her hair and started to put it in a ponytail as pretty pink similarities started to peek between the anger.

She remembered when she was a little girl and wanted a pink canopy bed like the one Dayja had. A pink room with imported pink shit like Dayja had. A big brother or big sister that loved her gigantically like Dayja had.

She remembered that she had feelings that kept her confused like Dayja had, and she remembered having a mother that kept her centered like Dayja didn't have. She went to her knees, folded her hands, and said, "God grant me patience."

Dayja's private line rang and she sat and watched it until the answering machine picked up.

"Hello, Dayja, this is Kelly. I was hoping I would see you in school today, but I thought you might go to court. I'm very sorry about what happened Saturday. We did a special prayer for Magic and Misery in church on Sunday. My Pastor's wife said she's gonna start a young woman's group because these little boys do a lot of things just to impress us, and we're too easily impressed. I don't know, but I told her we would attend. I'll call you back when I get out of school. Love you."

Dayja sat for a moment wondering how she got herself in this mess. Then she concluded that it really didn't matter. She just needed to get out. She got up, went to Porsha's room, and knocked softly on the door.

"Come in, Dayja," Porsha answered.

Dayja went inside, sat down on the bed, and for the first time that morning, their eyes met.

"Porsha, I really didn't mean to disrespect my brother. It just kinda came out the wrong way, and when Misery did that little thing with the bottle, I just lost it. I feel like I'll never be able to live that stuff down."

"Dayja, you ain't the only person that ever gave somebody oral sex and they told. People been sucking and telling since the beginning of time." Dayja smiled. "You're a smart girl, Dayja. Think," Porsha said while pointing to her head. "Not just about you, but how what you do effects everybody that loves you. Think! And then act. Now get out my room so I can take you to school, before that Kelly girl start going through Dayja withdrawals again."

Court

Mr. Kittles pulled into the underground parking lot of the 'Hall of Just Us,' he called it, looking every bit of an attorney. Very rarely did he come down here but when he did he wanted to give the white folks something to look at and all the little black faces something to aspire to.

The line was almost out the door, and it made him think about the Superman Ride of Steel at Six Flags. It didn't matter what day of the week or time of day, there was always a line.

Clear was saddened by this comparison because most of the kids that boarded this ride never got off. Statistics showed that most of them would return again and again.

Clear walked up the stairs at a medium pace, making eye contact with the mothers and their wayward children.

As he stepped off the stairs and onto the black marble floor that lined the foyer, he saw Peggy and Cory standing in line, waiting their turn to be swiped, checked and pushed through.

He had only seen Magic's mother twice. When he came to pick him up from their apartment building, she came down to meet the man her son was spending so much time with. The other time was when he saw her at the Department of Social Services the day him and Magic met.

"Hi, Mrs. Brown, how are you?" Clear asked and extended his hand.

"Hi, Clear."

He could tell she was questioning his involvement. She raised her hand, grasped his, and turned. "This is my girlfriend, Abigail."

"Pleased to meet you," Clear said with a slight nod. "Hey, Cory, nice cut man, who hooked you up?" Clear asked as he rubbed Cory's head.

"You did," Cory said with a big smile.

"That's right, gimme some, man." Cory stuck out his little fist and Clear tapped it, and like his big brother, Cory went back to observation mode.

"Can I speak to you at some point this morning?" Peggy asked Clear.

"Sure. In fact why don't you guys come with me."

They headed toward the metal detectors. Officer Cortez, who was on the Black Mob's payroll, greeted them. Clear didn't know the two other officers. And to his surprise there stood Sargent Schaffer, whom Clear hadn't seen in years, but asked about often. Big Shafe everybody called him back in the days, back when he was just an officer with no stars and no stripes and Clear was a new jack with no street credibility.

Officer Schaffer's eye's lit up and a little smile formed in the center of the salt and pepper goatee. Clear paused and touched his stomach, feeling nauseous as he was transported back to that day.

He'd worn his new brown Frost Masters and his brown leather bomber with the fur around the hood. Over a foot of snow covered the ground and the weatherman said it was seven degrees, which meant fifteen below given the wind chill factor. It was the first of the month; unemployed crackheads pay day. Clear hit his corner early, long before the mailman started dropping welfare checks in the mailboxes.

"The early bird catches the worm," Pit would repeat every morning when sitting at the table, fully dressed, reading the morning paper; planning, plotting and strategizing.
"Nothing comes to a sleeper but a dream, little nigga," he'd add as Clear hurried out of the house with a piece of toast in his mouth and comb in his head, looking bedraggled.

It was about noon and business had slowed. Clear had sold nine bags of weed and about six grams. He generally stashed his product in a little hole on the side of the store, but the snow had hidden the hole so he kept it all in his pocket.

Sunny, Michael and Irving stood on the corner lying about how many girls they had sexed and how much money they had stashed. Clear knew they were lying because every time they got money they gave it to him for weed or Mrs. Stevens, the owner of the corner store, for a six pack or a forty ounce.

All of a sudden, Michael screamed, "Pigs, pigs!"

"Shit," Clear said, turned and headed for the fence that surrounded the house behind the store. Clear jumped on the hood and over the fence just as Officer Schaffer pulled onto the sidewalk. Schaffer pulled his 6'2" frame from the passenger side of his cruiser and stepped onto the hood and over the fence in what appeared to be one effortless motion. Clear's house was only nine fences, four dogs, and a church parking lot away, but after the third fence and the first dog, it was apparent he wouldn't make it. He went into his pocket, pulled out the bag and threw it on the ground. He leaped trying to catch the top rung of the twelve-foot fence that surrounded the church parking lot.

Officer Schaffer grabbed the hood of his leather bomber and snatched him out the air. His head hit the asphalt and everything went black for a moment. He opened his eyes to find Officer Schaffer standing over him.

"Clarence Kittles?" Schaffer said.

"Yeah, what the fuck, man?" Clear said grasping his head with both hands and rolling over on his side in excruciating pain. "I got over a gee on me, man," Clear continued.

"I don't want your fucking money. I want you to stay the fuck off this block between the hours of six A.M. and three P.M. You understand me, Mr. Kittles? Because I ain't gonna be the motherfucker responsible for killing the last branch on a family tree."

"What?" Clear said as he tried to stand. Officer Schaffer grabbed him by his coat and hurled him into the fence.

"I was the first Officer to respond when your brother got his head blown off in the drugstore. I've arrested your Mama about five times for trying to sell her ass down on main, and I ride through some times and see that beautiful little sister of yours sitting on the stoop in front of your house. Somebody got to take care of her, so you got to do what you got to do. Just don't do it on my fuckin' shift," he said then turned and walked away, never even drawing his gun.

"How are you Officer Schaffer?" Clear asked.

The tall, studious officer turned, displaying his stripes.

"Sergeant Schaffer," he responded. "Good as yourself, I hear."

The radiant smile on his face seemed genuine. Clear felt favored, like a little boy receiving accolades from his dad.

"How can I help you, Mr. Kittles?" Sergeant Schaffer asked.

"I have a nine o'clock appointment with an attorney and I really need to see him before he goes into court," Clear responded.

"Are these gorgeous ladies with you?" he asked as he stared blatantly into Abigail's eyes.

"Yes they are."

"And I have a thing for tall men in uniforms," Abigail added.

"That sounds like solicitation to me," Sergeant Schaffer said.

Abigail stuck out her arm and responded enticingly. "Well cuff me then."

Taunts and snickers caused the Sergeant's composed caramel-colored face to crease and redden.

"I'm gonna let you pass with a warning this time," he said.

Abigail opened her mouth to respond but suddenly Peggy's glare torched the side of her face.

"Thank you," she responded. She laid her purse on the rotating belt and walked through the metal detector.

Clear was the last to walk through. "Thank you," he said and extended his hand to Sergeant Schaffer.

Surprisingly, the sergeant took his hand, pulled him to his chest, embraced him firmly, and whispered, "I'm proud of you."

Clear's head went down and he couldn't swallow. Emotion lodged herself in his throat, his eyes glassed over and try as he might he couldn't stop it.

"Thank you," he said pulling away. He pressed past all the too tough young black faces as he looked for the sign that read 'little boys room.' He pushed open the door and found picks picking and combs combing and motherfucker and son-of-a-bitches polluting the atmosphere before being sucked through the oscillating fan overhead.

The last stall was empty--the seat was saturated with urine. Clear leaned against the door and he felt ashamed. Ashamed of the lie. My whole life is one big lie, he thought as he loosened his tie and unbuttoned his collar. Then he heard Light tapping on the stall door.

"Yo dude, this lady said you alright?"

"Yeah, I'm cool, tell her I'll be out in a second." Clear responded.

A few minutes later he left the stall, walked over to the sink, filled his palms with cold water and splashed it on his face. "Get a grip, motherfucker. Get a grip," he said and put on his game face.

CHAPTER 31

Bullpen

Magic was in quiet awe as he walked down the hall cuffed and shackled. Astonished at how his peers seemed unshaken by the fact that this was how they transported slaves and housed animals.

Magic sat quietly on the bench observing all the craziness around him. His mind hastened in a thousand different directions as everyone talked about their case and justified their actions. This whole experience had him all fucked up.

At night when he closed his eyes the steel bars seemed to be stuck to his retinas, and when they locked him in the feeling of doom damn near suffocated him. In the morning when the sun forced its way through the thick Plexi-glass window he awoke feeling a rage and condemnation that was indescribable.

He had talked to Clear the night before and the conversation was full of air and basics.

"How you doing? How they treating you? You getting enough to eat?" That was the gist of it. Magic concluded that his focus should be on getting out of jail and everything else could wait, even Dayja. He looked up as the hallway behind him started to get noisy with the familiar sound of dragging chains.

"Line up against the wall," an officer said. "And as I uncuff you, park your ass in the fenced area."

Magic watched until his mind drifted back to the pre-trial release lady, his Jewish lawyer, and Dayja.

"What's up man?" someone said. Initially, Magic couldn't place the slightly taller and more rugged looking kid standing in front of him, but in a matter of seconds the file opened. It was Trife, one of the boys that jumped him when he first started school. He put his hard face on.

"What's up with you?" he asked.

"Nothing, just hollin' at you," he responded very unassumingly. Then he slid in beside one of the only white boys in the pit.

"What you doing in here, man?" he asked.

"Trying to get out."

"You'll get out. I'm surprised your daddy ain't bail you out.

"How you know my daddy?"

"Your daddy name Magic, your name Magic. He got that pretty boy shit goin', you got that pretty boy shit goin'. Do the math. And I know he ain't about to let his baby boy sit up in here, as good as he balling. Then again he might, I been here damn near a month with a funky ass thousand dollar bail."

"You sell for my dad?" Magic asked.

"I just said that," he responded.

"And you ain't got no money?" Magic said, which brought all that slick stuff to a halt.

"I was trying to get this fucking truck man, a '95 Expedition, the shit was mint. I sent my girl to try and get some of the money I put down on it, but the motherfucker wouldn't give it to her," Trife said. Then sort of 'as a matter-of-factly he added. "And I got a seed too. Between diapers, formula and clothes, he keeps my ass broke."

"You got a kid, man?" Magic responded, not meaning to sound so harsh but all he could think of was 'poor kid.' He didn't respond he just looked at Magic as if he had hurt his feelings.

When the big brass door opened the noise level dropped to about half. And when the deputy stuck his head in and screamed out a name, eyes started to scan rapidly, attempting to put a body with the name. 'Good luck man' was the only thing that could be heard over the clinking keys and sliding door.

"You think you getting out today?" Magic asked.

"Hell naw. I got a public defender, you know they get paid to keep this bitch at maximum capacity."

"How long you been working for my father?"

"About nine months before I got knocked down, I thought he would look out, but you really can't depend on nobody in this shit. Your own Mama will cross your ass if the price is right."

Not my mother, Magic thought as he panned the room, comparing the ratio of blacks to whites, young to old, loud to quiet. Watching as decadence spewed from mouths and oozed from the deputies pores like perspiration.

"How old is your baby?"

"He almost two, he'll probably turn two while I'm in this bitch."

"Damn," Magic said.

Magic stood up when his name was called, turned to Trife, and asked. "What's your name, man?"

"Trife, you know my name."

"No, your real name."

"Lance Spears," he responded as he extended his hand. "Good luck," he said.

"Thanks, man," Magic responded.

Magic walked into the courtroom searching for Dayja's face. Aunt Abigail's brilliant smile seemed to make her stand out amongst the apprehensive and gloom ridden faces that surrounded her. Cory and Clear sat way in the back, but no Dayja. Magic almost didn't notice his mother. He hadn't seen her in a ponytail and sunglasses since they'd left Alabama.

He pled not guilty, and was released to his mother's care.

CHAPTER 32

COURT

Clear, Cory, Peggy and Abigail met in the hall. Cory took Abigail's hand and Clear and Peggy walked side by side like two old friends as they proceeded toward the pre-trial release office.

"It'll be a minute before they get him processed and released. If you'd like we could go down to the coffee shop, get a bite to eat and talk," Clear said to Peggy.

"No, that's okay, I only have one question. What's going on with you and my baby?"

"Who, Cory?"

"No, Magic," Peggy responded.

"Oh, Magic's far from a baby. He's a young man, and you've done a fine job raising him. But I got him from here," Clear said, noticing the awful bruise peeking from behind her sunglasses. He made a mental note to check into it.

"What do you mean you got him from here?"

Likely response, Clear thought. He chose to ignore her question.

"I like Magic, I like him a lot," Clear said as he pulled a business card and a pen from his jacket pocket. He scribbled his cell number on the back and handed it to her. "If there's ever anything I can do for you and Cory, please call. But I got Magic," he repeated.

Peggy saw the masculine sincerity in his face as she took the card. It was a character trait she had seen often in Magic Sr. and had assessed to mean; I don't have to tell you shit, just trust me. She stood there and watched as Clear turned and headed down the hall like a modern day pharaoh, but she knew a God named Uncle Benny that would part his ass like the red sea. And she made a mental note.

Clear liked Magic from the first day they met, but Magic was soft. A 'share the sheep with the wolves' type soft, and that was unacceptable. But because Magic hadn't been fossilized by the streets at an early age, he was receptive to new ideas. He was teachable, and that made the possibilities endless.

Clear left the public safety building scrolling through the numbers locked in his cell phone then hit dial.

"Sergeant Cox's office."

"Is she in?" Clear asked.

"May I ask who's calling?"

"Mr. Kittles."

"Just a moment, please."

Clear hit the button on his key chain; lights flashed, the horn blew and locks popped.

"Mr. Kittles, how are you?"

"Fair, and yourself?" Clear responded, as he got into the car.

"Still broke, single and horny. Any suggestions?" Sergeant Cox said.

"Stop being so picky and hook up with one of them wide back Italian boys down there."

"I can do coffee with a touch of cream, but not the whole damn cow," she said and they laughed.

"And what's with this broke thing?"

"That was a joke, Clear. If I didn't have to watch over your crazy ass, I would be in the Bahamas sipping margaritas. This job sucks."

"Well, I don't know what to tell you about that horny thing, you wear a little too much blue for my boys."

"Is Blue the problem between you and I?" she asked.

"No, Porsha's the problem between you and I."

"Whatever, Clear. What can I do for you?"

"I need you to check your records and see if you have a police report from Canterbury Apartments, the Peek-a-Boo Club over on Lyell Avenue or something involving a Peggy Brown."

"Is that your new little protégé's mom?"

"Yeah, and his dad's name is Magic Warren Sr. Check on him too."

"I wondered if you had put the two together."

"Remember I was doing calculus when you were still doing basic math."

"That was school, Clear, this is life."

"It's all school, and I'm still doing calculus. But anyway, are you sure you don't need anything?"

"I'm a woman, I always need something. In a perfect world, it would be you laying in my bed when I got out of here at midnight."

"Aren't you breaking some kind of law talking to me like that?" Clear asked.

"Yeah, but I think it's moral not legal, consult Attorney Roebuck and I'll call you back," she said.

Clear shook his head, then closed the flap on his cell phone.

Magic walked out the door that said "pre-trial release," and down the hall and into the waiting room. Peggy looked up, and it was sort of like looking at Magic through new eyes. If he were any other kid or she was any other mom she would fight the voice in her head that said, you're looking at a man.

"Hi, baby."

"Hi, Ma." Magic responded.

"You okay?" Peggy asked.

"I'm fine."

"You ain't fine nigga, you look raggedy as hell. They ain't got no combs in here?" Abigail asked as she started rummaging through her purse.

"And a hardy good morning to you to, Aunt Abigail." Magic responded.

Peggy walked over and put her arms around Magic. She kissed him on the cheek, then stepped back and looked at him through her small-framed Fendi shades. Magic stood there then reached up and took the shades off her face.

"Did my dad do that?" he asked.

She took them from his hand, turned and said, "Let's go get something to eat. We'll talk about it later."

Magic walked over and picked up his little brother.

"You a jailbird, Magic," Cory said.

"You're a big mouth," Magic responded as he put him back down and reached for the small tuck comb Abigail was handing him. "I need to pick up my property, yall get the car and meet me out on Exchange Street."

"I want to go with you," Cory whined.

"Hurry up, Magic, because we'll never find a place to park," Peggy said, as her and Abigail turned and headed for the parking garage.

"Come on, man," Magic said to Cory, who smiled and slid up beside his brother. He knew he had at least twelve hundred dollars on him when he was arrested. He remembered sitting on his bed trying to decide how much a day at the mall with Dayja would cost. He pulled the yellow slip from his back pocket and handed it to the property clerk, who handed him two manila envelopes. One containing his shoe strings, his watch, his wallet, and a pack of double mint gum; the other contained twelve hundred thirty-seven dollars and fifty-four cents.

The judge had dropped Lance's bail down to five hundred dollars, he was told by the smiling brunette. She gave him back five of the ten hundred-dollar bills he had given her to bail him out. She also handed him the receipt and a small piece of paper that read 'Joy 555-3317.'

CHAPTER 33

Hoe By Design

Even his mother's constant please could not permeate the fixed idea in his head. His Aunt Abigail's logic and reasoning wasn't logical to him. He just wanted to blow his fucking brains out. And the fact that his blood pumped through his veins didn't mean shit. He burst through the doors and walked out to the street feeling nauseous. He found himself looking inside of every black and white car that passed although he knew the white Bonneville was parked in front of the building. He walked down to the Lake, to the Hess station and growled at the attendant just because he wanted to. He wanted him to say something, anything. Anything that even remotely inferred that he had a problem, so he could come across the counter and get at his ass.

"Can I help you?" he asked and Magic tossed the Mr. Goodbar on the counter. "Seventy-nine cents. You need something else?"

A twelve-gauge and a box of ammo, Magic thought. He tossed the dollar on the counter and walked out, leaving the change.

He noticed an old guy gassing up his truck and thought about his Uncle Benny and how pissed he would be at him now. He should've put a stop to this shit the first time it happened. The very first time Magic Sr. put his hands on his mother he should have done somethin', any fucking thing. But he just stood there like a little bitch. Not this time.

Magic started back down Lake Avenue and remembered that Muscle said he had a nine and Aunt Abigail had a pistol, too. Then the horn blew, the locks popped, and he got in.

Nothing was said. He just turned the car off, put his seat in a recline position, laid back, closed his eyes, and sat there for about ten minutes in silence.

"Magic, you got shit spewing off you like radiation, and it's fuckin' with the ambience in here," Clear said. "So what you gonna do?"

Magic just stared out the window and mumbled, "I don't know."

"You lyin'. Ya mama say you contemplating homicide. What cha gut say? Better yet, can you wake up in the morning feeling no remorse, knowing that your daddy's at the morgue."

"Fuck that motherfucka, I ain't got no daddy."

"That's what your head say. Whatcha gut say?"

"That motherfucka beat up my mom, that's what my gut say."

"Sources tell me your mother tried to cut his arm off."

"So what? He was fuckin' in our house, in her bed."

"Magic, your mother fucks for a living."

Magic's head turned so fast it hurt his neck. "What you talking about?" he asked.

Clear turned his head slowly and looked at Magic like he had shit on his face.

"You didn't know?"

Magic sat there staring at him, waiting for the next insult to come out of his mouth so he could tear this motherfucka up. Clear picked up his cell phone, scrolled down and hit redial.

"Hello, Peggy, this is Clear, and I'm not telling you how to handle your business, but your son needs the whole story. Because he's a bus ride away from twenty-five to life. So either he'll get it from you, or he'll get it from me. It's your choice."

Moments later, Clear closed the flap on the cell phone, did a U-turn and pulled over in front of Magic's apartment building.

"Listen, Magic, I'm gonna tell you this because your Mama is too emotional to realize it. First, your daddy was fucking a bank account, not a woman. Candy's a smart bitch and she got mad loot. Secondly, don't let nobody tell you they love you if they ain't ready to die for you, or make decisions that might forever alter their life. Love's a verb: open your eyes and see what you're looking at, don't just look at what you see."

Magic got out of the car, his hands and legs   trembling so bad, he could barely make it up the stairs. Cory and Aunt Abigail had apparently gone to her apartment and Magic's mother was sitting on the couch. Her eyes cornered him as he came through the door. Magic closed it, leaned against the frame and folded his arms.

"Have a seat," she said.

"I'm fine."

"I need you to have a seat, Magic."

Magic slowly began to walk over to the chair in the corner where she generally sat.

"First of all I want you to know that I love you Magic, and…"

"Mama, your love for me isn't in question here, what I need to know is how you livin'"

"No. How we livin'."

"Whatever, Mama," Magic said as he plopped down in the chair.

"I don't like your fucking attitude, Magic."

"Well I don't like what I'm hearing."

"What are you hearing, Magic? That you're the best-dressed boy in school, that you and your mama got a nice apartment in a decent neighborhood. What are you hearing?"

"I hear you hoein' to pay the rent," Magic said then sat back in his chair and glared over at her feeling fully justified. Her face plummeted, and tears started to gush from her eye's, she looked across the room at Magic, who looked away, because the pain he saw in her face was the same pain he saw in Clear's face, and there was no expiration date. She got up and went into the bathroom.

Magic sat there for a moment, and just like always Clear's words popped into his head. 'Magic, open your eyes and see what you're looking at, don't just look at what you see.'

Magic connected the dots and concluded his mother was a hoe. Case solved. He looked for the positives, like she was a good hoe or at least she had a job and wasn't on welfare, but none of these made him feel better. So he got up, walked to his room, closed the door, turned off the light and lay across the bed.

He thought about the woods in Alabama. The peaceful sound of leaves rustling and twigs snapping under his bare feet. The sounds of the birds chirping and crickets cricketting, but most of all he thought about the uninterrupted sounds of nothing. He had been in this city for a little over two years and had yet to hear the sound of nothing. There was always something up or something going down.

He thought about the crazy lady on the bus, and what she'd said about the demons, and his dark side. However obscurely, her babble started to make sense.

Amidst all the activity in his head, he heard the doorknob turning. A shadow walked into his room, closed the door, and disappeared in the darkness. He heard the sounds of denim sliding down the wall, and a faint grunt.

"Your Uncle Benny ran me and my mother out of Alabama when I was a little girl." The voice came out of the darkness. One morning we woke up, and he was standing at the foot of our bed with his shotgun thrown over his shoulder. 'You either leave, or I kill him'", he said.

My daddy was an old a pimp name Big Percy, and him and your Uncle Benny had been feuding for years. Some old Hatfield and McCoy shit, but when Aunt Brenda-Gail found out her sister was turning tricks, she went into conniptions. When Uncle Benny found out she was doing it for my daddy, they say he jumped up and down in the kitchen like a little boy and went forward and shook the foundation of Alabama like a giant.

"My father is like a myth to me and his myth ended somewhere between the time we boarded the Greyhound bus and when we arrived in Rochester. Your grandmother came here with a third grade education, she could barely write her own name. I remember her cleaning white folk's houses and waiting tables for a while. Sometimes she had to take me to work with her because she couldn't afford a babysitter. I was about six or seven then.

I remember the roach-infested dumps where we lived, sleeping on the floor under clothes, quilts, sheets, blankets, whatever we could find, because we didn't have gas and electric, or any furniture. I remember one night her getting all dressed up and putting on make-up and perfume, and telling me not to answer the door for nobody. Mainly, I remember the perfume, because I would wake up in the middle of the night, and if I smelled that perfume, I knew my mother was home.

In the beginning, it was nice. We moved into a decent apartment with no roaches, we paid cash for our furniture and we picked it out together. She bought me nice clothes and permed my hair so that the little boys in school would stop calling me peasy head. We would go to the Capitol Theater downtown on Sundays and then we would catch the bus down to Carrols and I always got the same thing. A milkshake, a hamburger and French fries.

Monday through Saturday nights I would stay by myself. Sometimes I would go down the hall to Miss Lulu's house. She sold beer, wine, and liquor after the stores closed. Sometimes she would let me pass the bottles through the hole in the door. And when my Mama came to pick me up, she would tell her what a good helper I was and give me a dollar or fifty cents.

"I was about twelve when I first started to realize that the stuff my mother did wasn't normal. On most days, when I was getting up for school, she was just getting home, and when I got out of school, she was just getting outta bed. She would get up, get dressed, and leave the house. When she came back, she would go in and out of the bathroom like she had diarrhea or something, and in the middle of our conversations she would nod off.

By the time I was fourteen, my mother was a full-blown heroin addict. We were being evicted every other month, but no matter where we moved to she would find the bums and bring them home. There was never any food in the house, and it was so filthy and stank."

His mother paused, and by now, Magic's eyes had adjusted to the darkness. She never raised her head, never raised her eyes, and never looked in his direction. It was as if she were reading a book and was afraid she would lose her place.

"I dropped out of school in the ninth grade, it was the second year and probably the seven hundredth time she'd told me, 'We'll go school shopping tomorrow.' I swore I would go back, because I was never going to sell my ass or use dope.

"I met your father one night at a house party in Fat Pam's damp, musty basement. Hormones were popping louder than Earth Wind and Fire, and we were ground permanent booty prints in the concrete wall. He stuck his tongue in my mouth, and it had to be about as big as a pop tart. I started to choke and he walked me outside to get some air. We sat in Fat Pam's backyard on top of some metal garbage cans. I was a virgin. Hell, I'd never even kissed a boy until that night.

"Your father was a brat," she said, and that thought must have been a bright spot in her life, because for the first time she raised her head and started to smile.

"Your grandmother was the only black supervisor at General Motors, and your grandfather was the only white custodian. Your daddy said they fell in lust on fish fry Friday, and he was conceived in the broom closet during a fifteen-minute break. When your grandmother found out she was pregnant, they got married, bought a house in the suburbs, and planned on living happily ever after.

"But one day your father found his way out of the suburban maze and ran into some people that didn't call him nigger behind his back. He was welcome at all our houses, and could hang out with all of us, because to us, he was black too. So he decided that this was where he wanted to be.

"Your grandparents would come to the city, find him, and have him put in shelters and boys homes, but he would always return to the ghetto more popular than ever. A month or so after the party he moved in with my dope fiend mother and me.

"Your father did whatever he had to do to get whatever we needed and whatever I wanted. He stole his mother's credit cards, jewelry, TV, stereo, everything. He would even get stuff from other girls and give it to me, and that earned him God-like status in my eyes.

"His parents finally got smart and had all the locks changed. And he started getting arrested for burglary, larceny, a bunch of different shit. His mother would come and get him from juvenile jail, give him some money and drop him back off at my house, because she knew that's where he'd end up anyway. The last time he was arrested he had just turned sixteen and was no longer a juvenile, so your grandmother couldn't come to his rescue. The judge said she was going to lock his ass up until he was twenty-one if he came in front of her one more time.

"By the time I turned sixteen I was fully developed. Thirty-two, twenty-two, thirty-two, a mini brick house. There wasn't a day that went by that I wasn't propositioned in some form or fashion. I was a magnet for drug dealers, and old men offered me all kinda' money to sleep with 'em. So your father and I formulated a plan; I would join my mother on the night shift, and we would get enough money to buy a half-oz of cocaine, and he'd take it from there.

In less than two weeks, I handed him fourteen hundred dollars, and he took it from there.

"Everybody liked your father, he was a real stand up person, and he always did what he said he was gonna do. His fair complexion and popularity pushed him straight to the top. The Dominicans and Puerto Ricans loved him, the Brothers respected him, and the Caucasians trusted him, and in less than a year he was supplying most of the dope smoked, sniffed, or injected on the East Side. Your father was the man, Magic, straight out the gate. Sometimes he wouldn't come home for two or three days, but when he did get home he would take off his pants and hand them to me with money in every pocket.

"Go shoppin', I'm going to sleep," he would say.

We moved into our own place after a while because my mother kept stealing from us, and all that she didn't steal I gave to her for some reason. I tried to make her get some help, she even went to rehab a couple a times, but she would get out and do the same shit all over again.

"Then you were born, and the future looked real bright. Your father loved you, Magic. You were the only thing that would keep his ass out the streets. I had absolutely no power over him, but when you started saying daddy he wouldn't leave the house until you went to sleep."

Suddenly the laughter that accentuated each syllable and punctuated each sentence was gone. Her tears glistened in the slight moonlight that shined through Magic's bedroom window, and an ugly overweight pause consumed the room.

"My mother was found dead in an abandoned building on Iceland Park," she said starkly. "The police report said she was found butt naked with a spike in her arm. Even though I had said to her a thousand times, 'they're gonna find your junky ass dead some where,' I still wasn't prepared, and it almost took me out. It probably would have if it wasn't for Uncle Benny and Aunt Brenda-Gail. Your father and I tried to pay for the funeral, but Uncle Benny wouldn't let us, even though he wasn't there. Aunt Brenda-Gail and Aunt Maulee came up and took care of everything. They wanted to bury her in Alabama but they said if this was where I was gonna be, then this is where she should be too.

"The funeral was big considering that most of my mother's friends were junkies. They came out in droves at calling hours, and some of them even gave me cards and money. But when I thought about it, I could remember my mother going to funerals. Aunt Brenda-Gail and Aunt Maulee stayed about a week after the funeral to make sure I was all right. Which I was, but approximately two months later, on March sixteenth, at nine p.m., for reasons that were unknown to me at that time, your father came home and locked himself in the bedroom. He stayed in there for three days, and when he came out he was at least fifteen pounds lighter and looked gray, like he was dying. Later, I found out that his mother's appendix had burst and poisoned her system. She died and was buried and he didn't found out until weeks later.

"In less than a year, I went from the plush lifestyle that comes with being the woman of a prominent hustler, to standing on corners selling my ass to support his habit. Your father had given me everything I wanted, and taught me everything I knew."

"I loved him with all the love that one person is capable of having for one person. The only thing that was or is comparable to the love that I had for him, is the love that I have for you."

"From the moment the doctor laid you in my arms, Magic, after twenty-nine hours of labor, I knew I would gladly give my life for you. I also knew the day your father stuck his head underneath my skirt, pulled my panties down, and made love to me in Fat Pam's garage that he would do anything for me and I would do anything for him. I became a hoe, a good hoe. I took care of my man and I took care of my baby."

"One morning I came home after doing an all night party for an escort service and found you sitting at the kitchen table, eating Captain Crunch cereal with red crunch berries and blue rat pellets. I took you to the hospital where I stayed with you for a week."

The Department of Child Protection Services tried to nail my ass to the cross. But I had witnessed too many of my friends being stripped of their kids and I was determined not to let it happen to me. The day before you were to be released in the custody of Child Protection, I asked could I take you down for an ice cream cone. They said yes. I took you out through the emergency room. We got on a Greyhound bus and went to Opelika."

"When we returned here from Alabama I tried to get a job. But I've never had a job and welfare wanted me to work thirty-five hours a week for five hundred dollars rent and a hundred dollars a month in food stamps. That's some slave labor shit, Magic, but I was going to go for it. Then I started looking at apartments that were in my welfare budget. And there was no way in hell that I was going to allow you and Cory to live in the same places that I was utterly ashamed of when I was a little girl.

When I first ran into Candy and she told me about her little establishment, I said hell no. But after the food stamps ran out, I wasn't about to move ya'll up in one of those rat dins."

The denim slid back up the wall as she opened the door and the light from the hall poured into the room. She looked at Magic, and the look in her eyes said listen up because this is it.

"I love you and Cory, Magic, and for you I will not only sell pussy, I will sell asshole, ankles and elbows," she said and turned and walked out.

At that moment, love became less of a mystery to Magic. He saw his mother in a completely different light. He laid there and recalled all the times he'd seen distress on her face and didn't know what to make of it. He couldn't see the emotions concealed behind the faint smiles or the feeble laughter. He never even asked himself why she sat in the dark in the wee hours of the morning, or why she stayed after the first ass whipping, or the second ass whipping, or the fifty-first ass whipping. Now he knew what Clear meant when he said, 'See what you're looking at, don't just look at what you see.'

Magic lifted his mattress, pulled out the money, and began composing a letter. He couldn't get pass Dear Mama, I love you. So he decided to let that do for now.

His mother's testimony was costly. Sleep eluded him. He lay there thinking about his father, his Uncle Benny, his grandmother he didn't even know, his mother, Dayja. Her mother, her father he didn't know. Then a whole conversation between Clear and him started to play in his head.

"I am the fuckin' problem, Magic. I'm the by-product of that dark, dark place where nobody wants to live, where nobody wants his or her children to live. Whole fucking countries have gone to war to keep from living in that place. The place is called 'Povertyville', where there is never enough of anything. And want, and need, and hunger carry pistols and pull triggers, a place where your environment forces you to make decisions, although you're too young to make good decisions. A place where your hunger pains are louder than the squeaking mattress where your mama is fucking just to get one more bag. A bag of groceries or a bag of dope."

CHAPTER 34

Training Day

Magic set his alarm an hour early, which was only two hours after he went to sleep. The last thing Magic wanted to do was see his mother. Actually, he didn't want to see anyone. He didn't want to go to school, he just wanted to partition himself off from the world.

He took a quick shower, half ironed his clothes, grabbed the money and the letter, sat them on the table and headed out the door. He walked toward his bus stop and a half dozen people seemed to be watching as he approached. Everything inside of him said they knew his mother was a whore.

When Clear pulled up he wanted to say, 'What the fuck you want, man? Stop fucking stalking me. Just leave me alone.' But he just got in the car. They rode in silence all the way through a Jaheim CD and as Musik began a love ballad Magic said, "I should be in school."

"You are in school," he responded, as they pulled into McDonalds and parked.

Clear ordered for both him and Magic; hot cakes with double sausage, a small cup of coffee for him, and a large orange juice for Magic.

"Always eat your breakfast, lil' nigga, and one day you'll grow up and be big and strong like me," he said with a too serious look on his face to be serious.

"Yeah, right," Magic said, looking at him.

For the first time Magic realized they were about the same size, but he quickly dismissed that idea because Clear actually towered over him. He towered over everyone Magic knew accept maybe his Uncle Benny. They were a lot alike in a city mouse, country mouse kinda way. But Uncle Benny was easy to read. You could almost tell by the look on his face how he felt. And what he was going to do in response to how he felt.

With Clear it was another story. Most of his responses seemed calculated and well thought out, almost as if he lived everyday twice and knew exactly how to handle each situation. He never looked ambiguous or doubtful; he marched through life as if he had the blueprint for heaven and the earth in his back pocket.

"What you thinking about, Magic?" he asked while Magic sat there sipping his orange juice.

"Everything," Magic said as he pulled the straw from his mouth.

"Don't blow a fuse trying to figure shit out. Answers come like opportunities, you just have to be ready when they arrive."

"Should I consider this an opportunity?"

"No, this is a blessing."

"I thought blessings came with no strings attached."

"Is that something you came up with, or did some broke motherfucker tell you that."

"My freedom is a hell of a price to pay." But Magic was just pitching. Trying to fill in some blank spots, darken some gray areas, but Clear didn't see it like that. He pushed his tray to the side and came forward. He got so close to Magic's face he could smell his breath mint. His response was short, and sweet, "I don't even pay parking tickets. I pay a lawyer, who pays a judge, who pays DA's-- that's the American way." Stepping from between the table and chair, he added, "I'll meet you at the car," and left the restaurant.

McDonalds got so quiet that all you could hear was the French fries sizzling. Magic sat there for a moment, then reached for his orange juice to wash that shit down. But his hands were visibly trembling so he decided against it, and all other confrontations with Clear. He got up and walked out under the watchful eyes of the patrons and the employees, feeling like the kid who had missed the lay-up and lost the game.

When he got back in the car, Clear smiled and pulled off. Magic had never met anyone who could be so hostile one minute and show no signs of hostility the next. This man transitions in and out of feelings like a chameleon, Magic thought. Clear turned the radio down, pulled in front of a flower shop, parked, pressed a button on the dash, got out and went to his trunk. Moments later he returned with a small safe and set it in Magic's lap. Magic turned to look at him. The look in Clear's eyes sent chills down Magic's spine. It wasn't a threatening look. It was a look that said, 'I am dead ass serious, so please don't take this lightly' and Magic didn't.

"Listen, Magic, I love you like a son, and anything I have is yours for the asking," he said. He leaned back and rested his head on the headrest. Then he exhaled heavily, took a deep breath and continued. "I'll take a bullet for you, and meet my maker with a smile. Because that's what love means to me." Again he paused for a moment, then, "Would you take a bullet for me, Magic?"

The bottom fell out. It shook Magic. He sat there for a moment wondering where does he come up with all this shit? But he just looked him straight in his eyes, because Uncle Benny said you always looked a man in his eyes. And he searched for words to express what he was feeling. He wanted to say, I love you like a father. He wanted to ask, why me? He wanted to say, I'm only seventeen and I'm not ready for this type of commitment. But once again his words rang in his head, 'If you don't have something or someone, a cause that you're willing to die for, then you don't have a life worth living. Right there in that instant Magic questioned everything that Clear ever communicated to him. Every comment, every inference, verbal and non-verbal, every expression of his face, every inflection in his voice, and all the concentrated truths compressed, packed down. 'Clearisms.'

"The whole fucking clip," he said. "Now what's the combination to the safe?"

He got him with that.

"Seven, two, seven," he said and sat there for a moment watching Magic turn the dial on the safe before he got out of the car. Seven right, two left, seven right.

Inside were eight stacks of hundred dollar bills, totaling forty thousand dollars. Magic felt a surge of power that was foreign to him; like he could leap tall buildings in a single bound, spit fire and make it rain. But he felt some other stuff, too, some warm bubbly stuff. Like when you sink into a tub of perfectly hot water, and you get that feeling in your stomach that makes you push, like when you're taking a crap.

He fingered through the stacks, savoring the smell of the crisp new bills. Then he realized: what he was feeling had very little to do with money. Because he'd started feeling it before he opened the safe. It was what initially clustered and forged a knot in his stomach. No man had ever told Magic he loved him, not his father, not even his Uncle Benny, and though it felt strange, it felt good. Those three words told him, everything is going to be alright, I got you, you're never alone, I'm here.

There was a little black book underneath the money. Magic pulled it out, sat the safe on the floor, and began reading. First he thought it was the manual that came with the safe. But by page three he understood what Clear meant by rules and regulations, procedures and protocol. By the time he got to page six he understood why Mack was murdered. He had broken damn near every rule in the book.

As a general, you couldn't have a wife or children. You were only allowed one house and one car. No flashy jewelry, and no flashy woman with flashy jewelry. You couldn't have a savings or checking account in your name. All internal conflicts were resolved during monthly meetings. And external conflicts were contracted out. The use of any mind or mood-altering chemical was strictly forbidden. This book went on and on and on. It put a new twist on the words organized crime.

Clear came back to the car with a bouquet of flowers and placed them on the back seat. Magic was just finishing page ten and continued to read as Clear pulled off. He had finished the book by the time they pulled into the hospital parking lot.

"Damn, are you sure you gave me the right book?" Magic asked. "This reads like a hand book for Presidential candidates."

Clear parked and took the key out the ignition. "A wise man learns from the mistakes of others. Turn to page three, the section on allies and adversaries," he said.

Magic opened the book and turned to page three.

"What's rule number one?" he asked.

"Never sleep until your adversaries are your allies. If you can't befriend them, buy them, if you can't buy them, kill them." Magic responded, reading from the book.

"Dayja created that shit between her and Misery. And he'll hurt you, Magic, if not kill you. Then I'll be forced to kill him," he said

"So what should I do?"

"What would you have you do, considering what you just read?"

Magic sat there for a moment aging rapidly, stretching mentally and summoning everything he had read, seen, or been told.

"He still in the hospital?" Magic asked.

"Third floor, unit thirty-four hundred, room eleven."

Magic reached down, picked up the safe, opened it, took out a stack of hundred dollar bills then reached for the door. Clear grabbed the flowers from the back seat and climbed out of the other side. As they headed toward the elevator, he handed Magic the flowers.

"I gotta give him flowers?"

"This ain't about image or ego, Magic, it's about damage control."

When Clear and Magic entered the room Misery was sitting up in bed watching a morning talk show. A tube protruded from his nose, taped to the side of his face. The blaring television almost drowned out the hum of the oxygen machine. Clear stepped from behind Magic and cast his shadow across the bed, Misery turned abruptly. Magic looked him straight in the eyes as he flung the sheet off and turned toward them. The hospital gown slid up revealing his balls, dangling from the side of the bed.

"What the fuck you want?" he asked.

Without hesitation, Magic said, "I want you to accept these flowers as a formal apology and some money for your medical bills."

Misery looked at Clear, then at Magic, then back at Clear, then back at Magic.

"I got Medicaid, what about pain and suffering," he said.

Clear laughed. "I ain't laughing, man, I can hardly fucking breathe."

Clear stepped forward and extended his hand. "What's up, Miz?"

"Your knife-slinging ass, homeboy. Don't he know motherfuckers carry guns these days," he said as he reached for Clear's hand.

"Magic, Misery, Misery, Magic," Clear said and stepped out the line of fire.

Magic set the flowers down on the food tray next to a half-eaten bowl of cereal, then extended his hand.

"I'm sorry, man. I was wrong to charge you like that. I wasn't aware that you and Dayja had history."

"No history, she straight shitted on me. The only reason she still breathing is because I respect her brother," he said and gently pushed himself back onto the bed. "But anyway man, I'm straight, you only stuck a hole in my fuckin' lung."

"No, actually you fell on the knife," Magic said.

"No. Actually, Dayja pushed me on the fucking knife."

At that point, Magic glanced over at Clear who watched this exchange in silence. Magic pulled out the stack of hundred dollar bills and dropped it on the bed. "Will this buy a big enough Band-Aid?" Magic asked.

He picked up the money and looked at the binder, which said five thousand. "Hell, yeah, and some pain pills too."

"Cool," Magic responded, then turned, and walked out.

Magic leaned against the wall just beyond the nurse's station and closed his eyes momentarily, attempting to gather himself. He wanted to snatch the tube out of Misery's nose and finish beating his ass.

He walked into the waiting room, stuck a dollar in the soda machine and pressed the button that said Pepsi. A Grape Crush came out. He left it there and walked back into the hall as Clear turned the corner wearing a smile about as big as his face.

"I don't like that kid," Magic said.

"He don't like himself. It's hard to like yourself when the whole world seems to hate you."

That was some real deep Clear shit, and Magic wasn't in the mood to be philosophizing with him, so he didn't respond. They pulled out of the parking lot and made a right onto Elmwood and a left onto Mt. Hope Ave. They passed the graveyard and the florist, then made a left onto the Clarissa Street Bridge. And for the first time in a long time Magic thought about the Cat-Food Man. He wondered if he was down there in the bushes, if he was still alive. He thought about the rusty rabbit's foot he'd given him, and how he used to cry and say, "They fucked me up, Magic, they fucked me up." Magic looked over at Clear as they pulled into the Mt. Zion Baptist Church parking lot. Surprisingly, Magic saw a resemblance of the same pain. Less caustic, but the same.

They parked facing a beautiful stained glass window, where multi colored angels, and long-haired, bushy-browed saints looked down on them. Clear turned off the car and they went in. They walked down the stairs and through a freshly painted hall until they came to a door marked Youth Rec. Area. Clear opened the door, and they walked into a dimly lit room filled with cots and reeking of feet.

They walked toward the far corner where someone sat reading. Gigantic painted murals covered the wall, one of which was Dr. Martin Luther King standing at a podium. Underneath, it read, 'If you can't be a tree be a bush, but never stop trying to be a tree.' Underneath it was a picture of Fredrick Douglas with a little boy in his arms. It read, 'It is easier to build strong kids than it is to repair broken men.' Murals of Sojourner Van Truth and Marcus Garvey graced the other side of the room, both of which had writing over their heads. Magic couldn't read what it said from here.

"I caught the young man that painted those defacing the side of one of our vans. I brought him in and gave him these walls," a voice in the corner said as they continued toward the desk.

His six-foot frame and coal-colored complexion startled Magic as he stood up and greeted them. He gestured for them to have a seat. Magic sat down in the chair on the right side of desk. Clear sat directly across from him.

"Reverend Stone, this is Magic."

"How are you, sir?" the Reverend responded.

"Fine thank you," Magic said, adding a little bass to his voice. He was really liking that "Sir" shit.

"I need you to take Mack off the payroll and put Magic on," Clear said. "He'll be the person you come to if there are any problems, financial or otherwise."

"Oh... that reminds me," the Reverend said as he excused himself.

He went through the door that sat between Sojourner, and Garvey. He returned moments later dragging a big sign. He leaned it against a cot in front of Clear and Magic. In red, black, and green letters it said, 'Kittles Afro-centric Day Care.' It was beautifully crafted, had a little black baby sitting naked in the grass surrounded by pink elephants, little bunny rabbits, and big balloons. The border was a traditional African design.

Clear smiled. A full smile. His chest swelled as delight danced in his eyes. Then out of nowhere, or from somewhere, came that look of pain. That, they fucked me up pain. He looked away toward the mural of Sojourner Truth.

"Reverend, do you remember when I was a little boy, and you had that old building on Scio Street?"

"Yes I remember," the Reverend responded tenderly, as if talking to a child.

"That was our harbor, the only safe place for us to go. I'd bring my little brother and sister down there as soon as we got out of school. Dayja would say, we going to the church, we going to the church, right Clear? There was no other place for us to go. That was our little raggedy stove, our TV with the aluminum foil on the antenna, our mismatched furniture."

"I didn't know that, Clear," the Reverend said. He looked pained.

"I know. But when we went there and the doors were locked, Dayja cried all the way home. She made me walk her there every day for a week straight. 'Knock on the door harder, Clear, knock harder,' she would say. If you want to do something for me, Just never close these doors. These doors should never be closed because there are millions of little Dayja's standing at doors knocking," he said.

Reverend Stone looked at Clear as if seeing him for the first time. "I agree," he said with equal resolve.

Clear stood and on his way up made a sleek transition from community activist to kingpin. "Anyway," he said and cleared his throat, "I just wanted you to meet Magic, and to make sure everything was straight for the Disney trip."

"Unless something has changed on your end, Clear. Nothing has changed, the kids are excited, consent forms are signed, and our vans are in tip-top shape."

Magic stood up and joined the two men at the front of the desk. The Reverend walked them to the door where they extended the normal pleasantries and headed down the hall.

"Hi, Magic," she said.

Magic looked up and saw her stepping onto the landing. It was the crazy lady from the bus.

"Huh? Hi," he said.

She walked over, caressed his face and kissed his forehead.

"The wild blueberries still grow fat and kiss the ground. Even in your absence," she announced, and turned to Clear.

"Hi, Granny," Clear said. He walked into her arms and they embraced. She stepped back, took both of his hands, and laid them crosswise on her chest.

"Even the angels are in awe of you," she told him with a smile. Then she turned and walked away.

They continued up the stairs and out of the building, and before Magic said anything he hopped into the time machine and traveled back two years just to make sure.

"Is that your grandmother?" he asked.

"No," Clear responded.

"Well who is she?"

"It's the old lady I told you about."

"What old lady you told me about?"

"The one that was there when the little girl got shot and I thought it was Dayja. She says her name's Presumptuous. I just call her Granny, it's easier to remember. Where do you know her from, yall seem to have quite a rapport."

"It's the crazy lady I met on the bus when me and my mom were on our way up here, but I've heard that name before."

"What you mean you met her on the bus?"

"She was on the Greyhound bus with me and my mother, she knew my name and knew I was a junior. She said all kinds of crazy shit like, 'dark angels rest on your shoulders, and don't be afraid of my dark side,' She weird, she scared the shit outta me."

"That's why you call her the crazy lady?" Clear asked, laughing.

Magic ignored his question. This was some major shit. Both of them were being stalked by an old lady talking about demons and dark angels and Magic knew that name from somewhere. He sat there frantically searching the seventeen years of archives stored in his head.

"There you go again, about to blow a fuse trying to figure shit out," he told himself.

Mercy High, 'All Girls Academy of excellence'

Tall trees and shrubs dotted the two acres of land. Vibrant colored fall leaves sprinkled the meticulously manicured lawn. And an almost tangible calmness lurked, camouflaged in open space, autumn leaves, and a big brick building that looked too much like a church not to have been one at sometime.

"Come on," Clear said as he got out of the car

Magic was too busy trying to figure out where he knew that name from to even consider where they were.

Silence greeted them as they walked in the front door. An arrow read 'Main Office This Way.' Magic followed Clear up a couple of stairs and down a hall. They made a right and another sharp right and walked into an office.

"Mr. Kittles, how are you, sir?"

"Blessed, Sister Beth, and yourself?"

"Also blessed, I must say," responded the beautiful, smiling black woman standing behind the desk.

This guy is a chameleon, Magic thought as he observed this exchange of caviar, escargot and spirituality.

"Beth, this is Magic, Dayja's boyfriend," he said in a joshing manner, but it didn't matter to Magic. He had answered the question that he was too afraid to ask. His jaws loosened and he felt as if he had drunk a cup of warm anticipation.

"Hi, Magic," she said.

"Please to meet you, ma'am."

Clear walked up to the counter and pulled an envelope from his jacket pocket.

"Beth, would you please give this to Mother Superior and tell her thanks for all she's done for Dayja? Tell her a portion is for Dayja's tutoring and the balance she can use to pave the parking lot or patch the roof, whatever yall do with donations.

She smiled, turned and placed the envelope on her desk.

"Would you like to see Dayja?" she asked.

"Yes, thank you. There's something she needs to take care of, but I promise to have her back here bright and early tomorrow morning."

"That's fine, she's a smart girl. The last thing we're worried about is her falling behind. If you gentlemen will have a seat, I'll get her for you."

Magic sat down in one of the cushy swivel chairs that lined the wall in the rather small, but nicely decorated office. Sister Beth picked up the phone and Clear turned to Magic.

"I'm going back to the car, you wait for Dayja," he said.

Magic nodded and Clear walked out. Magic couldn't believe how quiet it was in this school. He sat and listened as the second hand on the clock went tick...tick...tick...and his heart went tock, tock, tock. The ten minutes he sat there seemed like an hour. Sister Beth tried to engage in small talk, but he was being attacked by a battalion of emotions, and he had to stay focused to fight.

Dayja traipsed in and walked up to the desk, never even looking in his direction.

"You need to see me, Sister Beth?"

Sister Beth didn't even look up from her computer, she just pointed at him. By that time he was already on his feet. Dayja turned around and the expression on her face told him she had missed him as much as he had missed her. They met each other halfway, and he placed his arms around her waist, and with both hands she seized his face and their lips merged and their bodies fastened, like legs and short thigh connected at the gristle.

"Dayja!" Sister Beth cried out.

Magic tried to pull away, but Dayja wasn't having it. Her tongue continued to dance in his mouth and he graciously surrendered.

"Dayja!" Sister Beth screamed, "you got five seconds to get your tongue back in your mouth!"

Four point fifty-nine seconds passed and Dayja pulled away. The gleam in her eyes said what words could never transmit.

"Dayja, sign out!" Sister Beth roared, sounding amused but stern.

They walked down the walkway, Dayja gripped his arm, and laid her head on his shoulder. The sun was shining, the grass was growing, the flowers were fragrant, and all was right with the world.

"Sister Beth was going to jack your butt up back there," Magic said teasingly.

"Sister Beth wasn't going to do nothing. My brother has given this school so much money that I could slap her down, and the Board of Directors would make her send me an apology letter." Dayja sounded a bit disgusted.

"How's your leg?" she asked.

"It's straight, just a little flesh wound," Magic said stroking the side of her face. She looked up and kissed the side of his face.

"I'm sorry, Magic."

"It wasn't your fault. You reacted the same way I would have reacted."

"I wish you would tell my brother that," she said as they approached the car and got in. Dayja stuck her head between the seat, kissed her brother, and said, "Where we going, to the mall?"

"My days of taking you to the mall are over. That's what you got a man for," Clear said. He looked over at Magic, snickered, shook his head, and the atmosphere lightened.

"Dayja, you got your permit, right?" Clear asked.

"Excuse me, I got license," she said.

"Excuse me. You ain't got no damn car," he responded.

"Yeah, I got license, Clear," Dayja said as she slid back in her seat and out of his view.

After they pulled over in front of the barbershop, Clear looked at Magic and said, "Put that safe in the trunk."

Magic and Clear got out while Dayja sat there obviously trying to recuperate from that, "You ain't got no car," remark.

Magic followed Clear into the barbershop to holla at Daemon, Black and Marwon. They cracked jokes about Magic's incarceration and everyone laughed. Clear followed Magic out and they stood on the sidewalk watching Dayja bop her head to the music.

"Listen, Magic," he said. "Those are my friends, they will shoot the shit and laugh with you, but at my request they'll slow cook you over a cozy evening fire. You need friends like that. We're gonna call them Magic's first and second lieutenants." Then he turned and walked back into the barbershop.

Magic got back in the car and they pulled off. Magic laid the seat back and closed his eyes anticipating a trip to the mall. A few minutes later Dayja pulled over and Magic could feel the dark shadow of looming trees. Magic opened his eyes. A park? he thought.

Dayja got out, walked around to Magic's side, opened the door, took his hand and escorted him out of the car. She did a cute little spin-dip-dance move, and his arm ended up around her neck and hers around his waist. They walked down to a little bridge that stretched across the river and divided the park into two sections. He could tell she knew exactly where she wanted to go, almost like at the mall, but without the sense of urgency.

They came to a tall tree that leaned over a narrow strip of the river. Magic stood and watched as a squirrel scurried up the side with a big black walnut clenched between his jaws. He could hear the soft prattle of nothingness mingled with the slow moving tide, and the distant sound of traffic. For the first time in a long time he felt like there was nothing up or nothing going down. Dayja sat down, leaned her back against the tree, and gently pulled him down beside her.

"This is my favorite place," she said, "We're gonna take our wedding vows under this tree."

"Yeah, it's nice here," Magic responded, scooting out and over then laying his head in her lap. He looked up and watched the sunlight flash in her face as if it were taking snapshots and transporting her image back to God. She looked down into his eyes and slowly began tracing the edge of his lips with her finger.

"I love your lips... Your hair... Your eyes... Will you have my baby?" she asked with a smile that accentuated her beauty."

"Hell, yeah, when you wanna get started."

"Right after the wedding." she responded. Then out of nowhere, she said, "My brother's crazy, Magic."

Magic looked at her, looking for that sense of pride that was so apparent in Muscle's face when he diagnosed his Uncle Mack and labeled him crazy, but it wasn't there.

"Not Thorazine or Lithium crazy, a distorted perception of reality crazy. He's a fucking drug lord that wants to save the world. How crazy is that?" she said. "And he's gonna make your ass crazy, too."

"Nobody's gonna make me crazy, Dayja."

"My brother's gonna change you, Magic. He's gonna have you walking around here like his clone."

"Nobody's gonna change me, Dayja," Magic repeated, feeling a bit annoyed.

"My brother will change you, Magic."

"Your brother's not gonna change me. And what is this thing you have with your brother? When you're in his face you're rubbing his shoulders and kissing his cheeks. Now behind his back you're talkin' like he's some kind of maniac and shit."

"He is a fucking maniac."

"Why, Dayja, why is he a fucking maniac?" Magic sat up and turned to her. Her eyes started to open and close rapidly. Then she closed them tight. When they opened, moisture clung to her lashes like morning dew, and a reddish tint appeared on her pecan-colored cheeks. Tears rolled down.

"He killed my father, Magic."

"What?"

"I hate him sometimes, because I remember," she said wiping her eyes with the backs of her hands.

"You remember what?"

She sat there with her head down, twisting a rubber band on her wrist tighter and tighter until her hand turned puffy and red.

"You don't have to talk about it," Magic said.

"Yes I do." She let the rubber band go. "I never told anybody this, Magic, and the shit is killing me inside. Every lie I tell, every class I skip, every man I ever laid down with was in an effort to hurt him." She paused, and tugged at a patch of grass between her legs.

"They banged for a long time, as if they knew we were home. 'It's the police,' they said, and I hopped off the couch and answered the door. My mother was in her room and I tried to wake her but she wouldn't wake up. I remember shaking her and shaking her, but I don't remember if she finally got up or if one of the officers got her up. I remember hearing her scream and her sobbing when she took me down to Marge's house. I was crying, my mother was crying and Marge and her mother was crying. Somebody took me from my mother, carried me into the kitchen and gave me some Gingersnaps or Oreo's. Then Marge took me to her room and laid me in her bed.

"Sometime later Marge and my brother walked into the room. I played sleep because I didn't want to go home, for some reason I liked being at Marge's house.

"'I killed that motherfucker!' my brother said 'And I wish he was still living so I could kill his ass again. I'm the pit bull around this bitch now. I'm the pit bull.'

"I rolled over and sat up in the bed. My brother looked crazy. I had never seen him look like that or talk like that, ever."

"'I emptied this bitch in that motherfucker,' he said standing there with a gun in his hand. Then Marge picked me up and carried me out of the room. The last thing I saw was my father's necklace dangling around my brother's neck. I remember that necklace, Magic, I remember that necklace better than I remember my father for some reason. And my brother still wears that necklace around his neck today as if to torment me or some shit.

Everything changed after that. I never saw my father, my brother Brandon, and I barely saw my mother. She hardly ever came out of her room after that day. At her funeral, I didn't even recognize her. I remember saying to Marge, 'That's not my Mama.'"

Dayja laughed; a pain filled, runny nose, aching heart laugh. Then continued.

"The only thing I remember about my mother is her bedroom door. I have fucking nightmares about that door! A fucking door, Magic," she said.

Magic wanted to say something, or do something. Pick her up or lay her down, stroke her hair or something. But he sat there connecting the dots, making cross references as curiosity superceded concern.

"Does Clemar's mean anything to you, Dayja?" Magic asked.

"No."

"Was Marge white?"

"The last time I saw her she was."

"And when was the last time you saw her?"

"When my mother died I went into foster care. I haven't seen her since then."

Magic felt like a super sleuth. He was willing to bet his life that the Marge from the hotel and the Marge from Dayja's past, were the same. He remembered the card Marge left for him that said 'we have a mutual friend.'

Dayja sat there sobbing and sobbing as if this had happened yesterday. Magic took her hand to pull her up. He gave her a hug and they walked back to the car.

CHAPTER 35

Reality Versus Perception

The sign out front still read Clemar's. Magic had hoped to see the Cat-Food Man sitting outside doing lunch, but he didn't.

"Pull over right here," he said to Dayja, who was still sort of blue as she whipped the Lexus into a parking spot right beyond the hotel.

"Why are we down here?" she asked.

"I need to see a woman about a horse," Magic said as he opened the door.

"What?"

"Just come on."

"Magic, I'm not getting out. My eyes are all red and my makeup is all fucked up."

"Just come on," Magic said and closed the door.

She pulled down the visor, put on some lipstick and some eye shadow and got out.

Deep purple carpet covered the floor, and a lighter colored wallpaper caressed the walls. The ceiling fan turned silently, glistening in gold, and matching the do-dads and whatnots that hung on the walls and sat on the counter.

Everything was brand new and ritzy looking. Even the white girl standing behind the counter greeted them with a genuinely fake smile.

"Hi, is Marge in?" Magic asked.

"I believe she is. Let me check. May I say who's inquiring?"

"Magic and Dayja."

She picked up the phone and in less than thirty seconds Marge came running from the back. She stopped and looked at Dayja, then looked at Magic. Dayja's eyes lit up, and once again, filled with tears as Marge walked over and wrapped her arms around her. Magic received a so-so greeting; an offer to have a seat in her office and a less than friendly smile.

It had been a couple of years since he had seen Marge. But he had seen her aggravated enough times to know that she was doing all she could to maintain her poise. The thing that bothered him most was that he had no idea why.

"Marge, it's really good to see you again," Dayja said. "I think about you all the time. You haven't changed a bit, you look just like I remember you."

"It's good to see you too, Dayja. I ask your brother about you often."

"You still talk to my brother?" Dayja asked with an accusing look on her face.

"Not like that. But we talk on occasion," Marge responded.

"I kinda remember your mother. How's she doing?"

"She's doing great. And how's Dayja? How's school?"

"School's good, I'm graduating next year. And as you can tell, I grew up to be a beautiful young lady," Dayja responded jokingly..

"Are you talking about on the outside, because I hear a little bitch has taken up residence on the inside."

That caught Dayja off guard, but it confirmed that Marge and Clear had a well-established relationship. Because Clear called her a little bitch even when he wasn't mad at her.

Dayja hesitated. Magic could see she wanted to strike back, but she had no ammo.

"Is that what my brother told you?"

"Your brother don't have to tell me nothing. It's all over his face every time I ask about you. If you ain't in the street, you're locked up. Why is that?"

"I don't know." Dayja said and looked away.

"Should I just accept that response and conclude that you're as dumb as your choices make you seem?" Marge asked.

It took Dayja a minute to recover from consecutive body blows. She re-positioned herself in the chair, zipped on her big girl suit and tried again.

"I have some questions, Marge. You have some questions."

"This ain't Let's Make a Deal, Dayja. If I can answer your questions, I'll answer them."

Dayja re-crossed her legs and her eyes went from Marge to the picture of her son, little Brandon, in the silver frame sitting on the desk. Then to the yellow paper clip that glowed against the dark colored carpet and flashed as if it were saying, 'Proceed with caution.' Which Dayja ignored.

"Did my brother kill my father?" she asked.

If Marge was a smoker she would have reached for a cigarette, Magic could see the panic in her eyes. She reached for the Nextel phone that sat on her desk instead.

"Please don't call my brother," Dayja said leaning forward.

Marge sat with the phone in her hand, shaking her head slightly and glaring into Dayja's eyes.

"Why didn't you ask Clear, Dayja?"

"Because I'm afraid," Dayja responded softly.

"Afraid of what?"

"I don't know… Maybe the answer."

"So you think it would be easier to accept coming from me?"

"I don't know," Dayja repeated. Marge continued to hold her hostage with her eyes, and the phone.

"I don't know who or if your brother killed anyone," she said, then laid the phone back down on the desk in front of her. But, your biological father should have been born dead. His mother should have wrapped the umbilical cord around his neck and choked him to death. He didn't give a damn about you or your brothers. And he played your mother like a slot machine, and when she was empty, he bounced. Any other questions?"

"What about my mother?" Dayja asked.

"What about your mother?" Marge responded angrily.

"Why did she look like that when she died? And why are you taking this so personal?"

"Because it is personal. Your Mama was a dope fiend, addicted to crack, heroin, and fuckin' oodles of noodles. And because she was a dope fiend, you were born three months premature, and addicted.

"Your brother and I were at the hospital everyday watching your little ass shake like a leaf in a wind storm. Listening to doctors tell us shit that we didn't even understand. When you left the hospital, you were released in my mother's care, and the only reason my mother did that was because your brother swore he would take care of you, and he did. He also begged your mother to go to rehab or seek some kind of help.

When you came home from the hospital, she slowed down for a little while, but after your brother got killed she wanted to die, because guilt was eating her ass up. So she commenced to committing suicide, one bag, one bottle, one bundle at time. Now, is there anything else you think you need to know?" Marge asked.

"No," Dayja responded and got up to leave.

"Sit your ass back down because there's a few things I think you should know," Marge said.

Dayja crawled back into her seat and Marge commenced to blowing her wig back. "Dayja, life should be treating you like the bitch with the glass slippers, because that's all your brother talked about. How he was going to build a financial fortress around his little sister that not even the federal government could penetrate." Marge got up and walked over to the wall behind her desk. "You see these degrees, Dayja? Your brother paid for 'em. I'm one of the baddest bitches that ever embraced the concept of buying and trading stock.

Between your brother and I, there's enough money to run this fucking city." Marge smiled, a smile that screamed 'Incoming.' "I call your brother 'Sweat', Dayja, because he has tirelessly pursued his vision from day one. He calls me 'Tears', because I cry every time I see him because I love him, and admire him. But he's obsessed with this vision. He's building an empire Dayja... On a foundation saturated in blood, sweat and tears and it would be a real shame, if some of that blood was yours."

Dayja looked unbalanced. Marge had delivered a devastating left-right combination and knocked the legitimacy out of her resentment. She put her head in her hands and cried and cried and cried until Marge came and pulled her from the chair. "Magic, please excuse us for a moment," she said. Her face softened as she escorted Dayja out of the office.

Magic leaned down and picked up the paper clip from the floor, then turned the picture of Brandon slightly in his direction. It was a picture of him in a football uniform with a ball tucked under his arm. Magic got up and walked over to check out Marge's degrees, thinking how cool is that, she named her son after Dayja and Clear's dead brother.

Marge walked in as Magic was sitting back down. She closed the door, plopped one of her thighs on the desk right in front of him and leaned forward so that she was about a foot from his face. She looked at him, and if her intent was intimidation, mission accomplished. He wanted to hang his head, but he knew that was the wrong thing to do, so he looked at her, trying to appear hard.

"If Clear knew you brought his sister down here to question me about anything, by Wednesday they'd be dressing your ass for calling hours. That's if you were lucky enough to make the obits," she said. "Listen, Magic, and listen good, because even key players are expendable. Keep your pussy and your priorities in separate pockets. Save your feelings and your emotions for when you retire from this shit and take up poetry writing. Don't listen to anything anybody tells you. You're being groomed by a ghetto God, and you need to recognize it before it's too late. Now get the fuck out of my office."

Magic wasted no time accommodating her.

CHAPTER 36

When Allies Become Enemies

Dayja was sitting in the car fixing her face, which pissed him off even more. He didn't know who he was angrier with: her or himself, but he was fuming. He had gotten stabbed, jailed and reprimanded twice within seven days behind this girl. And he hadn't even had sex with her yet.

Not a word passed between them until they pulled into the parking lot at the mall.

Magic went into his pocket, pulled out the stack of hundred dollar bills, peeled off five and handed them to her.

"Meet me in the food court in two hours," he said.

"Thank you," she responded.

Magic got out the car and slammed the door.

He walked through the mall totally oblivious to everything that was taking place around him. Locked inside of his own head. Listening to his brain tell his heart to shut the fuck up. After about fifteen hundred dollars worth of stuff he didn't need, he realized this shopping shit didn't work for him. He sat down in front of a pretzel stand next to a deaf lady who was signing to herself. It seemed like she was rehearsing for a puppet show. He watched other people glance in passing, but he stared until she caught him. Her grunt sounded just like 'fuck you' and he assumed the gesture she made with her hands meant fuck you. She picked up her bags and stomped off.

Dayja walked past and didn't even notice him sitting there. She seemed to be deep in thought so he didn't bother to interrupt. Seeing her kicked his brain back into fourth gear. He appointed rationale as judge, selected a jury from past-experiences, and listened to his heart and his head plead their case. After about a half-hour of wandering aimlessly and listening to deliberation and dissertations, the jury declared no contest and sided with his brain. This told him he needed to let go of all reservations. He was locked in with only one way out; Death. And death seemed about as appealing as the coagulated grease and chunks of tofu swimming in the hot and sour soup at the food court.

"Sesame Chicken, taste. . .taste."

"No thank you," he responded, as the little Chinese lady pushed a toothpick with a piece of chicken dangling in his face. He walked over to Burger King and ordered a Whopper value meal.

Out of the corner of his eye he could see Dayja approaching. She stopped in front of Subway, briefly glanced at the meats, breads, and cheeses, then continued in his direction. She walked up behind him, put her arms around his waist and laid her head on his back.

"Thank you, Magic," she said.

Magic picked up his tray from the counter, she grabbed the bags that were resting against his leg, and they sat down in front of the carousel.

He looked across the table at her as he bit into the Whopper.

"You're scared, aren't you?" she asked.

"I don't know what I am," he said, and sat thinking for a moment.

The carousel turned and the carnival music played. A little white boy and a little white girl rocked from side to side on a mostly white pony. Holding on to the steel bar with one hand and waving to Dayja and Magic with the other. Magic waved hello to them and good bye to himself as the crazy ladies words reverberated in his head.

Evil hovers over you like a dark cloud, and the demons that are in front of you are far worse than the ones you left behind. Don't be afraid of your dark side. Your path was chosen prior to Saul's and dark angels rest on your shoulders."

For the first time in a long time his heart and his head talked to him in unison, and he dictated it to Dayja word for word.

"My Uncle Benny always told me that a double minded person is unstable in all that they do. I don't know where your brothers taking me, Dayja. But I believe he knows. And I'm going. I'm going whether you go or not." He hoped her response would be, 'If you're going, I'm going too.' But she just looked at him for a moment. Then she got up, picked up her bags, pushed in her chair, struck a Porsha pose and said, "I hope you get there before you're reduced to a number and they tattoo twenty-five to life across your fucking forehead." Then she turned and walked out of the mall as the carousel turned and the carnival music played.

A little black boy and a little white girl rocked from side to side on a mostly black pony, holding on to the leather bridal with one hand and waving hello with the other. Magic picked up his bags and left.

Her face was tighter than the Baby Phat jeans that underscored every blessed curve, even when she was sitting down. They pulled up in front of his house and he wanted to say something, but there was nothing to be said. There was no room for concessions or compromise. The terms were non-negotiable. He looked at her and she looked straight ahead as if he wasn't there.

"I got some stuff in the trunk I need to get," Magic said as they pulled in front of his building.

She hit the button to open the trunk and continued to look straight ahead. Magic opened the door, got out, walked around to the back of the car and took out the safe and his bags. She peeled off before Magic could even close the trunk.

Magic turned and saw Muscle sitting on the stairs.

"You look like you just spent the weekend in jail," Magic said with a grin.

"I need to ask you something, and I need you to tell me the truth."

Magic put the safe down, covered it with his bags, and sat down beside him.

"My aunt went shopping yesterday. She bought a brand new Range Rover. Rachel and Rocky is brand new all the way down to their fucking socks. A week ago she was asking me for money to buy milk for breakfast.

"My uncle and me talked a lot, Magic. I know him and Clear was beefin' even before he went to jail and I haven't seen my uncle in months. He's not in jail, I checked... So where's my uncle, Magic?"

Before he finished Magic had asked himself what would Clear say or do. He looked at Muscle determined not to lie. He took a deep breath, exhaled. "I don't know where your uncle is... But wherever he is... He's ain't with the living."

CHAPTER 37

Boot Camp

"So Peggy, what do you suggest I do with these feelings?" Abigail asked.

"Save 'em for someone who likes…"

"You like!"

"Not as much as I like dick."

"So what was all that moaning and groaning about the other night?"

"Abigail, I'm not saying that I didn't enjoy the other night."

"No, what you're saying is that I'm good enough to lick you, but I'm not good enough to be with you."

"No, that's not what I'm saying."

"So what are you saying, Peggy? Please tell me, so that I can walk up outta here and retain some dignity."

"Sleeping with a woman was never even an option for me, Abigail. Now you're talking about a relationship. Holding hands and walking through the park. I'm not ready for that."

"Okay, Okay," Abigail said calmly. Then she got up from the table and walked out the door as Magic walked in.

"Hi, Aunt Abigail," Magic said. He moved to the side as she slid past him. What's up with that? he thought. He turned and watched her disappear into her apartment and slam her door.

The house smelled like Sundays from long ago. Magic laid his bags down on the couch covering the safe, then rushed to the kitchen.

"You're home," Peggy said as she gently slid the plastic spoon back and forth in the meat gravy.

"What's wrong with Aunt Abigail?"

"You don't want to know. You hungry?"

Magic walked over to the stove to investigate. He looked at the gravy and the fried chicken then over to the rice, green beans and the watery Macaroni and cheese.

"Why is the juice in the green beans brown?" he asked.

"I don't know, maybe the can was rusty. It's been a long time."

"Yes it has," Magic responded with a smile. "I think I'll let you practice for a while."

"That's fine by me. Cory'll eat it," Peggy said.

"Don't be using my little brother as no guinea pig."

"He is a little pig, you see how chunky he's getting. He's gonna be thick, like his dad," she said, and the mood seemed to shift. Magic turned, left the kitchen and started down the hall toward the living room to get his bags.

The harsh memory of Cory's father had subsided over the years. For some reason, he just didn't seem so bad. Magic felt a surge of guilt every time his name was mentioned, or when Cory looked at him a certain way. He collected his stuff from the couch in the living room and started back down the hall.

Peggy stood in his way, arms extended. Magic stopped and leaned his bags against the wall. The sun shone through the window at her back leaving the generally dimly lit hall full of light. She held him firmly with arms strengthened by years of beating off bears, stroking male egos, and holding back tidal waves.

"I love you, Magic."

"I love you too, Mama."

Cory burst through the door with backpack and lunchbox in hand. He paused for a moment then dropped his school paraphernalia and joined them in a group hug.

"I bought you something," Magic said to his little brother as he reached down, picked up the bags, and headed toward their room. Cory left his backpack and lunchbox lying in the middle of the floor and followed him.

Magic noticed an envelope lying on his bed. He picked it up and fanned through it: All the money was still there, but no letter.

"What you buy me?" Cory asked.

"Find it," Magic said. He headed for the kitchen as Cory proceeded to tear into the bags.

Magic sat down and placed the money on the table in front of him.

"Ma, I really want you to have this."

"Believe you me, I really want it. I've never even seen seven thousand dollars at one time," she responded.

"Well take it, Ma."

"What kind of message would I be giving you if I took that money, Magic?"

"I'm seventeen years old, and any message that you're going to give me I've already got. You taught me to take care of my own, by whatever means necessary."

"But baby, I don't want to visit you behind bars, or have to come to the morgue and identify your body."

"Mama, death don't scare me, neither does jail but the thought of you selling yourself to feed Cory and I scares the shit out of me. Whether you take the money or not, nothing's gonna change.

"What's not gonna change, Magic?"

"Please don't start grilling me, Mama. Just take the money."

Peggy stood there leaning against the sink, obviously negotiating with herself.

"I can't, Magic. I just can't," she said and went back to stirring her gravy.

Cory came flying out of the bedroom dribbling his new NBA basketball and sporting his new Jordan's, laces dragging. He turned into the kitchen and the gleam in his eyes shined brighter than the hundred-watt bulb in the ceiling.

"Look, Mama!" he said, and stuck out his foot. "These the new Jordan's. Nobody in my class got these. I'm gonna go show Aunt Abigail."

"You ain't gonna thank your brother?" Peggy asked.

Cory let the ball roll under the table, walked over to Magic and put his arm around his neck. "Thank you bro," he said.

"You're welcome, man."

That done, Cory scooped the ball from beneath the table and dribbled out the door.

"That boy just got new sneakers less than a month ago. You're not gonna spoil him, Magic," Peggy said as the phone rang.

"Yes I am," Magic said. He got up, picked up the envelope and walked into the living room to answer the phone.

"Hello."

"What up, Magic?"

"Hey, Clear."

"How was your reunion?"

Magic paused, then, "Stressful."

Clear laughed. "Listen, man, I don't want Marge's name to cross your lips again. You don't go there. You don't call there. If you ever see her in the streets, you don't even acknowledge her presence. Is that understood?"

"Yeah."

"Okay, good. I'll be by to pick you up about one-thirty. Dress up, we're going out."

"One-thirty in the morning?"

"Yep, one-thirty in the morning."

Magic checked himself in the full body mirror behind his door one last time, rushed over to his dresser and drenched himself with the latest addition to his cologne collection. He left the door cracked a bit, light on. Cory wasn't quite over his fear of the dark. On his way out, he tapped gently on his mother's door.

"Be careful, Magic," she said.

"I will."

Magic walked out and turned the knob to make sure it was locked. He had no idea where they were going. As far as he knew neither him nor Clear was the nightclub type. He would hear kids in school talking about new clubs, fake ID's, and getting drunk, but for some reason, none of that appealed to him. A fun night for him was talking to Dayja on the phone until one of them fell asleep, or playing video games with Cory.

He stepped off the stoop and looked at his watch, thinking back to the time he walked into the barbershop fifteen minutes late for his scheduled haircut.

He found Clear sitting in his barbers chair reading. Marwon and Daemon were cutting and indulging in small talk with their customers.

"What's up?" Magic said but didn't receive a response from anyone except the two men getting their hair cut. Clear lowered the book slightly, looked at Magic, then raised it again.

Magic stood there for a moment then walked over to Clear. "You gonna cut me, man?"

Clear lowered the book again, looked at his watch, got up and took off his barber shirt. He walked past Magic, then turned as he approached the door, and said. "I had a four-thirty with Magic but I guess he came down with nigga-itis."

"Nigga-i-tis, What's nigga-I-tis, Mr. Rogers?" Marwon asked sounding childlike.

"Well the scientific community hasn't quite figured it out yet. They don't know the cause or the cure. But the symptoms are; not showing up and chronic fucking lateness."

"Damn, that sounds fatal, Mr. Rogers," Daemon said.

"Yeah, it is," Clear said and walked out the barbershop.

The streetlights made the red Lexus shine like glass as it silently pulled to the curb with three minutes to spare. Magic opened the door and was less than shocked to see the 45 automatic with a silencer lying on top of some papers on the passenger seat.

"Magic scooped up the papers and the pistol, laid them on the floor and carefully got in the car.

"Pick it up. It ain't gonna bite you," Clear said, pulling off.

Magic picked up the pistol, clicked the safety off and on three times, popped out the clip, laid it in his lap, screwed off the silencer, looked down the barrel, pulled back the handle and popped the clip back in.

"Not bad," he said.

"I forgot all you country boys know how to handle a gun. Now let me see how well you do on that job application."

Magic picked up the papers on the floor, pulled down the sun visor, and lifted the flap on the vanity mirror.

"What job am I applying for?" Magic asked, sticking the application underneath the other pieces of paper in the stack.

"Evening security at the church," Clear said.

"Cool. What's this other stuff?"

"It's a financial statement. Documentation of every dime earned from the time you came into the organization, and your cut."

"But I haven't done shit."

"You've done everything I've told you to." Clear responded just as his cell phone rang.

"Hello."

Magic could only guess who it was.

"Hey. What's up?" Clear said.

A pause, then, "Empty the club and keep him there, Clear said. "I'm just around the corner."

Magic sat reading the papers. Everything wasn't comprehensible, but the bottom figures said that they had made over four million in less than six months. His cut was a little over forty thousand. "Damn!" Magic said.

Clear didn't respond, he just smiled and pulled up in front of the Peek-a-Boo Club as patrons scurried out and rushed to their cars.

Magic saw the three Acura Legends for the first time since they'd been parked in front of his school almost two years ago. They were parked on the sidewalk, almost kissing the building, and looking like they hadn't aged a day. His father's black Cadillac was parked directly in front of them. His father's license plate read 'Magic J1.'

Magic braced himself and asked, "You gonna kill my dad?"

Clear continued to look out the driver's side window, "This ain't about me, it's about you."

"Are you gonna kill my dad?"

"Do you want me to kill him?"

"Why are you avoiding my question, Clear?" Magic asked, adding a little more intensity to his delivery.

Clear looked at him.

"For some reason, Magic, your father is fearlessly saturating my turf. I shoulda put a stop to it in the beginning. If he wasn't your father, I would have. If he wasn't your father it would take a forensic pathologist to identify his ass now. But

296

tonight isn't about me, it's about you. So if you want him dead, kill him," Clear said, his words void of emotion.

"Did you know Mack and my father were friends?" Magic asked.

"Keep going."

"I never saw them together, but Muscle said they picked him up one day."

"Why you just telling me this, Magic?" Clear asked quietly.

"Because it didn't seem important."

"In the future, let me decide what's important"

Magic sat there for a moment, then, "Muscle asked me about his uncle today."

"What'd you tell him?"

"I told him I didn't know where his uncle was."

"Is that all?"

"No, I told him he wasn't with the living."

"Good answer."

Three figures dressed in black from head to toe, exposing only their mouth, eyes and nose walked out the bar and insisted aggressively that the stragglers left from in front of the club. The most curvaceous figure dashed across the street with a twelve-gauge shotgun pointing downward pressed against her leg. Clear rolled down his window as she approached the car.

"Alright. It's all yours."

That's Officer Cox, Magic thought. After they got out the car she escorted them across the street like royalty. Magic looked over at Clear, examining his facial expression, his body language, even his well-polished stride. Before they reached the solid line in the middle of the street his modifications were complete.

Clear and Magic walked into the Peek-a-Boo Club. Magic Sr. stood in the middle of the floor with a twelve-gauge pump pointed at his head. His eyes darted from Clear to Magic Jr. from Clear to Magic Jr. He appeared humbled but not shaken.

Magic's eyes locked in on his father. Clear stepped away and gestured for Officer Campbell to lower his gun. Magic held his breath and tried with all his might to hold back the tears. A thousand words and phrases were loaded in, but only a choice few came out through his quivering lips.

"I was a good kid. I always got A's and B's. I made the honor roll for the last seven years, and you never even looked at a single report card... Do you like me, Dad?" he asked. "Do you like me, Daddy?"

"You my Jr. Magic."

"That's not what I asked. Do you like me?"

"I love you," his father responded.

"Well I don't like you. Not even a little bit, so please don't push me. Because I will kill you about my Mama," he said. And before the tears rolled from his eyes he walked out.

Magic Sr. stood there Xerox-ing the look on his son's face. He searched his memory because that look was familiar. Then he remembered--they were the same tears that sat in the corner of his eyes, the same quivering bottom lip, the same pain that consumed him at his mother's gravesite. The same pain that eclipsed the sun and made all things beautiful invisible. The pain that purged love and pounded the shit out of compassion.

Clear stepped off the barstool, walked over to the jukebox and stood there scanning the selections.

"Mr. Magic," Clear said as he turned and walked up to Magic Sr. and extended his hand, "your reputation proceeds you, sir."

"Likewise," Magic Senior said.

Clear walked over to the pool table, picked up the stick, leaned across the table and cut the six ball in the side pocket.

"Pool's a very interesting game, a gentleman's game. Do you play?" Clear asked.

"Never found any use for it."

"That doesn't surprise me. Is there anything in life you find use for?"

"Yeah, money and bitches. Is this personal or is it business?"

Clear walked over, stopped about four feet from Magic Senior and studied him. Searching for a soft spot or a panic button. But he found none. This didn't surprise him. Magic Senior was a relic, an urban legend. Him and Pit came up in the same era, an era of Dinobots. An era where all feelings and emotions were encased in impenetrable steel. "You fucking with my money," Clear said, "which is my business. Which makes this personal."

Magic Sr. didn't flinch. His eyes were still and sullen. Body sturdy and relaxed. He obviously knew that if Clear wanted him dead, he wouldn't have staged such an elaborate gathering. This wasn't about him or Clear, it was about Magic Junior.

Clear turned and walked out with Officers Campbell, Cortez, and Cox on his heels.

In front of the Peek-a-Boo Club, Clear briefly expressed his appreciation. Very few words were said, very few were needed. Nods and handshakes were sufficient. An envelope would soon follow, pressed down and running over with Franklins, for services rendered.

Magic sat in a meditative state. Popping out, and pushing in, popping out and pushing in the clip of his new toy while he stared at the flashing Budweiser sign in the window. He thought about the look on his father's face the Sunday morning they were reacquainted. The trip down south to pick up Cory and the awkward moments they'd spent together that didn't seem so awkward in retrospect.

Magic Senior watched as Clear hopped in his car and the red Lexus pulled away. And for the first time in almost eighteen months, he felt the need to alter his mood. The shit he was feeling wasn't foreign, just more intense, too intense. He walked behind the bar, poured himself a triple shot of Hennessy, dropped in a few ice cubes and began to stir slowly as he listened to the almost hypnotic sound of clinking ice cubes.

He looked up and into the small sliver of exposed mirror between the Courvoisier and the Johnny Walker Black. He saw his reflection and for the first time in a long time he questioned whether he liked what he saw. It was as if he was butt ass naked, fully exposed. The gold medallion, silk shirt, and tailor made double-breasted suit had stopped working. And carefully selected phrases began banging in his head like hard rock and heavy metal.

You'd sell your mammy for a new outfit. You're going to send me to an early fucking grave with your bullshit boy.

That's that nigga blood in you, that's what Niggas do. Rob, steal, kill and sell dope.

He bit down on his bottom lip, held his breath and tried to suppress the tears that sat in the rusty tear ducts. He turned to make sure. To make sure that nobody was there. That nobody was peaking through the window with the flashing Budweiser sign or passed out over by the pool table. He picked up the double shot of Hennessey and brought it up to his nose. The melting ice cubes had diluted the majestic smell of pure cognac. He lowered it to his lips and Mr. Ashby chimed in.

I'm gonna let you go a day early. In hopes that you'll return the day before your good looks and charming personality takes your ass back to the crack house.

He set the glass of quick fix back down on the bar because he knew that when he sobered up tomorrow, next week, next month or next year, Clear would be dead, and his son would be fucked.

Reluctantly, he pushed the glass of Hennessy away and grasped the cell phone that hung from his waist. It was time to perform his first unselfish act.

Clear looked at his phone, wondering who would be calling him this time of night with a restricted number.

"Hello," he answered.

"If you got a vest, put it on. If you don't, get one, and put it on."

"Are you threatening me?" Clear asked.

"Actually, I'm trying to save your ass."

"Save me from who?"

"Now you know that's a violation. But I have a fashion tip for you. Black's not your color, actually, it's not a good color at all. It tends to bleed and can ruin lighter, softer colors, like Marwon and Daemons. And here's a diet tip for you. Those Big Macs, it's enough envy and jealousy in them motherfuckas to kill a giant. You run a tight ship, man, too fucking tight. Put this word in your vocabulary--Mutiny." And he hung up the phone.

Clear made a sharp left, drove down Jefferson Avenue then turned onto Plymouth going in the opposite direction of Magic's house. Magic glanced over prepared to say, 'Please take me home,' but Clear looked twisted.

"What's wrong, man?" Magic asked.

Clear didn't respond for a moment, then, "The problem is that we fucked up, Magic. It's like the moment they cut the umbilical cord they stick a 'how to be fucked up' tutorial up our ass. And it doesn't matter whether we're in the White House or the Po' house, we still fucked up."

Clear looked over at Magic and the song changed on the CD. The lyrics and the beat seemed to web his words.

"I got a dream, Magic, and I used to think that only crackers waged war on niggas' dreams, but every time I look at the person staring down the barrel of the gun aimed at my dream, they look like me, they walk like me and talk like me. But they ain't me. Because if they were me, they would know not to fuck with me and my dream."

Clear pulled in front of the Canterbury Apartments, and as Magic opened the door to get out, he said, "You okay, man?"

"Hell no, but I will be. You just make sure you put that pistol in a safe place. We don't want Cory shootin' up daycare."

"Alright, man," Magic said as he got out.

Clear made a U turn in the middle of the street and headed back toward the Peek-a-Boo Club.

MASTERMIND

Magic walked up the stairs wondering if the they that fucked up the Cat-Food Man was the same they that cut the umbilical cord and stuck the 'how to be fucked up' tutorial up their ass.

CHAPTER 38

Next Day

"How dare you go and have a fuckin' fight and not invite me," Free said as he took his seat beside Magic in home base.

"It wasn't no fight. I did the Malcolm. Just stuck my knife in his ass."

"You niggas be on that West Side Story shit. You better graduate. Tec's and Nines, Nigga," Freestyle said, patting his waist. Magic looked over and saw the slight bulge beneath his shirt.

"Man ain't you scared you gonna get caught with that?" he asked.

"Hell, no. I'm scared I'm gonna get caught without it," he said and Magic just shook his head.

"How'd you make out in court?" he asked.

"I'm here, right."

"That don't mean shit. Here today, upstate tomorrow."

"I'm straight, man," Magic said as Miss Hutchins waltzed up to their desks.

"How you two gangsters doing today?" she asked.

"Just peachy Miss Hutchins, and yourself?" Freestyle responded.

"Don't get cute with me, boy," she said and shot Free down with her eyes. "You okay, Magic?"

"I'm good, Miss Hutchins."

"And you, peachy boy?"

"I'm good too, ma'am."

"Let's try and keep it that way," she said as she turned and walked back to the front of the class.

Magic looked over at Free as he watched the pinstripes shimmer across Miss Hutchins' ass every time her black pumps came in for a landing.

Magic studied him, wondering if he could be trusted. He watched him from first period to fourth, seeing how he handled his new notoriety, seeing if he acted any different with a pistol in his crotch. He was calm and charismatic. Slapping up people he didn't know and smiling, even at the ugly girls. Magic had put out an APB on Muscle, telling him to meet him at fourth period lunch. It was strange that he hadn't seen him all day, but everyone he asked said he was in school.

When Freestyle and Magic got to the lunchroom, Magic skimmed the tables, the lunch line and the adjacent hall where the gym mats and horny girls were stored--no Muscle. By the time they made it through the lunch line, lunch was half over. Magic sat down with his ice-cream sandwich, hotdog, and cold fries and began picking. He couldn't eat. It was as if he was full and the food just seemed to sit in his throat. He concluded that he was worried about Muscle, not stressed about Dayja. He pushed the tray forward, went into his pocket, pulled out a folded stack of hundred dollar bills, and started to count them underneath the table. His plan was to spark Freestyle's curiosity, but he pretended not to notice. Even when he poked Magic in the side with his elbow and pointed to the door.

Magic stood and called Muscle's name. Obviously too loud, because half the lunchroom stopped and looked at him. Muscle swaggered over to the table and slapped him up. Magic stood to do the male hug thing and as he did, he felt the bulge underneath his shirt.

"What's up, Free?" Muscle said.

"Chillin'," Free responded as he stuffed the last of the three hotdogs into his mouth. "Damn, you look brand new," he added.

"Yeah, they got this new spot over on Jay Street. Shit expensive but it's official though," Muscle responded.

"I called you about six times yesterday, your people didn't tell you?" Magic asked.

"Yeah, she told me. After she packed all my shit up and threw it on the porch."

"Git the fuck outta here," Magic said.

"That's what she said," Muscle responded.

"What happened?" Magic asked.

"Nothing, man, she just trippin'."

"Where you stay last night?"

"At a hotel downtown, a buck fifty. Room service and the whole nine," Muscle said caught somewhere between bragging and complaining.

"Oh, you got it like dat, for seventy-five, nigga, I would've gave you two hots, a cot, and a bag lunch," Freestyle said.

Muscle went into his pocket and pulled out a hand full of credit cards. "Plastic, baby."

"Who you rob?" Magic asked.

"Don't worry about dat," he said. He hopped up on the table and stuck the credit cards back in his pocket. "So what up? I hear you looking for a brother?"

"You whassup. You alright?" Magic asked.

"I'm straight," he said.

The lunch bell rang and the noise in the cafeteria escalated as everyone filed out.

"We got a spare room, man, you can spend the night at my house," Freestyle offered.

"Ya Mama take plastic?"

"Hell, yeah, my Mama take food stamps," Free responded and everyone laughed as they walked out of the cafeteria and into the hall.

"Yo, Free, let me holla at Muscle a minute," Magic said. "I'll see you in class."

"Cool."

Muscle and Magic walked until the second bell rang and the hall cleared. Although he tried to play it off, Magic could tell he was severely wounded. The new outfit and charcoal brown Timbs couldn't hide the slumping shoulders and the sullen, puffy eyes.

"Um' gon' kill your man," Muscle said.

"You ain't gon' kill nobody."

"Just watch. You and my aunt must be fucking him or something."

"Listen, Muscle, I know you all emotional and shit, but I ain't gonna stand here and let you disrespect me."

Muscle turned and stuck his hand up underneath his shirt and stepped in Magic's face.

"Fuck you, nigga, and fuck Clear too," he said, and headed down the hall toward the front doors.

Magic made a B line and headed for his fifth period class. He stuck his head in the door and motioned for Free. Magic knew Free saw the distress on his face because he wasted no time making his way into the hall.

"Give me your shit, man," Magic said.

"What?" He looked confused.

"Your pistol."

"For what?"

Magic didn't respond, but the look on his face must have spoke loud and clear. He pulled the pistol out, wiped it off with his shirt, and handed it to Magic. Magic took off down the hall stuffing it in his pants with Free on his heels. He flew out the front door and started across the parking lot.

"Where you going?" Free asked.

"I need to find Muscle."

"Let's drive," he said.

Magic stopped and turned around. "Drive what?"

"My car," he said as he tried to stick a key in the door of a white Honda.

"I didn't know you had a car," Magic said rushing over to the passenger side.

"I didn't. Where we going?"

"I don't know, man, just ride around the block."

As they pulled out of the parking lot, Magic saw Muscle turning the corner on Culver and Main Street. "There he go! There he go!" he said. "Pull in McDonald's parking lot."

"You gonna shoot Muscle, man?" Free asked as they headed up Culver.

"Hell no… unless…"

"Unless what?" he asked as he turned into McDonalds.

"Just stay here," Magic said, opening the car door before it came to a complete halt.

"Hell no, if my gun's going, I'm going," Free said as he slammed the car into park.

Magic jumped out, ran across the parking lot and jumped two fences with Freestyle right behind. They crept around the big brick apartment building on the corner. Magic saw Muscle standing at the bus stop. He walked up behind him, gun drawn and pointed at his head. He called his name and Muscle turned. Magic walked up feeling like 007, the surge he felt was unreal. He went from zero to a hundred in the time it took him to get from the side of the building to the sidewalk. He took Muscles pistol from his pants and stood there with a gun in both hands. The emotional overload made him high. His mouth filled with saliva and his heart raced. He wanted to pull the trigger, for no other reason than to pull the trigger. So he did. The bullet shattered the window of a car across the street and Freestyle ran up, snatched both guns from his hands and rushed away. Muscle and Magic just stood there staring at each other.

"I will fucking die for you, man," Magic said. "Don't disrespect me."

Freestyle pulled up beside them, rolled down his window and shouted, "Get the fuck in this car!" Magic heard sirens in the distance, so he hopped in the back. Muscle just stood there.

"You too, goddamn-it!" Free screamed.

Muscle hopped in the front and they pulled off. Slowly and inconspicuously.

"Now, can you two motherfuckers cohabitate for a minute?" Freestyle asked.

"Um-cool," Muscle said.

"What about you, Mr. Eastwood?"

"Just drive, man," Magic said.

Freestyle got on the expressway and got off at the Plymouth Ave. exit. Magic noticed Muscle watching him out of the corner of his eye as they turned into the park. The same park that Dayja and Magic had came to a day earlier, but they parked way down in a hole under a bridge somewhere.

Freestyle turned off the car, turned to Muscle and Magic and asked, "Now what's really going on?"

"I don't know," Muscle said.

Magic was still trying to figure it out so he didn't say anything.

"You don't know? Your main man just put a gun to your head and you don't know?" Free said.

"He know. nigga got all up in my face spittin' and shit, talkin' about fuck me."

"That ain't why you pulled out on me. You pulled out because I said I was gonna kill that faggot ass friend of yours."

"Nigga, Clear will wipe his ass with you. I don't know why you frontin' and shit."

"Not if I blow his ass off first."

"Wait, wait, wait, wait, wait. You telling me you niggas beefin' because of another motherfucker?" Freestyle shouted. The Honda went silent for a moment.

"You don't understand, man," Magic said.

"Please make me understand. Because I'm really not feelin' you niggas right now."

"Go ahead, tell him, Magic. Tell him about that grimy motherfucka you call your friend."

Magic's mind went straight to page three; Allies and Adversaries: 'Never sleep until your adversaries are your allies. If you can't befriend them, buy them. If you can't buy them, kill them.'

Muscle was presently on adversaries status, but Magic needed him. He was the only friend he had made besides the Cat-Food Man. Freestyle was yet to prove himself a friend, but everything about him seemed proper, he kind of reminded Magic of Superman fighting for truth, justice and an urban education. With him as second and Muscle as first lieutenant, Magic had a solid team, he thought.

"Let's go to my house," Magic said.

"For what?" Muscle asked, obviously pissed.

"Look, Muscle, and note it, because you might not hear it again. I'm sorry. Now get over it."

"Hell naw, nigga you put a gun in my face. I would never do that shit to you."

"I said I was sorry, man. What you want?"

"I don't know, but when I figure it out I'll damn sure tell you. Because that sorry shit ain't doing it for me."

"You niggas bicker like bitches," Freestyle said and started up his car. "Where you live, Magic?"

"On Lake Ave., Canterbury Apartments."

They took back streets and alleys all the way to St. Paul Street. "Make a right," Magic said as they approached Lake Avenue from Driving Park. "Pull in the driveway behind that black car," Magic said. He missed it and made a U-turn in the middle of the street.

Magic didn't see his mother's car so he assumed she wasn't home, which was good, considering they should've still been in school. They got out of the car and headed up the stairs.

"It's kinda nice in here, walls could use a fresh coat, carpet a little musty, but it's alright, though," Freestyle said.

Magic's mother was sitting in her favorite chair when they walked in. But this time she couldn't fool him. He saw the distress on her face as she tried to hide behind the faint smile.

"Hi, Magic," she said.

"Hi, Mama."

"Hi, Miss Brown."

"Hi, Muscle."

"Mama, this is Freestyle," Magic said.

Freestyle walked over and extended his hand. "Hi, Miss Brown, pleased to meet you."

"Hi, Free...Free?"

"Style, ma'am. Freestyle," he said, smiling politely.

"Nice. Pleased to meet you, Freestyle." She smiled back.

"Muscle, take Free back to my room. I need to talk to my mother a minute."

After they left, Magic sat down across from his mother and looked her in the face.

"What?" she asked.

"That's what I should be asking you. What's wrong, Mama?"

"Nothing's wrong, Magic."

"Mama, can we make a deal?"

"What kind of deal?" she said with a chuckle.

"You don't lie to me. I don't lie to you."

"Baby, I'm not going to burden you with my problems."

"They're not your problems, Mama. They're our problems. When you're messed up, we're messed up. Now tell me what's wrong."

She sat there for a moment, then picked up her coffee cup from the little table and took a sip. "It's really nothing, Magic. I was going to go to the mall and buy myself something this afternoon. Because I got up feeling real shitty. So I got dressed, went outside and my car was gone. I know your father came and took it. So I didn't even bother to call the police."

"Mama, I'll buy you another car."

"That's the other thing, I'm worried about you."

"Don't." Magic kissed her and headed to his room.

"Clear called, he said to call him," she said as Magic walked away.

"Thank you," Magic said.

Magic went into the room. Freestyle was kicking Muscle's ass in NBA 2000. From which Magic derived a great deal of pleasure because Muscle and Cory beat him on a regular basis. They were both perched on the edge of Magic's bed--he ducked and went under the cords.

"Naw, man, naw, that don't count. Magic impaired my vision," Muscle said.

"Impair this. Swish!" Free responded.

Magic heard the buzzer go off indicating that the game was over, so he reached into his closet and pulled out the safe. Muscle and Free watched as he turned the dial, opened it, and pulled out the stacks of hundred dollar bills. He shot one to Muscle and one to Free.

"You're a lieutenant or a Captain?" Muscle said.

Magic smiled, and he said it again. "You're a fucking Captain!"

Magic had never seen Muscle outwardly express that much joy. If Free wasn't there, he probably would've kissed him. Freestyle, on the other hand, just sat there in quiet contemplation, running his hand across the bills as if they were a deck of cards.

Magic leaned against the dresser and looked Muscle in his eyes.

"Look, Muscle, I love you like a brother, man, and I trust you with my life. You said that your uncle was going to make you a Lieutenant. Would you be my second in command?"

"Why you playing, man?" Muscle said, a slight smile on his face.

"I'm dead serious, Muscle."

"Hell, yeah," he said. His broad shoulders filled the platinum FUBU jersey. "I love you too, man. And I got you. I got you, man."

"What is you niggas talking about?" Freestyle asked as he tossed Magic the stack of money. "I don't know if I'm watching a Mafia movie or a chick flick."

Magic heard the telephone ring, but this situation had his undivided attention. He knew how Muscle was going to respond, but Freestyle didn't seem impressed at all, not even by the money.

"Magic. Clear's on the phone," his mother yelled. Magic left the room relieved, because he couldn't figure out which direction to go with Freestyle.

"Hey, Clear."

"You seen Muscle?"

"Yeah. He's here wit' me."

"I need to see him. Can you get him over here? Dayja just took my car."

"Yeah. My man Freestyle drivin', he'll bring us over."

"Your man?" Clear asked.

"Yeah, he cool, real cool."

"Alright," Clear said and hung up the phone.

As Magic approached his bedroom, he heard Muscle and Free talking. He slowed and stopped just outside the door.

"I don't know where he got the money from, probably that fucking Clear," Muscle said.

"That nigga got paper like that. Shit, I wanna be his friend, too," Free said.

That was all Magic needed to hear. He went into the bathroom, pretended to take a leak, flushed the toilet, rinsed his hands and walked back into the room.

He picked up the money off the dresser that he had given to Freestyle, along with another stack.

"Give me my shit, Muscle."

"I thought this was your way of saying I'm sorry," he said with a smile.

"Yeah, right," Magic said.

Muscle reluctantly handed him the cash. Magic put it in the safe and placed it back in the closet.

"So what's going on, man?" Free asked.

"I'll tell you later. Right now I need you to run me and Muscle somewhere."

"Where we going?" Muscle asked.

"Clear wants to see you."

"You didn't tell him what I said did you?"

"Hell, naw."

"Look, man, I ain't into all this riding in the dark shit. But since you my man I'll roll wit' cha'," Freestyle said.

"Well thank you kindly," Magic responded. He picked up a pen and wrote down the combination to the safe twice. He handed one copy to Muscle and they left the room.

Magic stopped in the kitchen where his mother was rattling pots and pans.

"I'll meet yall at the car," Magic said. He handed the other piece of paper to his mother.

"What's this?" she asked.

"It's the combination to the safe in the bedroom closet. There's thirty-five thousand dollars in there," Magic said and walked out.

CHAPTER 39

Let's Get One Thing Straight

They pulled in the alley on the side of the barbershop and parked next to Black's Expedition. Magic looked for Clear's Lex, but didn't see it. Marwon and Daemon both drove Escalades, one white, the other gunmetal gray.

The shades were pulled and the sign said closed. Magic knew Wednesdays were slow, but never slow enough to close the shop. As Magic approached the door, he heard chatter, but as they entered all conversation stopped.

Daemon, Marwon, and Black sat in their barber chairs, hands tucked underneath their long white barber shirts. Something was wrong. Clear sat in a patron's chair to their right. He watched TV, as Black, Marwon and Daemon, watched them.

"What's up, fellas?" Magic said

"What's up, Magic?" Clear said.

Freestyle walked in behind Magic, and Muscle was behind him. Clear clicked the remote as the door closed. The TV screen went blank. Clear got up and walked slowly toward Muscle. Magic eased back, guiding Freestyle with his arm, as his mind traveled backwards attempting to figure out what Muscle had done.

"You got a problem wit' me?" Clear asked as he stepped into Muscle's personal space.

Magic felt Freestyle's slight movement toward his pistol and in an effort to keep a bad situation simply bad, Magic tried to grab his hand. He felt a breeze on the back of his neck, and turned as Muscle collapsed like a deflated blow up doll. Clear bent over and pulled the gun from his waist.

Magic looked up and into the barrels of three pistols pointed at him and Freestyle. Freestyle's gun was pointed at Clear. Strangely, Magic thought, From this day forward I will never leave home without it. He turned to Freestyle and said, "Gimme the gun, man."

"Hell, naw!" he responded.

Magic stepped in front of him; the barrel of Free's gun pressed against his neck. Magic opened his palm and soberly asked, "Gimme the gun, Free."

Free looked around, weighing his odds. Then slowly lowered his pistol and placed it in Magic's hand.

Black, Marwon, and Daemon assumed their original positions. Clear walked over, locked the door and stuck Muscle's pistol in his pants.

Then he turned, walked over to the soda machine, got a bottle of water, opened it, took a drink, and started squirting the water in Muscle's face.

"Get up," Clear said when Muscle eye's fluttered opened. Muscle slowly came to his feet. Clear then turned to Freestyle and Magic. "Have a seat, Magic," he said, looking at Freestyle. They backed into the nearby chairs and Clear went back to his, allowing silence to create the mood and set the stage.

"So you're going to blow my fucking head off," Clear said to Muscle as he stood in the middle of the floor with water and humiliation dripping from his chin. "That would have been a novel idea. But you don't tell that to a person who I've sent a check to every month for three years straight," he continued as he walked over to his barber chair and sat down.

Muscle, crying now, watched him walk across the room.

"You killed my fucking uncle, man. You killed my uncle," Muscle said, tears flowing from his eyes. His chest swelled and his breathing was thick and hard. Clear's response was chilling, even to Magic.

"Yep, I sure did. But I didn't just wake up one morning and decide your uncle had to die, Muscle. He was stepping outside the mirage, fuckin' with the illusion. And when the illusion is gone, we're nothing but lofty street thugs, headed for the penitentiary."

"Who the fuck do you think you are, Clear? God?"

"That depends on what you mean when you say God. If you mean, Good Orderly Direction, yeah I'm that. First and foremost, I'm an entrepreneur with a vision. A vision I've carried like a baby all my fuckin' life. It consumes my every waking thought. It regulates my blood pressure and my pulse. See, if I ever thought that this vision and I couldn't co exist, I would pass the baton and blow my fucking brains out. I'd do likewise to anyone that I felt stood in the way of this vision. Present company included," Clear said. He paused and looked at Marwon, Daemon and Black."

"This wasn't just your vision, Clear," Muscle said. "It was you and my uncle's vision. You didn't have to kill him."

"I didn't kill him," Clear said. He went into his back pocket and pulled out the little black manual. "This is what killed him." He held the book in one hand and poked it with the other. "Your uncle co-signed every rule and regulation in this book into law. Muscle, there is no organization without rules. Absolute compliance to these rules is what keeps our asses immune from prisons and morgues. Your uncle couldn't follow his own fucking rules. Can you? Can you follow rules, Muscle?"

Muscle didn't respond, he just stood there, eyes dry but red. Chest deflated. Breathing normally. Clear didn't advance. No proposition came forward. But Muscle knew. Because Magic knew. The question cloaked the invitation. The invitation he had waited for since he was thirteen. The invitation that forced him out of bed every morning and made him do his homework every night no matter what time he came in. The invitation that made him accept shit that was unacceptable in an effort keep his grades up and his nose clean.

"Yeah, I can follow rules."

"Well here's the first rule you need to learn, never bite the hand that feeds you."

Once again, he turned to look at Marwon, Daemon and Black. "Now I want you to go home and take your aunt her shit back. Then come see me."

Muscle turned to leave and in a deep but sympathetic voice, Free said, "Yo, Muscle."

Muscle stopped, but he didn't turn around.

"You need a ride, man?"

"Naw, I'm straight," Muscle said and continued out the door.

No one said a word as Clear paced from one end of the barbershop to the other, composing himself, gathering his thoughts, obviously questioning his actions. Then all of a sudden he stopped, walked over to Free and extended his hand. Freestyle stood before accepting it.

"Clear."

"Freestyle."

"Pleased to meet you, Freestyle."

"The pleasures all mine, Mr. Clear," Free said.

Clear smiled faintly. Then he turned and introduced Freestyle to Black, Marwon and Daemon. Free walked over and shook all their hands, looking impressed and impressing.

I got him, Magic thought. He walked to the back room to get the mop. He mopped up Clear's footprints and the small puddle of water in front of the door. Clear opened the shades, then took a broom and started sweeping the floor.

"Freestyle. Sounds like a hip-hop tag. Does that mean you can flow?" Black asked.

"Um, nice, man," Free responded, moving his head to an imaginary beat.

"Yeah, yeah, yeah, every little nigga in the ghetto from eight to eighteen a rapper and from eighteen to twenty-five a fucking pimp, and from twenty-five to forty-five a fugitive from child support," Black said.

"And from forty-five to the time their asses are stuffed in a coffin, they're saved, sanctified, full of shit," Daemon said. He went in his pocket and pulled out a stack of money neatly folded with a rubber band around it. "I got about two hundred that says you can't impress me."

"Money on the wood makes the game go good," Free said.

Daemon tossed the money on the floor. Freestyle didn't hesitate. He went straight into performance mode. He rapped about his life. How his brothers got gunned down and his mother worked two jobs. How he was a bastard and the hook was some shit about, 'This is my house, built on stress and strain, heart ache and pain, I'll invite you in, but don't touch a damn thang.'

When he was finished, everyone sat in silence moving their head up and down as a sign of approval. Staying true to his character, Daemon, in a soft sincere voice, sniffling as if he were crying, said, "Damn, man, that shit was therapeutic."

Then, as Freestyle walked over and picked up his money off the floor, everyone started laughing.

Then things got a little strange. They started talking about college and goals and future aspirations. Freestyle sounded like Puff Daddy or Berry Gordy or somebody as he talked about the music business.

"I want to be a studio engineer, but I'm veering toward an entertainment attorney. Artists get shitted on in the music business," he said. Then he started talking about percentages and royalties. Music studios, tracks, mixers, and drum machines. He even had Magic on the edge of his seat talking about 'The Business,' as he called it.

Magic really didn't see this one coming, and he felt like Freestyle and him were being placed side by side and measured.

"What about you, Magic, what you want to do?" Clear asked, sitting in his barbers chair with a score card in his lap.

Magic paused for a moment and placed his hand on his chin.

"I haven't given it a lot of thought. But my favorite subject is people, which would fit narrowly in anthropology or psychology. Secondly, I love money and power. So I think I want to be you."

Maybe that was the wrong answer because Marwon and Black's faces went sour. Clear smiled proudly and a knock on the window stole Magic's moment, because he was going to rap too.

Daemon got up, unlocked the door and Dayja walked in. Magic put on his hard face.

"Would you believe that that hair dresser put someone else in my slot? I walked in and she was doing this multi-colored peacock looking weave shit." Dayja stopped, pulled the rubber that was on her wrist and popped herself. "Ouch," she said and everybody looked at her as if she was crazy.

"Sorry. It's a Porsha thing. She says mature women don't use that type of language. So she went out, bought me a bag of rubber bands, and instructed me to wear one around my wrist every day. Every time I say a bad word, I pop myself. It's working, too. I've only said six bad words all day."

Black, Marwon and Daemon tried hard not to stare at her gorgeous ass that fit so perfectly in the low rider jeans. Freestyle didn't even try to play it off. Dayja sat down beside him never even looking in Magic's direction.

"Okay, yall can continue your conversation now."

"Hi, I'm Freestyle," Free interjected.

"Nice to meet you, Freestyle," Dayja said, smiling.

Magic sat there still and cool like he was sitting on an ice pack.

"We were talking about college Princess Di, I mean Princess Dayja," Marwon said.

"Keep it up, Marwon, I'm gonna have your ass deported," Dayja said.

"Shut up and pop yourself."

"Ass ain't no bad word."

"Ass is a bad word," Magic said.

"You wouldn't know bad if it was standing in your face." Dayja grimaced, and every eye shifted in Magic's direction. He picked up the magazine in the chair next to him and pretended to read.

"I thought so," Dayja said as she sat back in her chair. "And what about college?"

"What you gonna do when you graduate?" Marwon asked.

"I'm going to Spelman for fashion design; full scholarship as long as my GPA is at least a three point five at the end of the year. I got an acceptance letter and didn't even apply."

"You go, girl," Marwon responded with the overhead three snaps and all, sounding like a mentally ill homosexual.

"Don't do that," Dayja said, scowling.

"Don't hate," Marwon responded.

"It's really time for me to go. Bro, I'm after the peacock lady and I'll probably have your car a little longer that I expected to."

"That's cool, just bring your ass straight back as soon as you get out the chair."

"I can do that," Dayja said as she started for the door. "I'll see yall later."

Magic reluctantly took the magazine down from his face, hoping what he was feeling inside wasn't apparent outside, but he could tell by the way Free looked at him that he had failed.

"You sprung, nigga. She got your ass whipped," he whispered. Then in the same breath, he asked, "She got a sister?"

"Naw, you can have her."

"Yeah, right… I got to bounce, man. My mama be trippin if I don't check in after school. You staying here?" he asked.

"Yeah, I need to talk to Clear about somethin'."

"Cool, but come to the car with me for a minute," he said.

Free got up and worked his way around the barbershop doing the manly hug, handshake combination. Clear looked him in his eyes and spoke with sincerity.

"Look, Free, a lot of talent is wasted in the ghetto, let's make sure that don't happen to you."

"It won't, Mr. Clear."

"And let's drop the mister."

"Okay."

Magic followed Free to the door, then Clear said, "You leaving, Magic?"

"Naw, I'll be right back. Can you drop me off?"

"No problem."

Free and Magic stood at the corner and watched the steam rise from the black top. It was summer time in the ghetto, and chromed out cars cruised the city streets just below the speed limit. Riders and Ridees watched gorgeous girls set the side walk ablaze.

The boys that were too young to drive and the girls that were too young to ride, stood in front of the corner store where blunts are fifty-five, and loosies are twenty-five and you can get a twenty-five automatic for a hundred and thirty-five. Where everybody with something is trying to sell it, and everybody with nothing is trying to get it. And little, little kids play kickball, hopscotch and hula-hoop and little bigger kids rush somewhere to meet somebody to do nothin'.

"So what's up, man?" Free asked.

"What you mean, what's up?"

"Come on, man, don't play wit' me."

"To be perfectly honest, I don't know. I thought I knew."

"What you mean?"

"I don't know, man. One minute I'm dealing with a gangsta. The next minute I'm dealing with a motherfucker who cuts kids hair on Sunday for free and questions my academic pursuits and shit."

Free was silent for a minute. Then he sort of slid in his next question.

"Where you get all that money from?"

"Clear gave it to me."

"For what?"

"For nothing."

"Nothing, my ass. Nothing is for nothing these days."

Magic wanted to just start talking. Tell him everything, but that didn't seem wise. He felt that he could trust him and all, but he didn't want to scare him.

"I don't know, man, but yesterday he picked me up at about seven-thirty in the morning when I was on my way to school. He gave me a safe filled with forty thousand dollars, a pistol and a copy of that book he had in his back pocket."

"What's in the book?"

"A bunch of rules about everything."

"Everything like what?"

"I don't know, man, some old drug dealer shit. But... but... I don't know, man,"

"Stop saying you don't know, sounding all retarded and shit."

"I don't fuckin' know!"

"You know, Magic, and when you get ready to tell me you will... I gotta get home."

"Cool," Magic said. They slapped up and Magic headed to his car.

CHAPTER 40

D-Day

At one point during the day, Clear was so messed up he almost cut a lady's eyebrow off. His hands were trembling and something was floating around in his stomach, but of course, not butterflies. He attributed it to fatigue, because he had stayed up half the night listening to music and waiting for Blast to get in from New Jersey. He didn't really feel tired, he felt apprehensive, and that was foreign. He hopped out his seat and placed the magazine in the chair behind him, choosing compliance over defiance.

When Magic walked into the barbershop the stage was set. Everyone was in place.

"Yall can bounce," Clear said. "I'm gonna wait for Dayja to get back with my ride and I'm coming up outta here too."

"Bet," Marwon responded, as him, Black and Daemon prepared to leave.

"Peace," Magic said.

"Peace," they responded in unison.

Clear walked to the door behind them and stood there for a moment. Then he walked over to the corner at the entrance of the alley and yelled, "Yo, Daemon, Marwon, I need to holla at yall a minute." Then he turned and walked back into the barbershop.

Daemon and Marwon followed moments later and stood by the door.

"What's up?" Daemon asked.

"Have a seat," Clear responded. Marwon and Daemon sat down at their stations. Magic stood looking at the pictures of all the fresh cuts that lined the wall. Thinking that maybe he should change his image with a skin-fade and a curly-top.

"What's up, man?" Daemon asked again.

Clear grasped the medallion that hung from his neck.

"What's wrong man?" Daemon asked

"Shh," Clear said, pressing his finger against his lips.

Magic sat down slowly while Daemon watched the door and Clear. Clear rolled the medallion around and around in his hand. His forearm bulged and he could feel the veins pop from his temples. Marwon opened his mouth to say something, but the explosion drowned him out. The windows shook, and the shades nearly came off the hinges. Magic hit the floor. Daemon ducked, his pistol drawn.

Marwon flinched, but never took his eyes off Clear.

"Black..." Marwon said.

Clear looked over at Daemon who was still standing next to the chair with his pistol in his hand. The air was so thick the flies were flying in slow motion, banging their heads up against the windows and door trying get out. Clear let the medallion drop and wiped the sweat from his palms on his pants. Then he looked over at Magic, to do a gut check.

Magic looked back showing no signs of an unfavorable review. Black was one of the faces that looked like him, walked like him, and talked like him. One of the faces staring down the barrel of the gun aiming at his vision.

"You alright, Magic?" Clear asked.

"I'm straight."

Clear looked again at Daemon, then down at the gun. Daemon hurriedly stuck the gun in his pants and covered it up. He cleared his throat and licked his lips.

"So when was yall gonna tell me to start making funeral arrangements?" Clear asked bitterly.

"Come on, man," Marwon said.

"Come on, my ass," Clear responded.

Stillness reigned as utter chaos erupted outside. Magic watched detached as people scurried by on the other side looking for casualties and running for cover. Marwon found cover under Black's dead body.

"Clear, man, Black been talking shit since the day we killed Mack," he said. "We all get pissed off at you and talk shit, but doing something was never an option. I don't mean to question your actions, but are you sure this was the right thing to do?"

"You are questioning my fucking actions, but obviously that has become the norm. So what I need to know is why?"

Why what?", Marwon responded.

"What could ya'll possibly be pissed off at me about?" Clear asked. Marwon looked away. "Come on, let's expose all this bullshit to the light."

"It wasn't just one thing, Clear, Marwon said. "First, it's the millions of dollars that we never see, nor do we see any evidence of. We don't even know where it is. Once every three months we get some papers telling us we have X amount of dollars. We don't know if that shit's real or not."

"What reason have I ever given you not to believe me, Marwon?"

"You've never given me a reason. I'm straight. But Mack was always tossin' salt on your name. He claimed you were fuckin' his baby's Mama. That you iced him out when he went to jail, and when you killed him, like it wasn't nothin', in some peoples eye's that made you suspect."

"I haven't seen his baby's Mama in almost five years. When he went to jail I sent her money to take care of those fuckin' kids. The same thing I would do for your people if you went to jail. Mack was crazy, Marwon, he would've had all our asses locked up."

"He was crazy, Clear, because he was tired of being in your shadow. It's not easy groveling in your shadow, and that little book you're so proud of locks us in."

"I don't believe this shit. I picked you niggas up out the sewer, wiped the shit off, and made you rich. You were straight off the boat, Marwon. Fighting deportation. I paid out my ass to get you a green card. And Daemon, if it wasn't for me, your ass would be wearing lipstick and a cut off T-shirts up in Attica some fuckin' where."

"Clear, that's your version of our story," Marwon said.

"There is no my story, or your story. It's our story, and their story. They have multi-billion dollar businesses. They give billions to research diseases that plague their people. When have you ever heard of a national fuckin' telethon to fund research for sickle cell anemia? They have high schools and junior-high schools that are better equipped than some colleges. We have unemployment, the highest death rate, and we send our future doctors and lawyers to cramped classrooms with no textbooks. You ain't got no fucking story. You're just an insignificant participant in somebody else's story. And you always will be, until you stop thinking like a nigga."

"I'm thinking like a nigga because I want to see some of the money I been saving for twelve years?"

"If I gave you the money, you'd spend it on grimy bitches, platinum chains, and stretch Hummers, because you think like a nigga. Now get the fuck out my face!"

Marwon slid out of the chair and slithered to the door, Daemon right behind.

Clear turned his chair toward the mirror that stretched the full length of the back wall and simply sat there with his eyes closed, and his face expressionless.

Magic wanted to say something or do something, but found no words or deeds within his reach. So he just sat there skimming through a magazine and making mental notes to refer back to later, when he was running shit.

Officers Cox and Campbell walked in, in uniform. Clear got up and they all walked out together.

The merging sounds of police cars, ambulances, and fire trucks had a music all their own. And the generally quiet alley sounded like a major highway with a multi-car pile up.

Magic watched as Clear and the two officers turned the corner and headed down the alley. He watched as the police blocked off the street and people started to gather out front. He watched until his mind started taking him places he didn't want to go and people started asking him questions that he didn't want to answer.

He walked back into the barbershop, closed the blinds, locked the door and walked over to the mirror to see how much he had aged in the last half-hour. He turned away from his reflection, picked up the remote, and started channel surfing. He found his long lost friend Bart Simpson hanging out on channel thirty-one. Bart provided a temporary diversion as he waited.

Clear, Magic and Dayja rode in silence all the way to Muscle's house.

"I'll call you later, man," Magic said.

"Do that," Clear responded.

"See you later, Dayja," Magic said. She ignored him.

Some stuff you just can't keep from your best friend, Magic thought. He opened his mouth and it all came pouring out.

Muscle's only response to Black's demise was, "Maybe both of us can be Captains."

Muscle's aunt was no longer mad at him; she came out on the porch and talked to them for a few minutes before her, Rachel and Rocky got into their new truck. She told Muscle that there was some cold cuts in the fridge, and some money on her dresser if he wanted to go to McDonalds or something.

Muscle and Magic walked over to the Adams Street Recreation Center and played basketball and shot some pool. After the Center closed they walked back to his house and sat on the porch for awhile. Magic caught a cab home about 11:30

and sat down in the living room in his mother's worry chair. Cory was on the couch. He talked a lot of junk, but he wouldn't get in bed if Magic wasn't home. Not even if the light was left on.

CHAPTER 41

DAEMON

Daemon stood leaning against the back of his truck sipping on a Heineken. He knew mind and mood altering chemicals were taboo, according to the Black book. But he had tried everything: sex, working out, a massage. Nothing worked.

It was midnight and he couldn't escape the picture of the smoldering truck, or the visual his mind had created of Black broiling inside. He wished that it hadn't happened like that. He had argued vehemently with Black and Marwon in Clear's defense, because he hadn't forgotten.

Although it was nearly ten years ago, he hadn't forgotten. Every time he looked at Clear, whether he was across the table or across the street, the twenty-five to life sentence he was facing would pop into his head. One of his fondest memories was when he told his public defender that he wasn't copping to shit and he had a real attorney.

He remembered how good it felt when him, Clear, and Attorney Roebuck would show up in court together. He remembered Clear insisting that he wear a suit, and then taking him out to buy one.

Clear was the only person in the world who ever believed in him enough to take a risk, he thought. Turning up the Heineken bottle, he felt humbled by the memories but shaken by reality. The reality that it could have easily been him toasting in his Cadillac Escalade. Or even worse, locked away from the rest of the world for twenty-five years.

His cell phone ringing startled him. He pulled it from his hip.

"Damn, it's Clear," he said. He set the Heineken under the truck behind the tire as if Clear had pulled up.

"Hello."

"What's up D?" Clear said, sounding subdued.

"Ain't nothin' man," Daemon responded, waiting.

Clear didn't say anything so Daemon said, "Clear, I need you to understand, man, that that wasn't my deal."

"That shit is history, Daemon, if I thought it was your deal, you wouldn't be here to tell me it wasn't.

"I'm thinking that maybe I need to revisit some of the shit in this book," Clear said.

"Clear, it ain't that book, man, it's us, you're right. Soon as we get a biscuit above a donut, we forget. We forget how it feels to be starving for some shit you should already have. And that prisons are bursting at the seams because little niggas want what they should already have. We forget, Clear."

"But we can't forget, Daemon. We can't forget," Clear said. "Peace, man."

"Peace," Daemon said.

CHAPTER 42

Marwon

Marwon lived in Corn Hill, where mostly middle class white folks lived. It was once a rustling, bustling, thriving ghetto, but one day they realized that they had a bunch of niggers living in Victorian mansions, in a prime location, just a hop, skip, and a jump away from downtown and the expressway. So, they came in with checkbooks and major development plans. They bought up all the property, moved out all the niggers, constructed streets to separate them from the rest of the niggers and built beautiful town-houses to complement the Victorian mansions.

At first, the only way a black man got inside one was if he was doing a burglary, and a black woman if she was providing maid service. Then someone realized that Benjamin,

Washington, and Jackson's weren't white, they were green. And Marwon had more than his share of them. So many, that they wouldn't even fit in the briefcase with all the platinum and gold jewelry he had never gotten to wear.

He dumped drawers, socks, and T-shirts onto the black silk sheets and carried the Samsonite over to the last of three safes.

"Who the fuck needs clothes? Where I'm going swimming trunks is the only necessity," he said as he raked the contents of the safe into the small carry-on, closed it and tossed it on the bed. He walked over to the walk-in closet, tore through the middle, pushing aside the rack of black and white barber shirts Clear insisted they wear every day. Next was the rack of designer jeans, jerseys and shirts. Some with tags still dangling from the sleeves. And there they were. Shiny and beautiful. Big and small. Nickel plated and blue steel. An arsenal missing only a nuclear warhead. There was even a cannon from the eighteen hundreds that he had purchased off E-Bay that sat in the center of the arrangement.

He walked over and took an M16 off the wall, stroked it and gazed at the barrel as if he was about to perform oral sex on it. Then he turned like Tony Montana, his hero.

"Let me introduce you to my little friend, da,da,da," he said with a smile as he carefully selected the weapons he would take. Then making his way back through the wasted wardrobe, he opened the Samsonite and laid the pistols on top of the undetermined amount of cash, wrapped the automatic rifles in a towel and headed for the door.

Fuck Clear!, he thought as he pulled out of the driveway.

As he passed the county jail, he took his cell phone from his waist and dialed 911.

"911, may I ask who's calling?"

"No, you may not," Marwon answered.

"Sir, I need to know who I'm speaking with."

"No. This is what you need to know. A truck exploded behind a barbershop on Dewey Avenue today. It was a hit. Put out on a guy named Irving Calloway-aka-Black, by a guy name Clarence Kittles, who they also call Clear. He owns the barbershop. He supplies about fifty-five percent of the dope in Buffalo, Syracuse, Binghamton and Albany. The hit was carried out by a guy named Blast, I don't know his real name, but he's outta New Jersey. I got some other shit for you, but that should be enough for you to lock his ass up," Marwon said and hung up.

Just as he turned the corner and got on the expressway, his cell phone rang. It was Clear.

"Hello Mr. President," he answered.

"Hello," Clear repeated.

"How may I be of service to you, Mr. President?"

"Marwon?" Clear asked.

"No. I'm sorry, Mr. President, but Marwon has left the building. You're speaking to the nigga that's about to crush your empire and blur your vision."

"You don't know enough to blur shit or crush shit. I told you nigga, you ain't nothin' but a peon."

"I know enough to put some heat to your ass and to place you outside of the illusion," Marwon said. He kissed the cell phone and dropped it out the window. He hit the gas and the gun metal gray Escalade accelerated. He was trying to put as much space between him and Clear as possible, as quickly as possible. He'd just changed lanes when he heard his name.

"Marwon?"

He looked around frantically.

"Did you forget why I'm head nigga," the voice said.

Marwon continued to look around until he realized the voice was coming from the speakers in the dashboard. "Close your mouth. I meant to tell you a long time ago, that when you get nervous your mouth hangs open"

"Clear?" Marwon said.

"Naw, this ain't Clear. It's Mr. President, and I'm sitting here in the Oval Office about to press the red button and nuke your ass."

Marwon thought about Blast and how efficient he was when it came to blowing up shit and wiring up shit. He hit the brakes and reached for the door.

Old Joe had been driving tractor-trailers for over twenty-five years. He had an unblemished tractor trailer license and he was on his way home. Home to his plump wife and a house full of kids. He had been driving for about twelve hours and just didn't see the truck stopped in the middle of the expressway. He rammed it so hard that his recently emptied cab almost jackknifed. The Escalade exploded and flew over into the next lane only to be plummeted by oncoming traffic.

The morning paper would read, minor injuries, one fatality.

CHAPTER 43

Un-Clear

"Fuck!" Clear said as the monitoring screen went blank. He slammed the remote down on the couch and pounded his fist on the pool table. He paced back and forth from one end of the basement to the other. Evaluating and re-evaluating, assessing and re-assessing. Considering every angle of the worst possible scenario. He picked up a rack of CD's and threw them against the wall. He sat down on the couch to think, then got up off the couch to think. He grasped his head with both hands and shouted, "Why? Why? Fucking why?"

And the answer to the first why pounded on the basement door.

And the answer to the second why came running from upstairs and began shouting his name.

"Clear? Clear? Clear?"

As best he could, he composed himself and headed up the stairs.

"What the fuck is the matter with you?" Porsha shouted.

Dayja stood with tears glistening. "Why what, Bro? Why what?" she asked.

"Why are you banging on the basement door like you ain't got good sense," Clear said. Then he put his arms around both of their shoulders and pulled them to him.

"I'm alright," he said. "I'm alright." Then he went back to the basement.

He laid back on the couch and drifted between past, present and future, looking for answers to questions he never thought he'd ever have to ask.

CHAPTER 44

My Brother and I

The house was empty when Magic got home from school, so he just laid on the couch thinking about what Clear had said about the fucked up tutorial in their ass. He was seventeen and he understood perfectly what he was saying, it was more psychological than physiological.

99.9 percent of the time when he turned on the TV he saw white people. He'd go to the hospital and 99.9 percent of the time he'd see white nurses, white doctors, white administrators, and black janitors and food service workers. When he went to court, he saw predominately white lawyers, white judges and black criminals. When he went to the corner store, he'd see Arabs on the inside and the black faces he'd eventually see on the six o'clock news standing on the outside. If that wasn't enough to fuck up his psyche, he didn't know what was. Except for the fact that the most important building in the United States was called the White House.

"I remember hearing my Uncle Benny say it's gonna take an act of God to straighten niggas out, white folk got us so damn confused it ain't funny. They raped Africa, colonized and enslaved Africans. Brought us over to America, worked the shit out of us for over four hundred years and ain't give us a plugged nickel. Yeah, it's gonna take God to even that score" he would say. But how do we move beyond here? That's the question Magic asked himself as he fought sleep.

Maybe money's the answer, he thought. It was one of the most necessary things in a capitalist society, because how could you live in a capitalist society without capital? But what about all of that other high-fallutin' shit, like morals, ethics, values and unwavering principals, respect and dignity.

His Uncle Benny used to say, "Stand for something or get knocked down by anything, If dat's' what you believe then stand on it, until you start believin' somethin' else. You got to walk with purpose, Magic. With purpose. You can't just walk through life like you ain't got no damn place to go. Find a need and fill it."

If he hadn't been raised by him how would he have turned out? he wondered. Probably just like Misery and Trif, not standing for nothing and getting knocked down by everything. The stuff Uncle Benny taught him you couldn't buy, his thought continued as he drifted off into a KKK nightmare.

His mother and Aunt Abigail came through the door laughing and talking. He was half awake and half asleep. The back of the couch was to the door so he just lay there hoping that they would quiet down or leave. He wanted to get a little rest before Cory came home. He had plans to spend the day with him.

Then he thought he heard pre-sex noises, like lip smacking, heavy breathing and the sound of clothing being tugged on, but not quite torn off. Then he heard his Aunt Abigail say, "I love you," but there was no response, so he kind of figured that there was a man in the house. Then she said, "Let's go to the bedroom."

"No, Cory will be home in a few minutes," his mother responded.

"It'll only take a few minutes," Aunt Abigail said.

His initial response was shock, and soon as the door closed to the bedroom he sat straight up. Then it was funny, then nasty, then weird. He just sat there afraid to move. Then it hit him. His mother was happy. Happier than he had ever seen her before. She was looking good. Her, Aunt Abigail and Cory were always gone or planning to go somewhere. And Aunt Abigail treated Cory better than both fathers put together.

At some point, the whole atmosphere in this house had changed and he hadn't even noticed. That concerned him more than the fact that his mother was engaged in some sort of deviant sexual act with his Aunt. It bothered him that he was so consumed with what was going on with him that he was oblivious to what was going on with the people around him.

He got up, tiptoed out of the house and sat on the front stoop. Before long, Uncle Benny popped into his head again. He wondered if he would have run his mother out of town for sleeping with a woman, even though she was happy and Cory was happy. He tried to remember if he ever heard him say words like faggot or cracker or spic or dike, but he hadn't. He had a real problem with white folks but he never called them crackers and he never let them stand in his way.

He'd call them, them damn white folks, and his tone would let you know that he wasn't pleased. He talked about black people bad, but he was always trying to help, sort of like Clear in his own twisted way.

Cory and a bunch of other little kids got off the bus across the street. He had on the red Polo shirt Aunt Abigail bought, some black jeans and the sneaker Magic had bought him. He looked so handsome pulling his little Scooby-Doo book bag.

He noticed Magic just as he crossed the yellow line and he could see the smile form on his face and his little eyes light up. He had never seen that before. Though he was sure it happened often, he had never seen it, and it did something to him. Something emotional, but it also stirred something mental.

For the first time, it occurred to Magic that something could possibly happen to him. He could get hit by a car right now as he walked across the street. He wasn't looking for cars, just trusting that he was in good hands. Having perfect faith in the judgement of the bus matron, he could eat the wrong thing, or caress the wrong person, become sick and die, or just be at the wrong place at the wrong time. Magic got teary eyed and had a sharp pain in his chest as he fought back the tears.

Cory traipsed up to him in a foot dragging sort of motion, as if his book bag was weighing him down. Magic pulled Cory to him and held him close and tight, and he didn't let him go. He didn't ever want to let him go. He wanted to let him know that he could have perfect faith in him. That he was going to take care of him. But the most powerful thing he could think of to say was I love you. Considering all the things he had gone through and all the possible things that he could go through, I love you just didn't seem like enough.

As they walked up the stairs, Magic carrying Cory's book bag and holding his hand, he thought about his mother, and her mother, his Uncle Benny and his mother and father, Dayja,

Clear and their mother and father, Muscle, Free and Cory and him, and last but not least, the Cat-Food Man. And once again, he found himself redefining love. Because somebody at some time told all of them that they loved them, but what happened to that love because if 'I love you' there is no way you should die because you want a new pair of sneakers, or have to sell your body to keep from living in the slums. And nobody should ever, ever eat cat food for dinner.

CHAPTER 45

In the Perfect World

Cory wanted to play video games, and he was kicking Magic's ass in Smack Down when the doorbell rang. And Magic wasn't moving.

"Get the door, Cory."

"You get the door."

"Get the door, Cory!"

"You gonna cheat?" Cory said.

"I don't even know how to play, how am I gonna cheat, boy?"

"I'll get the door," Magic's mother said as she pranced across the floor in her new pink silk pajamas. "Daaayja," she said a few seconds later.

"Hi, Miss Brown," Dayja said as she walked through the door.

Magic didn't even turn around, he had been trying to talk to her for over a month and got nowhere. So he knew she must have been here to see Cory and his mother. His mother liked Dayja, you could tell by the way she said her name, and she hugged and kissed her every time she saw her. But after what Magic had seen today, he questioned her motives.

"Hi, Dayja, I'm kicking your boyfriend's butt," Cory proudly announced.

"Hi Cory." She walked over, twisted his little head and kissed him on the cheek. She placed her hands on Magic's shoulders and began a gentle massage. Frederick's of Hollywood's Peaches and Cream. She always smells so good, Magic thought as the multi-colored flashing letters appeared on the TV screen: "YOU LOSE." Which confirmed that Magic sucked at video games. He felt fatigued, as if he was the one getting body slammed and pinned on the screen.

"You suck, Bro. Dayja, you wanta play?" Cory asked.

Magic looked up at Dayja, who looked kinda lost.

"Cory, if you beat me like that, I would be crying, and with tears in my eyes, I couldn't see how to drive my new truck."

"Oooohh...you got a new truck, a Cadillac Escalade?" Cory asked. Dayja and Magic laughed. Magic noticed his mother from the corner of his eye as she leaned against the doorframe between the living room and the hall, a smile on her face.

"No, not a Cadillac Escalade, an Explorer."

"An Eddie Bauer?" Cory asked.

"Yes, Cory. An Eddie Bauer."

"How you know so much about trucks, boy?" Magic asked.

"I don't know, I just know stuff. Can I see it?"

"Sure. You wanna go for a ride?"

"Yeah! Can I go, Mama?"

"I don't care," Peggy said.

"Would you like to come, Miss Brown?"

"Thanks, but no Dayja. I don't have a truck fetish like you young people."

"No, she has another fetish," Magic said. And before he could get it all the way out, he wanted to kick himself.

"And what might that be, Magic?" his mother asked. She didn't wait for a response. She turned on her heels and headed to her bedroom. Magic had hurt her feelings, although he was referring to something she didn't even know he knew.

Magic followed her to her bedroom and closed the door behind her. "Mama, I love you, and everything you did to make sure me and Cory would be okay makes me love you more. And if I can be as committed to my children, or my family, as you are to us, I will be one hell of a man." She looked at him as if he had changed colors right before her eyes.

"Magic, don't tell me Dayja's pregnant."

"No, Mama!" Magic said. She exhaled and sat down on the bed.

"What I'm saying, Mama, is…"

"I know what you're saying baby, now that I know what you aren't saying. And I really needed to hear you say it."

"Okay...I think."

"So what other fetish do I have?"

Magic was really hoping she wouldn't ask him that. Especially after he just said you don't lie to me and I don't lie to you. He braced himself and spit it out. "I was home today when you and Aunt Abigail came in. I was lying on the couch. But I don't care who you sleep with, Mama, as long as they're good to you." He could see the tears welling up in her eyes. They hugged and Magic walked out of the room.

Cory had chosen the Rock and Dayja some old guy named Hulk Hogan. But when he saw Magic standing at the edge of the couch he turned off the machine.

"I'll put the smackdown on you later, Dayja," he said. He took the controller out of her hand and nearly pulled her to the door.

Magic walked over to the TV and started taking the Play Station apart as Dayja and Cory watched. It was his turn to play hard, but it didn't last for long.

"I need to talk to you, Magic," she said. She walked over and took his hand. Cory took his other hand and they successfully pulled him out of the house, down the stairs and into the back seat.

The truck was canary yellow, the same color as Porsha's. The license plate read Princess D. Tinted windows, sunroof, plush black leather interior, navigational system, CD player, DVD player with an eight inch screen that slid out of the dash. It was a beautiful truck, not Magic's first choice as a color, but a beautiful truck.

Cory sat up front, and they rode around for a while, then stopped and went into a little ice cream parlor. Cory and Magic had triple scoops. One maple walnut, which was Magic's idea, a bubble gum and a strawberry shortcake, which was Cory's idea. Flavors Magic didn't even know existed. They sat at one of the picnic tables out front.

"Who bought the truck?" Magic asked as Dayja sat down beside him with a cup of frozen yogurt that would have been just enough to make him mad.

"My brother bought it, and Porsha picked it out."

"Yeah, I can tell who picked it out," Magic said.

"You don't like it?"

"Yeah I like it. It's you."

Dayja paused as if she was stuck then looked at him. "Magic, I think something's up with my brother."

"Why you say that?"

"He hasn't been the same since we dropped you off that day."

"What day?"

"You talking about Clear?" Cory asked.

Magic looked over at Cory, remembering the times his mother said to him, 'You always got your nose stuck up in other people's shit.' Echoing the sentiment Magic said, "Cory, didn't I tell you about sticking your nose in other people's business?"

"That's okay," Dayja said. "We'll talk later."

"You ready to go home?" Magic asked Cory.

"No, I can't get in Dayja's new truck with this ice-cream," he said and kept on licking.

"You have to go to school tomorrow, boy."

"So do you," he said as he successfully balanced all three scoops of ice cream, almost managing to cut off any drips before they reached his elbow.

Cory finished his ice cream while Dayja got more napkins. She cleaned him up and they waltzed back to the car hand and hand. The 'so do you' remark kind of rubbed Magic the wrong way, so he was removed from his place of privilege and downgraded to the back seat. Which he didn't too much like, but he didn't too much care.

About two blocks from the ice cream parlor the sugar kicked in and Cory couldn't be quiet.

"Y'all getting married? Because I'm getting married. This girl in my class call me her husband. My teacher say she fas'. Say her mama ain't got no business putting no weave in her hair, and that's why she fas'. But I thank she pretty and she call me her husband. Let's got to Sea Breeze. Mama and Aunt Abigail took me to Sea Breeze, but they wouldn't let me ride on the Jack Rabbit. They said I was too little. But this boy in my class the same size as me said he rode the Jack Rabbit and he the same size as me, almost." Cory didn't stop talking until he drifted off to sleep, but by that time Magic had tuned him out and directed all his attention to Dayja.

The mood was perfect, his little brother was breathing softly in the back seat, and he could just barely hear him over the Best of Baby Face CD spinning in the CD player.

The moonlight seemed to lie on the hood of the canary yellow Ford Explorer. And the words to illustrate how he felt about Dayja eluded him. But the feeling sat somewhere between his heart and his throat, waiting to be defined. But to say he loved her would be an understatement.

"What's wrong with my brother, Magic?" Dayja asked, her face riddled with confusion.

"Whadda you mean?"

"I mean, he, he," she said and sat up in the seat, "he just hasn't been the same."

"Whadda you mean he hasn't been the same?"

She just sat there, and Magic wanted to rush in and reiterate his question, because he hadn't seen Clear for about a week. They had talked on the phone and Magic had stopped by the barbershop a couple of times and it was closed. He said he was just regrouping and assured him that everything was okay.

"Ever since that day I came to the barbershop."

"You always come to the barbershop."

"The day I had his car, and all the cops were in the alley."

"Oh," Magic said.

"He hasn't been the same since that day. He's like five-star fucked up. He sits in the basement for hours just listening to music. Sometimes he walks past me and Porsha in a fog, and it's like he's not there, mentally or physically. Porsha says he's not eating or sleepin'. People stop by and go straight in the basement. I don't even think he's left the house."

"Your brother's fine Dayja. He's just got a lotta shit goin' on right now. The thought of having to make some of the decisions that your brother has to make scares the shit out of me. Just give him some space, baby girl," Magic said as they pulled up to the Canterbury Apartment building.

"Okay, Magic, but I've never seen my brother like this."

"He's fine," Magic said again and leaned over and gave her a kiss.

Magic pulled Cory's chunky butt out of the truck and woke him up so he could walk.

"Oh, and for the record, I don't know where my crazy ass brother is takin' you," she said. "But if you're going... I'm going too."

CHAPTER 46

What's Really Going On 2

Magic didn't hang out with Clear for nearly a month after Black was killed. He saw him when Muscle, Free and him would go by his house to meet Dayja and Kelly. Something was up with him, but every time Magic asked, he would say that he was okay, just regrouping. Magic believed him because at some point he saw all the people that he had been introduced to, either ascending from or descending into, the basement. He saw Marge, Officer Cox, Officer Campbell, Pastor Williams, Reverend Stone, Daemon, Attorney Roebuck. The only person that was missing was Marwon.

Magic, Dayja, Porsha, Kelly, Muscle and Free hung out a lot. Dayja and Free were teaching Magic and Muscle how to drive, until Muscle hit a parked car in Dayja's truck. Clear didn't even get mad, he just said shit happens and went back in the basement with Daemon.

Kelly was leading Muscle and Free on. But Muscle was leading Angie and Sandra on. And Free was leading Monica and Wendy on. And Magic's mother was leading his father on so much that he bought her a brand new Cadillac. It looked just like his, but it was white. The first time he showed up at their house Cory answered the door, and yelled.

"Mama, this woman beater out here."

Magic's mother didn't let him in, they talked in the hall while Cory and Magic stood with ears pressed against the door. He talked about Candy like a dog and his mother kept saying, "You made your bed now sleep in it."

Magic's mother took Cory's Play Station for being disrespectful to his father. But Cory said he didn't mind. He said it was worth it.

Porsha was worse than Dayja. Most of their outings either began or ended at the mall. For some reason every time they went to the mall she would stop in the children's section and look at kids clothes. She would stare at mothers and their small children in silent envy.

One day they were in Sears or J. C. Penney's and she followed this lady and her baby around the store. The lady told security and that was the first time Magic saw Porsha really get ghetto. Later on in the truck, they managed to convince her that she was following the lady. She made them promise not to tell Clear. After that episode, Magic could tell Porsha wanted a baby. She treated him, Muscle, Dayja, and Kelly like they were her children. He wondered if she knew babies were out of the question, according to the Little Black Book.

Some of the stuff in that book dumfounded Magic, initially. He couldn't see the logic behind no wife or children. But now he kind of understood. Fathers were as scarce as virgins in the ghetto. No one had a father, at least no one that he knew. Well…some had fathers, but they were either dead, in jail, cracked out, or simply missing in action like his was for all those years. But when he looked at Muscle, Clear and Dayja, who didn't have a mother or a father, he felt blessed.

CHAPTER 47

D-Day 2

Clarence Kittles' day started at eight. He stood waiting in the kitchen staring out of the window, considering The Promise. He listened as Dayja stirred upstairs in preparation for school. Then he heard her flying down the stairs, and imagined her turning the corner into the dining room.

She saw him standing there. Or at least something or someone who looked like her brother. But this man looked empty, like a hologram. Lifeless... No spark... No fire... No flame... Just there. Even the gigantic smile on his face wasn't real. That wasn't her brother's smile. Those weren't her brother's eyes. Those weren't the eyes that she quietly feared, and defiantly respected. That wasn't the posture of the man who had given her everything. He opened his arms and she longingly walked into his embrace. She moved in so close that she could hear his heartbeat. And she knew that that was her brother's heartbeat. And although the words were vague, the way they vibrated in his chest was like a familiar lullaby.

"I'm gonna tell you something, baby girl, and I need you to bury it deep, because everything you hear after this day will lead you to believe otherwise. I love you, and I will never leave you," he said and pulled away.

He walked slowly up the stairs to his bedroom and sat down next to Porsha. Her eyes fluttered then opened, and almost immediately tears started to flow from them. Clear pressed his finger to her lips, "It's okay, baby. It's okay," he said, then got up and slid open the closet door.

"What are you looking for, Clear?" Porsha asked, lying with her back to him.

"I don't know," Clear responded.

"Get in the shower, Baby, don't I always lay out your clothes?" Porsha said as she flipped the covers back and sat up.

Clear walked into the bathroom and got in the shower. He stood there underneath the almost too hot water and contemplated the knot in his stomach. The knot that replaced the gut wrenching pain. The pain that he had learned to love and depend on. The pain that serenaded him when he crawled out of the dumpsters behind McDonalds. That romanced him in the wee hours of the morning when the crackheads wouldn't stop knocking on the door. That pain he'd married and promised to serve, honor and respect until death did them part. He needed the pain. He needed the pain to legitimize his actions. Without the pain, he was no more than a murdering drug dealer. No better than Pit. No better than Mack. No better than the system that perpetuated the pain. He needed the pain. Not the <u>knot</u>. Because the knot didn't know. The knot wasn't <u>there</u>. The knot wasn't fucking there when the refrigerator was empty and the heat was off and Dayja said, Clear, I'm hungry. He placed his hands over his ears, trying to quiet the knot.

"Where's the fucking pain?" he shouted, "Where's the fucking pain?"

Porsha stuck her head in the bathroom door. "Your clothes are ready," she said.

Clear got out of the shower, dried off, wrapped the towel around himself and walked into the bedroom. Porsha lay across the bed, a bottle of lotion in her hand. The smile on her face didn't match her eyes. Her eyes looked so sad and pain-filled that they almost evoked jealousy. So Clear avoided her eyes.

She beckoned him seductively with her pointer finger, and uninterestedly, he sat down on the bed. She began to lotion him down and every so often kissed his neck and sniffled softly, wiping the tears on the back of her hand. She climbed off the bed, walked out the room and hurriedly went downstairs.

Clear tied his boots, tucked his shirt, and cuffed his sleeves. Then he walked over to his nightstand and pulled out a copy of the Little Black Book, stuck it in his pocket and headed down.

"You want a bagel, or some coffee?" Porsha asked. She reached into the fridge and took out the carton of orange juice.

"Naw, I'm good," Clear said.

"Clear, baby, you look terrible. Are you sick? Please tell me you're sick and you're on your way to the hospital for some medicine."

Clear walked over, put his arms around her and kissed her and kissed her. He kissed her all over her face. Then he looked into her sad, swollen eyes.

"I'm gonna tell you something," he said, "and I need you to bury it deep because everything you hear after this day will lead you to believe otherwise."

"What it is it, baby?" She moaned as she lay her head on his chest.

"I love you, and I will never leave you," he said, pulled away and headed out the door.

The three Acura Legends were parked out front, and when the red Lexus pulled out of the driveway, they fell into formation. And as Clear turned onto Genesee Street, his cell phone rang.

"Good morning."

"Good morning," Officer Cox responded, and took a breath. "Clear, you still have about a month before your indicted and with Marwon dead they really don't have a case. Why don't you think about this for a minute?"

Clear simply hung up.

CHAPTER 48

Regroup

"What's wrong, baby?" Candy asked.

"You won't shut the fuck up, that's the only thing I can see wrong!" Magic Sr. snarled, and hit the gas. He had places to go, people to see and a web to untangle. He knew that there was more to this than met the eye. Cops didn't spend all night kicking in doors, confiscating product and not takin' nobody to jail. All five gates? He could see two out of five, even three out of five. But all five? Hell no, he thought. And when they pulled up in front of the Peek-a-Boo Club, the web started to de-tangle all on its own.

The red Lexus and three Acura Legends were parked across the street, green stickers plastered all over the windows and doors of the Club.

Magic Sr. sat in observation mode. He pulled his pistol from his crotch and held it in his hands down between his legs. He believed that if you don't know what to do, you don't do nothin', so that's what he did... Nothin'.

He heard someone rap on the window, turned, let his window down. "Mr. Warren, Mr. Kittles would like to speak with you," Officer Cox said. "And please leave any weapons in your car."

Magic Sr. slid his pistol underneath the seat, got out and followed Officer Cox across the street. She opened the car door and Magic Sr. leaned over and glanced inside.

"Good morning, Mr. Warren," Clear said.

"What the fuck's good about it?" Magic Sr. said.

"You breathing. Get in."

They rode in silence for a couple of minutes, both men sizing each other up and deliberating with themselves. Clear checked his rearview mirror and a slight smirk appeared on Magic Sr.'s face.

"Entourage still in tow?" he said.

"Always," Clear said.

"So I can assume that somehow all of my spots getting busted last night is connected to this day."

"Make no assumptions. Its only connection is this day."

Magic Sr. snickered and shook his head. "When I grow up I want to be just like you."

"Today's the day you should grow up then."

Clear pulled into the Blood of the Lamb Baptist Church parking lot and parked.

"Come," he said as he got out.

Magic Sr. followed.

Clear stopped as they entered the church and waited for Officer Cox, Officer Campbell and Officer Cortez.

"Take Mr. Warren upstairs, make him comfortable and gimme me about ten minutes," Clear said.

The four of them headed up the stairs as he started down. Clear was sure Pastor Williams had taken care of everything but he felt the need to double check.

The pastor's door was open, but Clear tapped gently on the frame. The pastor's eyes were sad when he looked up from his book. His generally hardy hello was reduced to "Please come in."

"No, Pastor Williams," Clear responded. "I just stopped by to make sure everything was set."

"I've done what you've asked me, if that's your question."

"Is there a problem, Pastor?"

"No, I'm fine, Clear."

"No you're not."

"Yes I am. It has taken countless hours of prayer, but I'm fine," the pastor said. Then he smiled and confessed, "No, I'm not."

Pastor Williams closed the book, leaned back in his chair and closed his eyes for a moment before he spoke. "I'm sixty years old, Clear... And I've been in somebody's church since I was five. Singing in the choir, Jr. Deacon, usher board, you name it... I did it...

Now I look in the face of a man who's far from a law-abiding citizen. The only time he comes to church is to have meetings about criminal activity, and to drop off money like it grows in his backyard... And I look into his eyes... And I see more God in him than I see in my whole congregation. You asked me to do you a favor, and after everything that you've done for me, this church, and this community. I question whether I should have done it or not. My spirit tells me no and convicts me, but that little orphan boy in me that wishes like hell you were around when he was searchin' for a hero says to me, how can you not? That makes me question, me... my stewardship... and even my God."

Clear grunted, and leaned against the doorframe.

"Pastor, I don't know heaven... Don't know your God... Not convinced the two exist... But I know hell... Spent a lotta years there... And if there's some God in me, he must of showed up when I was paroled from hell, because he damn sure wasn't there when I was serving time. I'm trying to get people up out of hell. Because until you're up outta hell, heaven isn't an option if all the rules apply that are in that book," he said as he pointed to the Bible that sat on the desk in front of Pastor Williams.

"That's the piece I think you and your God's missing," Clear wanted to say. There was just so much he wanted to say, though, so much he didn't understand about this God thing, but the discomfort from the knot returned with a vengeance so he bid the pastor farewell and headed down the hall.

Unless his eyes were deceiving him, she was glowing. Not a fluorescent glow, but a slight shimmer of light radiating from her silver hair. It faded slowly as she walked toward him.

"The knot is the essence of God that resides in you. It has always been there submerged in the pain. In your case, the pain of purpose. In the celestial realm we call it the petrifier. It strengthens and prepares one for a purpose. Man's purpose is to serve God. Not the God of the heavens, we serve that God, but the God that resides in man. My message to you is from the Father, the God of old, the God of fires, floods and plagues.

You have served valiantly. What you do by choice... Magic will do by design. Your destiny is fulfilled and the heavens await your arrival." She turned and walked away.

Clear stood there doubtful and mystified. He touched his stomach gently and once again the knot was gone. He sat down at the foot of the stairs to consider who this woman was. This woman who just showed up one day and...and...

Officer Cox's hormones were probably popping like Movie-Time popcorn, and Magic Sr. had a 'cash the check bitch and give the money to me' look on his face. Officer Campbell, who had gotten the panties, but wasn't grown up enough to capture the heart, looked rather amused by the non-verbal, non-contact sex sport between his co-worker and Magic Sr.

Officer Cortez, who had received a check every three months last year for doing absolutely nothing, while Clear and Officer Cox observed his character, sat in pure glee.

The day after Officer Cox gave him the envelope that contained his first three months pay, he came to her office with tears in his eyes, and said, "Nobody could understand the pain that a man goes through when he can't adequately take care of his family. Sometimes the shit makes you wanna run away from home."

Clear walked in and sat down across the table from Officer Cox. She sat at the far end of the table where Mack once sat. Clear wasted no time.

"Mr. Warren, the reason you've been asked here today is because I've become a topic of discussion in the wrong circles. And as a result, the gate keeper needs to change. And after a thorough search, I've found no one worthy to take my place, including yourself. So I gave up on worthy and adopted capable. Now that's where you come in. You are sorely lacking in ability to handle your personal affairs, but this is business and in that regard you have my utmost respect.

I run a multi-million dollar operation. And I run it without deviating from the tried and true. The long-term goal of this organization is more important than any individual sitting here, including myself. I will kill me, so I have no problem killing you, and might I add anything that looks like you. Having said that, I would like to extend to you an opportunity. An opportunity to be me.

Magic Senior didn't see this coming. He knew that Clear had killed two of his lieutenants and Marwon was found a couple of weeks ago sprawled out on the expressway raggedy as a Mango seed.

He'd figured Clear would've offered him a position, which he would promptly refuse, but this was some lotto shit. Maybe a hustler's hallucination. He pinched himself underneath the table and smiled slightly in response to the pain.

"Hell, yeah, I want the job. Do I look like a fool to you?"

"Good," Clear said. As everyone exhaled, he went into his back pocket, pulled out the Little Black Book and threw it on the table. "This is your Bible. It is what governs you in my absence. I suggest you read it, re-read it, and read it again. And if you're ever in doubt, refer back to it. Because ignorance is not a recognizable defense. That book contains the procedures and protocols that will govern your life, and if they fail to govern, you won't have a life. There is no standing eight-count, no three strike rule. You make a mistake, you die. In the eyes of the world, we are law-abiding citizens, and that's by necessity not by choice. We are cloaked by our good deeds and our up-rightness."

Clear stood and said, "Okay, I know all you C- trick people need to get refreshed for your cops and robbers adventure tonight." He walked over to the door. Officers Cox, Campbell, and Cortez got up, nodded slightly in Magic Sr.'s direction, shook Clear's hand and headed out.

Clear closed the door behind them, then took a seat across the table from Magic Sr., in one of the side chairs.

"How you feel?" Clear asked.

"I feel great."

"Good. But I'm a bit uneasy. Because I know the more you got the more you want. The more you want, the more you want and the less likely you are to share. And at some point things become more important to you than people. What you think?"

"I think you're right."

"I'm a fair man, Mr. Warren. I don't believe that my need to be okay is any greater than your need to be okay. At my table everybody eats, and eats well. Because hungry people, like greedy people, are unpredictable. Do you understand that analogy?"

Magic Sr. placed his hands on the table, locked his fingers and licked his lips.

"Mr. Kittles, I'm neither hungry nor greedy. I just wanna' eat... And eat well."

"People like you and I weren't meant to just eat," Clear said.

"And what the fuck do you mean by that?"

"Some eat... Some are eaten... And some feed... Eating isn't a problem for us," Clear said.

Magic Sr. leaned back mulling over what he'd just heard. That was a compliment he concluded. But it didn't feel good. Clear was almost eight years his junior and he struggled with the concept of being the pupil. But he had learned early that life was a puzzle, and you never know who was gonna hand you a piece that fit. He'd also learned during his many years of tutelage that you never bite the hand that's about to feed you.

But there was a difference between a bite and a nibble. So he decided to nibble...

"What about our son?" he asked with a growl.

"He's a feeder, like his daddies," Clear said emphasizing the S. "And for the record, I never intended for our son to see a bag of dope, so selling it is out of the question. I have major plans for your son. But I'm starting to feel like in the big scheme of things, my plans don't mean shit." Clear looked away.

Good fucking answer, Magic Sr. thought. And with that the animosity he held for Clear subsided. Only a tinge of residue was left and that he equated to jealousy. Not jealousy of anything purchasable, or fuckable. It was some other shit. Some shit only found in folktales and fables. That larger than life shit you find in black history books. That Marcus Garvy, Malcolm X, Sojourner Van-Truth shit. Then he remembered a long, long, long time ago, when he had some of that same shit.

"I'm out," Clear said, rising from his chair. "On the corner of Magnolia and Jefferson there's an abandoned building; meet me there at midnight. Until then, go spend some of my money you've collected over the last couple of years. You ain't gonna need it."

Magic Sr. rose and Clear held the door open. They walked down the stairs, out of the church and stood on the stoop in front.

"Can I drop you somewhere?" Clear said.

"Naw, I'm gonna call and have Candy pick me up,"

"Cool," Clear said, and Magic Sr. turned and headed out of the parking lot toward the intersection of Genesee and Bronson Avenue.

"Hi, Magic," she said smiling. "I'm Presumptuous."

"Hi" he said, looking at her sideways, as if to say, "do I know you?" while reaching for his cell phone.

She extended her hand and Magic Sr. stopped in mid-motion and grasped it. Gray matter swirled... Time reversed... Perception shifted... And he remembered.

He remembered leaving the beautiful suburbs and coming to the city to get a haircut and seeing all the dilapidated buildings, raggedy streets, and broken happy people that looked almost like him. He remembered how he felt when he read about the colonization of Africa, Apartheid, and the struggle for civil rights. He remembered seeing Roots and wanting to go outside and beat up all the little white kids in the neighborhood. He remembered the day his daddy called his mama a nigga, and he grabbed the knife out of the kitchen drawer, ran into the living room, shoved his father over the coffee table and screamed, "I would rather be a nigga than a savage who murdered, ravaged and plundered his way into the history books." He'd forgotten the day he put on all black and tried to recruit the other three black kids in his neighborhood for a new Black Panther movement. He'd forgotten meeting Peggy in Fat Pam's basement, when wanting to touch her was secondary, and primary was never letting harm, want or need near her again. He remembered that most of his young life he had that shit that Clear had. That return to the plantation and lead other slaves to freedom shit. But somewhere between then and now things got twisted, and he'd forgotten. The light turned red and he looked around. She was gone. But, That shit was back.

CHAPTER 49

Roll Call

When Miss Hutchins gave Free and Magic passes to the office, Magic panicked. He knew it had to be something him or Muscle had done, so the first thing he did was start interrogating him.

"So whatcha do, man?" he asked Free

"I ain't do nothin'. What you do?" Then they both looked at each other and said, "Muscle."

When they got to the office Muscle was already there. He looked at them and said, "What y'all do?"

They joined him on the bench and sat backtracking. Retracing their activities over the last couple days, trying to figure out what they were doing here. He knew if either of them had done something they would be in a huddle concocting a story to cover their asses.

Although they really didn't have to, there wasn't a faculty member in the entire school that had anything bad to say about them. They had just enough flair to impress the girls and not piss off the teachers. The boys were another story. They concluded that it wouldn't matter if they made a vow of celibacy and passed out pizza and wings in the lunchroom every day, they weren't going to like them. So they stayed close, and with very little persuasion convinced Muscle's aunt, who Magic had started to call Mom, to get them cell phones. They never turned them off, but they kept them on vibrate while we were in school.

They had a few problems with people saying things behind their backs and making comments when they passed in the hall. So, Magic gave Muscle and Free his rendition of Clear's 'who in the fuck is Dayja' speech. "Who in the fuck are they, are their pictures on the front of some foreign currency or is their name on the bag of some new cuisine? Because if you can't spend it, chew it, digest it and shit it out, I don't want to hear nothin' about it. Unless it's gonna turn my B's to A's or do my fuckin' homework."

They had become like brothers, even Siamese twins or maybe Siamese triplets. Magic could be thinking about Muscle or Free and out of the blue they would show up or hit him on the hip. They had started finishing each others sentences and even feeling each others pain.

One Saturday Cory woke Magic up about eight o'clock in the morning. He was fully dressed in his Southwest Colts football uniform. Magic had promised him that if he made the team he would teach him how to throw the football. But not at eight o'clock on a Saturday morning. He said he didn't want to learn anything except how to throw the football really far, because he was going to be the team's quarterback.

He dragged Magic out of bed and they headed over to number seven school. The boy had a better arm than Magic thought. He started throwing the football a lot farther than he expected him to. Magic was running backwards to catch the ball when he tripped over some little boy's action figure and twisted his ankle. That following Monday, Muscle and Free came to school limping, and neither of them could recall doing anything to injure their leg. Same swelling, same leg, same day. Eerie.

When Mr. Morgany stepped out of his office with a big smile on his face, it eased the discomfort Magic was feeling. He ushered them in and said, "Please have a seat." Then he sat across from them and just stared for a long time with a big stupid smile on his face.

He picked up a piece of paper from his desk, stared at it and said, "I don't know how, and I don't know why, but I received a phone call that I didn't believe, so I asked them to send me a fax. This piece of paper says that all three of you knuckleheads have been accepted into Morehouse College, full tuition paid."

Free jumped up and snatched the paper out the principal's hand and began reading it out loud. Muscle and Magic just sat there waiting for him to finish.

"This is the college that Bill Cosby went to, the number one black college in the world. I gotta call my mother," Free said.

Mr. Morgany pushed him the phone. He then turned his attention to Muscle and Magic. Magic smiled at him, not knowing what else to do, because he wasn't goin' to college. He was gonna be the president of the Black Mob. He looked at Muscle and he could tell he was feeling the same thing he was feeling, and thinking the same thing he was thinking.

"Aren't you boys excited?" Mr. Morgany asked.

Neither boy answered. Magic had seen advertisements for the 'National Negro College Fund.' He thought it said, 'A mind is a terrible thing to waste.' So is time, he thought. The purpose for college was to put you in a position to make money, and he had money, and ain't had to do nothin' for it but pay attention.

Free was standing there moving like he had to pee, waiting for his mother to come to the phone.

"Hello, Ma', are you sitting down?" Free asked. "I suggest you sit down, Ma... I just got a full four year scholarship to Morehouse College... Fo' real, Ma, fo' real, Ma. I'm not lying. Here talk to my principal," Free said as he handed Mr. Morgany the phone.

It was very amusing, Magic thought, to watch the generally calm and professional Mr. Morgany turn into this rosy-cheeked ambassador of great good tidings. Free turned and looked over at Muscle and Magic. The smile on his face slowly disappeared and he looked confused. Like when you go to the kitchen to get something then forget why you were in there. Magic looked him straight in his eyes all the while, asking himself why he was so mad. He literally wanted to shake this kid and didn't really know why. Sure, he had his own plans for him. He was going to be his lieutenant, or second lieutenant, or Captain or something. But that wasn't it. Then it hit him, that damn Clear, their conversation after Mack was murdered.

"It has nothing to do with you, but everything to do with your uncanny ability to know what X+Y-D to the third power means. And if you have your way, you'll get your little college degrees, and your corporate executive job, move out to the 'burbs and lobby for more prisons, welfare reform and against affirmative action."

That what it was. He was afraid that Free would forget.

Magic got up and shook Mr. Morgany's hand; Muscle followed suit. Then Magic shook Free's hand and said "Congratulations."

Muscle just walked past him as if he wasn't there, still a mental health day at the mall wasn't out of the question.

Dayja and Free blew up Magic's cell phone, so he ended up putting it on vibrate. Muscle hated not answering his phone. But he stopped after Dayja called him a lying bastard when he told her he didn't know where Magic was. Free called him a couple of times but he called Magic every fifteen minutes for about four hours straight. If Clear wouldn't have told Magic never to turn off his phone he probably would have dropped it in the wishing well.

Muscle bought a couple of CD's, and they had a sale on sneakers; two pair for eighty-nine dollars. So he bought him and Magic a pair, of course he wanted the same kind Magic got, and Magic couldn't talk him out of it. He bought us Taco Bell meal deals and pretzels. They didn't talk about college, Free, Dayja, Clear, the Black Mob or none of that. They just walked around the mall, sparingly talking to each other.

Magic got home about ten o'clock. Cory was asleep on the couch with the play station remote in his hand, and a bag of popcorn stuffed between his legs. Magic was exhausted and just plopped down in his mother's worry chair, which he hadn't seen her use in awhile. After about a half hour of sitting there with this college thing bouncing around in his head like a bad check he decided to go to bed.

Cory had gotten too big to carry so Magic sat down beside him feeling real sentimental. He rubbed his head and whispered his name. "Cory… Cory."

Cory opened his eyes and stretched. "Hi, Magic." He yawned.

"Hey, little bro', let's go to bed."

Cory got up, staggered into their room, pulled the covers back, crawled in his bed and wasted no time falling back to sleep. Magic peeled off his clothes, turned out the light and attempted to do likewise.

He could hear his mother's TV playing in her room as he lay there. He could here Cory's soft shallow breathing. Then all of a sudden it got loud, the committee had assembled in his head. Guilt slammed its gavel. Shame declared court-in-session. And the committee started bringing into question all his action and reactions over the last few years.

"Why aren't you affected by Black's death? Why was the urge to pull the trigger so great when you held the gun to Muscle's head? Why do you want to be just like a man who murders his friends and distributes poison? Why did you kill Cory's Daddy?" Why this, and why that, and why this, and why that, and on, and on, and on.

"You got angels over your bed."

"What?"

"You got angels over your bed," Cory repeated.

Magic looked checked every corner of the room, then got up and turned on the light. He walked over to Cory's bed. His eyes were closed and he appeared to be asleep.

"Cory," Magic said, but he didn't answer. "Cory," Magic said again. Cory moved slightly, adjusting his head on his pillow. Magic smiled, turned off the light and crawled back into bed.

The moonlight shined through the trees and cast an eerie shadow through his window onto the wall where Cory slept. Magic lay there and watched it sway as the night air tossed the leaves. He concluded that if Cory saw anything, that was what he saw.

Magic felt a calm, not a 'everything is going to be okay' calm. It was more like a, 'all this can wait until tomorrow' calm. He stretched and curled up as sleep found him eagerly awaiting its arrival.

Then he heard a voice say, "Come." He opened his eyes and saw the Crazy Lady standing in his bedroom. She extended her hand. Magic opened his mouth to say something, but nothing came out.

"You're not afraid," she said, and he wasn't.

He took her hand, and she pulled him into her bosom, and it was as if someone said, 'we now conclude broadcasting on this station.'

When Magic opened his eyes he knew he was somewhere closer to heaven than earth. And something stood before him. Its shimmering shades of darkness and light constantly changed, like when the moonlight rests on the ocean bed and a gentle breeze shifts the tides. But it was patterned, like a woman. Its eyes were black, transparent and shaped like his. They mirrored the radiance of the sun that sat at its back and the clouds that drifted in the distance. And he was not afraid.

"I am Presumptuous. Matriarch of the vision. Guardian of destinies. Spoken into existence by the word."

She raised her arms, and on the right and left of her rose two rostrums, formed from the air. And up from obscurity with the grace of swans and a power that stirred everything in this domain, soared two winged creatures. Up, and up, and up until they were almost out of view, and like raindrops falling from heaven, they descended, kneeling on the rostrums.

"I am A-dark-us, your dark Angel. Spoken into existence by the word. I guard your steps," one said.

"I am Dark-us, your Angel of light. Spoken into existence by the word. I go before you illuminating your path," the other said.

They were embellished in the most beautiful shade of brown, with long, lustrous black hair that flowed and kissed the air which canvassed their beauty. No tucks. No zippers. No buttons. No flowing garments. Naked. Arrayed only with swords and shields that shined like gold and beckoned the light.

"Close your eyes," Presumptuous said, but he didn't.

"Don't be afraid, Magic," she said.

Magic closed his eyes and saw the place where wild blueberries grew fat, bending branches and kissing the ground. And birds soared from weeping willows to oaks, to pines. And in the distance he saw winged creatures flapping their wings in front of the big oak tree, and he could feel the a cool breeze danced around his neck.

As he approached the tree, their wings rescinded into their backs. And he saw himself sitting beneath the oak tree. And he wept, and she was there. And she wept, and they were there, on his right and his left.

He opened his eyes and she was there with Cory's head resting on her lap, gently stroking his forehead. This time she didn't move her lips, but her words rang in his head like church bells.

"Your spirit was present and dwelled in high places long before your flesh found form. You were chosen and preordained by him who buildeth up, teareth down, and forsaketh no man. Your spirit is one of nobility, and savagery. You will do by design what those who came before you failed to do by desire.

"I am Presumptuous. Spoken into existence by the word. Matriarch of the vision. The vision which bears the signatures of many. Remember my words and forsake them not.

Three pillars have fallen, the foundation has weakened, the house rest on your roots. But you are the true heir. You will journey to the home of the savants and your mind will be honed like the blade of an ax. You will emerge with your hammer and the wisdom bestowed upon you by him who maketh wise them who he chose to be wise. You will tear down the house and rebuild.

You will plant, you will harvest, and all will eat... I bring to you a message from the God of old, 'Feed my sheep and restoreth my flock,' sayeth He."

CHAPTER 50

I See

Magic woke up the next morning, went straight to the phone and called his Uncle Benny. He told him he had met his angel. Benny asked Magic what did she tell him, and reminded him that she told him to come home and raise some men. Magic told him he would call him back as soon as he figured it out.

Mostly everything was clear to him. All of it pertained to Clear and the Black Mob. The pillars were Mack, Marwon, Daemon and Black. Clear was the foundation, and he had obviously cracked. Magic couldn't visualize him crumbling. He sat for a moment and thought about the part about the house resting on his roots. My roots...My roots, he thought. The roots of a tree, roots. A family tree, his family. He gave up on that one and decided to come back to it later. The only other thing that had him confused was--savant. What was a savant? He scurried around the house looking for a dictionary, and of course, he couldn't find one. He hadn't forgot how Muscle and him had dissed Free the day before, but he was the next best thing to a dictionary, so he decided to call him anyway. He went to his room, got his cell phone and hit speed dial.

"Yo, Free," and that's as far as I got.

"Yo, Free, my ass. What's up wit' you and that little fuckin' dwarf? My momma been savin' up money for years for me to go to college. I don't care how much fuckin' money you make, if you ain't smart enough to keep it or do somethin' wit' it, your' ass gonna end up broke. So if yall wanna' kick me to the curb because I wanna' get an education, then be my fuckin' guest."

He hung up and Magic hit speed dial again.

"What the fuck you want, man?"

Magic could hear his mother screaming in the background, "Do you think because you got a cell phone that you can curse in my house?"

"Sorry, Mama. What you want, man?"

"What's a savant?" Magic asked..

"What?"

"A savant, What's a savant?"

"A savant. I don't know. I don't know what it is, that's why I'm goin' to college, smart ass nigga."

He was really pissin' Magic off. And he planned on tellin' him as soon as he looked up this word. "Get that big raggedy ass dictionary out your book bag."

"Wait a minute, man, just wait a minute," Free said. Magic could hear him riffling pages. "And why you ain't call your homeboy, Muscle?"

"Because I called my homeboy, Free," Magic said, trying to defuse him.

"Savant, a person of learning, one with detailed knowledge in some specialized field. Like a professor at college. You know a college...Like Morehouse."

CHAPTER 51

D-Day 3

Clear took Plymouth from Main down to Magnolia, made a left on Magnolia and pulled over on the side of an abandoned building. He turned the car off, pulled Machiavelli from his CD case and pushed it in the CD player. Then he adjusted his seat to a reclining position, leaned back and stared silently at the building. He closed his eyes and began searching for the tomb marked 'Toxic-- Buried Alive--Excavate at Your Own Risk.'

He forged his shovel, broke ground, and began digging into the recesses of his mind. Rummaging through the memories. Then the cell phone rang. He flinched, and waited until the last ring as he brought himself back to the present.

"What's up, D?" Clear answered.

"I don't know, man."

"What you mean you don't know?"

"I just got this feelin', Clear," he said and paused. "I'm not afraid of dyin' man', I'm really not. But the thought of you doin' me fucks me up. You the only nigga that ever believed in me."

Clear felt as if he had sunk to monster status. He really wanted to take off the stainless steel. Just break down and tell Daemon that he was veering toward suicide, and trying to stay as far away from homicide as earthly possible. But he couldn't tell him that. He couldn't tell him that every night for the last six weeks, before he laid down to endure another sleepless night, that he placed a hollow tipped forty-five slug in his old Smith and Wesson, spun the revolver, put it to his temple and pulled the trigger. He couldn't tell him that he missed the shit out of Mack's fat ass, and that it wasn't supposed to end like this. He couldn't tell him that, or maybe he could. Just not today.

"I got two things to say to you, Daemon, feelin's lie--and please don't flip the fuck out on me now."

He just held the phone to his ear wanting a response, but none came, so he hung up.

Magic Sr. pulled up on the side of him and rolled down his window.

"Park," Clear said, looked at his watch and got out of the car.

He walked down the side of the building to see if the cherry tree that was in the yard next door was still there. He remembered the vehement arguments he would have with the neighbors because Brandon wouldn't stay out of their tree.

'The branches are in my yard so it's my tree too,' Brandon would say.

Clear almost tripped over the piece of plywood Daemon had taken off the door. It bothered him that Daemon didn't trust him. He wondered if Daemon was coming. Then he wondered if he'd come if the situation were reversed.

Magic Sr. was standing at the door with his pistol in his hand, not quite on display, but definitely not concealed. Clear pulled the key from his pocket, unlocked the door and walked in with Magic Sr. on his heels.

Little slivers of light shined through the cracks in the door from a room down the hall. Clear didn't need any light; the layout of this building was as familiar to him as Porsha's curves. Magic Sr.'s pistol was now on display, cocked and ready as he followed Clear down the hall, and up the short flight of rickety stairs.

Clear opened the door to the living room of his old apartment. Two lamps sat in the far corners. And a chalk board sat in the middle of the room, almost blocking from sight the two bodies slumped over the chairs positioned against the far wall.

Clear walked over, took the medallion from his neck and put it on the neck of the corpse to his right. A thirty-seven year old black male, approximately Clear's height, weight and complexion. He'd made the wake, the funeral, but had skipped his burial. To his left was a twenty-two year old male, one of the many murdered over the last six weeks, from which Daemon had to choose.

"What the fuck is this, midnight Mass?" Magic Sr. inquired as he scanned the dimly lit room.

"Naw," Clear responded. "These cadavers represent the two ghosts that's gonna be on your ass twenty-four-seven. You can't hide from Casper."

"I thought Casper was a friendly ghost."

"He is, until you cross him," Clear said and looked at his watch.

Magic Sr. lifted his shirt and stuck his pistol back in his pants. Then he sat down in the only unoccupied chair in the room and pushed it against the wall. "Are we waiting for somebody?" he asked.

"Naw. You not officially on the clock until midnight. You got about five minutes. Relax."

Clear walked out of the room into the hall down the corridors of his past. He could hear Dayja screaming, "Clear, we ain't got no toilet paper." He could smell the stench that came from that closet. The stench from the pile of dirty clothes piled so high they'd pushed through the closet door as if they had hands. He could see Dayja playing dress up in the filthy clothes that reeked of unwashed ass. And the memories that were buried inside of harsh realities started to scratch their way to the surface. He dug in with his shovel and they all came pouring out.

It was March 1980, the third of the month. And the calm after a storm had come and found us salvaged. The constant knocking on the windows and doors had ceased. And we were left to fend for ourselves, which was nothing new.

The welfare check had been spent, the food stamps cashed in and sold for half their value. The cupboards were bare and the antique icebox had long expired and found rest in icebox heaven, its carcass left to house the dead and dying rodents who also occupied our two-bedroom flat.

I went to my mother's room to get the WIC checks. She never sold the WIC checks. Somehow she had convinced herself that if she could supply us with a bowl of Trix for breakfast, and at the very least, a hot dog or baloney sandwich for dinner, she had performed her motherly duties. But as of recent she was unable to even do that.

I opened the door to her room. I never worried about waking her. Three days of non-stop partying with her crack-head friends left her comatose for at least twenty-four hours. This was the room of the living dead, a life-sized, live-in coffin where dead dreams, dead hopes, and dead aspirations lay amongst the dingy sheets, dirty clothes and a stench that discouraged entrance.

I opened the top dresser drawer, and wrapped neatly in a soiled face rag was a glass stem, a broken coat hanger, and a Bic lighter. I closed the drawer, and as I turned to look around, my eyes became transfixed on the picture. . . the picture of me that hung on the wall above the nightstand with no drawers. It was my first grade school picture. Blue shirt, black tie, and a smile that revealed two missing teeth, which were worth a whole bunch of money in those days. Yeah, shit was good in those days.

Jiffy cornbread was my favorite, and I could smell it as soon as I disembarked the little yellow school bus, that was said to be for retarded kids. But I knew better, because I was the smartest kid in my class. My mother would say, 'You come from a long line of psychos, schizos, kleptos and assholes, but you're going to be a goddamn genius.'

She would cut me a big chunk of cornbread and I would sit down at the kitchen table and do my homework while she finished dinner. 'Horton Hears a Who,' ' Green Eggs and Ham,' and ' The Little Red Wagon,' are permanent fixtures in my mental archives. She could read, cook dinner, and stroke my ego all at the same time.

On your mark! Get ready! Set! Go! A's on my report card always meant an all out race to Warren's drug store, where I could get anything I wanted from the toy wall, and a pack of Now & Laters. I was always baffled by the fact that my mother could outrun me, even when I had on my new P.F. Flyers. Pizza, popcorn, and Law & Order on Fridays. Amusement parks and Chinese food every other Saturday. Shit was real good then.

After Brandon was born, our mother had to work more hours, but she never complained. Every minute she wasn't fluffing pillows, drawing blood, and passing out medicine at the hospital, she spent with me and Brandon. She would say I was her man, Brandon was her little man, and we were all the man she would ever need.

I turned to leave my mother's coffin, and I noticed an old purse half-hidden by her tattered bedspread. I picked it up and poured the contents on the floor. A pack of unopened Double Mint gum, eyeliner, a razor, and a picture. A picture of 'that bad man,' as Dayja called him. I raised the picture to my face and immediately my heart began to palpitate and my hands started to quiver. I walked over to my mother's dresser, took the lighter from the drawer and set the picture on fire. I watched as it turned to ashes on the hardwood floor. This was like a narcotic to me, but provided only temporary relief from the sadness that resides in the memory of that man.

He came bearing gifts: Flowers, bicycles, tricycles, he even gave horsy back rides. In the beginning, it was like Christmas every day. He would come by and bring us all the latest Star Wars shit, pay the babysitter, and slip us a couple of dollars. Then him and my mom would ride off into the sunset in his candy-apple red Cadillac Brougham.

One day we were sitting at the table eating, and my mother asked the bad man where he was from, and what he did he for a living. He looked at her, laughed and said, 'If a man is paying your bills, and bestowing on you all kinds of lavish gifts, you shouldn't ask a lot of questions. Or he might stop.' Then he slammed his fork down on the table and walked out.

He called himself Pit. And around his neck was a 24-karat gold medallion with diamond lettering that read, Pitbull. He loved that medallion, wore it everywhere; never took it off. It was like that Samson and Delilah hair thing, or the God and Moses' staff thing.

His friends called him Dog Man, and in the end, I understood why. He was as warm and friendly as a well-trained house pet in the beginning. When he saw Brandon and I, he would wag his tail and throw his paws around our shoulders. For my mother he would fetch, play dead and roll over. To her he was like a Seeing Eye Dog.

His disposition said, 'Follow me--I know the way--I will guide you through the darkness.' And she did. Like a blind woman, she followed him straight to the gates of hell, where he paced the floor like a pit-bull on a choke chain. He would have that medallion in one hand and a 9-millimeter in the other, evoking a terror in me that procreated and gave birth to a monster.

He turned our world upside down and left. January 1979 was when he moved out, and I came home from school and found my mother sitting in the middle of the floor smashing ten-milligram Valiums with a hammer. He left her with a crack habit, a felony conviction for drug-trafficking and stripped of her nursing license.

By September 1980 the house had fallen on me. I was thirteen and trying to hold it together. Brandon was eight, and out of control.

On this particular day, Brandon punched the little boy down the street in the mouth and took his bike. He went in the basement, got a can of spray paint, and painted the whole bike, handlebars, tires, chain, and all, candy-apple red.

"Why, Brandon?" I asked.

"Because he had two bikes, and wouldn't let me have one. And I need a bike, too," Brandon said.

Pit stopped by again in 1981 to drop off some semen.

In 1982 Dayja was born.

It was December, 20th 1983. Dayja was small for one, but big enough to grab, rip and spill. Brandon was eleven, and still out of control. On this particular day, he broke into the church and stole all the Christmas presents and distributed them throughout our apartment building.

"Why, Brandon?" I asked.

"Because last year Santa brought me puzzles with pieces missing and a Thundercat with a broken paw," he said.

I just looked at him, thinking back to the time he got kicked out of school for hitting his best friend in the head with a stapler. His friend had called our mother a crack-head. Thinking back to when Dayja was born, and Marge and I went to the hospital and found her in intensive care, shaking like a miniature earthquake had taken up residence in her little frail body. She was going through withdrawals.

With tears in my eyes I pulled my little brother to me and wrapped him in my arms.

"I'm sorry, Clear," he said.

"I'm sorry to Brandon," I said, "but I promise you that one day, I'm gonna put a wall between us and poverty so thick that not even God can penetrate it."

It was June 1987, I was nineteen, and working toward becoming a manager at McDonald's. Making five dollars and seventy-five cents an hour, I bought food, clothes, shoes, barrettes and supplied milk money.

Dayja was four going on forty, and her favorite words were bitch and faggot. Brandon was fourteen, and hadn't smiled in at least a year, but I believed that one day I would get it all together and Brandon's smile would return.

The last thing Brandon said before he left for school that morning was, "Clear, I need some new sneakers, man. My shit busted."

"I need some new sneakers too Brandon, and so does Dayja. Stop being so fucking selfish," I said. "You just got those sneakers a few months ago."

That afternoon Brandon stood in the drugstore on the corner of Rugby and Arnett Blvd. waving a pellet gun demanding sneaker money.

The proprietor of the store pulled out a 45 semi-automatic and splattered the balance of my little brother's young life all over the family size boxes of Tylenol and Advil.

When my mother walked into McDonald's and told me that Brandon had gotten shot and that I needed to come home, to me that day she died. I left her standing there and walked into the manager's office and cried like a baby.

I went home and found out that my little brother was dead and that was the last day I flipped hamburgers or asked, "Would you like fries with that?" I cried until all the good boy inside of me was gone. I cried as I retrieved the hundred and seven dollars that was stuck in the curtain lining in my room. I cried as I walked into the Arab store and bought a .25 semi-auto and a full clip. I cried when I knocked on the door and said to the bad man, it's Clear. I cried when the bad man opened the door and I pulled the trigger and didn't stop pulling until the clip was empty. I cried when I snatched the gold medallion from around his neck. I cried as I ran around the house collecting all the money, all the drugs, from all the stashes that I had helped establish as stashes, when this bad man didn't seem so bad.

I got thirty-one thousand in cash, and six ounces of 90% pure fish-scale cocaine. I hooked up with Big Mack and the smart ass white girl down the hall. We cut the nine ounces with Jupe from the smoke shop and turned them into eighteen. Mack and I super-sized the bags, and within six month we had the neighborhood locked down.

I switched our apartment from a place to come and smoke, to a place to come and buy. And I sold dope day in and day out, stopping only to shit, shave, and bathe. Six months later I bought my little brother a headstone with a pair of Nike Airs chiseled into the black marble. Less than two years after that, I buried my mother on the other side of the graveyard, as far away from Brandon as possible. A blood vessel burst in her head. Cocaine overdose. She wanted it, I gave it to her. Child Protective Services took Dayja. The smart-ass white girl down the hall went off to college to learn about stocks, bonds and Dow Jones reports. While Clear (Little Clarence Kittles existed no more) and Big Mack stacked paper faster than we could count it.

Clear walked back into the room where Magic Sr. sat. He picked up the chalk and drew a big X on the chalkboard. On the top right he wrote, Mt. Zion Baptist Church, top left, Saints and Sinners Baptist Church, Bottom right, New Life Fellowship, Bottom left, Aenon Baptist Church. "It's now twelve A.M. and you are officially on the clock. But someone else is doing your job, and will continue to do your job for the next thirty days. You have thirty days to put four captains and four lieutenants in place. I would suggest your captains be thoroughbreds because they will determine how high you rise or how hard you fall. They will be the only ones with enough information to implicate you in any thing.

"North, East, South and West," he said pointing to the four names of churches at the end of the X. "We don't run'em, in name we don't own'em, but our money flows freely through them, No audits, no taxes.

"Each church has three vans, but not like ours. Our vans are custom made. Seats, ceilings and all side panels come out. A coolant system separate from the air conditioning, runs throughout the whole van, and comes on automatically when you stick the key in the ignition. Every van was constructed to hold three to four hundred kilo's of cocaine, twenty children, four adults and a driver. Twice a year these vans are loaded with kids and they're taken on an all expense paid trip to Florida's Disney World. The number of vans taken on the trip is determined by the amount of dope confiscated by the Florida DEA. When they arrive, the vans are parked in a predetermined location where they're picked up and loaded down"

"On the day that the trip is scheduled to be over, the vans are returned to their original location and everyone is brought back to the church. The vans are then taken to Serenity Hills Funeral Home. We don't run it and we don't own it in name. The vans are parked in the garage with the hearses and coffins. That night the contents of the vans are unloaded, inventoried, divided into boxes and labeled as donations.

"By the following Wednesday, product is ready for distribution. Your lieutenants will place their orders with your Captains. Your Captains will in turn, give their orders to you. For now, you simply need to drop the orders off at the church on the side of town that it is to be delivered to, with an alias and an address. Between the hours of nine a.m. and twelve noon, a UPS truck will deliver the product to them. For which he or she will sign. You will never touch a bag of dope, neither will your captains"

Clear paused when he heard the door downstairs open. Magic Sr. adjusted his chair and put his hand on his pistol. Whoever it is sounds like they weigh about five hundred pounds and can barely make it up the stairs, Clear thought, as he glanced at his watch.

Daemon walked through the door carrying two five gallon gas cans. Clear couldn't remember the last time he was so happy to see anybody. Especially when they were late.

Daemon dropped the gas cans on the floor. "Sorry I'm late," he said, wiping his hands on his pants. "Where we at?" he asked. Clear smiled. Daemon smiled. Magic Sr. watched.

"Why must we remain cloaked, Daemon?"

"Why must we remain cloaked?" Daemon repeated as he joined Clear in the middle of the room.

"Because we distribute a chemical that gives miserable broke motherfuckers a euphoric feeling of happiness and well being. This chemical was traded and consumed as early as 1500 BC. Before the period of grace was ushered in we were sucking on coca leaves. But unfortunately it's illegal, and until the federal government is able to box it, bag it, can it, track it, and tax it, it will be illegal. And they're putting motherfuckers in jail forever for selling it. So we do nothing to draw attention to ourselves."

"Very good. What's the General's responsibility?" Clear asked.

"Your responsibility, Mr. Magic, is to keep your captains in check, collect money and make sure it gets to its proper destination."

"What's his Captain's responsibility?" Clear asked, really having fun with this.

"To collect money and keep his lieutenants happy, and the lieutenants responsibility is to keep foot soldiers happy, and the foot soldiers responsibility is to keep customers happy and coming back. It's all in the book," Daemon said regurgitating the things he had heard Clear say at least a thousand times over the last eight years. "And I suggest you read it, re-read it, and read it again. Because in this army ignorance isn't a recognizable defense."

It took everything inside of Clear to stay composed. Things were happening inside of him, some happy, bubbly shit. Stuff that he hadn't felt since the races to Warren's Drug store and the big chunks of Jiffy corn bread. He didn't want to be Clear anymore, he wanted to be little Clarence Kittles, A plus student.

"Any questions?", Clear asked, looking for signs of confusion or doubt.

Magic Sr. shook his head slowly. "No," he said.

"Okay, then you're free to leave, and I'll be in touch."

As Magic Sr. rose from his chair, Clear added, "Spend some time with your son, soon he'll be away at college," and Magic Sr. turned to leave.

Clear sat down in the chair, leaned back and closed his eyes. Daemon stood at the chalkboard and just watched him for a second, then he walked over to one of the dead bodies and started taking off his jewelry and placing it on the corpse. When he turned around, Clear was staring at him with his pistol in his hand. Daemon just stood there, in the spotlight of the two lamps. Clear stood and walked in his direction and Daemon closed his eyes as Clear's hand left his side.

"I miss Mack's fat ass," Clear said as he bent over to stick his pistol in the corpse's crotch.

Daemon opened his eyes and exhaled loudly. Clear looked at him and laughed. "Let's burn this bitch down and go fishin'," he said.

Then he walked over and picked up one of the five gallon cans of gasoline, and headed down the hall.

THE END

Madd Bricks • Raw Chicks & Charges That Won't Stick!

TEFLON

A LINCOLN LEE Novel

TEFLON

A LINCOLN LEE Novel

SNEAK PREVIEW!

CHAPTER 1

ENDING OF '96

THE GIFT AND THE CURSE

The closing of the county bars was all very real to Cleofis Jackson, having been to prison already at age seventeen. He quickly adapted to the county jail rules. April secretly ratted him out to collect on a thousand dollar reward. Sergeant Fox couldn't wait to pull the van over that chauffeured him in the back under tinted windows. The top floor of the county jail is where he was stationed, where they kept some of Kankakee's worse criminals. Cleofis was in the north east cell block where there were ten cells, five on one side, and the same on the other. You had to walk in a circle to view all ten cells. Cleofis was housed in the fourth cell with a cellmate named Bootleg that he woke up to every morning. The fifth cell was the last cell before turning the corner to go to the other side, which had cells six, seven, eight, nine, and ten.

More than anything he stayed on the phone in the day room trying to get his fifty thousand dollar bond lowered by his lawyer Mark Galante. The normal bond for a person being charged with attempted murder was twenty-five thousand. But because Detective Diamond and other law enforcement spoke with the State Attorney, they went for the highest bond possible.

A lot of inmates thought Cleofis still had money, and figured if he didn't bond himself out, then Bruno, his ballin' ass cousin, would come to the rescue. But they were sadly mistaken, and Cleofis drowned himself in shame, not able to bond out for what some felt was nothing to him. Very few expected his stay in the county jail to be long and in a strange way, considering how much money he once possessed, Cleofis felt some way some how he would bond out before coming to the actual terms of exile.

Ninety-seven rolled around, and it was kind of chilly waking up in the morning "BREAKFAST", the trustees yelled, "Naw I'm straight", Cleofis replied. Splashing some water on his sleepy face, he recognized his cellmate was still asleep. Looking in the tainted small mirror the inmate noticed a change, "Shit this filthy ass county breaking my face out." His face looked nasty, and it was spreading rapidly! Taking off his white tank top he searched his upper body to make sure it was just on his face. "What's wrong with you?", asked his cellmate. "Man this damn county breaking my face out." He responded, jumping on the top bed of the bolted in the wall bunk. "I need me a request slip." He bent between his swinging legs and said.

Bootleg looked up at him from the bottom bunk with his eyes half way opened. "It ain't like they gonna do shit, you gonna have to see the nurse."

Bootleg was fighting a secret indictment. He was a chocolate complexioned, cocky fella with braids. He enjoyed being housed next to the widely spoke about Cleofis Jackson. "Man if I find a way to break out this bitch, they'll have to kill me to get me back", Cleofis said, tired of the living conditions. "Well if you find a way out let me know 'cause I'm coming with cha", replied Bootleg.

Bo Pete was out in the world running his big mouth, smoking crack and telling the triple murder story that involved Cleofis, to anybody who would listen. "I was there, CJ killed all three of them boys, and da nigga woulda killed me if I wouldn't of jumped out of the window", Bo Pete continued, "I'm telling you, that boy is a cold blooded killa, with silencers and all. That's why nobody heard anything...I'm for real. The nigga had silencers, no bullshit!"

The story started in a crack house and in no time it was all over the city. Disco couldn't control his tongue, neither. "I'm telling you Cliff, CJ is a killer. The nigga killed Toby, Muddy, and them niggas in that townhouse."

"I thought Marvin killed Muddy", Cliff said naively. "Naw stupid, I just told you, I don't know how he got outta it, but CJ smothered dude and set his body on fire. Toasted the nigga, motherfucka looked like a skeleton", Disco exaggerated a little.

"I know Cleofis Jackson killed my boy", the mother of the little white boy Toby cried. "Everybody knows it! Why isn't he being charged with my son's murder?" Detective Diamond tried to calm the lady. "We have no proof, ma'am, but were working on it, just give us some time."

Every actual murder Cleofis did, that was uncertain to people, eventually became certain to them. Bo Pete spoke about him as if he was some myth. Hustlers spoke about him as if he was Robert Di Nero off the movie 'Heat'. Gangsters talked about him like he was one of them. Women pictured him as a gangstafied Tupac figure or something. The newspapers described him as notorious, after Marvin yelled, "Cleofis Jackson did this shit, not me", in court, while he was on the stand. Citizens thought of him as a monster, and vengeful family members of the victims prayed for his death or life imprisonment. His absence gained him street credibility beyond his childhood dreams. "If CJ was out, this...., if CJ was out, that...", was some of the things his followers would say to eager listeners. Plenty of niggaz talked shit though, but the majority who talked shit feared him in physical form. His presence was felt, even though his body was locked inside a cell.

In Chicago, he would be just another gun-slinger, but in Kankakee to get away with that many murders without being charged was genius, especially considering the fact that murder was hard to get away with in the small city.

Majority of all the murders from the early nineties was brought to justice by a right hand man who caught a case and chose to rat on his homie, or simply from killers having big mouths. It was a few silent killers that dwelled in the night, but for the most part the late nineties was full of big mouths, bragging about murders they didn't do or see. Once you was suspected or charged with a murder the gossipers would implicate you in other murders. The stories about Cleofis was so added and subtracted, by the time it would reach a different set of people, it was a totally different story than the first. Kankakee was full of gossiping, miserable people that would lie about a cup of coffee just to hold conversation.

"Mail", she yelled, handing out mail to the first cell. Cleofis jumped anxiously off the top bunk, squeezing the steel bars impatiently, I better have some mail, he said to himself before seeing her. "Jackson", she yelled when approaching his cell. And there she was, Natalie Knowles, and for a second, Cleofis' heart skipped a beat. The encounter was brief, but it was breath-taking. *Damn she bad!*, He said to himself after making the eye contact.

Natalie reached out to hand him his mail, "Quite a bit of mail you got there Mr. Jackson."

Delighted by her comment and appearance, Cleofis replied, "Thank you, and how do you do today? You look a little tired to be new, 'cause I haven't seen you before."

Natalie checked on cell five and remembered that Cleofis' money order receipt was in her shirt pocket. "Here you are Mr. Jackson, I almost forgot", she said, handing him his receipt. "I never worked this floor before that's why you never seen me before."

"Well you need to work it more often", Bootleg yelled as Natalie walked off and over to cells six, through ten to finish handing out the mail.

Natalie was 5'4" with caramel skin, honey brown eyes, full luscious lips, and plenty of cleavage. She didn't have big hips, but she did have a very large bottom that stuck out as if it was swollen. No garments could hide it! Besides the small gap between her top front teeth, she had crazy sex appeal. She had long black hair that reached the middle of her back, even when she wore it in a ponytail. Her ears almost looked like elf ears, how pointy they were at the top, but Natalie was still a very attractive woman with a round baby face. Her thin textured hair she'd been growing since birth was a fairly decent strain, which she usually kept professionally done.

"That bitch raw ain't she?", Bootleg replied, star-struck. "She decent", Cleofis merely expressed, not wanting his cellmate to know he was head over heels, and didn't even know her name yet. "Who wrote you?", Bootleg asked, trying to be nosey. Cleofis sat on a stool, built into the wall along with a desk, "None of ya business, chump", he replied jokingly, "Jus' moms and a couple of folks."

Looking at the fifty dollar money order receipt, Cleofis smiled thankfully. *"Gabe always lookin' out for me, man that's my nigga"*, he said proudly to himself, opening a letter from Shawndra Coleman.

Hey little Bro,

This is your big sis Shawndra. I was just thinking about you, I've been trying to come see you but this job has had me working crazy hours. My little girl still asks about you, saying "Where Cleo at momma?", I tell her you're at school. It's amazing how she still remembers you. I hope they lower your bond soon, so that you can get out,' cause I miss your little bad ass. Call me as soon as you can. Take care of yourself and I'll keep you in my prayers.

From your big sis Shawndra

Cleofis set his mothers letter to the side, for an unknown letter caught his attention. It had no name, no address, and no city state or zip code. *Who could it be?*, he thought. Opening the small folded letter, he was instantly curious because it was an anonymous sender. But he didn't recognize the hand writing, so his first thought was it was an old fling or female he probably was involved with in the past, so he started to read.

How are you doing Cleofis Jackson?

Preview

I don't think you know me, but I know you. You're the one that killed my little brother. I've dedicated my life to tracking you down, and I hope so bad they set you free. No need to know my name now. Just pray you never meet me, 'cause I will never grow to accept your presence on this earth. You a dead motherfucker, and you don't even know it yet.

Bootleg could see the displeasure in Cleofis' face. "You straight 'Moe'?", he asked concerned as Cleofis balled the letter up into a compressed paper wad, and threw it in the toilet aggressively. "Who was that?" Bootleg asked.

Cleofis jumped distraughtly on the top bunk, laid on his bed and replied, "Nobody."

When the inmates on his cell block went to the day room, Cleofis stayed in his cell in deep thought about what victim's brother that letter came from. Staring at the graffiti covered ceiling, it dawned on him. "CHOPPER! Travis' older brother, I bet that's who it is", he spoke out loud to himself while he tried to picture the man's face.

"Jackson you have a visit", a white guard yelled. He was so into thought, he didn't hear the big key they used to open the northeast door. "I bet you that's Kim", was his thoughts as the cell door rolled back. "Let's go Jackson", the white guard yelled again.

The visit was in a first floor room, with thick glass in between the visitor and inmate. Communication was by phone, sight and sign language, if hearing impaired.

Kim was already sitting waiting when Cleofis arrived, as a streak of joy came to his face, when seeing the woman he loved. Wanting so bad to know why Kim hadn't written him, Cleofis took a seat in the hard chair and grabbed the phone that strongly resembled a pay phone.

"I hope you got a good explanation young lady", he said sarcastically, "You haven't written me and you haven't been to see me in a while. What some nigga got ya time or something?" Cleofis was becoming frustrated with her complete silence, and her lack to look him directly in the eyes. "What the fuck is wrong with you?" he yelled.

Kim stood erect and Cleofis knew what it was before she could get it out, "I'm pregnant can't you tell?"

He sat with a confused look on his face before asking, "By who?"

Kim glanced totally in a different direction, "Gillmen", she spoke in a low nervous tone. "I'm sorry CJ..... I still love you no matter what."

His heart felt like it was ripped out of his chest, the phone slid slowly through his fingers, as a force field of sickness rattled his body making him feel very weak. Gathering strength, his mouth could barely muster the words, "Get outta here", he began in a hollow whisper, "I betta not ever see yo' face again, you filthy disgusting bitch. I hate you!" The last words came out hoarse for the thought of betrayal took his breath away. *'Out of all the niggaz in the world, she had to sleep with my enemy,'* he thought hurtfully banging the phone on the thick glass, as Kim walked out of the visiting room in tears. Cleofis sat their for a minute visualizing Gillmen on top of Kim and how happy he must of felt impregnating the young woman that he loved.

The guards physically escorted him from the visiting room, trying not to have a conflict with the infuriated young man. Cleofis went to his cell and threw a tantrum, throwing all of his cosmetics all over the place.

Bootleg was in the day room with the other inmates, wondering why Cleofis didn't come out of his cell.

"Ay 'Moe' you coming out today?"

Cleofis corrected his sobbing voice into a stern reply, "Leave me the fuck alone!" he yelled in response.

The broken heart brought many sleepless nights and many refused meals. The thought of Kim made him sick to his stomach, and resulted in him losing weight.

Finally, after weeks of staying in his cell twenty four hours a day, by choice the sick villain was recuperating. He grinned and laughed like an old hoodlum when receiving news of Bruno's widely discussed murder. Cleofis knew that Chicagoans got word back to

Preview

the powerful figure that they tore off in Maywood, because of the dice game incident, along with Bruno not bonding him out and for sleeping with Kim. Cleofis vowed to disclose Bruno's role in the tremendous come up. The hit men practically turned Bruno's five hundred Benz around with choppers, leaving Bruno's body riddled with heavy artillery. You could barely identify him because pieces of his face were missing. Kankakee's king pin was dead, and the funeral brought in tons of women from many different states and dealers, who wanted a last look at the street legend.

Inmates thought the news would send Cleofis back into depression. They all were naïve to the fact Cleofis was the cause of the murder, and that he could barely control his smile around them. After reading an influential book on John Gotti, the villain decided to call himself Teflon, The Untouchable. And the name stuck to him in no time, the whole cell block referred to him as Teflon, But Cleofis was still a number one fan of Al Capone. He mentally noted that he was going to call his crew the Capone gang, when touching down.

Cleofis was now fully understanding his power to control, and became a master at manipulation. He used to do it unconsciously, but now he was fully aware of what people expected out of him -- leadership, money and to feel protected. And he wanted something in exchange, the assistance to murder anyone who stood in the way of him getting money.

The mafia bosses he read about all had a similar past to his own, and Cleofis came to the conclusion that, that's what he was, a boss.

"What's up lil bro? I tried to call you earlier, but nobody answered the phone."

"Who the hell is, Teflon", Gabe asked in a joking tone, "I started not to accept the call, till I recognized your voice."

"That's what niggaz call me now, but when you write me, don't use that name 'cause them people try to read every square inch of my mail. And I don't want them having that alias before I get out. But anyways lil bro I was calling to tell you thanks for the cheese. It was right on time and them bitch ass niggaz out there gonna make me fuck them up if they don't start matching what you bring down here."

Gabe listened carefully, to his friend that some people was

starting to forget about, "Man I don't mean to cut you off, but I seen this fine bitch the other day with that thick bitch you used to creep with, Makeela."

"Oh, and thanks for reminding me, the fine bitch you talking about is Kiara, and she told Makeela she wanted to holla at you."

"Stop lying nigga", replied Gabe not believing his friend, "You serious, straight up."

"Would I lie to you? I talked to Makeela last night, and she said the bitch asked about you."

"Man that bitch, bad she look like a fuckin' model."

"I know lil bro", Cleofis spoke through a slight giggle, " And I think she a virgin, so don't mess this up, 'cause I tried to get her but she wouldn't go, and she went back and told Makeela like that's my woman or something."

Gabe broke off into a humorous laugh, "How do I get up with the chick? Where she stay?"

"Don't worry I'll have that all hooked up by tomorrow, thanks to you big bro Teflon, 'The Untouchable'."

Gabe and Shawndra started coming to visit him together and Gabe was getting close to Kiara in a way Cleofis could only dream about. Kiara most definitely looked like a model, it's like she just hoped out of a magazine or TV. She was a tall beautiful light skinned girl with Chinese eyes and long hair. Gabe was appreciative for Cleofis putting in a very good word with Kiara, and when visiting him with Shawndra, Cleofis could see his friend was full of joy and happiness.

"I heard about that guy Bruno, somebody said that was your cousin", Natalie said, observing Cleofis as he was reading a book in the library."

"Yeah, that was my cousin", he replied with a straight face, "Did you know him or something?" he lowered the book from his squinting eyes.

"I've seen him around, when I was younger, but I didn't know he was this big time drug dealer that everybody's talking about."

Preview

Cleofis stood up, and walked to the bars that locked him in the library, "Tell me something. Why are you working here? You seem too intelligent for this job." Natalie gave a bashful look, "'Cause the extra money really helps, and work takes my mind off of other things."

"Is that right, Ms. Knowles?"

"That's right, and how come you don't ever smile? To be so young, I never seen you laugh since I've been working this floor."

Cleofis put up the best happy smile he could produce showing all thirty two teeth. But his smile could not hide his heavy heart, and Natalie could tell he was stressed.

"See I knew you could smile", she continued, "I came up here to see if you were ready to go back to your cell block?"

"Do I have a choice?"

"I'll let you stay out a little bit longer."

"I appreciate it pretty lady", the eye contact between the two sent chills down his spine, and Cleofis went off the Scarface theory, "The eyes never lie, chico." Cleofis almost forgot about Natalie in his time of heartache, but now was open to a mutual encounter of flirting with the eyes.

"Look at her", he said to himself in a low tone, "She know she wants a thug in her life." She looked just a little too long, and that's all Cleofis needed to build off of.

Time plus pleasure has granted me this golden opportunity to correspond with a lovely lady such as yourself, I couldn't help it I had to write you regardless of a response or not. The flirting going on between us is obvious, and a nigga want to know, how can he get the time of day? I know you probably get a lot of attention from guys but I'm definitely a unique one. I didn't see a ring on your finger, so I would assume you don't belong to a man. I'm about to shake it out of here soon, and it would be nice to have your friendship out in the world.

Cleofis was waiting on a response from this letter he wrote Natalie, but never got it. He didn't let it bother him though because his trial was coming up, and he was trying so hard to get in touch with Gillmen over the phone. "You got his number?"

"Yeah I got it", Shawndra answered.

"Well, click over and call him on three way."

Gillmen's cell phone rang until the last ring finally he answered.

"What it is man?"

"This Cleofis homie, my trial is about to start and I was wondering what you was going to say."

"What'chu mean, what I'm gonna say? You shot me, you bitch ass nigga. I'll be in court before the scheduled time." Gillmen hung up the phone after the statement.

"Hang the phone up Shawndra, that nigga hung up on me." Shawndra clicked Gillmen's line off. "Damn he wild, I thought he was a street nigga, how he just gonna come to court on you like that?"

"'Cause they stool pigeons, what'choo expect, but fuck it. I'mma still take it to trial, 'cause everybody else say it wasn't me, and that rat ass nigga know he was coming to kill me."

It took an all white jury no time to find Cleofis Jackson guilty of attempt murder. Gillmen came to court, and gave a partially false statement of what happened. Cleofis went to his cell and contemplated all night on hanging himself. And the double digits the judge was going to give him were hard to swallow. More sleepless nights came, but this time not from Kim's heartache. He didn't feel like Teflon the untouchable anymore, and the verdict seemed to take the fight out of him.

Until a wise old inmate took a look at his case, and enlightened him to a lot of errors. The old man gave Cleofis life again, when he felt like it was over. He immediately went to work, reading anything in the law library, that had something to do with his case and situation. Cleofis started showing the old man more errors that were made. The old man advised him to set a meeting with Mark Galante as soon as possible. Mark was stunned by the intelligence of the young man for recognizing things that he didn't. He presented the errors to the judge on the sentencing date.

Preview

HUSTLIN' BACKWARDS

By Mike Sanders

SNEAK PREVIEW

Prologue

San Juan, Puerto Rico

Surrounded by darkness, I glance over at the nightstand beside the bed and notice 3:26 AM is illuminated on the digital clock. Lying on my back, I sigh aloud as I fold my hands beneath my head and stare towards the ceiling. *Damn, how did I end up here, like this?* I think to myself as I feel someone stir beside me and place a warm, feminine hand on my chest.

"Capone, what's wrong? Are you okay?", Consuela's sleep-filled voice breaks the silence of the night.

"Yeah, I'm cool. I'm just thinking. Go back to sleep"

"You seem worried", she says, in a deep, Spanish accent.

I ignore her comments and within minutes I hear the sound of her steady breathing which confirms she's asleep. As I ease from beneath the comforter, slipping out of bed making sure not to wake her, I tiptoe across the plush carpet to the restroom and quietly close the door behind me. Once inside, I search for the light switch, squinting once the room is filled with light. When my eyes finally adjust to the brightness, I make my way to the large mirror and stare at my reflection as if I'm seeing a stranger.

Preview

"Damn Dog, you fallin' off!", I comment to the person staring back at me in the mirror.

I see a 5'10, 170-pound light brown skinned complexioned brother with a tight Caesar-style tapered cut. Observing obvious changes in my appearance, I pat my short, Caesar Afro and wonder how long my dreads would be if I hadn't cut them a year ago. I surveyed my arms where the *'704'* and *'Queen City Hustler'* tattoos once resided and realize how glad I am to be rid of them along with the *'Fuck The World'* which was tattooed across my stomach. Taking a deep breath, I begin to reminisce about the days when I use to don the Presidential Rolex, Coogi gear and Gators before hoppin' in my Range or Benz, so I could floss the streets of Charlotte.

Charlotte, North Carolina, is the 'Queen City' to many, but in reality it's a city for a King. And that king was ME!!

Well, that was exactly one year and ten pounds ago. It's still hard to believe that a chain that was so tight could all come apart with the weakening of just one link. Never in a million years would I have thought I would be here, in Puerto Rico living the life of a fugitive!

At twenty-six years old, my life is just beginning. And here I am, on the run from the Feds!

As I continue to stare into the mirror, I ask myself, "How did it all go so wrong?"

Chapter One - Da' Early Years

Charlotte, NC

At the Little Rock Apartments, a group of dark-brown brick, three-story buildings that doubled as living quarters for the not-so-fortunate, is where it all began for me. Little Rock was just one of many neighborhoods located on the west side of Charlotte that was labeled ghetto. If you weren't from my projects, or affiliated with someone there, you couldn't come there. Everyone knew each other and looked out for one another to the extreme. Growing up, if I did something I wasn't supposed to do, it was open season for an ass whuppin' from not only my mother, but also anybody's mother in the neighborhood that caught me slippin'. As with any other projects or hood, the day just didn't go right unless we heard sirens or saw some drama going down. The babies were having babies at a rate so phenomenal that Social Services couldn't even keep up with them. Every first of the month was like a small Christmas Celebration because ninety-five percent of the people in my hood were on welfare. The five percent that weren't on welfare just didn't care! *'Live for today, we will worry about tomorrow when it arrives'* was the ghetto anthem we lived by. Life was fairly simple and we did what we had to do to make the ends meet, regardless of the consequences.

My mother, older brother and I lived in a two-bedroom hotbox, the size of a sardine can. The heat barely worked in the winter and there was no air conditioner for the summer. Our fans only blew hot air, so my mom used to put them in the windows backwards so they could suck all of the hot air out of the apartment. At least that's what she said, but I couldn't tell one way or the other. Hot is hot! My brother Bernard and I shared a room so small that we bumped into one another any time we both tried to move around at the same time. I mean, it wasn't much, but to me it was what I called home.

The fall of '93, I was seventeen years old and didn't have a care in the world! Like so many other teens in my hood, I couldn't wait to turn sixteen so I could quit school. And as soon as I was able to do so, I did! *What could those up tight ass crackers teach me that I couldn't learn from the streets?*

My brother Bernard and I were like night and day, we didn't have anything in common other than the fact that we had the same mother and lived in the same house. Bernard is a year and a half older than I am and has a totally different mind-frame from me. While he's somewhat passive and naïve, I'm always the aggressor and can recognize game coming a mile away. Bernard was a homebody-- never, ever got into any trouble. On the other hand, I was always in the streets and stayed into some shit! I guess you can say I was the Black Sheep!

Bernard had just graduated high school and considered himself to be lucky for getting hooked up with a job with the City. I considered him a fool for being content working his ass off for those crackers, for pennies. Me? I was just laying back and going with the flow! I had a couple of partners who apparently shared similar thoughts and viewed life the same way I did. One of my boys was Jared, but we called him Junebug or June because of the shape of his head and the way his eyes bulged like a beetle's whenever he was excited. June was just a year older than me, but thought he knew more than me because of the mere twelve-month age difference. In actuality, it was the other way around. He was slightly overweight and sported a baldhead because he had inherited a receding hairline. June was the typical follower of the group and was very easily influenced.

My other partner was Vonzell -- we called him "V" for short. He was by far the closest thing I ever had to being a best-friend! V was the same age, height and weight as me, but whereas I'm light brown skinned, he was two shades darker than me with short, wavy hair. V was the only nigga I ever knew that had a temper worse than mine and I guess that's one of the reasons we've stayed so tight for so many years. We'd been partners ever since elementary school. We were so tight of friends, everybody thought we were cousins. V knew a lot of girls and had so many liking and trying to get with him, that naturally he declared himself a young pimp. The only thing that stopped him from being a young Don Juan was the fact that he was just like June and I. Neither of us could talk to a girl without ending up cursing her out or getting cursed out!

Ever since I'd quit school, my mom had been on my back about getting a damn job. But work and I didn't get along, AT ALL!! To get dough, my two partners and I were doing petty stick-ups. Basically, robbing low-scale hustlers for little of nothing. Because of our capers, we had earned a reputation of being stick-up kids without a conscious. Sometimes we wore masks, sometimes we didn't. It depended on the situation or the mood we were in at the time. Luckily, we hadn't been caught by the cops or any of the dope-boys we had been laying down. If a nigga or chick had money or dope, better yet both, we were going at them ruthlessly.

For me, robbing a nigga was an adrenaline rush! I loved to see the look of fear in a person's eyes when they stared down the barrel of my pistol and wondered what I was going to do next. Most of our robbing sprees went smoothly, without any problems, but there were also times when we had to make examples out of those who tried to buck. One thing I can say about my two road-dogs is that they were just as trigger-happy as me and I respected them for their, *'Shoot first – fuck the questions'* attitude. When niggas on the block saw us coming, they knew to get missing unless they wanted to be left facedown with their pockets out like rabbit ears. We used to hear cats whisper, *"Oh shit, here come Mike and 'nem"* and watch as they scramble to leave. That was a feeling of pure POWER!

Late one night, June, V and I were sitting on the stairwell of June's apartment building smoking weed and talking shit to each other while enjoying the brisk air. It wasn't warm, but it wasn't exactly cold either because winter hadn't yet arrived. The neighborhood was fairly quiet and virtually no one was out side on this night, which was unusual for our projects. I was seated on the bottom step while June and V were one or two steps higher. While June and V clowned each other, I started thinking about our last lick and a potential problem we would possibly have to handle.

Two nights earlier, we had hit our biggest lick ever, thanks to Keisha, one of V's girlfriends. She put us up on some hustlers from New Jersey that were selling dope out of her aunt's house in the Pine Valley neighborhood on the south side of Charlotte. Keisha told us to come through right after midnight because they would be sold out by then and have the most money on them at that time. So, we ran up in there a little past 1:00 AM, just as a customer was exiting the back door. Ski-masked-up'd and waving gats, we rushed that shit like a swat team. Everything was right where Keisha said it would be -- pistols under the sofa and money underneath the kitchen sink in a cereal box. We got away clean with 6-grand and two gats, which was a major sting for us at that time. We broke Keisha off and split the rest three ways. But the problem was the fact that Keisha wasn't satisfied with her share.

As I grabbed the blunt from between June's thick fingers, I interrupted their joking, "Yo, y'all remember how them niggas eyes almost popped out when we ran up in there? I thought both them niggas was gone shit on they self, straight up!"

Thinking back to the episode I was referring to, both V and June laughed. Between chuckles, June said, "Yeah, dem niggas was scared as shit!"

"Y'all know I started to dump on that tall nigga for not movin' fast enough. I 'on like New York niggas anyway!", V added.

"You mean Jersey?", I tried to correct him.

"New York, New Jersey – same shit, ain't no difference! I should've put hot-balls in that nigga's ass!", V said, sounding regretful.

"Nah, fuck them niggas! Let me tell you 'bout yo' bitch! Keisha know she can act! I almost laughed at her, the way she was on the floor cryin' and shit", I spoke to V as I watched him smile with pride.

June snatched the weed from V as he said, "Speakin' of yo' bitch, I ain't givin' dat skunk no mo' money. If dat trick want some mo' dough you gonna be da nigga to give it to her"

"Ain't no question 'bout that, 'cause I sho' ain't givin' her ass none!", I added.

"Y'all niggas need to quit trippin' 'cause y'all know I'm a handle that shit!", V said looking at me and June with a nonchalant smirk.

"Oh nigga, we know that! But you need to handle that bitch before she opens her big-ass mouth. 'Cause you know if them niggas find out who laid 'em down, we gonna have to deal wit 'em!", I explained to my ace.

"Didn't I just say I got that? That bitch ain't gone cross a nigga 'cause she'll be puttin' herself on front street. Besides, I'm fuckin' her too good for her to flip like that. 'Cause that's what I do – fuck'em, breed'em and mislead'em!", V responded while simulating a doggie-style sex act, complete with his hands spanking the air like it was her ass.

I had given the blunt to June. V was watching him baby-sit it. V grew impatient and whined, "Damn! Can a nigga smoke wit 'choo? Fat muh-fucka you!"

Realizing he was hogging the chronic, June finally passed it to V and he took a long drag, slowly letting the smoke out through his nostrils blending it with the night air. Savoring the sweet taste of sticky green, V admired the blunt in his hand like a damn weed-connoisseur as he offered his critique of the herb, "Damn my nigga, that boy Jo-Jo got some good shit! This is fire right here!"

"Yeah, dude got some chronic. And you know what? I been thinkin' 'bout touchin' dat nigga", June said, replacing 'that' with 'dat' as he often does, as he rose to his feet and brushed his wide ass off, ridding it of possible dirt.

"Who? Jo-Jo?", both V and I asked in unison.

"Damn right Jo-Jo! Dat nigga slangin' much weed and I know he sittin' on a few G's up in there", June replied while shaking his left leg, trying to get the blood circulating again. Because of his weight, his leg had gone to sleep from sitting in one position for such a long period of time.

At that moment, I saw June look past me and V with puzzling eyes and it caused a chain reaction. I looked back and then V looked back. I stood up and reached beneath my sweatshirt for my pistol as Ron-Ron, the neighborhood crack head appeared from the shadows.

"Ron-Ron, you better quit sneaking up on niggas like you crazy!", I barked at him for startling us like that.

"My bad, lil' Al Capone", he replied sarcastically, while smiling and revealing his badly stained teeth. "I'm tryin' to get straight. Y'all holdin'?"

He was clutching a few crumpled bills in his hand. Neither one of us had any more dope, so I toyed with him.

"Yeah dirty ass nigga, we holdin' P.S. and if you don't get the fuck away from here you gone get some"

Not knowing what P.S. was, but judging from my tone, he decided he didn't want any.

"Aiight Al Capone", he said again with sarcasm as he turned on his heels and did a foot shuffle, imitating James Brown, before shuffling off in the direction in which he had come from.

All of us laughed at him as he walked away.

"What in the hell is P.S.?", June asked, once Ron-Ron was gone.

I lifted my sweatshirt and pulled out my pistol and began explaining with the blunt dangling between my lips.

"I call this mutha-fucka right here 'Problem Solver'! Ain't no problem too big or too small for this bitch to handle. KnowhatImsayin'??", I finished my explanation by turning the pistol over in my hands, watching as the chrome sparkled whenever a small piece of light bounced off of it.

Passing the blunt to June, I tried to remember what we were talking about before Ron-Ron had interrupted us. It finally came to me as I began to contemplate what June had said about Jo-Jo. What he'd said was indeed true -- Jo-Jo was serving an awful lot of weed at his spot. I thought about agreeing with June to rob him, but then I decided against it because Jo-Jo and I went back too far.

"Nah, we ain't fuckin' wit Jo-Jo. That nigga cool wit me", I told my partners, while bringing the subject back up.

June and V both looked at me at the same time before June said, "Nigga who you 'pose to be? You tryin'a tell a nigga who we can't jack?"

"Yeah nigga, you getting' a lil' beside yo' self. You don't run nothing", V laughed while putting his two-cents in.

"Dat nigga Ron-Ron was right. Dis nigga think he Capone or somebody. Nigga you don't call no shots!", June added.

"Yo' name gon' be Capone from now on, aiight gangsta?", V joked.

"What's up Al Capone?", June laughed.

They meant it as a joke, but the name ended up sticking! From that day on, Mike was dead and Capone had just been born.

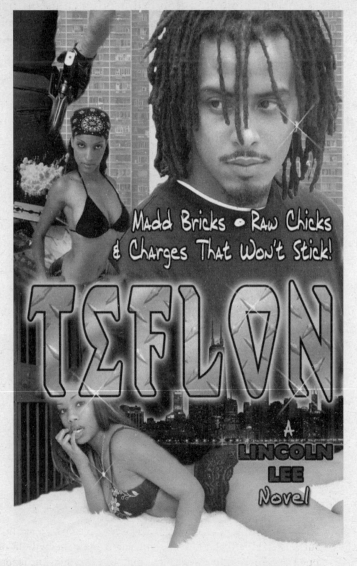

" T E F L O N "
D E S C R I P T I O N

Cleofis Jackson a.k.a. **"Teflon the Untouchable"** is a young hood-rich hustler that the FED's have not been able to make murder-charges stick.

Having been trained by one of the best, **Bruno** (his cousin), the #1 Kingpin in Chicago destined for the 'Hood Hall Of Fame', Teflon desires to achieve everything Bruno has! Blood is normally thicker than water. But when Teflon finds out that his main-girl and first-love (Kim) is about to become Bruno's baby-mama, it's about to be on!

Teflon is ruthless and murder is his calling-card -- but it doesn't detour a steady stream of raw ghetto-girls all dying to become his ride-or-die chick.

Natalie is a thick 5'3", gap-toothed, big-booty part-time correctional officer that has a thing for thugs and does many favors for Teflon. **Holly** is a grimey gangsta-chick that's all about the dollar, but doesn't like competition for Teflon's attention and ain't never scared to hand-out a beat-down. **Shawndra**, 10-years older than Teflon, works for Bruno as a 'mule', while simultaneously getting dangerously close to Teflon when she begins visiting him during a short-stint in jail. **Kim**, though a chicken-head, is the only women that Teflon has a weakness for, having known her since they were 15-years old.

When Teflon forms his own crew, 'The Capone Gang', and sets out to control the street, his crew's loyalty and honor gets tested. Everyone knows that if you fail Teflon's test, you'll never see tomorrow's daylight.

Gabe is Teflon's protégé and one of his boyz from the block that he's now puttin'-up on game, just as Bruno had done for him. Everything between them is all good, that is, until Gabe starts making his own moves, calling his own shots and begins gaining power.

When Teflon makes the cardinal mistake of starting to use some of his own product – he begins to become paranoid -- about everyone and everything!

Adding gas to an already red-hot fire, a long-kept secret of Teflon's is found-out! Teflon is then threatened, which is the last thing that anyone should do!

Feeling like his hand is forced, Teflon resorts to planning a set-up and murders. But his new drug-habit is scratching and denting the hell-out of his normally sound and rock-solid judgment – putting everything in jeopardy, including his freedom and his life! – Proving it's possible for anything to be penetrated – even Teflon!

" C R I M I N A L   C O D E "
D E S C R I P T I O N

Jorge Gomez, a Miami-bred black-Cuban hustler believes in living by the 'Code' and dying by the 'Code'. After serving a 5-year bid on drug-possession charges, refusing the Fed's offers for him to become a snitch, Gomez gains an early release due to the recommendations of a corrupted Correctional Officer that he'd done favors for while in jail.

Though Gomez' is true to his code of loyalty to his friends and family, he returns to find that Doris, his wife and baby-mama to his two kids hasn't been faithful to the code.

After his release, Gomez decides to relocate, setting his sights on virgin drug territory. He meets **Mark Goodman**, a drug dealer himself, who helps Gomez get back into the only game he's ever known. But when the script gets flipped and it's Goodman needing Gomez, a double-cross creates a deadly situation between the two.

Donna Schultz a.k.a **'Iceburg'** is a real down-a** chick that falls for Gomez, but her wealthy father (Bruce) wants her to have nothing to do with a hood-gangsta.

Bruce Schultz (Donna's dad), a Cadillac dealership owner who long-ago turned his own dirty-money into a respectable business is dead-set on making sure that his daughter will not be put in jeopardy by Gomez' lifestyle and is willing to do anything to ensure it --- even murder! Having many connections, he enlists the help of Federal Agents and Local Police to try take out Gomez – permanently!

Kiki, a life-long friend of Gomez from Miami, is nicknamed **'The Friendly Ghost'** because of his ability to get into cars, houses and pockets undetected. A true believer of the code, Kiki's always down for whatever – whenever.

Sexy **Sandra Perez** is a law-school student and in debt to one of Gomez' boyz (Jimmy). She's forced to work as a phone-sex operator for Jimmy as a way to repay her debt of school tuition. Gomez has a soft-spot in his heart for Sandra and buys her freedom from Jimmy. Later, when a botched-hit attempt on Gomez' life fails, Sandra lives up to the code, as she's now an Assistant District Attorney with crucial information on witness identity that she supplies to Gomez.

Gomez has vowed to never see the inside of a jail again! When he learns of a former drug-associate who's considering becoming an snitch for the Feds, putting in danger everything he's achieved, it's time to live by the code, die by the code or kill by the code!

" M A S T E R M I N D "
D E S C R I P T I O N

Clarence Kittles a.k.a. **'Clear'** is the mastermind behind his New York crime-crew, The Black Mob. But, he's more than just street-smart. Clear knows exactly how to organize and keep his biz on the down-low, disguising his true identity through a legitimate business, a barbershop.

Growing up in poverty, he vows never to go back to that life again. Anyone trying to hook-up with him better understand one thing -- Clear is a stickler for rules! Understanding that most hustlers get caught by not following them, he has no patience for rule-breakers and quickly turns into the most ruthless man when dealing-out punishment. On the flipside, most people in the community have come to know Clear as the *'Ghetto Robinhood'*, an up-standing businessman who gives away free haircuts to kids of women on welfare and donates money to churches.

Magic Jr. is a smart-youngster who basically grew-up without a father just like Clear. When they meet, Clear can't help but think about how much Magic Jr. reminds him of his deceased brother, Brandon. He begins to treat Magic Jr. like a younger brother, even hooking him up with his sister (Dayja) while schooling him on the game.

Dayja is Clear's little hot-mama sister that he's trying to wrestle free from the grips of the Child Protective Services system that he'd originally had her placed into because of her wild ho-like behavior. She's also the main reason that he works so hard at the game, so that he can provide her with anything that she wants.

Magic Sr., was a drug-addict during Magic Jr.'s early childhood. It wasn't until Magic Jr.'s teen-years that he even knew the man that he was named after. Having endured the bad-side of the game, Magic Sr. cleans himself up and decides to now profit from the very same game that had him strung-out by becoming a dealer. When he chooses to set-up his operation on drug-turf that belongs to Clear, that action could lead to a deadly conflict.

Big Mac is the co-founder of The Black Mob and Clear's boy from way back. But, just because he was there at the beginning doesn't mean that he's immune from the rules that he helped to create – Clear ain't having it!

Porsha is Clear's ride-or-die chick that is like a mother to Dayja. She is no stranger to thugs and the drug-game. She says that she's down for whatever and will do anything for Clear, but has never been tested.

Candy is a booty-shakin' stripper turned conniving strip-club owner. Despite her name, there ain't nothin' sweet about her, as her only goal is to take care of #1 – herself! And she's so grimey, that she'll do it in anyway possible.

As Clear becomes frustrated by some of his crew's lack of discipline that can threaten his freedom, he begins to systematically reduce the size of The Black Mob, one-by-one. He knows that even though he's got cops on his payroll -- that may not be enough to overcome careless mistakes.

At times, Clear feels like he's the only one who truly understands that 'The Game' is chess, not checkers!

"LEGIT BALLER"
DESCRIPTION

Jay Bernard has been dedicated to his craft as a baler. That is, until his deeds land him a 14-year bid in the Federal Pen on drug-charges.

Kim, Jay's supposed 'Bonnie' to his 'Clyde' wastes no time in cutting ties after his sentencing by moving her game to the new Baller-Kint (Paris).

During Jay's incarceration, sexy Summer Foster, proves to be a better friend than anyone who'd benefited from Jay's life-style. Though from the same hood, Summer has managed to rise-up, earning a college degree and currently an M.B.A. student at Harvard.

After his early-release, Jay finds it hard to avoid the only life he knows, even with the love and encouragement from an old-friend (Summer) for him to go 'Legit' – Old habits, just seem to die hard!

The complete opposite of Jay's gangsta, Summer views him as much more than just hard-rock – but a true diamond-gem! However, Jay's past and the streets keep calling him.

Paris views himself as a street-rival of Jay's even before his stint in prison, and now feels threatened that Jay may want to re-claim everything back – his drug territory and his woman (Kim)!

When the inevitable confrontation arises between Jay and Paris, the next move could be the last!

" H U S T L E R S "
D E S C R I P T I O N

Popcorn & Bay-Bay have been boyz for what seems like forever. Since they were 'shorties' growing up in Richmond-VA, as the crowned Street-Prince-boys to their OG-fathers who carried notorious reputations in VA's streets as true hustlers, nothing separated the two of them -- until both of their fathers fell victim to the hood.

After the deaths of their fathers, Bay-Bay's mother decides to relocate to Miami, Florida – temporarily ending their contact.

Several years later, Popcorn & Bay-Bay are all grown-up and reunite with plans of taking 'The Game' to the highest level – fulfilling their destiny as Street-Royalty.

Peaches, a hood-sophisticated dime-piece and Popcorn's wifey, is thoroughly satisfied with the kinky-work he's puttin'-down in the bedroom, but suspects that Popcorn is cheating on her with his life-long female friend (Yolanda) who he seems to always be around.

When Popcorn suddenly starts disappearing at night and begins flashing more cash than his 'lawn-business' could possibly provide, Peaches doesn't feel like she even knows who he really is.

As Popcorn seeks to gain revenge for his brother's murder, he wants to know if he can totally put his trust in Peaches? Is she just a dime? Or is she truly his 'to-the-grave' Ride-Or-Die chick?

Out for her own personal-revenge to satisfy her suspicions of Popcorn's indiscretions, Peaches makes a decision that will come back to haunt both of them.....maybe forever!

Money, Betrayal and the constant Struggle-for-Power are just the normal territory for Real Hustlers!

"This Joint Is So Hot!....Ghetto-Fab!....
...Game Has To Be Recognized!"
- Terry Shropshire, Rolling Out Magazine

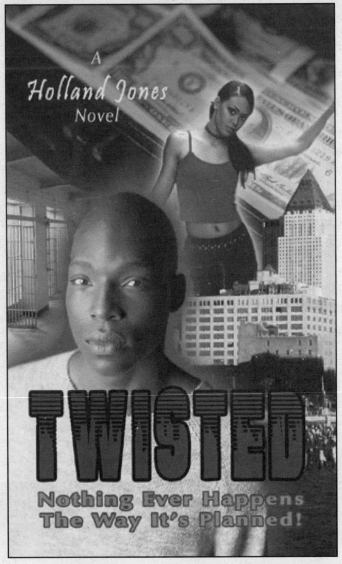

"TWISTED"
DESCRIPTION

Nadine, a sultry, ghetto-fine conniving gold-digger, will do whatever it takes to make sure that she is financially set for life -- even at the cost of breaking-up a family.

When Wayne, Nadine's man since high-school, is sentenced to two years in prison for a crime he did not commit, he's betrayed by the two people he trusted the most—his woman (Nadine) and his cousin (Bobo).

Asia, a curvaceous diva and designer-clothing boutique owner with a wilder-side sexual-preference becomes an unlikely confidant to her best-friend Nadine's man (Wayne) during his incarceration.

Meanwhile Bobo, one of VA's most notorious and most successful Street-Entreprenuers, manages to hustle his way into staring down a possible life sentence.

Now that the roles are reversed, it's Bobo who's now facing some serious prision time, as Nadine tries to do whatever it takes to keep her hands on the secret stash of cash hidden in a suitcase that Bobo left behind.

Money, greed and sex always have as a way of gettin' things **Twisted!**

"Daaaaayummmmmmm! Holland Jones brings it! A hood-licious story that combines deceit, murder, freaky sex and mysterious-twists! You gotta get this one!"

-- Winston Chapman, Best-Selling Author of *Caught Up!* and *Wild Thangz*

"Hustlin' Backwards"
DESCRIPTION

Capone and his life-long road dawgz, June and Vonzell are out for just one thing…. To get rich!….By any means necessary!

As these three partners in crime rise up the ranks from Project-Kids to Street-Dons, their sworn code of "Death Before Dishonor" gets tested by the Feds.

Though Capone's simple pursuit of forward progression as a Hustler gains him an enviable lifestyle of Fame, Fortune and all the women his libido can handle – It also comes with a price.

No matter the location – Miami, Charlotte, Connecticut or Puerto Rico – There's simply no rest for the wicked!

WARNING: HUSTLIN' BACKWARDS is not the typical street-novel. A Unique Plot, Complex Characters mixed with a Mega-dose of Sensuality makes this story enjoyable by all sorts of readers! A true Hustler himself, Mike Sanders knows the game, inside and out!

"Fast-Paced and Action-Packed! Hustlin' Backwards HAS IT ALL -- Sex, Money, Manipulation and Murder! Mike Sanders is one of the most talented and prolific urban authors of this era!"

" N A S T Y "
D E S C R I P T I O N

Life-long friends, Nate & Moe, are certified players! Both have used their jobs in the entertainment industry to their advantage with the women they meet.

Moe is a well-known radio DJ in New York, while Nate is doing his damage with a pen as a magazine writer in Baltimore.

When Nate loses his job in B-more and moves back to New York to freelance for one of the hottest urban magazines, a controversial article he writes about star music artists that are using drugs could lead to his permanent down-fall.

Moe warns Nate about releasing the article, but Nate's regaining of success has him feelin' himself too much – Now he's making big-cash and begins feeling like he's untouchable! Playing women may only get him slapped, but playing with the industry's hottest hardcore rappers that have millions to lose from the article could get Nate 'slumped'!

Kaneecha (Moe's girl), is a sexy-diva clothing model and nympho without a conscience. Kaneecha's always gotta have it, whenever, where-ever! But a horny-night decision may come back to haunt her.

Tierra is a blunt-smoking, hood drama queen from Queens, NY. Though she's known Nate for a long time, it wasn't until he resurfaced in New York years later that she recognized that she wants a piece of that! Later, she views Nate as the answer for her baby-daddy drama.

Janettea (Nate's 'main-girl') is an independent sophisticated-dime that's doing her own thing with interior designing, but can also cop an attitude with a quickness! And, she ain't above giving a beat-down to a hoochie she thinks is sexin' Nate.

All the dirt Nate's doing begins to catch-up with him. Having twice narrowly escaped the hardcore rapper's crew of henchmen seeking revenge against him – he might not be so lucky the next time! Doing the ultimate dirt to his boy Moe, has serious consequences of its own! And, his player-ways gets him played!

It's just the price you pay for being NASTY!

"DRAMA!"
DESCRIPTION

Destiny Smith, a young sexy diva, is intent on living the wild-life – a path that puts her on a collision course with nothing good! Spoiled by her boyfriends and protective brother (Chicago), she feels like the world owes her and she'll settle for nothing less.

Sexin' a ball-player, fightin' hoochies, back-stabbin', lyin' and cheatin' are all fair game in the ordinary day of Destiny.

When Destiny's wild behavior catches-up with her and lands her in serious trouble with the law, it's up to her brother (Chicago) to again rescue her. Having no choice, Chicago accepts a favor from a rogue cop -- a favor that he'll soon regret taking – one that will cost much more than they're willing to pay!

Though Chicago takes it upon himself to look-out for his full-grown sister, especially after the broad-daylight murder of their mother – he's also struggling with his own personal-demons. On-and-off relationships with hoodish girlfriends, money problems, court battles, consistent drama-situations in Destiny's life and the rogue cop's increasing strong-arming of him – all of these things are beginning to wear him down to a breaking point.

Chicago tries his best to hold it together – keep from going gangsta, and solving problems in his normal way...with a gun! – But when the tables are turned on him and he smells a set-up that threatens his life, he's forced to take matters into his own hands!

And, when an unexpected event reveals the identity of his mother's killer, placing him face-to-face with them, it's definitely gonna be ON!....There's NO WAY and NOBODY that can stop the *DRAMA*!

"DYME HIT LIST" DESCRIPTION

Rio Romero Clark, is an Oakland-bred brotha determined to remain a Playa-For-Life!

Taught by the best of Macks (his Uncle Lee, Father and Grandfather), Rio feels no woman can resist him. And he knows that his game is definitely tight, considering that he's as a third-generation Playa.

It is Rio's United-Nations-like appreciation for all types and races of women, from the Ghetto-Fab to the Professional, that leads him to the biggest challenge of his Mack-hood, Carmen Massey.

Carmen, a luscious southern-Dyme, at first sight, appears to be just another target on Rio's *Dyme Hit List!* Possessing a body that's bangin' enough to make most brothas beg, mixed with southern-charm that can cause even the best playa to hesitate, Carmen's got Rio in jeopardy of getting his Playa-Card revoked.

Burdened with the weight of potentially not living-up to the family Mack-legacy, Rio must choose between continuing to love his lifestyle or loving Carmen.

Unexpectedly tragedy strikes in Rio's life and a dark secret in Carmen's past ignites a fire that threatens to burn-up their relationship, permanently.

"*Dyme Hit List* is On-Fire with Sensuality! This story is pleasingly-filled with lotsa lip-folding scenes! Curtis Alcutt is a bright new star in fiction!"

-- Winston Chapman, Best-Selling Author of *"Wild Thangz"* and *"Caught Up!"*

"SHAKEDOWN" DESCRIPTION

Paris Hightower, is a sexy young thang who falls in love with the man of her dreams, Tyree Dickerson, the son of very wealthy Real Estate tycoons. But there's a problem.... Tyree's mother (Mrs. Dickerson) thinks that her son is too good for Paris and is dead-set on destroying the relationship at all costs.

After Mrs. Dickerson reveals a long-kept secret to Paris about her mother (Ebony Hightower), a woman that abandoned Paris and her brother more than fifteen years ago when she was forced to flee and hide from police amidst Attempted-Murder charges for shooting Paris' father --- Paris is left in an impossible situation.

Even though the police have long given-up on the search for Ebony Hightower (Paris' mother), the bitter Mrs. Dickerson threatens to find her and turn her in to authorities as blackmail for Paris to end the relationship with her son.

Paris knows that Mrs. Dickerson means business – she has the time, interest and money to hunt down her mother. Left with the choices of pursuing her own happiness or protecting the freedom of her mother, a woman she barely knows, Paris is confused as to the right thing to do.

As the situation escalates to fireworks of private investigators, deception, financial sabotage and kidnapping, even Paris' life becomes in danger.

Just when Paris feels that all hope is lost, she's shocked when she receives unexpected help from an unlikely source.

"Be careful who you mess with, 'cause Payback is a ......! *Shakedown* combines high-drama and mega-suspense with the heart-felt struggle of the price some are willing to pay for love!" -- Winston Chapman, Best-Selling Author of *"Wild Thangz"* and *"Caught Up!"*

"BUSTED"
DESCRIPTION

Arianna, Nicole and Janelle each have met a charming man online at LoveMeBlack.com, a popular internet-dating website.

Arianna Singleton, a sassy reporter who moves to Philly to further her career as a journalist, finds herself lonely in the big 'City of Brotherly Love' as she seeks a brotha-to-love online. After several comical dates with duds, she thinks she's finally met a stud.

Nicole Harris, a sanctified Public Relations Executive residing in Maryland puts her salvation on-hold when she begins living with a man that she's met on-line. Stumbling across her new beau's e-mails, she realizes that his Internet pursuits didn't end just because they now share the same zip code.

Janelle Carter, a Virginia Hair Salon Owner spends her nights cruising the Web taking on personas of her sexy, confident clients. A business arrangement that she makes on-line brings her face-to-face with a man she thinks is her destiny.

The lives of Arianna, Nicole and Janelle collide in a drama, as they discover that they've all been dating the same man....Chauncey, a brother that makes a habit out of loving and leaving women that he's met thru LoveMeBlack.com.

The three of them plot to exact their revenge on the unsuspecting Chauncey, as an unforgettable way of letting him know that he's been **BUSTED**!

"Rhonda Swan 'brings it' in this comical story that's a warning to wanna-be players as to what can happen if they ever get **Busted**!"

-- Winston Chapman, Best-Selling Author of *"Wild Thangz"* and *"Caught Up!"*

" S l i c k "
D E S C R I P T I O N

Dana & Sylvia have been girlfriends for what seems like forever. They've never been afraid to share everything about their lives and definitely keep each other's secrets ... including hiding Dana's On-The-DL affair from her husband, Jonathan.

Though Sylvia is uncomfortable with her participation in the cover-up and despises the man Dana's creepin' with, she remains a loyal friend. That is, until she finds herself attracted to the very man her friend is deceiving.

As the lines of friendship and matrimonial territory erodes, all hell is about to break loose! Choices have to be made with serious repercussions at stake.

If loving you is wrong, I don't wanna be right!

"SLICK!!! .... Ain't That The Truth! Brenda Hampton's Tale Sizzles With Sensuality, Deception, Greed and So Much Drama – My Gurrll!"

- MYSTERIOUS LUVA, BEST-SELLING AUTHOR OF
SEX A BALLER

"Wild Thangz"
DESCRIPTION

Jazmyn, Trina and Brea are definitely a trio of Drama-Magnets - the sista-girlz version of Charlie's Angels. Young & fine with bangin' bodies, the three of them feel like they can do no wrong – not even with each other.

No matter the location: Jamaica, Miami, NYC or the A-T-L, lust, greed and trouble is never far from these wanna-be divas.

Jazymn has secret dreams that if she pursues will cause her to have mega family problems. Though the most logical of the group, she can get her attitude on with the best of them when pushed.

Trina wasn't always the diva. Book-smarts used to be her calling-card. But, under the tutoring of her personal hoochie-professor, Brea; she's just now beginning to understand the power that she has in her traffic-stopping Badunkadunk.

Brea has the face of a princess, but is straight ghetto-fab -- without the slightest shame. As the wildest of the bunch, her personal credos of living life to the fullest and to use *'what her mama gave her'* to get ahead, is constantly creating drama for Jazymn and Trina.

When past skeleton-choices in Brea's closet places all three of them in an impossible life-and-death situation, they must take an action that has the most serious of consequences, in order to survive!

The very foundation of their friendship-bond gets tested, as each of them have the opportunity to sell-out the other! The question is, Will They?

Wild Parties, Wild Situations & Wild Nights are always present for these Wild Thangz!

Best-Selling Author of "Caught Up!", Winston Chapman weaves yet another suspenseful, sexy-drama tale that's a Must-Read!

"Wild Thangz is HOT! Winston Chapman shonuff brings the HEAT!"
-- Mysterious Luva, Essence Magazine Best-Selling Author of "Sex A Baller"

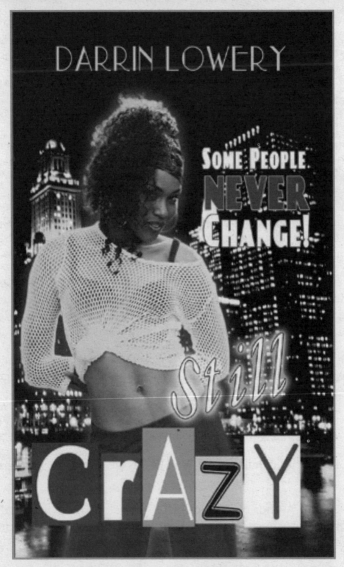

"STILL CRAZY" DESCRIPTION

Kevin Allen, a rich, handsome author and self-reformed 'Mack', is now suffering from writer's block.

Desperately in need of a great story in order to renegotiate with his publisher to maintain his extravagant life-style, Kevin decides to go back to his hometown of Chicago for inspiration. While in Chi-town, he gets reacquainted with an ex-love (Yolanda) that he'd last seen during their stormy relationship that violently came to an end.

Unexpectedly, Yolanda appears at a book-event where Kevin is the star-attraction, looking every bit as stunningly beautiful as the picture he's had frozen in his head for years. She still has the looks of music video model and almost makes him forget as to the reason he'd ever broken off their relationship.

It's no secret, Yolanda had always been the jealous type. And, Kevin's explanation to his boyz, defending his decision for kicking a woman that fine to the curb was, "She's Crazy!".

The combination of Kevin's vulnerable state in his career, along with the tantalizing opportunity to hit *that* again, causes Kevin to contemplate renewing his expired Players-Card, one last time. What harm could one night of passion create?

Clouding his judgment even more is that Kevin feels like hooking-up with Yolanda might just be the rekindling needed to ignite the fire for his creativity in his writing career. But, there are just two problems. Kevin is married! ....And, Yolanda is *Still Crazy!*

"Darrin Lowery deliciously serves up…..Scandal & Sexy-Drama like no other! *STILL CRAZY* has all the goods readers are looking for!" -- *Brenda Hampton, Author of "Slick"*

"Sex A Baller"
DESCRIPTION

Mysterious Luva has sexed them all! Ball players, CEO's, Music Stars -- You name the baller, she's had them. And more importantly, she's made them all pay......

Sex A Baller is a poignant mix of a sexy tale of how Mysterious Luva has become one of the World's Best Baller Catchers and an Instructional Guide for the wanna-be Baller Catcher!

No details or secrets are spared, as she delivers her personal story along with the winning tips & secrets for daring women interested in catching a baller!

PLUS, A SPECIAL BONUS SECTION INCLUDED!

Baller Catching 101

- Top-20 Baller SEX POSITIONS (Photos!)
- Where To FIND A Baller
- Which Ballers Have The BIGGEST Penis
- SEDUCING A Baller
- Making A Baller Fall In Love
- Getting MONEY From A Baller
- What Kind Of SEX A Baller Likes
- The EASIEST Type of Baller To Catch
- Turning A Baller Out In Bed
- GAMES To Play On A Baller
- Getting Your Rent Paid & A Free Car
- Learn All The SECRETS!

BY THE END OF THIS BOOK, YOU'LL HAVE YOUR CERTIFIED BALLER-CATCHER'S DEGREE!

"CAUGHT UP!"
DESCRIPTION

When Raven Klein, a bi-racial woman from Iowa moves to Atlanta in hopes of finding a life she's secretly dreamed about, she finds more than she ever imagined.

Quickly lured and lost in a world of sex, money, power-struggles, betrayal & deceit, Raven doesn't know who she can really trust!

A chance meeting at a bus terminal leads to her delving into the seedy world of strip-clubs, big-ballers and shot-callers.

Now, Raven's shuffling through more men than a Vegas blackjack dealer does a deck of cards. And sex has even become mundane -- little more than a tool to get what she wants.

After a famous acquaintance winds-up dead -- On which shoulder will Raven lean? A wrong choice could cost her life!

There's a reason they call it HOTATLANTA!

"HYPED"
DESCRIPTION

Maurice LaSalle is a player – of women and the saxophone. A gifted musician, he's the driving force behind MoJazz, a neo-soul group on the verge of their big break. Along with his partner in rhyme and crime, Jamal Grover, Maurice has more women than he can count. Though guided by his mentor Simon, Maurice knows Right but constantly does Wrong.

Then Ebony Stanford enters Maurice's world and he begins to play a new tune. Ebony, still reeling from a nasty divorce, has just about given up on men, but when Maurice hits the right notes (everywhere) she can't help but fall for his charms.

While Maurice and Ebony get closer, Jamal is busy putting so many notches on his headboard post after each female conquest, that the post looks more like a tooth-pick. When a stalker threatens his life, Maurices warns him to slow his roll, but Jamal's hyped behavior prevails over good sense.

Just as Maurice is contemplating turning in his player card for good, stupidity overrules his judgment and throws his harmonious relationship with Ebony into a tale-spin. When it appears that things couldn't get any worse, tragedy strikes and his life is changed forever!

A Powerfully-Written Sexy-Tale, *HYPED* is a unique blend of Mystery, Suspense, Intrigue and Glowing-Sensuality.

"Buckle Up! HYPED Will Test All Of Your Senses and Emotions! LUKE Is A Force To Be Reckoned With For Years To Come!" -- WINSTON CHAPMAN, ESSENCE MAGAZINE BEST-SELLING AUTHOR OF "CAUGHT UP!" AND "WILD THANGZ"

"CRUNK"
DESCRIPTION

Imagine a Thug-World divided by the Mason-Dixon Line……..

After the brutal murder of four NYC ganstas in Charlotte, the climate is set for an all-out Thug Civil War – North pitted against South!

Rah-Rah, leader of NYC's underworld and KoKo, head of one of the Durty South's most ferocious Crunk-crews are on a collision course to destruction. While Rah-Rah tries to rally his northern Thugdom (Philly, NJ & NY), KoKo attempts to saddle-up heads of the southern Hoodville (Atlanta, South Carolina & Charlotte).

Kendra and Janeen, a southern sister-duo of self-proclaimed baddest b*****'s, conduct a make-shift Thug Academy to prepare KoKo's VA-bred cousin (Shine) to infiltrate NYC's underground, as a secret weapon to the impending battle.

The US Government, well-aware of the upcoming war, takes a backseat role, not totally against the idea that a war of this magnitude might actual do what the Government has been unable to do with thousands of life sentences -- Rid society completely of the dangerous element associated with the Underground-World.

Suspensfully-Sexy, Erotically-Ghetto and Mysteriously-Raw. CRUNK will leave you saying, Hmmmm?

"Get Ready For A Wild & Sexy Ride! Twists & Turns Are Abundant! An Instant Urban Classic Thriller! Tariq, Rudd & Jones Are Definitely Some BAD BOYZ! Errr'body Gettin' CRUNK!"

BLACK PEARL BOOKS INC.

ORDER FORM

Black Pearl Books Inc.
3653-F Flakes Mill Road- PMB 306
Atlanta, Georgia 30034
www. BlackPearlBooks. com

YES, We Ship Directly To Prisons & Correctional Facilities
INSTITUTIONAL CHECKS & MONEY ORDERS ONLY!

TITLE	Price	Quantity	TOTAL
"Caught Up!" by Winston Chapman	$ 14. 95		
"Sex A Baller" by Mysterious Luva	$ 12. 95		
"Wild Thangz" by Winston Chapman	$ 14. 95		
"Crunk" by Bad Boyz	$ 14. 95		
"Hustlin Backwards" by Mike Sanders	$ 14. 95		
"Still Crazy" by Darrin Lowery	$ 14. 95		
"Twisted" by Holland Jones	$ 14. 95		
"Slick" by Brenda Hampton	$ 14. 95		
"Hyped" by Luke	$ 14. 95		
"Dyme Hit List" by Curtis Alcutt	$ 14. 95		
"Busted" by Rhonda Swan	$ 14. 95		
"Shakedown" by Nubian James	$ 14. 95		
"Hustlers" by Ronald Quincy	$ 14. 95		
"Legit Baller" by Jerry Blackshear	$ 14. 95		
"Street Games" by Eric Myrieckes	$ 14. 95		
"Nasty" by Rahsaan Ali	$ 14. 95		
"Drama!" by Tia Hines	$ 14. 95		
"Criminal Code" by Jorge Landrian	$ 14. 95		
"Freak Unleashed" by Cindy Cox	$ 14. 95		
"Mastermind" by Robert Ricks	$ 14. 95		
"Teflon" by Lincoln Lee	$ 14. 95		

Sub-Total		$	
SHIPPING: ___ # books x $ 3. 50 ea. **(Via US Priority Mail)**		$	
GRAND TOTAL		$	

SHIP TO:
Name: _____
Address: _____
Apt or Box #: _____
City: _____ State: _____ Zip: _____
Phone: _____ E-mail: _____